THE WANTON LIFE OF MY FRIEND DAVE

TRISTAN WOOD

PARTRIDGE
A Penguin Random House Company

To order additional copies of this book, contact
Toll Free 800 101 2657 (Singapore)
Toll Free 1 800 81 7340 (Malaysia)
orders.singapore@partridgepublishing.com

www.partridgepublishing.com/singapore

To Nino Funfa, for meeting me between here and now, but especially to my True Poet, for never abandoning that place.

And to my mother, always. I know you're watching from above.

If our friendship depends on things like space and time, then when we finally overcome space and time, we've destroyed our own brotherhood! But overcome space, and all we have left is Here. Overcome time, and all we have left is Now. And in the middle of Here and Now, don't you think that we might see each other once or twice?

—Richard Bach, *Jonathan Livingston Seagull*

PROLOGUE

The first time Dave and I met, we had a spread of tarot cards between us. If I were to say that everything changed from that moment on, I would be lying, because it took us six months and the other side of the world for that to happen.

One thing you need to know, though, is that Dave and I were never lovers—and we never, ever were meant to be.

We were soul mates of another kind.

PART I
BECOMING DAVE

CHAPTER 1

THE POES

The thing about families is that you rarely get to choose them since you tend to be born into one and be a part of it. The family, on the other hand, tends to choose you and become a part of you, whether or not you grow to like it or will yourself to want.

The Poes weren't much different. They too chose you, but you were either a Poe or you weren't. You could never *become* one.

Dave was a Poe.

He was the middle child of an upper-middle-class couple who got married because they mistook shared interests for love and ended up divorced after Dave's father's more-than-expected midlife crisis. As a result, Dave grew up in that misplaced piece of attention that is reserved for middle children, wedged between a gifted older brother who inhabited a world of his own and a gay younger brother who strangely fulfilled his mother's need for a daughter. Dave's upbringing, however, was never one of neglect or lack of love.

Dave's mother was an eccentric woman who breezed through life with no sense of guilt or awkwardness, purposely oblivious to anything that would pose as a hindrance to her perception of the world. Or so she seemed, I mean, as I came to realize during the years that I had the pleasure of knowing her.

She was, in fact, a very singular woman. She would constantly project an image of herself that would make everyone around her think that she was futile and fragile, vain even, and that she was unavailable to see beyond the obvious, that she was incapable of any deeper perception other than what was unequivocally laid down for her. And this would lead everyone through a presumptuous path of disdain toward her capacities, making others feel safe and unaware of her every conquest of their concealed thoughts and secrets . . . until it was too late. They finally realized that sometimes they had been utterly exposed to her and that, at some strange level, she owned a fragment of them. It was bewildering; I can tell you from experience.

Dave's mother took upon educating her three sons with the same resolve that she put on making a shopping list or choosing new curtains for the living room. To her, there were no middle terms, only will, so whether curtains or her sons' education, everything mattered. She loved her sons more than anything in her life. There was no doubt that she was to every one of them the self-image of kindness and fragility and their imprinted ideal of what a woman should be. And there lay a part of the problem, as I came to realize, since she was one of a kind. She was a single soul that no one could have ever matched or tried to measure up to, because no one can take the place of a perfect mother who gives you the world as you know it and makes you believe that it is yours to take.

Dave always spoke of his mother with that almost worshipful tone that parents use to speak of their children, which made me wonder if he had ever suspected that sometimes she could see right through him.

He told me stories of his childhood, such as when his mother nurtured his younger brother's homosexuality by dressing the three boys in her clothes and highest heels so that they would know how difficult it was to be anything different than what they were expected to be. Or how she would take them to every museum and library to appease Dave's older brother's need of knowledge. And how she would let Dave have an entire chocolate cake for dinner when she forgot to pick him up from school. Or even how, to Dave's father discontent, she would call their school and tell their teachers that they all had gotten the flu so they wouldn't be attending classes that day, and then she would take them on a trip somewhere or invent a game that would last all day.

She really was one of a kind, but never a Poe.

Despite Dave's mother's strong will to give the children everything she thought made a good home and a sense of world—her world— the boys were often wrapped in the whirlwind of events that was their parents' marriage.

From a very young age, Dave and his brothers were accustomed to seeing their father ignore their mother's tantrums when she demanded from him the love that he never felt for her. She was, Dave told me, quite dramatic on her quest, but she would always succumb to a bouquet of flowers or a box of chocolates presented by her husband. Then the late hours at the office and his constant absence would be forgotten, because his romantic gestures numbed the certainty of her unrequited love.

Despite all, Dave's father was not an absent parent. Well, he was, but not in the literal sense of the word. Notwithstanding Dave's mother complaints, his father spent a lot of his free time with his sons, and he was considerate enough to engage with them in activities that they all appreciated, such as sports and going to the cinema or a concert.

He just didn't truly mean it, and he'd do it out of obligation rather than out of love or will. He loved his sons because they were his, but for nothing else. And that was why he knew that if he could go back in time, he would not have gotten married or had them. In the course of time, all his sons, and Dave in particular, began to feel the burden of their father's regretful love on their shoulders.

Fortunately, the lack of understanding wherewith God blesses the innocent allowed Dave and his brothers to ignore this painful truth about their father most of the time while they were growing up. Sadly for his father, and for Dave himself, Dave matured faster than the usual boy and became aware of his father's regrets far too young. That, along with Dave's perception of his father's lack of love for his mother, made Dave's relationship with his father a tough one, where forgiveness was never an option.

However, not even that prevented him from being a Poe.

Dave was born on one of those cold days of February, looking like a ball of fat littered with hair. He was, as his grandmother put it, "no angel to see." Eventually, he grew up to become a squab brown-haired boy with crooked teeth and a mischievous smile that accompanied him through life.

He did have the "bad boy" thing going for him, but he was not what you would call a beautiful child. In fact, the first time I saw Dave's yellowish old childhood pictures, I recall thinking him rather tubby, and I could not hold back the surprise that hit me when I realized how distant from those images he had grown. Years later, while looking back at those pictures, I was even more surprised when I learned that Dave's first sexual experience had occurred at the innocent age of six. Not that his looks at the time had anything to do with it, but then again, I was always the one to make the weirdest synapses.

Dave was already in first grade, he told me, when his mother started attending some ceramic classes every other afternoon and left him to the cares of an older cousin when he wasn't at school. His brothers were saved by the piano lessons that Dave himself refused to attend. The older cousin, who was facing extreme hormonal puberty at the young age of twelve, was very keen about playing house in a literal sense. Dave told me, with that crooked smile of his plastered all over his face, that she said she was going to teach him how to "be a good daddy." Then, in a childish way, she would let her wild pubescent imagination take the lead and perform her very own impersonation of the birds and the bees. No flowers were involved, though according to Dave, his "love stick" took part in it. Dave and I would never refer to his penis in any other way than that, since that was the bashful—and very much mocked by me—term that Dave used the first time he recounted one of his sexual adventures to me. So we kind of decided that we would stick to it. Pun intended.

"Dave, did you just tell me that you were abused? Have you ever told this to anyone else?" I asked, half-amused and half-astonished, for I knew that my friend wasn't revealing a dark secret; he was bragging.

"What? Abused? No!" Dave barked, as if such a thought had never crossed his mind before.

"Then what do you call that? Lovemaking at the age of six?" I teased, unsuccessfully trying to keep my curiosity at bay. "Which of your cousins was it? Was it that one that seems to have something dark going on?"

"What? No! And it wasn't like that. I didn't feel abused. I kind of liked it at the time, you know? I didn't like all of it. Some parts I recall

6

being uncomfortable . . . and kind of stupid, when I think of it. Two brats in a situation like that . . . You can picture the whole mess, can't you, Izzy?" Dave wrinkled his nose at me.

"And you never told anyone this?" I asked, raising a doubtful brow at him.

"Of course I did! I told my friends. I was the first one of the group to get laid!" he replied proudly.

"I don't think that that counts as getting laid. And you told me that you lost your virginity when you were fifteen, at the city park . . ."

"At six o'clock in the morning, on the thirteenth of June, on the bench farthest from the kiosk that sold ice cream," he said, cutting me off.

"Sooo?" I urged him.

"So I lost my virginity at fifteen. That's it. At six, I just got laid," Dave said this matter-of-factly.

"That is not getting laid!" I almost shouted, eyeing him sternly and crossing my arms as if preparing to charge.

"Well, technically, it was. It just doesn't count as losing my virginity, because I didn't come," he said dismissively.

"If we're going down that road, I can come up with some seriously twisted logic and tell you that you technically lost your virginity to your right hand . . . Wait, you're not left-handed on those matters, are you?"

"Hmm . . . Just when I pretend that someone else is doing it to me." He let a faint smirk escape from his lips.

"Does that really work? Honestly, does that happen or is it just some sort of manly joke?" I asked, truly interested as to the outcome of that.

"Izzy, you'll just have to find out that one for yourself," he said with a wink and a stupid smile plastered all over his face.

Despite this or due to this incident, as I referred to it (and honestly, I was never really able to make up my mind on the subject), I never doubted that Dave grew carefree and rather happy within his abnormally large and hormonal family.

Dave's family was far from being limited to his parents and his two brothers. In fact, Dave's family was almost a community by itself, with an uncountable number of cousins, several crazy uncles and aunts, and, go figure, very conservative grandparents.

From what I learned myself and from what Dave told me himself, his family could not be described as less than, for lack of a better word, eclectic. Many of his relatives seemed to have come out of a novel. From a maiden aunt of seventy who kept a wedding dress in the closet and wore it on her birthday every year, to an uncle who farted in public and excused himself by saying that he had to give the farts away since nobody was willing to buy them, Dave had all sorts of uncommon relatives. As a result, his sense of family bonds and boundaries was completely misfit or, in some situations, inexistent. This made his ability to restrain himself from hooking up with a cousin—voluntarily, I mean—until he was twelve, the age when puberty struck him hard, a most impressive feat.

In fact, as Dave used to put it, he didn't pass by puberty; puberty moved in with him. And it was not the unruly growth of facial hair, the pimples, or the voice changes. It was actually a bad case of sexual urges and untamable hormones, with all the implications that that had among Dave's family.

Dave's sexual education, if you could call it that, was initiated by one of his great-uncles who, noticing Dave's unequivocal stares at all passing pairs of breasts, decided to take upon himself Dave's tutoring on the birds and the bees. Unfortunately, Dave's great-uncle was not very literate when it came to birds and bees, since he had been breeding cows for most of his life, so he had to adapt a bit.

"Dave, come here. It is time for us to have a men's conversation."

Dave froze when he heard his great-uncle's serious voice calling him to what he would recall as one of the most awkward sex talks of his life.

"You know, Dave, you are becoming a young man. I see that you are starting to notice women." There was a long pause that allowed Dave to feel overwhelmed with the fear of anticipation over what was about to come next. "Have you seen a woman yet, Dave?" And as Dave stood there staring, not knowing what he was expected to answer, his great-uncle kept on going. "I mean, do you know what a woman is?" he asked, letting Dave know that things just weren't getting any easier.

"I guess," Dave decided to say, as he would say anything that would stop the course of wherever that conversation was heading for.

"You know, Dave, women are like flowers," Dave's great-uncle said, probably sensing that his lack of knowledge on flowers might compromise the intents of the analogy he was trying to pull off to explain to his grandnephew the mysteries of womanhood. "I know that things are changing in you now, and that you are noticing women and that makes you feel . . . things that you didn't feel before, and that make you want to do things or think things . . ." As the old man fumbled, panic must have been obvious in Dave's eyes, because his great-uncle decided to go for a not-so-straightforward approach.

"Bulls know when cows are ready, Dave. Have you seen the bull near the cow when it's mating time? The bull goes to the cow and releases his seed in her . . ." While saying this, Dave's great-uncle made sure his message was coming through by mimicking the act and passing one of his arms through an imaginary channel and opening his hand while saying the word "releases."

Dave remained mute and silently prayed to all saints he'd heard of that all the awkwardness of the moment washed away. But it didn't, because his great-uncle kept on going.

"I was young too, you know? And I remember when I was your age and when I started noticing women. I remember seeing your great-aunt for the first time . . . Ah, the things we did when nobody was watching us! Back in those days, we didn't have the freedom you young boys have nowadays. We had to be creative. And we weren't less naughty because of that." At this point, Dave was certain that his great-uncle had lost his focus somewhere, but the old man was nowhere near stopping.

"A man has his needs, Dave, and you must always show women who is in charge. Women like men who take the lead and know how to boss them around. One day you will have to say to your wife to iron your shirt, to prepare your dinner, or to lie down in bed and fool around with you. It's a man's prerogative, Dave. A man's prerogative!" As he emphasized this, Dave looked for an escape out of this talk of shame.

Eventually, one of his cousins saved Dave, but the conversation would be engraved in his memory for as long as he lived—first as an embarrassing moment and afterward, when maturity overcame puberty, as a good story. And what's the purpose of a good story if you can't share it with anyone?

As Dave told me once, despite the uselessness of his great-uncle's awkward conversation, most of his insights on women came from his family. Not that he realized it at the time, but his family behavior ended up being an inexhaustible source of knowledge in that aspect, and it was the catalyst to many of Dave's destructive behaviors as well.

By the age of ten, Dave knew for sure that at least three of his uncles had extramarital affairs, one of which was with one of his elder cousins. He also knew that his grandparents from his father's side did not sleep together and that one of his single aunts liked to kiss women. He just wasn't aware of the meaning of it all at the time.

Dave's grandparents from his father's side started to sleep in separate rooms when Dave's grandmother was confronted with the strange devotion of Dave's grandfather for her younger sister. This happened way before Dave was born, so when he was growing up, he didn't find it odd that his grandparents inhabited different rooms in their house. In fact, for a long time, he took for granted that elder people lived like that, and since his grandparents from his mother's side had passed away before he was born, he couldn't quite compare situations. He was an adult already when we gained full knowledge of the strange love triangle that was his grandparents' life story.

Dave's grandfather was a young lawyer when he saw Dave's grandmother for the first time. He was at the churchyard with some friends when Dave's grandmother was closing a window at her father's house, just across from the church, and for a brief moment, their eyes met. Many things were said about the women of that house, kept under lock and key by their father, but he had never laid eyes on one of them before. When he did, it took him just one single look, that one glimpse that fate allowed him to have, to have her grave face and the abandonment in her eyes carved in his soul forever. His life therefore irreparably changed. He thought he was in love, maybe because there was something noble and detached about her that made her seem almost ethereal.

Three days later, he was knocking on her door and requesting her father's permission to court her. Fortune, or the lack of it, made her father like him and agree with the courting. After all, she was his eldest and the only one the old man had intended to marry. He had other plans for the other daughters. This was how Dave's grandfather started attending the house to visit his bride, and he soon realized that his infatuation was all but love. Love, and lust in particular, came after, when he met his fifteen-year-old soon-to-be sister-in-law, only to learn that he could never have her. That was not his father-in-law's plan for her, nor was Dave's grandfather in a position to exchange brides honestly. So Dave's grandfather did the only thing a man in his situation could do: he married the available sister, hoping to come closer to the unavailable one under the sacred protection of holy matrimony.

Family bonds proved to be tight, and eventually, upon his father-in-law's death, Dave's grandfather took under his and his wife's care and roof his beloved single sister-in-law. As a sign of gratitude, she cared for her nephews and nieces, helped with the house, kept her sister company, and loved her brother-in-law whenever chance gave them the opportunity. This arrangement lasted years and was only broken when an unfortunate lapse from Dave's grandmother occurred and she inadvertently caught them in what could be called a compromising position. She didn't mean to, and mostly she didn't want or intend to catch them. She'd always known it, she'd complied with it, and she did whatever she could and was in her power to ignore it. However, once faced with the facts, Dave's grandmother couldn't keep up with the pretense, nor could she fail to react as she was expected to. So she did the only thing that seemed fitting and moved her husband's things to another room, this way silently ending their marriage but keeping up the appearances.

No one asked questions since no answers were supposed to be delivered, and no one really had doubts regarding the doings, so things happened as if actually programmed and order was not disturbed. In the silence of her room, Dave's grandmother grieved her nights of solitude, though. It was not the loss of her marriage or of her love that upset her. Truly, she had never loved her husband or cared that he had made her sister his mistress. She missed his warmth in bed at night and the assurance of his company to fight the demons and ghosts that tormented her during the night.

You see, Dave's grandmother was one of those singular creatures that lived between two worlds, bridging them and listening to the solicitations of the dead. Unfortunately, and since she refused to nurse their requests or address their existence, the dead refused to make her nights peaceful. Dave's grandfather's skepticism seemed to calm Dave's grandmother's misery, and for that she missed him. He, regretfully, only missed the "ifs" that life hadn't allowed him, and for that he blamed her. He blamed her for being the eldest, for her father's despotic behaviors, and for her superior attitude that misled his feelings. Mostly, he blamed her for never letting him be able to love her.

As I came to realize over time, mistaking love with other things, or the inability to perceive love itself, was very common among the men of Dave's family, and rather than a flaw in character, it was regarded as a character's feature.

Dave shared the feature.

CHAPTER 2

THE ART OF WAR

D ave's adolescence could be called a typical one. It summed up to the inevitable family awareness, seasoned with that pinch of teenage drama contemplating sex, drugs, and rock and roll. To this added a fruitless quest regarding the meaning of life around the age of eighteen, when, for all purposes, Dave was already supposed to be an adult.

By the age of fourteen, Dave's concerns were undeniably girls, pot, and hearing the latest musical hits. But contrary to most teenage boys, sexuality was not a discovery to Dave. It came along with being a Poe. Sex and sexuality were a constant presence in Dave's family. Either subtly or more overtly, they were there. It was almost as if every family member, family story, attitude, or event had a connection, no matter how apparently small, to sex or sexuality.

Dave had a bachelor uncle, his father's younger brother, who was a charmer by flaw and a womanizer by virtue, as strange as it might sound. You should be advised, though, that neither Dave, who grew up knowing him, nor I, who grew by knowing him, were ever able to provide an unbiased opinion on the man. To me, he was a poet, but you must understand that to Dave he was a hero.

The man was the personification of charm. He walked, talked, and breathed charm. He was a devastatingly handsome man, but that was just a small detail, because he was so much more. Everything about him was charming. Everything he said or did was charming. It was inebriating.

After he introduced me to his uncle, Dave mocked me for weeks because I made a fool of myself cracking stupid jokes and laughing nervously. I even found myself giggling, which is actually one of my least favorite words in English; therefore, I avoid promoting such action in order to prevent the use of the word. But to my utter embarrassment, I giggled, because I had never seen such a fine specimen of Man. That's right, capitalized—for he was the personification of manliness. Hell, he was every woman's wet dream and more. It was so extreme that Dave and I just accepted as an irrefutable truth that he would be able to charm away the devil himself. Therefore, in its extreme, Dave's uncle's charms became a flaw and a hazard to women, for he loved them. All of them and everything about them, and, as the charmer he was, he could not help himself around them.

In his defense, I must say that he did not use or abuse women's trust in him. He misled no one. He made no promises, nor fed any hopes. Moreover, in his peculiar way of loving, he truly loved every single woman with whom he got involved. He loved them because he meant to. He was in it heart and soul—every time. So it could last a day or it could last a year, but whoever she was, during that time, she had him all, no restraints, no restrictions, no reserves, and above all, no regrets.

When it ended, because it always ended, he just walked away. No explanations given, no excuses made, and no forgiveness asked.

Even the more desperate or heartbroken would not get more than an "I don't love you anymore." They never heard that he was sorry. He was never sorry, and neither should they be. He had no regrets. They eventually nurtured a few. He essentially couldn't force himself to apologize for his feelings, or lack of them, since it was not up to him to control them. He knew every time that he would stop loving them eventually. Because he knew that, along with no restraints and no regrets also came no forever. Even so, he hoped every time to find his. And it was that hope that washed away any guilt, for he could not be blamed for stopping loving them when he believed, with all his strength, that the love that he'd found would last him a lifetime, even when he knew deep down that it wouldn't.

As odd as it may sound, one thing that I came to respect about him was that though he didn't need to be, he was a womanizer. Woman fell at his feet, but he felt compelled to chase them and pursue them, because he was, after all, a gentleman. Any other man in his position would have just taken the easy path and taken advantage of what life had so generously offered him. But not him. He wanted to earn it, because he wanted it to be real. You see, he was a romantic, as was Dave.

I always believed that that was why Dave was his favorite nephew. Somehow, despite all their differences, he saw himself in him. He had a lightness about him that Dave would never be able to sustain, but each shared, in his own particular way, the secret belief that he was meant for a love bigger than life. Or so he hoped.

I nicknamed him Uncle Casanova (not particularly original, I know, but in my defense, I must say that eventually everyone succumbs to commonplaces) because he was and knew how to be gallantly and irremediably attentive to women. And he saw it as an art, which he cherished; hence, he considered it his duty to pass his knowledge along to his nephews.

Merit must be given to Uncle Casanova, though. Anyone can teach two or three tricks on how to seduce women and unveil the basic principles of how women think and act. The former is pure common sense, and the latter is basic psychology. But truly understanding how women react and knowing how to act around them is a master's task. And the man—truth be said—was the Master Ioda of seduction.

That was how Dave, by the age of fourteen, had already learned and experienced that a woman will run from a man who runs after her and run after a man who runs from her.

Her name was Clara.

Clara burst into Dave's life like a pimple on a teenager's forehead: loud, furious, and instantly. She was transferred from another school and appeared in class next to him without the courtesy of a notice. He wasn't ready. She didn't care.

She was blonde, pretty, and extremely developed for her age. At fourteen, she already knew that she held power over men. Unfortunately for her, and as history has shown countless times over its course, inexperience and presumption were never the wise companions of power.

It took Dave one look to feel his entire body be overwhelmed by a feeling that he had not yet experienced with such intensity. It came as a blow to his heart, making it skip a beat. It was sharp and brutal. In a second, it spread down his body and focused with all its glory between his legs. Fairly enough, given his inexperience and lack of knowledge in the love organs department, he thought it was love. It took him some time, but eventually he realized that it was lust at its most. Clara had the biggest pair of breasts he had ever seen on a girl her age. From that day onward, all his thoughts revolved around those melon-shaped protuberances.

He drooled when he was near Clara, once even literally, so his embarrassment took the best of him whenever he was near her. He couldn't bring himself to say anything clever or witty around her. If it weren't for the fact that he had already made a fool of himself in front of his classmates by staring into her breasts with his eyes and mouth wide open and a little line of drool peering through, he would be certain that she failed to acknowledge his existence.

As days turned into weeks and weeks into centuries (in Dave's teenage time measurements), Dave's urges did not fade. Despair started to get the best of him. He would toss and turn in bed at night, consumed by fantasies and desires of Clara, and when he finally managed to fall asleep, it would be to wake up later in the middle of a wet dream, soaked in puddles of semen and sweat. He was obsessed with her, and fueled with the hype of teenage drama, he thought he was doomed.

Dave did his best to disguise his torment, but by the third week of Dave's despair, everyone in his family had noticed what was going on, and by the fifth week, the happening had turned into a novella among Dave's uncles and older cousins. Apparently, it was impossible not to notice the constant sighing and Dave's big cow eyes, filled with loss and abandonment. Moved by curiosity at first and by mercy once he learned the story of Dave's doom, the Casanova uncle took it upon himself to help his nephew, for everyone's sake, since the situation already bordered on the ridiculous.

Uncle Casanova, the charmer he was, offered Dave a copy of Sun Tzu's *Art of War*, telling him enigmatically that he would find the answers that he was looking for in there. Of course, the subtlety was wasted on the boy. A week later, Dave had read the book from cover to cover and still didn't understand shit of what was written in there. He even searched for a handwritten page by his uncle, hoping to get some answers, but as he found none, he drew what seemed to him to be the only logical conclusion: his uncle had given him the wrong book!

When he approached his uncle and shared his brilliant insight with him, the man realized that the boy lacked the maturity to understand the book and a more straightforward approach was in need. Therefore, he delivered it.

"Dave, the first thing you have to do is get this girl's attention. Make her notice you. Once you accomplish that, you can start ignoring her."

"But how? Why? She doesn't even know I exist. Well, she knows, but she ignores me."

Uncle Casanova took a long breath and probably assessed the dimension of the task that he had ahead of him. This was not going to be easy. The boy was, at this point and as far as he was able to guess, dumb as a brick in what concerned women.

"Okay, I'm going to break this down to you step by step. You will do exactly as I tell you." And Dave did exactly as his uncle told him.

Dave first studied the "enemy." He looked for a flaw, a weakness, and eventually, as goes for women in general and pretty women in particular, he noticed that looks are always important. It didn't really matter if there was truly something wrong with them. What mattered was that someone thought there was.

Next, as instructed by his uncle, Dave started to look at Clara's ears when he was seated next to her in class, and he would smirk and add a little grunt to that so that she could hear it. And that was it. Once a day, whenever he had a class where he would sit next to her, he would do just that. By the end of the fifth day, when Dave was already losing hope but grunted nevertheless, Clara snapped.

"What? Do you have a problem, kid?"

Dave focused all his energy in looking cool and absentminded. "Sorry, did you say something?" he asked dismissively.

Clara rolled her eyes and threw out one of those annoying teenage "whatevers." Then she tried to refocus on what she was doing. Dave counterattacked with another dose of a smirk and a grunt. Clara, of course, reacted.

"What. Is. The. Problem. With. You. Kid?" She spelled it out for him, putting special emphasis on the "kid" part.

It was now or never. He bent his head to the left and stared at her ears as if they were something out of this world.

"It's just that you have really big ears. I bet that's why you never wear your hair up." He laughed straight into her face.

She clearly couldn't believe the outrage. "You really are stupid, you know?"

Dave had a response ready for that. "Yeah, but that's a phase for me. Those jumbo ears are a lifetime for you, darling!"

At this point, the poor girl was furious. "I do not have big ears, and I am not, and never will be, your darling!" she cried. "Not in a million years. Kid!"

Dave gave her an assessing look with a mocking smirk plastered on his face, shrugged his shoulders, faced the front of the class, and delivered the final blow.

"Don't worry about that. I don't even find you attractive anymore, Dumbo!"

Even if Clara wanted to retort, she just couldn't. It seemed that every single soul in that classroom had heard their conversation and was now laughing at her. Even the teacher's efforts to calm the class down seemed fruitless. Dave was a hero. She obviously hated him.

The next day, Clara showed up in a ponytail, trying to prove Dave wrong but accomplishing only to give him, on a silver platter, the importance that she was trying to deny him. Dave had won the battle, and now he was all in for war, knowing that because of his uncle's lessons, all warfare, in the words of Sun Tzu, was based on deception.

Dave started to ignore Clara without an inch of subtleness. He made it loud and clear, as he managed to exchange seats with his peers in every class in which he had sat next to her. He left no room for doubts that he wasn't interested in being near her. He praised every girl he could, with the exception of Clara. He flirted with them and wooed them with his sweet talks and the pickup lines that his uncle had taught him. He became a success with the girls and a hero among the boys.

Make no wrong conclusions, though. Dave had always been a popular kid. He was a natural at it. He was smart, intelligent, well bred, and had a witty sense of humor. But now that he'd learn to add reason to instinct, he was becoming very much aware of his social skills and how to put them to proper service.

Dave learned how to fight his battles correctly, which pawns to sacrifice and which moves to avoid. It was rather easy at the time since he had no match to his skills. A curious thing is that when you teach children to play chess, most of them will quickly pick up on the game and easily memorize entire chess moves. However, few will think and anticipate moves of their own; therefore, by creating distractions, you can rather easily beat them at their memorized games. You see, you can teach them the game, but it's up to them to learn how to play.

Clara, unfortunately, didn't know how to play chess. Her initial rage against Dave quickly turned into irritation when she realized that he did not seem to want her, as opposed to every other boy. Irritation, on the other hand, soon faded away when she became aware of his interest in every girl but her. Envy and curiosity then took its place.

At this point, Dave had already earned a reputation of being a good kisser among the girls in his school, and Clara, by this point, was already eager to confirm it. That's the thing about women: if you play your cards well, most of them will easily eschew pride for the sake of infatuation.

So when Clara, not that randomly and despite all his deceptive contempt, paired with him at gym class, she saved no efforts to draw his attention. She breathed hard, she stepped close, she brushed at him, and she jabbed her bazookas. She drove him crazy. Hormones, at these ages, are not to mess with. Dave, who by now had the necessary confidence and ease to pull it off, made a bold move and went for checkmate.

"Are you going to John's party this Saturday?" he asked.

"Yeah, probably. Why do you ask?" she countered conceitedly.

"No reason," he said.

"Oh. Are you coming?" she asked, her smile falling.

"Haven't decided yet. Why? Will you miss me, Clara?" Dave asked smugly.

"Maybe," she teased.

And that was it. In that moment, Dave knew he had her, and honestly, half of the fun was gone. It was the first time he experienced that feeling—that instant when you know you've got it, the momentum thrill that inflates your ego, that tiny hiatus of joy before your interest starts to fade away, because you already know that you're going to get what you want.

Saturday arrived as scheduled.

Spring had sprung, and it was a bright day, with the sun peeking through the big white clouds that crept slowly across the sky. The day was warm, and the hopes were high. The party began at four in the afternoon.

Dave showed up around seven, knowing that Clara would be waiting for him. She was. And she looked magnificent. Her blonde hair was down, and she was wearing make-up. She looked older, much older. She was wearing a miniskirt and a tight top. All that anyone could see were breasts, so imagination didn't need to make its appearance there.

Dave was in for the final kill, so he kept ignoring Clara. He rambled around the house, speaking with the guys and messing with the girls, and got a few more than interested in him. He occasionally glanced at Clara, who was sending him no mixed signals. She wanted him, no doubt about it.

But he kept playing it cool, as his uncle had told him to.

"You see, Dave, people always want what they can't have," Uncle Casanova had said. "If this Clara girl thinks she cannot have you, she will want you bad. So don't be hasty and don't go chasing her. Let her chase you. Let her come to you but remember to bait her. Make sure she notices you but feign disinterest. This is all about deception."

That seemed to work. Since he'd started using his uncle's tactics, things had improved a lot. Talking to a girl was easier than ever. Either he pointed out a flaw that made her self-conscious and then ignored her until she tried to prove herself to him or he just commended her outright. The latter strategy worked better on girls who, albeit smart, were not that sharp about their looks. Looks, though they don't always matter, always play their part.

Once the bait was out, Dave just needed to wait for the fish to come and feed, which eventually happened.

Dave was by the food table, grabbing something to eat. When he got what he wanted, he sat at a nearby table, eating a slice of pizza. That's when Clara approached him.

"So you came," she stated, trying to sound uninterested.

"I did," Dave said flatly. He was having too much fun to let it go easily. "You were waiting for me?" This slipped out sounding more like a statement than a question, but it produced the desired effect nevertheless.

"What if I was?" she said, leaning over the table while she rolled a lock of hair around her middle finger. Her voice had become lower and had gained a sugary tone that drained from her tongue and numbed Dave's senses while hardening other parts of his anatomy. Still, he kept his cool and his facade of indifference, even though Clara stood in front of him, merciless. Later on in life, whenever Dave saw that look or deep cleavage on a woman, he couldn't help himself from fearing the threat of being overflowed with meats.

He didn't answer her. At that point, he wasn't able to coordinate the muscles of his tongue to articulate a sound, much less his brain to come up with anything that would resemble a phrase or even a word. So he opened his mouth and took another bite of his pizza. Then he chewed. Slowly. And since his blood was all housed in one part of his body, he kept repeating the mechanical process over and over.

He couldn't bring himself to do anything else. His uncle hadn't taught him that far. Sure, he knew how to act around other girls, and he normally got to kiss them at least. But Clara was different. She was experienced. Everyone knew that. What if he made a move and she rejected him? All the certainties that he had had so far were now gone. Insecurity took over him and filled every limb, every organ, and every cell of his being.

So he kept chewing.

Fortunately for Dave, it seemed that chewing was easily mistaken with scorn, or at least Clara made that interpretation. And you see, we women have a problem with being ignored. It bothers us.

Naturally, Clara was pissed out of her mind. She abruptly stretched her arm and knocked the pizza slice from Dave's hand, making him drop it to the floor. She then grabbed him by the collar of his shirt, pulled him toward her, and kissed him. In truth, she slammed her teeth into Dave's. He was stunned by her boldness and strength but soon recovered from the impact and kissed her back. Unfortunately, their abrupt motion made them fall over the table that stood between them, and it was not strong enough to support their weight. The table eventually crashed, but the music was loud enough to prevent them from becoming the main attraction, and only a few passersby saw the fall. They rapidly pulled themselves from the floor, regained composure, and wandered to a dark corner where they could continue their activities. Those did not involve the destruction of any more furniture. I asked, just in case.

Dave had never felt so turned on. It was not every day that a boy his age could reach second base with a girl who wore a D cup. Normally, the girls that he had been able to fondle had boobs that resembled mosquito bites. Clara's were teenage boy heaven.

Dave's pubescent dreams regarding Clara became true that night. No detail spared. When Dave told me this story, I clearly remember picturing those old ladies that squeeze the melons at the supermarket to see if they're ripe and end up bruising them, such is their eagerness for the watery fruit. Clara didn't complain, though. And everything was going fine until Dave started noticing that he had his face covered in Clara's saliva.

She was a drooler!

One thing is a bad kisser—most people can handle that—but a person that has to wet you all over just to give you a peck, well, that's just bad. There's nothing worse than a drooler. It's just too much unneeded lubrication. And with that, Dave simply lost all his interest in Clara.

Once he got what he wanted, Clara had nothing else to offer him. The challenge was gone and, with it, all the attraction that he had felt for her. Well, not all, but it was no longer consuming him. During the following days, once Clara noticed his detachment and lack of interest, hence becoming clingier, Dave did his best not to deal with the drama of the heartbroken girl and avoided her at all costs.

I don't personally believe that Clara was ever heartbroken. Piqued? Definitely. But not heartbroken. At this phase of life, love is as rare as unicorns.

In the end, their affair, if it could ever be called that, summed up to that one brief encounter. But contrary to many other encounters that Dave had had and would have, this one was the one time where all but the encounter mattered. Despite never knowing it, Clara played her part in Dave's "becoming," for it was because of her that Dave was christened as a bad boy and lived up to the reputation. And naturally, she was the one who set a type for him—the busty, voluptuous, blonde type. Not very original, but hey, who truly is?

Oh, and so that you know, at that time, Dave didn't know either. How to play chess, I mean.

CHAPTER 3

THE POP OF A CHERRY

"Was it good for you? I mean, was it what you were expecting?" I asked.

"Yeah. I guess so. And you?" Dave countered with a conceited smile.

"Hmm, it wasn't that great for me," I answered, adjusting my back on the couch, looking for a more comfortable position.

"Sorry . . ."

"Why are you apologizing to me?" I asked, cutting him off.

"I dunno. Force of habit, maybe." Dave laughed.

"Do you normally have that many complaints from the girls you bed?" I teased.

"Very funny, Izzy," Dave said sarcastically.

"It kind of is." I smirked.

Our laugh filled the room for a brief moment before the silence dropped its heaviness on us, forcing us to stare at the ceiling and get lost in our own thoughts. This was one of those moments that we had grown accustomed to, but that would be awkward to most people. We were sharing confessions. Well, in truth, Dave was spilling his guts out and I was carving it all in my memory, managing to keep what was mine to myself. Old habits die hard, you see.

I shifted again, propping myself up on my left side and resting my head on my hand while I looked down at Dave, who was lying across the floor on the carpet, his head resting on his hands and supported by a pillow.

"Would you just stay still?" Dave said in a grouchy tone.

"I can't. These pants are too tight."

"Why don't you wear something that actually fits your ass?" he mocked.

"Hey, I have a fine ass! And besides I lent it all to you . . . Delicious."

"Delicious?" Dave voiced, intrigued but discreetly sneaking a glimpse at my behind, which he actually couldn't see since it was facing the couch, as if checking my statement about by ass.

"Yeah," I snorted. "Stop trying to check out my ass!" I scolded. "You never thought what your travesty name would be? If you were one, I mean."

"Of all the stupid things that crossed my mind every day over the past few years—and in the years prior to those, before you get the chance to ask—my travesty name was never on the list." Dave was clearly trying to sound incredulous.

"That's a pity, Dave. You would make a damn fine *shemale*. And I like Delicious. Sounds flirty and fun, don't you think?"

"Sounds wonderful, honey!" Dave said with an affected voice, waving his hands in a sissy way. "How about you? Do you have a travesty name?"

"Travesty women aren't as fun as travesty men. I mean, you can't even compare it. But yeah, if I were a travesty, I would be named Roberto."

"Unbelievable. You actually put thought into that!" he exclaimed.

"You have no idea," I said with a mischievous smile. "But hey, we are rambling here. Let's get back to our discussion."

"I don't know, Izzy. As much as I would like to know the circumstances in which your cherry was popped, I must confess that I am very tempted to ask you about your Roberto side . . ."

"Oh, please! If I had a real Roberto side in me, I would score more girls than you," I deadpanned. "You know that, don't you? I'm such a waste as a heterosexual."

"I couldn't agree more!" Dave teased.

"Very funny, Dave," I grumbled.

"It kind of is." He winked.

"Okay, we can cross that one out. There's never been any girl-on-girl action for me," I said, trying to put an end to that conversation. "I wonder if lesbians who never had sex with men can be considered virgins or if their cherries are popped anyway."

"Uh, that's a good one," he agreed.

"Okay, let's focus and get back to your cherry," I said, snapping out of my ramblings.

"Technically, I don't think that my cherry can be popped, since I am a straight guy," he pointed out.

"For the sake of argument, let's say that you could and you did have your cherry popped, in a straight way, I mean. Do you remember how it felt?" I asked.

"Honestly? No, I don't," he said blankly.

"Who was she?"

"I don't even remember her face, much less her name."

"Dave?"

"Hmm?"

"You suck!"

Dave's honesty was overwhelming. Losing his virginity had been a goal and had meant nothing to him, as with so many boys. But strangely, that bothered me and, I didn't know exactly why. Truth be told, I never knew why it bothered me, but I always assumed that it was because it somehow stained the bit of hope that I had stashed away for him in my pool of guilt, as the good Christian I never was. He'd done far worse and would do far more unforgivable actions with my connivance. He was no saint and I was no prude, but I guess that at some remote level, I wanted to hold to a shred, as tiny as it might be, of his innocence, one that would justify and amend his actions . . . and my omissions.

After Clara, there was no stooping to Dave's bad boy reputation. He scored more girls than he could manage and with very few effort or merit, I might add. And the more aloof he became, the more women he attracted. Naturally, the more women he fooled around with, the closer he got to convince one to let him pass the final frontier. And beyond. Literally.

However, these were still the times when being easy was not a compliment to a girl, and I have to take my hat off to Dave, because even at this age, he wasn't the guy to go for the easy catches. Well, at least not recurrently. There was normally more to his women, even when he didn't remember them.

The girl to whom Dave lost his virginity was older than he was. She wasn't much older, but three years did make a difference when a boy was that age. She was eighteen and a senior. She was no hottie and had no special attributes, so Dave said. Apparently, she was rather plain. And despite Dave's lack of memory regarding her name and her face, he remembered the one thing about her that had drawn his attention: she was funny.

It was June, and Dave was hanging around at the city park with his friends on one of those lazy summer nights littered with that thick humid air that seems to hold time in abeyance. The stillness of the trees made them seem frozen in time, and even the birds seemed bothered by the hot air, for you couldn't hear a chirp cutting the night.

The only noises to be heard were of people and the eventual car that passed by on one of the surrounding streets. Nearby, a group of girls was also lazing around on the benches near the football field. It didn't take long for the boys to notice the girls. They seemed older but not much older. Naturally, the guys started to show off their abilities on their skateboards, as the good adolescent males overflowing with hormones that they were. And thank God for clichés, which keep ensuring the reliability of some things, because it worked. Half an hour later, the two groups had become one.

There was laughter, talk, and fun going around with the easiness that is proper to these ages but doesn't come around very often in adulthood. The boys were younger, but the girls didn't seem to mind. They were having simple fun with no strings or labels attached. Age and gender didn't seem to matter.

"Does anyone know why all the other numbers are afraid of number seven?" A girlie voice asked between the bustle of voices that was cutting through the silence of the night.

The lack of response prompted her to give the answer.

"Because seven, eight, nine! Get it? Seven *ate* nine?" she blurted out, laughing hysterically. The joke wasn't that funny, but her laughter infected everyone around her, and soon they were all laughing. This was when Dave noticed her.

She exuded sheer energy. She was not pretty, and she looked plain and timid. She had a pale complexion and lifeless blonde hair that seemed to fuse with her skin, not to mention one of those faces with forgettable features. If you had to use a word to describe her, it would be beige. She was beige. But she was one of those persons who has the ability of growing on others and stunning them with an unexpected poise. She was one of those persons who, once you meet her, you can no longer say is plain or unattractive, because you no longer see features; you only see personality.

As the night wore on, Dave became more and more aware of her personality. She was hilarious. She cracked dirty jokes with the same finesse that she gave her opinion about starving children in Africa. Yes, at some point during the night someone brought that up for no valid reason whatsoever. And at some other point during the night, Dave found himself sitting near the girl and talking to her.

"I love Supertramp! They're the best band ever," she said.

"They're great, I'll give you that. But they are far from being the best band ever," Dave said matter-of-factly. When it came to music, Dave held his ground as few did. It was one of his true passions, and music came to him as fundamentally as breathing.

"And here I was thinking you were still listening to *Sesame Street* songs," she mocked. "Who's your favorite band? And before you answer, please remember that Big Bird is not the lead singer of any band!"

"You don't say? You just killed all my beliefs," Dave said, pretending to be ravaged.

"No, I didn't. Not yet!" she jeered. "I'm sorry to also be the one to tell you this, but—brace yourself—Santa Claus is not real either!"

"Noooooooo! Stop. Just Stop! You're slaying me here! Have you no heart, woman?" Dave sneered dramatically.

She laughed at his mockery. "Nope. And I've known it since I was eight."

"Well, at least I had that figured out—by myself, I might add—when I was five."

"Jeez, so you've known that for, like, what? Three, four years now?" She winked at him while dazzling him with a mischievous smile.

"Do I look that old? I'm only six, you know." Dave tried to exhaust the subject. She obviously knew that he was probably much younger than she was, and that seemed to be a problem that he needed to work around.

"I do eat my vegetables, which explains my overdeveloped body, and I listen to good music, which actually includes Supertramp . . ." He was baiting her.

"See? Told you! They're the best," she said, cutting Dave off.

Dave continued, despite the interruption. "But as I was saying, that includes Supertramp and bands that are much more awesome, such as . . ."

"Please don't say AC/DC!" she screeched. "That's just noise, you know."

"I wasn't going to mention AC/DC, but thank you for reminding me of them. They are beyond awesome! So besides AC/DC, you have Depeche Mode, Queen, INXS, Peter Gabriel, Def Leppard, you name it, who are way better than Supertramp." Before she could retort, he continued in a purposely cocky way. "And I'm not even including the gods. I'm not gonna pull into this conversation Dire Straits, or U2, or the Rolling Stones. I don't want to humiliate you."

"U2?" she said excitedly. "Aren't they those guys who released an album last year named *The Fire* . . . something? The one that has that song 'In the Name of Love'? I love that song!"

"*The Unforgettable Fire* is what the album is called, and the song is Pride [In the Name of Love]."

"Well done! Want me to give you a treat, sweetie?" she teased, talking to him as if he were a little boy who had just done a trick.

Dave looked her in the eyes, all mockery gone from his face, and he licked his lips lingeringly before answering her in a low voice. "That depends on what you're offering." And he lowered his gaze from her eyes to her lips. And back again.

Her face gained a serious expression as well, and she swallowed hard, never leaving Dave's gaze, though. "You know Supertramp's 'Give a Little Bit'?" she asked, not really wanting an answer. "The one that goes 'I'll give a little bit . . .'" She hummed the rest of the verse and sang only the last verse, the one that says to send a smile and show you care. She sang it in a sweet voice, still never leaving his eyes.

Dave stood, looking at her, and he smiled broadly to let her know his answer. He sang the lyrics that followed the ones she'd sung. He sang with all his heart and reached for her hand when the words "Take his hand, you'll be surprised" left his mouth.

And she did take his hand. They stayed there hand in hand, talking about music and joking while one after the other, people started fading away. It was almost dawn when they realized that they were about the only ones left. Everyone else had gone home or was hooking up nearby. Some of his friends had been lucky (too).

"You wanna get out of here?" she asked.

"Yeah, sure," he said, trying to sound cool.

They strolled through the park, revisiting their early conversation about music groups, but awkward silence filled most of the gaps. This was the dead man walk. They both knew where they were heading, and there was no turning back. Well, at least Dave hoped there wasn't.

They settled down on a bench near the ice cream kiosk, the farthest and most secluded one. She sat and Dave stood in front of her. He was nervous now, not knowing if he had interpreted her invitation the right way. Girls always pulled the friendship card in the worst situations. But she had thrown a lot of dirty jokes and innuendos at him during the night. She had complimented him. He'd heard her say to her girlfriends that he was cute, and that she bet he'd be strenuous in bed. Well, she hadn't said it so bluntly, but what else could she mean by saying that she'd put down her money if he weren't a two-pump chump?

These were still the days when Dave had a shred of innocence left in him. Soon after, it would all be gone, though not that night.

"So how old are you?" Dave asked, trying to break the silence but regretting the words as soon as they left his mouth. That was a dumb move. He should know better than to ask questions that he didn't want to answer himself.

"I'm eighteen. And you?" And there it was—the ugly question that could jeopardize his hopes of getting laid, properly and willingly this time, right there and then. What does one do in critical times like these? Lies! What else? There's no point in trying to deflect the question. It's out there, and going around it will only raise suspicions. Answering it truthfully will most likely get you nowhere, at least nowhere near where you want to be. So you lie. You lie through your teeth and cross your fingers that you sound every bit convincing as you think you do in your head.

"I'm almost eighteen," Dave stated.

"You don't look eighteen," she countered.

"That's because I'm not. I'm almost, but I'm not eighteen yet." Before she had time to dissect the implication of Dave's words, he carried on. "You don't look eighteen either."

"What do I look like, then?"

"You look beautiful," he said, staring her in the eyes. Sometimes the best defense truly is a good offense. He had nothing to lose but hope. And his virginity.

"You're cute," she teased, averting her gaze before silence overcame them again and left them hanging on the moment. It was that awkward moment before you kiss someone, when a heavy silence overpowers everything, anxiety grows, discomfort seizes all movements, and all you hear is your breathing.

"Can I kiss you?" Dave asked, and I must confess that to this date, this is a debate that was left unclosed between us. Who in his right mind spoils the moment with an asinine question like that? She was there, alone with him, on June 13, at six o'clock in the morning, on the bench farthest from the kiosk that sold ice cream. Of course he could kiss her! What did he think she was doing there? Knitting? Dave, however, always argued that this was a good move when one wasn't sure, and he thought it was enticing, that it could spike the tension. He used it often.

To me, however, the enticement was lost, as was the tension of not knowing when or if it was going to happen. It also added the risk of getting a no for an answer when he had the possibility of sweeping her off her feet. The memorable kisses are always the unexpected ones, don't you think?

"Yes," she said in a whisper, and the next thing Dave heard was her moan when he pasted his lips to hers.

The connection that had started shy and slow soon developed into something more desperate; in fact, it became so fast that, if needed, one could beat the egg whites for a cake with it. Dave's words, not mine. The desire quickly consumed him, and he, with the eagerness of the inexperienced, hurriedly started fumbling around with his fidgety hands. The fondling went on for a while, and when Dave couldn't take the pressure anymore, and she had her girls feeling like dough from all the kneading, she pushed Dave away. Dave's first time sounded a lot like baking, I suppose.

"Do you have protection?" she asked.

"Yes." This time, the whisper came from him, and as soon as the realization of what was about to happen hit him, Dave started clumsily looking for the prophylactic that he kept in his wallet. One never knows, and he thought it looked cool to carry a rubber around. As soon as he reached it, he quickly ripped the packet foil with his teeth, forgetting to be careful not to tear the precious content inside it, such was his eagerness. Fortunately, the wiener wrapper was intact and no irreparable harm was done, as far as he was able to ascertain. Exhaling deeply, Dave mentally reviewed the technique of gloving the love stick. Definitely easier said than done. He had tried it at home once or twice before, just to be prepared, but now, with the pressure, he was starting to fear that he might not manage it.

"Here, let me do it," she said, taking hold of the situation in a literal sense. "Have you ever done this before?" She seemed a bit concerned.

"Sure," Dave lied, summoning all the confidence he could gather, under the circumstances, to pull it off. No pun intended. He was nervous and excited, and all he had ever imagined about that moment was happening! All the films he had watched were proving to be useless in this moment, for nothing could have prepared him for the real deal—except experience, but he had none.

Most girls he'd been with so far were less experienced than he was, and even the ones that weren't didn't let the necking go very far, at least not that far. This being said, all that Dave had been able to touch so far were breasts, Clara's being on the top of his short list. And now there he was, ready to go the whole shebang, and he was scared to death of it. Well, he truly was scared of a bad performance, and I could honestly never fathom how he could even hope for a non-mortifying one, much less a decent one, under the circumstances.

First times are, by nature, supposed to be awkward and low in expectations, if you are a down-to-earth kind of person. If you're a dreamer, they'll just be hopeless and desperate. And if you're neither, they'll be, hopefully, endearing and heartwarming. But they're rarely good. Nevertheless, they always leave their mark.

Dave's didn't last long, and he jumped the poor girl's bones literally, hard and clumsily. He jumped on top of her so much that she skinned her butt on the bench and got a splinter stuck in one of her thighs. No encore followed on that or any other day, and sadly, he never saw her again. Dave's first time remained the first and only for a while, allowing him to engrave the memory of it deep down in his mind as a detached and clumsy sexual experience. But it was his first real one.

"That was it?" I asked.

"What were you expecting?" he countered, raising a brow at me.

"Well, you said that it had been good," I said. "How in the hell was that good? You jumped on her and stuck your love stick in her—and I'm guessing that it wasn't an easy task, given the absence of foreplay!"

"I'm a guy. It was good!" Dave said, rolling his eyes as if his statement had been self-explanatory.

"If you're into trampolines, I guess it might have been. I have a friend who deflowered—I love this word—two guys, and not at the same time, before you ask, and she told me that they jumped on her a lot. It must be a virgin guy thing."

"Yeah, right, call it a *friend*, Izzy," Dave said sarcastically.

I shifted to adjust my position, laying my back on the couch again and no longer seeing Dave's face, and I resumed my staring at the ceiling, where he had been looking all along. We remained like that for a while, just hearing each other breathe.

"You came in her hands when she tried to put the condom on you, didn't you?" I asked, my eyes glued to the ceiling as I tried my best not to burst out laughing.

"I will neither confirm nor deny it," Dave said with faked solemnity.

And he never told me.

CHAPTER 4

HERE'S TO YOU, MRS. ROBINSON

Have you ever had one of those moments where you inadvertently locked eyes with someone and the world around you suddenly ceased to exist? A pang blasted through your heart, making it skip more than a beat, your breathing became erratic, and you knew, deep in your soul, that something had broken free and changed in you forever? Me neither. But this was how Dave fell in love for the first time.

He fell in love under a tree, waiting for the autumn rain to pass and without any other expectation than to see time run its course. His eyes were stuck on the ground and his mind was lost in the depths of nowhere when he heard the steps that brought him back to this world. He looked up, toward the sound, and her eyes were all he saw. Everything else faded away as his body was consumed by the flush of feelings that ran through him, and the certainty that reason was abandoning his heart struck him. All he managed was a gasp.

She looked right back at him, keeping her eyes on his as she passed by under her pink umbrella, her pace slowing down but never stopping. Then she broke the stare, and he could swear he saw her lips slightly curling up in a faint smile as she turned her head forward and walked away, resuming her pace.

He saw her walking away and followed her with his eyes, stuck in the moment, unable to move. She never even glanced back. He never gathered the nerve to go after her.

When Dave came to his senses, the rain was gone and he couldn't tell how much time had passed without his noticing. It was night already. Now that the days were shorter, it seemed that there was never dusk. The night came without warning, as if it were something doomed to happen. So he headed home, her eyes never leaving his thoughts. It was all he got. He hadn't seen her face properly, but those big brown eyes were engraved in his soul.

The thought of it, the bizarreness of the entire situation, overwhelmed Dave during the following days. How could he be so obsessed with a girl whose face he might not even recognize? How was it possible? For all he knew, she could be utterly boring or ugly. But why couldn't he think of anything else? Why did he feel so needy, so desperate of her? Was this love at first sight? Did he even believe in such a thing?

At that time, Dave was still naive. Well, at least part of him was—the part that still held the belief in the constancy of feelings. He'd met his share of girls over the last two years. He was now a young man with far more broken hearts at his account than he should have, but in the matters of love, true love, he was still raw.

The girl in the park had become a turning point once the inglorious memento with her stopped eroding Dave's brooding memories. Since he'd made his peace with his shameful performance, Dave made it his mission to pursue nothing less than all a girl could give him. In fact, he had become merciless at it. Since that day in the park, more than a year ago, he'd bedded several girls, and none had truly mattered to him. He liked the sex, that was granted, but he realized that he loved the hunt. Once he had what he wanted, the thrill of the hunt wore out and he lost all interest in his prey. He would immediately move on to the next one without giving it a second thought. He had figured out that bad boys truly are the ones who have the most fun.

But he wasn't having fun now. He was looking for her eyes on every girl, on every street, and in the weeks that followed, nothing else mattered to him. The beauty of the situation, and for me personally, the purity of Dave in it all, was that he didn't fear the unknown. It consumed him, not out of ignorance but out of distress. He was more than willing to free-fall into whatever this was with no regard for his own heart, as do all dreamers and lovers who haven't experienced the hardships of pain. The helplessness of it all was only despairing him.

Who was she? Where was she?

Then one day, unexpectedly, he saw her. Her eyes again. The same electric rush that had drowned him in anguish so far washed over him with the fury of a hundred tides. All air was sucked out of his lungs, his stomach dropped a thousand miles, and his heart burst into a million pieces; she was holding some guy's hand. Her gaze was frozen on Dave's, and her smile was lost in a clash of astonishment. The guy, who was speaking to someone, was oblivious to the exchange, but he yanked her out of her daze once he started saying his good-byes and walked toward the school building.

This time Dave followed her. *Them*. The guy left her at a classroom doorway, planting a kiss on her mouth and giving a swat to her backside but failing to notice that her eyes were looking at someone else. They were looking at Dave, who stood a small distance away, experiencing the burn of desperation crawling under his skin and a surge of irrational rage erupting through him. Dave was jealous.

He walked past her, who still stood at the doorway facing him, and forced himself not to glance in her direction. He was mad. She had a boyfriend. And it had never occurred to him that that was a possibility, that she had a life beyond him. That she wasn't as affected as he was. That he was alone in his distress. That she was real.

Once the wrath washed away and reason slowly stepped in, Dave allowed himself to think things through. She had a boyfriend, which made him have a problem. Perhaps not that big of a problem, though, judging by the way that she'd looked at him. He'd felt it. She had held nothing back, and he was almost certain that what he had seen in her eyes was a reflection of his own feelings and longings. He knew it in his gut. But he had to do things right, which took time. As his uncle Casanova had taught him, good things come to those who wait.

So he waited. Then he started encircling her, breaking her resistances, placating her internal war and the fears that he saw in her eyes when he caught her looking at him. But he did all this from a distance. At first, he looked at her, and then he looked away from her to see if she searched for his look. Finally, they couldn't keep their eyes from each other. She was so beautiful, more than he could have hoped or imagined. Her eyes were so big, bright, and full of life that her soul gushed through them. Her eyes spoke volumes; they could give you a thousand words with one look only. And more, much more.

Inevitably, their silent communications started being heard by her boyfriend. Naturally, Dave was pleased with that. Wreaking havoc was one of his goals, and it seemed that he had already shaken their foundations. The only problem with a jealous and insecure boyfriend was that he was now constantly hovering around the wide-eyed girl, whose name, by the way, was Sarah, as Dave managed to find out.

The silent courtship took its time, more than Dave cared to admit or wished to endure, but it had a motivational effect on him. More than ever, he was enjoying the hunt. So when the time came for him to take his prey down, he was ready. Or so he thought.

It happened at a crowded Christmas party that someone had thrown. All of Dave's friends were there, as was she . . . with her boyfriend. He didn't look at her, though, despite her pleading stares at him. He didn't want the boyfriend to be on the lookout. So he feigned indifference, and once the boyfriend neglected his attention and left her on her own, sitting on a chair at the end of the room, Dave crossed the dance floor toward her with a swaggering pace and a wild determination. She never saw him coming. When she noticed him, he was already bent over her, had one hand cupping the nape of her neck and the other one placed on the wall behind her, caging her, and his lips were brushing her ear. She never stood a chance.

"I'm Dave," he said, and without hesitation or warning, he grasped her face with both hands and kissed her with all he had. She kissed him back, questionless. Time, space, people, and everything else vanished. When they broke the kiss, they were standing in the middle of the room, not knowing how they'd gotten there, and looking into each other's eyes. It was a memorable kiss.

The next thing Dave felt was also memorable. It was her boyfriend's fist punching his nose and breaking it, gracing Dave with the bump that gave all that personality to his thereafter crooked snout. Blood gushed everywhere as Dave fell down on the floor, the raging boyfriend ready to pounce and beat him into a pulp.

"You earned that one, but if you touch me again, I'll break your teeth," Dave managed to say as he raised himself from the floor, wiping the blood from his nose to his shirt as a crowd surrounded them.

Honestly, Dave knew that the poor guy was more than entitled to punch him. Repeatedly. After all, Dave did go after the guy's girlfriend, stepping all over him. But as they say, all's fair in love and war.

It helped that the boyfriend was smaller and thinner than Dave was. Nevertheless, Dave was, well, Dave. He was a reputable and popular bad boy who had all his friends to back him up there. But even so, the boyfriend had something bigger than that, which was a bruised ego and the stupidity that naturally flows from it. So he went for the killing. Surprisingly, he managed to throw in a few more punches and give Dave a black eye and a split lip to go with the broken nose before they were broken apart. He was, of course, in a much worst state, with at least one broken tooth and several other injuries to go with his torn heart.

And Sarah? Sarah never hesitated. She stood by Dave and didn't let go, as if it had always been like that. As if he were the prince charming that had rescued her from the claws of the evil . . . well, not prince. The boyfriend wasn't a bad guy. He just wasn't Dave. This being said, there was never an official breakup, or any kind of conversation regarding the start of a new relationship. It all went as natural as breathing to all of them.

From then on, when you saw Dave, you would see Sarah. They were inseparable. They fit well together. Dave's tall frame and, at the time, almost broad shoulders seemed to fill her smallness. She was petite and curvy. She had a doll face, with her big brown eyes framed by untamed curly brown hair and a smile that radiated sympathy. She was quite lovely. My words, not Dave's. According to Dave, when he showed me her picture, she was hot as hell and the most beautiful girl in the world, at that time. She was his first girlfriend and, as he truly thought then, the love of his life. Potentially. Nonetheless, she was his first love.

She was different from all the other girls that he'd known so far. He couldn't get enough of her. Everything she said or did was interesting to him, and he could spend hours, literally, just looking at her or hearing her talk. They spent all their waking time together, and yes, one could say that he had it bad. He even took her home to meet his parents and went to her home to meet hers. Well, her mom at least, since her father was currently working on a project that kept him away for long periods of time. The man was a well-known psychiatrist who, it seemed, did justice to the myth that to be a shrink, one has to be a bit crazy. The "it takes one to know one" kind of thing. According to Sarah, however, he wasn't crazy at all. He was just a bit eccentric sometimes and absentminded the rest of the time. She thought he was great, and contrary to what others thought they had a close relationship.

Sarah was an only child and the devoted center of her parents' undivided attention. Although her father was away, Sarah's mother tried her best to fill the hole that the momentary absence of her husband caused in both of them. So above all, she strived to make their house cozy and inviting. Dave said that the house always smelled of baked cookies and cakes, which gave him a sense of belonging. He liked it there. Besides, the house seemed to attract movement; it was always busy with people, mostly Sarah's mom's friends.

Sarah's mother, being a homemaker by marriage and not by choice, since she often mourned her lost Latin teacher's career openly, liked the fuss. It made her feel less empty and helped her forget about her lost dreams. So the house was frequently packed with middle-aged housewives who, to Dave's delight, openly shared the juicy details of their torpid marriages. Moreover, being the only man around not only gave Dave insight to the amount of sexual frustration those women nurtured, but it also made him the ladies' eye candy and object of teasing. He loved it. Especially because some of them were seriously hot and sassy, even if the flirting was, of course, quite innocent and mostly joking.

Truth be told, at this time, Dave was already quite a charmer, courtesy of Uncle Casanova, but Dave's merit nonetheless. As expected, the ladies raved about Dave's gentleness. He was, in their words, such a fine and well-mannered young man. And indeed he was. Independently of Uncle Casanova's advice about charming the pants out of women and Dave's own bad boy tendencies, his upbringing had been exquisite. Therefore, Dave managed to pull off effortlessly his badass attitude while squandering sympathy. It was quite a feat.

The ladies loved to have him around, and he liked it as well, especially when they did those Tupperware parties there. Not that he would attend them, but both Sarah and him soon realized that those busy times were the best for sneaking into Sarah's room and having some hot and steamy make-out sessions without being noticed. Apparently, plastic containers of multiple sizes and purposes somehow got the ladies more excited than he did.

But with or without Tupperware parties, Dave did his best to respect Sarah. He tried to take it slow. She was a virgin, and he wanted to make it special for her. He wanted her to feel ready to take that step. This was a trait of character that I always appreciated in Dave: the keen ability to delude himself. And he was genuine at it too; he believed in every word he professed. He truly wanted to be *that* man, the one who waited and didn't push his way. However, despite all his good intentions, after three months of dating Sarah and a severe case of blue balls, Dave was becoming impatient. He wanted more, and she kept teasing him, never making up her mind about it. So fighting about it became inevitable.

"Stop pressuring me," she growled under her breath.

"I'm not! I just want to know, Sarah," Dave said, a bit peeved.

"Well, I don't know. I'm just fifteen, Dave. I'm too young to be having sex." Sarah was visibly upset.

"Fine, have it your way. But when you're old enough, don't come find me, because by then I'll make damn sure that I don't love you anymore." Dave turned his back on her and stormed out of her house.

"Dave!" she cried out as she followed him out the door, but he didn't even flinch. He kept on going and didn't turn back, ensuring that he left her with the right amount of drama dripping from their teenager love. It was the first time he'd said he loved her, and if he'd played his cards right, it would serve his purpose. During the following days, Dave ignored her and gave her the cold shoulder but made sure that she saw him talking to other girls. At this time, Dave was already sufficiently self-assured to hold his bluff and wait for her to break. He knew she loved him and wasn't proud enough to give him up, especially when there were so many other girls ready to take her place.

He was right. After not even one week had passed, Sarah showed up at his place, wanting to talk and willing to hand him her virginity, which he took one week after that. Dave made it special, though. Or so he hoped. Genuinely.

Once sex got into the equation, Dave reinforced his belief that Sarah was the love of his life, for the time being. They didn't do it as often as Dave wished, but they were finally having sex, mostly rushed, sticky missionary encounters during Tupperware meetings. But it was sex nevertheless. Sarah seemed okay with it, and she assured Dave that she enjoyed it and found it pleasant.

The truth was that Dave had had his share of sex so far, but he didn't know how to please a woman. He'd only had shoddy sex in dark alleys and other similar uncomfortable places and taken the virginity of a few girls under the utmost strangest situations, which mostly didn't even have encores. I recall Dave telling me the sad case of the baker's daughter, whose innocence was stolen on top of her father's sacks of bread flour at the rear of Sunny Bakery in the middle of the night. Or even Red Sonya's story, whose nickname—well known and made popular throughout the school—drifted from the unfortunate fact that she'd had sex with Dave while having her period. They had gotten caught by the school janitor, who rushed them to math class, both unaware that their clothes were smeared with her menstrual blood. Consequently, Red Sonya got the slutty nickname and Dave got a reinforcement of his bad boy reputation. Eventually in life, we all learn that the world is a cruel and unfair place—and that nothing nice ever comes out of sex during menstruation. Pun intended.

So as time went by and Dave and Sarah's relationship settled down uneventfully, Dave realized that he was appeased and content with the course that his life was taking. He was, in his own words, numbly happy. He was preparing to go to college, he had a girlfriend that he really liked, and he had great friends. He had it all.

If I didn't know Dave any better, I would tell you that that was the problem . . . his problem. However, that wasn't it. Surely he was, by nature, dissatisfied. But there and then, that wasn't it. It was something else. Have you ever had that feeling that your life is happening just as it should? That everything is perfect and then, just because you can, you blow it all and ruin everything just to indulge the rush of the moment? That was the problem. Dave, as Oscar Wilde had wisely put it, could resist anything except temptation.

So one afternoon, similar to hundreds of others before it, Dave walked up to Sarah's house to see her, knocked on the door, and let himself in without waiting for anyone's say-so. Neither Sarah nor her mother was there. Only a friend of Sarah's mother was there, the hot blonde woman who kept giving him the stare of a wildcat.

"Dave, how nice to see you!" she shrieked.

"Hi. I'm looking for Sarah." Dave looked around searching for her.

"I'm sure you are, but she's not here. You just missed her. Her mother took her to see a math tutor. Seems she's been neglecting her grades since she started dating . . ." She spoke languidly.

"Oh." Dave was unsure if he was bothered about not knowing about her grades or not having been told that she was going to a math tutor.

She responded as if she'd read his mind. "She didn't know it either. It was a last-minute thing. Her mother got word of this new tutor and rushed Sarah there."

"Oh," Dave said again.

"I see that you have a way with words, young man," she said sarcastically. "I hope your way with other things is more . . . diversified." She'd whispered this in a hoarse voice, and she moved in his direction like a feline, her gaze never leaving his.

Dave swallowed hard and felt his heart thumping like a drum in his chest as the woman approached. It all happened so fast and unexpectedly, and when he realized that she was already inches away from him, this was when they heard Sarah's mother entering the house. The woman jumped back, fixing her hair with both hands and plastering a wide-open fake smile on her lips.

"Oh, hi there," she said as Sarah's mother looked at both of them with a questioning look. "You almost scared me. I think that the cake is ready. I'll go get it out of the oven." "There's no need. I can do it. You don't need to worry about that. Thank you so much, darling. I'll not keep you any longer. I'm sure you have things to do." Sarah's mother said this with an equally fake smile, dismissing the woman courteously. She knew.

Sarah's mother was an odd woman. She was cheery, nice, and supportive, but she had a fire in her eyes sometimes—a fire that she seemed desperate to put out and light up at the same time. Dave had seen it before and was seeing it now. She thought something happened there or at least had been about to happen. He didn't know what to say. He'd done nothing, but he didn't know how that had looked like in the eyes of the beholder.

"You want a slice of cake, Dave?" Sarah's mother asked, but Dave knew it wasn't an invitation to eat.

"Sure." Dave followed her down to the kitchen and stood silently by the freezer as he watched her unmold the cake. Sarah's mother grabbed a knife and sliced the steaming cake that now rested on a plate.

"Now, be careful and let it cool for a bit. We don't want you having any gripes, do we?" she asked, but not really asking again. "Milk?"

"Sure," Dave managed to say, getting fidgety.

"Sarah went to math tutoring. She'll be back in an hour or so," she offered, not looking at him.

"Okay," he muttered.

She moved past him and accidentally brushed her heavy chest against him as she reached for the refrigerator handle to take out the milk. Sarah's mother was one of those busty women with wide shoulders who carry their weight in their upper bodies and normally have nice legs. Sarah had her eyes, but her mother's hair was straight and a lighter shade of brown. She was average-looking, but she was voluptuous and there was something about her, when you looked at the whole assembly that made her attractive.

"You've been sleeping with my daughter," she said flatly.

This undoubtedly wasn't a question. Or a statement Dave wished to address, for that matter. So he didn't. He just stood still, waiting for her next move.

"Have you been with other women?" Sarah's mother asked as she moved toward him. He felt the air in his lungs vanishing and unease rushing through him as he pressed his back against the freezer in the hopes of putting more space between them . . . or running. She stood before him, a foot parting them, staring into his eyes. And there it was again, the fire, burning more than ever. She raised her hand and put her forefinger over Dave's mouth. "Do you want to?" she asked. And to this question, he knew the answer instantly.

Everything went down fast. Dave opened his mouth abruptly, and her finger clumsily plopped into it. He gasped at the unexpected intrusion, but he didn't dwell on it since the next thing he noticed was her grabbing his face and kissing him. She removed the finger first, in case you were wondering about it. I did.

"No way!" I said, my mouth hanging open from the shock. I turned to where Dave was sitting near me on the ground. We were shitloaded drunk, in the middle of the night, sitting on the ground in a public park somewhere I couldn't brace myself to name. I recall the day having started out normally: my going to work, working, leaving work . . . Dave waiting for me outside my office with a bottle of whiskey. Ah, yes! From there on, everything was sort of a blur, until we ended up at that park, sprawled out on the ground, drinking whiskey from the bottle.

"Way, Izzy!" Dave exclaimed, burping.

"You are shitting me!" I cried out, burping as well.

"I shit you not."

"You did not kiss your mother's girlfriend."

"I did! I swear to God, Izzy, I did," Dave said, putting a hand over his heart.

"Say it again, looking at me," I demanded.

"What, you gonna look into my eyes and know if I'm lying?" he sneered.

"No, that's bullshit, and I'm way too drunk to get your eyes focused anyway. But you have a tell when you lie, so let's have it. Say it again." I faced him.

"What's my tell?" he asked, eagerly.

"I'm not telling you; otherwise, I won't be able to know when you're lying to me!" I retorted.

"I don't lie to you," he said, offended.

"Yes, you do. Or did. Anyway, it doesn't matter. Say it again."

"I slept with my girlfriend's mother. There." He said it with all seriousness.

"Ah! You really did, you bastard. And you lied to me!" I cried, still astonished with Dave's revelation.

"I'm telling the truth," he stammered, sounding confused.

"Yeah, I know. But you lied to me before. I was fishing, and you fell for it when I said you'd lied to me before. I suspected it, but now I know for sure. You didn't refute it. That's why I know that you did it. Lie, I mean. Boy, I'm so drunk. But I will remember this conversation tomorrow. You know that, don't you, Dave?" I was rambling.

"I wouldn't expect it otherwise. Now, may I continue my tale?"

"There's more?" I asked, astonished.

"Of course there is! I slept with Sarah's mother for a solid month or two. Or three." He said this deadpan.

"Did she teach you everything you know in bed?" I asked mischievously.

"I have to admit that she was a life lesson, so yes, she taught me a lot, but not everything," Dave confessed.

"Are you any good in bed, Dave?" I asked softly.

"Wouldn't you like to know? I haven't had complaints, Izzy," he bragged.

"You do know that women fake orgasms, don't you, Dave?" I asked with an innocent smile plastered on my face. Or so I thought I did, but it was more likely that I got my idiotic drunk face on. "You know, I was just wondering when's Simon and Garfunkel's 'Mrs. Robinson' is going to start playing."

"Shut up, Izzy!" Dave scolded, nudging me in the ribs. "Do you want to hear the rest of it, or do you just want to sit there cracking stupid jokes?"

"I don't think it can get any better, but I do want to hear the rest of it, Dave. But first I need to know if you were covered in chocolate that day . . ."

"What?" Dave asked, cutting me off and, I sensed, starting to get really annoyed with my drunkenness.

"Well, you had to be covered in chocolate that day; otherwise, how do you explain being attacked by two middle-aged women in the same day? I mean, come on, Dave. That's kind of unrealistic, yet strangely, I have no doubt that it happened. But you have to agree that it's almost surreal. There has to be an explanation to that phenomenon! Care to share it?"

"When you're hot like me . . ." Dave started out in a cockish tone.

"Cut the crap, Dave, and give me the goodies!" I demanded, proceeding to hum "Mrs. Robinson."

As it turned out, Sarah's mother's rampant kiss, which was followed by the best sex Dave had had in his life so far, which wasn't all that surprising or difficult given Dave's and Dave's sex partners' lack of experience in the field, wasn't all that out of the blue. And Catwoman (the blonde lady who almost attacked him before Sarah's mom actually did it, and whom I refused to picture any other way than a foxy middle-aged blonde dressed in animal print, despite Dave telling me otherwise) was frisky and had been on to him for a while, but opportunity was only presented that day. Regretfully.

Sarah's mother had gone from being a wild and carefree girl to a frustrated woman trapped in a marriage that had lost its sparkle many moons ago. Her husband had become a distant man entwined in his eccentricity, and he failed to give her the attention and love that she longed for. The woman was a pit of need and want, clinging to a dream of a career that had never happened and a marriage that was long gone, although she managed to mask all of this under a busy shallow life. In the end, it was not about the lost career or the unfulfilling marriage; it was about the entrapment in a life that she felt didn't fit her but that she was forced to accept as hers.

Probably when she saw Dave's willingness and desire to fall into her friend's arms that day, she didn't prevent the fire from her private hell from burning inside her chest, and maybe she thought of herself before thinking about the others. That's how what started with a raw and animalistic kiss developed into desperate kitchen table sex with hair spread over a steaming banana cake. It was quick, needy, and unsatisfactory for her. Yet it wasn't shameful to either of them. Even when Dave was pulling his jeans up or Sarah's mother was straightening out her skirt without any exchange of words between them, there was no shame or discomfort in that silence.

That's probably why the next day that Sarah went to her math tutoring, Dave went to her house and to her mother. He knocked on the door and let himself in, and just as he had wished, he found her alone.

"Hi," he said, thrusting his hands in the front pocket of his jeans and looking at her as if all hope from Pandora's box was trapped in his eyes.

There was a moment of hesitation, when perhaps guilt and morality made their claims into Sarah's mother's thoughts, but they never reached her heart. Her fire burned higher. She took Dave's hand and led him into her bedroom, where she made sure that this time he did good by her.

During these encounters, Dave's unseasoned eagerness toward sex was tamed and refined. He learned that women's bodies are not like vehicle motors; they need time and dedication to get started and the right touch to become ignited. He quickly learned that sticking or rubbing fingers into holes or squeezing the girls as if they were rubber ducks would not get him the right kind of shriek. And he finally became acquainted with foreplay.

The oddity of it all was that these exchanges occurred without much verbal communication to entertain them. They would touch, lick, kiss, claim, and grab each other, but they would rarely speak, parting their own ways once their longings were appeased. Time was precious, and they really did not have that much to talk about, apart from the obvious, which they opted to ignore. As if the fact, since not addressed, would not become real.

Nonetheless, the few words they exchanged ended up being relevant and meaningful.

"*Abyssus abyssum invocat,*" Sarah's mother once told him with a hoarse voice while she rode him. Those words were engraved in his mind and tattooed on his arm forever.

Sarah was oblivious to these encounters, and not even Dave's enhanced sexual performance and repertoire, or her introduction to the wonderful world of orgasms, made her suspect that something might be wrong. However, as time went by, Dave's detachment started to show, and then, only then, did Sarah start to feel the unease that was growing between them.

Dave, being Dave, was choking on his guilt and suffering from the lack of conflict between his love for Sarah and his desire for her mother. Not feeling it made him question his humanity. But mostly, it made him fuel the growing weight of the unspoken affair in his conscience as a way of compensation and self-punishment. To top it all, the then smothering effect of Sarah's love gave Dave the undeniable certainty that he and he alone had tainted their love. The stain was there, and he could not bring himself to overcome it, thus their love was irremediably ruined. The reason it that as strange as it might be, and like his uncle Casanova, Dave was, above all, a hopeless romantic.

"What's wrong, Dave? You've been acting weird," Sarah said.

"Nothing's wrong," Dave lied.

"Don't lie to me," she scolded softly. "I know you better than that. You've been distant."

"It's nothing. I'm just worried about all the college stuff, you know."

"I know that there's more than that." Sarah paused, assessing his mood, and then she went on. "I know that something is worrying you and that things with your parents are not very well . . ." And before Dave, who was already opening his mouth to interrupt her, could say anything, she raised her hand in a clear shut-up-and-listen-to-me sign and raised her voice one octave. "I was thinking that it would be good for you if you talked with someone. Someone who could give you some guidance and counseling, you know, help you to deal with these matters. So I talked to my father and asked him to see you when he comes home next week. He said yes."

Dave's balls dropped to the floor. Hard. This could not be happening to him. Yet it was.

"What?" Dave shouted.

"Calm down, baby. It will be good for you," Sarah reassured him.

"Are you crazy? I'm your boyfriend!" he shouted. "He's your father! I'm not going to talk with him about my life. It's weird!"

"He doesn't know you're my boyfriend! I'm only going to tell him when he comes home, because I want to do it in person." Sarah said. "Besides, whatever you say to my father will be bound by doctor-patient confidentiality."

I don't know if it was a self-inflicted need for punishment or plain stupidity, but Dave went to that appointment. He sat in front of the man whose daughter and wife he was screwing and poured his heart out to him. God only knows what possessed him to succumb to a severe and painful case of mental diarrhea.

According to Dave, he blocked when he saw Sarah's father. And he was so nervous that the connection between his brain and his mouth seemed nonexistent, so he had no control over whatever woes burst from him. Leastwise, he managed to omit the names, which softened the blow, but aside from that, he gave the poor man all the sordid details. Moreover, he knew, at some point if not from the beginning, of whom Dave was speaking. He knew whose daughter and whose wife Dave was talking about, even if he didn't want to admit it.

Dave sat in Sarah's father office for the longest hour of his life. When he finished speaking, he was sweating as if he'd run a marathon and he felt nauseated. Sarah's father looked at him from behind his desk for what seemed like the longest minute of silence in the history of humanity. His stare was blank and devoid of any emotion.

"Your time is over." That was all he said to Dave.

And Dave knew without further words what that meant. He knew that his time with Sarah, with Sarah's mother, and with pure love and naivety was over.

Nevertheless, he still went to Sarah on the following days, dodging all her attempts to introduce him to her father as her boyfriend. But the guilt and the angst became unbearable and too much for him to bear, so he forced himself to do the inevitable and broke up with her. He told her that he was going to college soon and didn't believe in long-distance relationships, so breaking up now was for the best.

Sarah cried her heart out and begged him to reconsider. He died a little that day, but he did not back down. He couldn't change things, and he had to live with the guilt that he alone had ruined them.

*   *   *

"What does it mean?" I asked, motioning my chin in Dave's arm direction, and though he didn't need clarification, I offered it. "Your tattoo."

"Hell calls to hell."

CHAPTER 5

THE MEANING OF LIFE

Murphy's Law: If anything can go wrong, it will go wrong. And left to themselves, things tend to go from bad to worse.

After Dave's and Sarah's breakup, he saw her very little and her mother even less, and only from a distance. Sarah gathered the necessary pride to mourn her heartbreak silently and managed the strength to cut all ties that linked her to him. There was anger, regret, and resentment in her eyes, but Dave could tell that there was no acknowledgment. As he expected, her father hadn't said a word. He couldn't, of course, but more than that, Dave knew that he wouldn't. He knew that ignoring the truth was far more convenient than to be forced to act upon it. Dave knew that Sarah would never learn the truth and that she would end up hating him, though not for the right reasons.

Sarah's misguided hate scarred Dave more than he thought possible. In the beginning, it cut through his soul and ripped all innocence that he had left there, for she mattered to him. She was the first woman he had ever loved. And knowing that he was the one causing her all that suffering just because he had been selfish made him feel vile. I asked him once if he regretted it. If given the opportunity, he would have done things differently. He told me that he regretted it tremendously, but even if he could, he would not have changed a thing. I knew him well enough to understand what he meant. That was who he was and how he lived—with regrets but no doubts.

The breakup with Sarah took place around the same time that Dave's parents divorced. Dave's father moved out and left his mother crumbling in despair and self-pity. After his share of affairs, Dave's father decided to fall in love with a younger woman who was half Dave's mother's age. Albeit lacking tremendously in originality, Dave's father had chosen the easy path of midlife crisis to sustain his decision—or lack of it, since truly, the man just wanted out of his meaningless life. He neither hated nor pitied the life he lived. He just disliked the numbness that he felt by living it and the apathy that the people who were in it evoked in him. Worse than feeling hate, self-pity, or sadness was not feeling at all, so he wanted out desperately.

Dave saw his father's reasons better than anyone, for despite beating himself up for it, he not only understood them, but he felt them too. That made him loathe his father even more. Dave blamed him for being so alike him and for his own flaws, as if they were a hereditary disease. But it was Dave's mother's diagnosed depression (not by Sarah's father, by the way) that broke the last strings of respect that bound father and son. Dave cut all ties with his father then.

As Dave felt his world shatter around him, he began to develop what would become his typical behavioral pattern toward problems: he acted out. Not that uncommon, true, but in Dave's case, ignoring his problems and resorting to drugs, alcohol, and sex to cope with them was already a normal behavior in him. Dave did not need any sorts of problems to use drugs, alcohol, or have vast amounts of sex with a great variety of women. Yet this complicated things.

With Dave, it was all about the small details. The changes were slightest. He always had the same fire burning inside him; only what fueled it changed. He would act edgier, he would risk more, and he would surrender control, albeit subtly. And as he became more carefree in his actions, it would be clearer that whatever was eating him had taken over.

Dave normally ignored his real problems by not addressing them or acknowledging their existence with the person or thing that caused them. As if by doing that, they'd cease to exist. But inside, he would brood them to exhaustion. He would close himself to the world and dwell with his demons until they conquered him, and they normally did, even when I was there to help him fight them.

It was around this time, while he was still feeding his share of guilt over Sarah and his home resembled the spoils of a war, that Dave started to use heavier drugs. And it was under the influence of drugs that his first two tattoos were made. He tattooed Sarah's mom's words—*Abyssus abyssum invocat*—on the inside of his left forearm to remind him not that the first step toward the temptation of simply letting go was hard to avoid, but how pulled he felt to the deeps. To Dave, the attraction of the abyss was inexorable, so he needed a constant reminder.

I believe that Dave must have tried almost every drug available in the market at the time, except heroin. He didn't inject it, I mean, but he smoked it. Dave's self-destructive ability and abyss attraction had the double effect of scaring and fascinating me, because the line that prevented him from free-falling into the depths was all but existent. Yet he held himself there, on the razor's edge, nevertheless. He always juggled that fragile balance, and I learned to admire that trait in him because it takes great effort and strong character to acknowledge one's weaknesses and dwell with them on a daily basis without giving in. You see, Dave's demons might torment and conquer him, but they never ruled him. He did. He was always his own master and commander.

In his attempts to numb the darkness that consumed him, Dave did all that was at his reach to make Sarah hate him, which I believe he accomplished with great success given the amount of women he managed to sleep with at the time. Shamelessly, I might add, taking advantage of the wounded bad boy type that he personified, since women's obsession with saving men from themselves is timeless.

During this time, Dave had at his disposal a girl who would follow him like a dog. He even named her Lassie. Eventually, he took pity on her and forced her to get a life that did not involve him. Eventually, she grew some self-respect and got one. He also dated a gothic college girl who was into some kinky business. It didn't last long. But Dave recalled fondly the day she asked him to pin her to the bed, slap her, and call her a whore, which he promptly did and treasured as the only time he'd hit a girl. I told him that it probably wouldn't classify as such, since it had only occurred because she requested him to do it. The fact that he took pleasure in it was irrelevant. Regardless, he liked to think of it as the only situation when a man could hit a woman and actually be proud of himself for doing it.

I used to tease Dave about it, saying that that had been the inspiration for his second tattoo. It hadn't, but it could have been. On top of his heart, it read, "Give a little beat" in a spiky font that resembled the waves of an ECG. Of all Dave's tattoos, this one was always my favorite because it assured me that he would never lose his hope. I also liked the double meaning that linked the tattoo to the girl in the park, the one to whom he had lost his virginity. It wasn't the Supertramp song title, but it sounded the same, and I believe that it was intended that way. He got this tattoo while he was still high after a crazy night of partying that made him question a lot more than the flaws in his character.

He'd started drinking with his friends during the afternoon, which was quite normal then. They were listening to music and simply hanging out. The beers kept coming, and then some weed tagged along, and after a while, they were all laughing like crazy. It was one of those moments when you're so high that even television static is funny as hell. Incontrollable laughter rushed through him, and he was crying from laughing so hard. It went on for three hours or maybe ten minutes. He couldn't tell which.

It only stopped when he felt the stinging pain in his stomach reminding him that he was starving. Weed always made him hungry. Next thing he knew, they were eating hamburgers at some old diner that smelled like grease and had yellowish walls covered with corny framed platitudes. From "Time heals all wounds" to "Every cloud has a silver lining," they had them all. Dave couldn't help but notice the one that was directly on the wall opposite of where he was sitting, framed in gold and written in what seemed like embroidery. It read, "What goes around comes around." He couldn't help wondering if it really did. I guess that years later, when he met me, he got more than the answer to that question.

Dave and his friends left the diner after paying for all the burgers they managed to shovel down their throats and every possible consideration about the platitudes on the walls had been made. After all the laughter, a philosophical mood stepped in and took hold of them.

Whether it was the remains of their baked state or the profound thoughts about the meaning of life that adolescence invokes in all of us, the truth was that high or not, they just couldn't get any deeper.

"Life's a bitch!" one of them said, roaming down the street to nowhere in particular as the rest of them followed him.

"Yeah!" someone else agreed.

"You really think everything happens for a reason? Like everything you do is because of something?"

"That would mean that you have no control over what happens in your life, man."

"Yeah, and that God exists. That's definitely a proof that God exists."

"I don't believe in God. I think that's all bullshit. I think that God is man's invention to make us control each other, you know? Like making us do the right thing out of fear of going to hell."

"My grandmother says hell is right here on Earth . . ."

"What's the right thing?" Dave asked as they kept wandering the empty streets.

"The right thing is what society tells you to do."

"See? I told you guys. It's how they control us."

"Yeah, like they castrate our own ideas and tell us they're wrong because they don't fit the parameters."

"Castrate? Parameters? Man, where did you learn those words? Have you been reading the dictionary or something?"

"You should try it sometime. Girls dig smart guys."

"Guessing by the number of girls you scored so far, either they don't consider you all that smart or you've just been meeting the dumb ones."

"Look who's talking . . ."

"Have you ever wondered what we're doing here?" Dave asked.

"Talking?" one of them offered without a trace of humor in his voice.

"No, I mean, what's our purpose in life?" Dave clarified.

"Sex, drugs, and rock and roll."

"Now, that's a good purpose, man."

"What if we could do anything we wanted and go unpunished?"

"I already do that, man."

"You know what I mean. What if we could live without rules and do whatever we wanted, no regrets, no penalties . . ."

"That's anarchy, man."

"That's freedom!"

"But do you want to do anything illegal and not get punished? We're all over eighteen now, so there are, like, real consequences! All of us can get punished and stuff."

"Yeah, we're adults now!" one of them stated proudly.

"No, I want that possibility, but not to do illegal stuff. Just imagine living life doing all the things you like without concerns, just being happy."

"According to my father, I'm already living that life."

"Have you ever thought about what happens when you die? Like, if there's a heaven?"

"Yeah, but what would be heaven like?"

"Heaven is like what you imagine it would be in your dream life. To me, heaven would be surfing all day and then having all the girls I wanted and all the pot I could smoke . . ."

"You don't know how to surf . . ."

"I don't know how—yet."

"Well, imagine that to that fat girl who's been chasing you, heaven is having a relationship with you. So would you, like, be stuck in her heaven with her? Or would you be in your heaven and there would be, like, another you in her heaven? But if you were aware of that, wouldn't that be hell to you?"

"Hey, man, that was low. You just ruined my heaven fantasy."

"You know what would be heaven right now? Drinking something with alcohol in it," Dave said.

The next thing they knew, they were at a bar downtown, drinking and talking—not the profound gibberish that they'd covered earlier, though. The bar was full, and they had managed to enter without any problems since a cousin of a friend of his worked as a doorman there. The walls were covered with bright colors, everyone seemed chatty and friendly, and they had no difficulty ordering drinks. Soon enough, they were all drunk again. At some point, one of Dave's friends handed him something and told him to pop it in his mouth and enjoy the ride. He didn't even give it a second thought as he did it.

The next thing Dave recalled were the walls around him starting to blister and drip big fat drops of paint while they wobbled to the sound of the music. And he could see the music—waves of music coming and going; people twisting like screws as the sound hit them. It was the most amazing thing he had ever seen. He danced while the paint drops dripped down. Big yellow, blue, and green drops were seeping down in zigzags. Smiley sappy people swayed and spun as the sound swatted them. Everything was so pretty; everything was so good.

Then or thereafter—who knew?—they went out to the streets in a flood of voices and laughter. People, lots people, and the dark night and no more colors draining from the walls. There was just darkness and the sound of steps. Steps stepping stones. Dave was still high, but it was slowly fading away by then.

"Where are we going?" Dave asked one of his friends.

"We're going to that guy's house," his friend said, pointing to some guy who was leading the way.

"Oh. Who's he?"

"He's this guy we met at the bar. Don't you remember? He says he has drinks and other stuff at his house, so we can continue the party there." Dave's friend wiggled his brows as he said the words "other stuff," as if trying to make a point.

"Cool," Dave managed.

The guy lived nearby, in a two-bedroom apartment with a big balcony. It was on a high floor and had a nice view. Apart from Dave and his three friends, there were around ten more people there. Dave's friends started mingling and talking to the girls, but Dave went to sit on the balcony. His daze was fading, and he was getting drowsy. The music and the people sounds from the room behind him became a buzz, and he must have dozed off. When he was coherent, he realized that there was only a dull sound of jazz music playing in the back and a dim light coming through the glass doors that led to the balcony. He could see the shadows moving inside, but where he sat, it was dark as pitch.

It didn't take him long, though, to notice that he wasn't alone on the balcony. He heard the noises first. There was the sound of two persons pushing into each other, moaning and groping with urgency. Dave stood there listening, the darkness allowing him to see only silhouettes, the groans building his arousal. He only noticed his panting when the two figures stopped and looked in his direction, the silence enveloping the three of them. Then the taller one made a subtle head motion in Dave's direction, as if giving a silent order to the other.

There was a pause, as if the smaller figure was assessing the request, and then Dave could only see the shoulder-length hair stirring and the slender figure moving in his direction and kneeling in front of him. He closed his eyes, not wanting to see anymore, and then he felt a pair of hands sliding up his thighs and stopping at his fly. He moaned, giving his approval, and dropped his head back while his hands clasped firmly at the chair arms. The figure lay at his feet, nestled between his thighs, and moved the zipper in his trousers down slowly, as if to entice him, and the figure that stood at the balcony corner watched them. Then he felt the soft hands searching for him, freeing his woody self, and then stroking him . . . once and then twice. A velvety tongue caressed the tip of his love stick and moved up and down his length before engulfing him with the softest lips ever. He gasped.

He felt the head in front of him moving up and down, up and down, and the arousing sensation of that wet tongue moving along him as if he were an ice cream cone. And those lips enwrapping him . . .

It felt so good. But what made it even better was the knowledge that the eyes of the figure in the corner were upon him, that his moans and groans were being heard. That someone was feeling aroused by watching him. He could hear the figure panting, and by the way that its contours writhed when he'd open his eyes to steal a glimpse, he could tell that it was touching itself. That knowledge acted like a fuse to his own arousal. He liked it. A lot.

So he reached for the bobbing head, sliding his fingers through the smooth hair and grabbing it to guide the movements at his own rhythm. The figure in the corner kept watching in the dark. He ran a hand down the hair that spread over his lap, stroking it, while his other hand kept a firm grip on the bobbing head. He released it and trailed the tips of his fingers down her forehead, her nose, her beard . . . Dave froze, an adrenaline rush running through him, the hand that rested in the hair grasping it and pulling it to stop the rocking motion, his other hand brushing a stiff beard.

The person blowing him was a man.

With his mouth ajar, he locked his gaze with that of the guy kneeling in front of him, who still had him in his mouth. A glance of hesitation and confusion crossed the guy's eyes. And then fear.

Dave breathed deeply and exhaled lingeringly. His grip on the guy's hair loosened, and he dropped his head back, closing his eyes again. "Don't stop," Dave said. And then he finished in the guy's mouth.

When he opened his eyes again, he noticed his friends standing at the balcony entrance. He stood up, zipped his fly, and left the balcony, walking past them without acknowledging their presence. They followed him out of the apartment and into the streets without a word.

They walked in silence. One of them lit a joint and, after giving it some puffs, passed it around. Once the high started to kick in, they started to relax and it became inevitable.

"Fuck, Dave!"

"Yeah, man. What was that all about?"

"Are you gay or something?"

"God, no! I didn't know it was a guy until . . . Listen, I don't want to talk about it. Things have been rough, and that's it." Dave was trying to kill the subject.

"But . . ." one of the guys started.

"I don't want to talk about it. Ever!" Dave's shout silenced them all, not to mention any attempts of development on the topic.

"Okay, man." They all acquiesced, though only one of them voiced it.

They kept wandering through the paved streets in silence. After a while, their errant walk led them to a little tattoo shop with a bright pink neon sign that read Nighttime Tattoos. Dave didn't think twice. He opened the store door and went in, followed by his friends. The space was small and stunted, covered from top to bottom with photos of tattoos and reeking of cigarettes. Unsurprisingly, a bald guy covered in tattoos sat behind a small counter with a cigarette hanging from the corner of his mouth. Dave picked up a pen and drew what he wanted, more or less. The guy looked at it for a while, gave it some polishing, and then, when they were both satisfied, pressed his tattoo pistol on top of Dave's heart and gave him his "Give a little beat" tattoo in a spiky font. Nobody asked him for any explanations, because they all knew they wouldn't come and because that's what friends do. They stick by you no matter what.

They never talked about or even acknowledge it thereafter. It was as if nothing had happened, but not to Dave, though. Being Dave, he obsessed about it for a long time, and he only found some peace when he spoke about it with his younger brother. And not because his brother shed any light on the matter or assured him of his straight sexuality. He didn't. Dave didn't really need any assurance regarding his sexuality. However, this was the touchstone of the close relationship they developed afterward. It made Dave truly understand and accept his brother and, most importantly, be befriended by him without reservations

More than anything, this episode was the last straw in Dave's hope, at the time. He dwelled on it and went totally numb, independently of the peace of mind that the newly found bond he had formed with his younger brother gave him. So Dave did what he did best. He pressed the eject button and ran from it all. He roamed the country with a backpack, camping and hitchhiking his way around, alone and adrift, overthinking the importance and meaning of his every action and questioning where it would lead him. He brooded about the consequences of his steps and anticipated their outcome. But he never forgot the freedom of letting go. Simply. Letting. Go.

It took him four weeks and a severe case of skin rash to make him find his paths back to hope and home (they weren't the same). Truly, I think that the paths found him and not the other way around. But one thing was for sure: he'd finally acknowledged his contradictory nature, though he didn't accept it, and he had stopped searching for the meaning of life.

The conflict between what he did and what he thought was ever present and a trait of his character that he would never nurture but would always feed for it was primal and instinctive. He couldn't run or hide from it; however, he could fight it, and that was meaningful.

When Dave told me the balcony story, my only remark to him was that that was certainly a blow job to remember. And I meant it. There was something poetic about it, though I realized Dave didn't see it like that. I noticed him staring at me with an incredulous look in his eyes that was bordering on a hurtful one, and he asked me bitterly, "Really, Izzy? That's all you have to say?"

It was. I knew that anything else I might say, he wouldn't want to hear it. So there was really nothing else to say or talk about, because we both knew that I knew why he had done it. Not saying it, though, allowed him to sustain the illusion that he alone kept the truth.

I knew that he'd probably known all along that it was a guy blowing him, and that he would always refuse to admit it—to me and even to himself. I knew that he had stupidly struggled for ages with doubts about this event just to mask his real fear: numbness. I knew that he had let the guy blow him because he desperately wanted to feel anything . . . and because nothing else had mattered then. And I knew that his tattoo was his desperate cry to his own heart not to lose hope and let himself feel.

Anything at all.

CHAPTER 6

GREAT EXPECTATIONS

So how do you come back from numbness? Well, in Dave's case, he went away to college.

It was that time in life when madness was the normalcy, and it resumed to parties, drugs, and women.

Again! Or, if we're going to be accurate and include Dave's particular case, yet.

And that was basically it.

College, to Dave, summed up to that and to majoring in arts.

Dave recalled those years in a fragmented and disconnected way, such were the gaps in his memory when it came to it. Although I firmly believed that he'd vilely murdered most of his brain cells at the time, things didn't blur in his mind when the subject was broached. They flashed. So every time he mentioned college in my presence, I would be immediately compelled to sing the *Flash Gordon* theme song's chorus.

And yes, it did get old, but I'd do it anyway, mainly because I liked the sound of it.

Despite the apparent randomness of Dave's flashbacks, I always managed to find the connecting thread in his stories that gave us the rationale we both needed when it came to his life.

To me, Dave's college experience seemed something out of a book. He'd done the mundane things associated with it, of course. He'd gone to class, done laundry, eaten crappy food, made friends, dated girls, gotten drunk and high, stressed about exams, embraced ideologies, and gained a purpose in life. While most of us this did this, because that's what college sums up to, Dave did it fully, as he tended to do all things in his life. Except love.

He never loved fully. Not because he didn't want to, but because he was, as I said before, a romantic. It's true. He wanted a love without boundaries, limits, or doubts. A love that would last him a lifetime even if he only had it for a day. A love that would be so unequivocal that no questions remained. He wouldn't settle for less than that, because he couldn't settle for anything. And less than that would be nothing. So he lived fully because he couldn't do it any other way and because that was the only path, he thought, to find what he believed in. Not that he searched for it, though. He tended, unwittingly, to put his faith in the universe and wait for it to hand him whatever he was supposed to deal with. Sort of.

"Flash! Aha!" I sang, cutting off Dave's ramblings about college experiences between two bites of cake.

"Threesomes!" he exclaimed suddenly, swallowing a barely chewed piece of cake that almost made him choke.

"For real?" I asked, ignoring his distress.

"No, it only happened in my head. But I thought about it a lot and touched myself while I did it, so it felt real," Dave retorted sarcastically, already recomposed. I laughed.

"That's every man's fantasy, Dave. It's serious business!" I said, still laughing. "Did it live up to your expectations?" I asked, genuinely interested.

"Jeez, Izzy. I don't know why I keep telling you these things."

"What?" I snorted.

"You never ask the right questions," he deadpanned.

"Sorry, let me take it down a notch so that I can tune in to your line of thought," I mocked. "Were they, like, really hot girls? Did they have, like, big tits?" I added, chewing imaginary gum and acting dumb while I twirled a strand of my hair with my fingers.

"Keep it down, will you?" Dave said, shushing me and looking around to see if any of the other patrons in the coffee shop were looking at us or showing any signs of having heard our conversation.

"Nobody's listening," I told him dismissively. And then it hit me. I had an epiphany. "Holy crap on a cracker! You had a threesome with a man," I whispered.

"Who the hell still says 'holy crap on a cracker' nowadays, Izzy? Where do you dig that stuff up?" He sounded dumbfounded.

"You're getting better at this!" I said, eyeing him almost respectfully. "But I don't need to take you off guard to know that you had a threesome with a man . . . and a woman?" I said, purposefully pausing and adding the last part as a question just to pester him.

I must say that at that time, I still hadn't gained knowledge of Dave's balcony story. In fact, he only told me about it years later. If I'd known it by then, I trust it might have compromised my epiphany.

"You're such a . . . witch," Dave said smugly, winking an eye at me and confirming my suspicions.

"That's why you love me!" I exclaimed, regretting the words as soon as they left my mouth. Our awkward talk was still too fresh in our minds for me to be so carefree about things like that. Dave was still very sensitive about it, and my attempts to clear the air had failed to be anything but uncomfortable. Despite our best efforts, things hadn't been the same between us since we had addressed the elephant in the room. And I was still overwhelmed by how easily putting into words what we both felt could cause such damage to how we acted around each other, even if we felt the same and wanted the same. But Dave didn't know that at the time.

"My first threesome was—and yes, there was more than one—with two women," Dave said, clearly trying to deflate our awkward moment.

Going back to our initial conversation was the wiser thing to do, so we stuck to it while we drank our coffees. Besides, what could there possibly be about threesomes that might not be fun to know?

A lot, apparently.

First of all, if you're a man in bed with two women, just embrace the fact that what you imagined in your head will not become real unless (a) you're Superman; (b) you're high on Viagra; or (c) in your fantasy, only you get to have fun.

Now, if you're a woman in bed with a man and another woman, please read the last paragraph again and adapt the options accordingly.

That's it!

Well, honestly, that's what I drew out from Dave's first threesome experience.

The odd thing, as if there was only one oddity about it, is that Dave's first threesome story did not start as his other stories usually did. He was neither stoned nor drunk, and it was sort of a ladies' and gentleman's agreement, to my utter delight.

It all started one day when Dave sat at the esplanade of a bar, where he and his colleagues used to hang out, with two girls who were friends of his. They were drinking beers and making small talk about this and that. They had known each other for a while then, and they shared the same musical tastes, liked the same movies, and had the same visions about life, liberty, and Fruit of the Loom commercials.

"What do you think about *Wild Orchid*?" one of the girls asked.

"I think I liked *Nine and a Half Weeks* better," the other one said.

"I still haven't seen *Wild Orchid*. I'm thinking of going to the cinema this weekend. You girls recommend it?" Dave asked.

"I most definitely do. It's . . . intense."

"Ehh . . ." The girl that had liked the first movie better frowned.

"Oh, come on! Don't tell me you didn't find it at least interesting?" the other one asked, a bit startled.

"I found it surreal. Sex in these kinds of movies is always pretty and intense, therefore lacking reality."

"I didn't know you were such a purist."

"I'm not. I'm simply a realist. Come on, it does not happen like that in real life. It just doesn't!"

"What do you mean by that?" Dave asked, totally taken by the talk that was going on in front of him.

"I think you should be asking her who she has been doing and not what she means, Dave."

"Very funny! You know what I mean. In real life, nobody has sex between sheets! Nobody comes like that, and when you finish, there's always that awkward moment when his fluids run down your thighs. Yeah, so go ahead and tell me that I'm a purist."

"Hmm, I'll have to agree with you on that last part. The fluids thing is gross, and you don't see it in the movies. The first time it happened to me, I was beyond mortified."

"And whose fault was it? The movies, I'm telling you. In the movies, they always make sweet love and come at the same time, and in the end, they cuddle and nothing comes out of the girl's vagina. Nothing. Never!"

"True," the other girl acquiesced, clearly won over by her friend's arguments.

"You don't always come?" Dave asked, as if that had been the only thing that had caught his attention or proved to be the point of the entire conversation.

There was a moment of silence while the two girls faced each other and then Dave with confused looks on their faces before they answered no. Most of the time they didn't come at all.

"Now I want to know who have you been doing, ladies," Dave said conceitedly.

"Look at you, Mr. Hotshot!"

"Well, I don't have complaints," Dave said, raising his hands in a defensive gesture.

"Is that right?"

"I don't want to brag, but yeah, that's right," Dave bragged.

"You do have a nice reputation—I'll give you that."

"How would you know?" Dave asked, suspicious.

"I heard a girl in my economics class talking about you . . . and she was saying nice things, to put it shortly."

"Hmm, who was she?" Dave asked.

"I don't think I know her name, but she's a cute blonde with a nice smile . . ."

"That could be a lot of people," Dave said, scanning his mind in search of the blonde.

"With big breasts?" the girl added.

"Ah, the swimmer!" Dave shouted, snapping his fingers as soon as he heard his friend mention the identifying element.

"Hmm?"

"She's a blonde girl who is on the swim team," Dave clarified.

"I think so, yeah."

The swimmer was uneventful, apart from the doubt that was forever nestled in my mind regarding the feasibility, in practical terms, of a competitive swimmer having large breasts. What can I say? I lose myself in the details. Dave dated her for a while and then got bored, as he always did. So he moved on, and so did she. There was no damage resulting, since no one had deep feelings or high expectations regarding the affair. And as there was nothing remarkable to remember about her or the brief period of time in which they shared each other's company, Dave lost memory of her name and would have forgotten completely about her if she hadn't been the catalyst to his first threesome. Apparently, there are many ways a woman can leave her mark on a man.

"What did she say about me?" he asked, curious.

"You know how they say that curiosity killed the cat."

"Yeah, but they also say that satisfaction brought him back," Dave promptly replied.

"Is that so?"

"It is. So, what did she say about me?"

"Well, she said you made all her wildest fantasies come true. At least that's what I overheard her saying."

"Well, now I'm wondering what those fantasies were. Do tell, Dave!" the girl who had been mostly silent urged.

"A gentleman never tells, ladies."

"Oh, come on! You're not going to leave us hanging here now!"

No matter how much of a gentleman a man might be, the allure of bragging about his sexual abilities will most certainly overpower his manners at one point or another. Good thing Dave was not a gentleman; he was a hunter. And he was already foreseeing the possibilities that lay in front of him. Literally. He was offered their curiosity, and now he needed to gain their trust.

"There's not much to tell," Dave mumbled, playing hard to get.

"Dave! You have to tell us!"

"I'll tell you this: her fantasies were not that wild." He sighed, feigning exasperation.

"What do you mean by that?"

"Exactly what I said. There wasn't anything special about her fantasies. They were pretty . . . standard."

"Standard? What the hell are standard fantasies? You're killing us here, Dave!"

"Wait, what would you consider a wild fantasy?"

"Well, by my standards there's really not much that I would classify as wild." Dave smirked, averting the girls' piercing gazes.

"Wow! I don't even know how to interpret that. Tell me one thing that you would consider wild."

"Let's do it the other way around. I don't want to shock you. What would be a wild fantasy to you? A threesome?" He was trying to sound hesitant.

"Hmm, I don't know," one of the girls said, looking at the other, who was also mentally debating on the theme, as if in search of support or validation for her own thoughts on the matter. "Yeah . . . maybe a threesome, right?" She said it tentatively, continuing to look at the other girl.

"With two men or with another woman and a man?"

"I don't know . . . I think both."

"But how do you think you would feel more comfortable?"

"I think I would rather do it with another woman and a man," one of them said.

"Why?" he asked.

"I don't know. I think I would feel less slutty."

"I hadn't thought about it that way, but now that you mention it, I think that you might have a point," the other girl said. "I guess I would also rather do it with another woman and a man."

"Ah, ladies, there is where the problem lies! You are more worried about what you think about it than what you feel about it."

"Well, that's easy for you to say. You're a man. If you do something like that, you're a stallion. If we do it, we're sluts. Plain and simple as that."

"What if nobody knew about it?" Dave said. "Ever."

"Yeah, right. What guy would keep his mouth shut about it?"

"I would." He shrugged.

There was a moment of silence between the three of them while they absorbed the implications of Dave's words.

"Yeah, right," one of the girls said dismissively.

"How long have you known me? How many times have you heard me brag about the girls I sleep with or the stuff I do?"

"That's not the point . . ."

"I know it's not! The point is, would you do it if you knew that no one would ever find out about it?"

"I don't know. I never really thought about . . ."

"There's your problem. You think too much instead of seizing the moment," Dave pointed out.

"I would!" the other girl, who had been silently listening to the conversation for a while now, blurted out.

"You would? I didn't know you were so forward."

"Well, I am. We only live once, and there are a lot of things that I would like to try. Especially now, when we can still blame it on our young age and immaturity."

"She's right. This is the time in life where we owe it to ourselves to be wild," Dave said.

"Hmm . . . What if you do something and then regret it after?"

"If you don't go, you never gonna know!" Dave said, phrasing what would become one of his life mottos.

"Yeah, let's do it!"

"What? Like, the three of us?"

"Yeah! Why not? We've known each other for a while, so it wouldn't be weird. We trust each other, so it would be established right here and now that this is never to be mentioned to anyone. Ever! And Dave, having quite the reputation with the ladies and being our friend, would be the perfect guy to do it with. I mean, think about it!"

"Hmm. I don't know. What do you think, Dave? Is this too crazy? Aren't we going to ruin things between us?"

"I don't see how. But I will only do it if you're sure about it."

"Hey, would this classify as a wild fantasy to you, Dave?"

"Honestly?" Dave asked, deliberately pausing for suspense. "I'll tell you later." He had a mischievous smile plastered on his lips.

It didn't require great effort on Dave's account to seal the deal. Once stoked to do it, the girls didn't take much convincing on the details of the doing itself. Dave knew, however, that he had to act quickly and couldn't let the thought die. This kind of zest for life outbursts tended to fade away in a blink of an eye. So Dave stuck by them all day and went home with them at night. And it happened!

It was not great at all.

For starters, they were all nervous and hadn't had the good sense to drink themselves into the stupor that would allow them to relax. The girls were all hands and sloppy fingers, grabbing anything that stuck out in an attempt to lighten the air. Dave, on the other hand, was feeling the pressure of having to please two women who were his friends at the same time—or at least with a short time frame between . . . pleasings. Moreover, the entire thing was driving him insane because he had two naked women in front of him, touching each other and him, though awkwardly, and he had to last. For the life of him, he had to last!

It didn't go well. He didn't last.

Honestly, I think Dave's hopes on this were much too high for his own sake. And expectations, when that great, tend to overshadow the true value of things. In fact, even no expectations at all can leave the bittersweet taste of disappointment in your soul when greater things come to view. As they did.

Given Dave's state of mind at the time, he didn't allow himself to succumb to the frustration that poured from his flunked threesome. However, he needed validation—or his male ego did. So he would seek it in the countless female bodies that he managed to enjoy afterward with complete and utter detachment and no remembrance. Until one night.

One night the music was blasting through the speakers in a tiny room packed with bodies that brushed against each other to its sound. It was impossible to dance, given the tight space and the mood that filled it. If sex were breathable, it would have filled every pair of lungs in the room. Dave was there. Breathing. He was either drunk or high. Or both.

He must have left the room at some point, for the next thing that flashed back to his mind was being highly engaged in a conversation with a girl who sat at a table near the bar. She was drunk too, and she had eyes that shined. She had eyes like Sarah's.

They kissed. Then they left the party, staggering through the streets and clinging to each other, laughing and kissing. She lived nearby.

They stumbled around the house until they found her room. She tottered inside, and Dave asked to use the bathroom. Then he went back to her room, with his bladder relieved from all the beer that it had been nestling. The room had a lot of pink—pink pillows, pink comforter, pink rug. Even she was pink. She had silky pink skin that almost blurred with the sheets under which she hid coyly.

Dave undressed himself and lay on top of her, the sheets between them. Like in the movies.

He couldn't close his eyes. Everything spun when he did. So he kept them open, glued to her shiny stare. She seemed nervous now and far more sober. Dave slid under the fabric slowly, keeping her covered, his eyes never leaving hers. He lay on his left side, bringing himself near her and pasting their bare bodies together. He felt her naked under the fabric and started trailing his hand down her body, grabbing and groping.

He reached for her hips and then slid his hand south, caressing. That's when he found the emptiness that hid there. He fumbled with his right hand, insistently searching for what he was missing, and when he realized that he wouldn't find it, confusion and fear struck him. The girl's eyes now shined with the unshed tears that pooled in them, shame covering her face as she bit her lip in an attempt to prevent those tears from falling. She clung to the sheets with a fierceness that immediately faded when Dave gently released her hands and slowly pulled the fabric down, uncovering her body and exposing the stump. Right there, just below the middle of her left thigh, her leg was missing; all there was to see was the pink stump with its pink scars and its slightly folded skin wrapping it up.

Dave sat up in the bed, feeling a wave of nausea, caused by the sudden movement and the remains of his drunkenness hitting him. He forced his eyes to move from her residual limb and roam the room in an attempt to calm himself down. But they froze when they landed on the prosthetic leg resting in the corner near the headboard. His mouth was ajar, and shock was plastered all over his face, as if the vision of the fake limb made it more real.

"I'm sorry," she said, the tears flowing down her face now as she saw Dave's panic. She tried to cover her nakedness with the pink sheets.

Dave inhaled sharply, trying to compose himself. As he looked into her pleading eyes, he felt deeply ashamed of himself, not because of his reaction but because he was repulsed by the vision of her stump and realized that he was prejudiced against sleeping with a handicapped woman. All of a sudden, she'd become deformed in his eyes.

He managed to speak even as he did his best to hide his feelings. "No. I'm sorry. It's just this was . . . unexpected."

The awkward moment filled with silence as they lay there unmoving and not knowing what to do. Dave wanted to flee and not look back, wipe that moment from his existence. Erase it. But when he looked at her again, into those shiny eyes mortified by shame and misplaced guilt, he was overwhelmed by pity. He ran his fingers through his hair, fighting the ignominious feeling, but he couldn't. He pitied her, and he felt bad about it. Therefore, he did the only thing that he thought would appease his conflicting feelings. He made love to her. Gently. Then he grabbed his things and disappeared into the night, crying all the way home in the light rain.

He cried because of all the things he'd done so far, this had felt the noblest and the most despicable of all. He had slept with women out of lust, out of love, out of fun, and even out of opportunity—but never out of pity or obligation. He felt bad about it because, for the first time ever, he had felt like a whore. He'd done it out of pity, but above all, he'd done it to prove to himself that he was not prejudiced. Yet he was, because despite all his efforts, he'd failed to prove himself wrong.

The reality shock numbed Dave for a while, the stump haunting him in his dreams. Eventually, he let it go, and he surprisingly developed the habit of subtly touching women's thighs and limbs in general before taking them to bed. It reassured him.

For a while, but not that long of a while, Dave abstained from having random sex with strangers. In fact, he abstained from having sex at all. He was tired of its emptiness. He had periods like that, and as I grew to know him, I reckon that they worked as a sort of spiritual catharsis, where Dave would expunge most of the ghosts that he clung to. Dave submersed in these states of mind and physical restraint, and most of the time, he came out of them believing he was in love. Those periods normally ended with the start of a new relationship. At least, with time, that became the great expectation of anyone close to Dave—and to Dave himself.

Not long after, like a phoenix reborn from the ashes, Dave felt compelled to love a French dancer who was attending Dave's college for the semester under one of those foreign exchange students programs. As with all affairs with an expiration date affixed on them, their infatuation was intense and consuming. Dave would spend countless afternoons just listening to her talk. He loved how the words sounded in her French pronunciation, how the *r*'s rolled almost endlessly from her mouth. They would read to each other and then make love in public spaces (in that order) because they both thrived on the hazard of being caught. As for the reading foreplay, I must say I never understood it myself, so I'll leave it with God.

They shared the same taste in movies and music and revisited every classic movie in the book. She taught him how to hold a woman and lead her on the dance floor, with great success, I might had. Dave was a great dancer.

Above all, in those few months they were together, they shared themselves entirely. It was one of those perfect loves that time would crystallize and allow them to only revisit in their memories, for that would be the only thing left from it: an enhanced memory of a flawless love to treasure for a lifetime. As with all perfect things . . .

When their time came to its expected ending, which they had been ignoring as one ignores the certainty of death, they divested themselves of all their unreasonable expectations and mourned their affair. She cried all night, and Dave remained stoically composed, holding her in his arms. But inside, his heart was bleeding.

The next day, he took her to the airport, embraced her firmly, and kissed her as if his life depended on it, as if that kiss was their last. Because it was. They never saw or spoke to each other again.

As Dave saw her disappear into the restricted area of the airport, reserved for passengers only, and lowered his arm from their last good-bye wave, he felt at peace. It was over. He turned his back to the place she had lost herself into and walked away without giving it a second thought.

He was numb again.

So how do you come back from numbness?

You don't.

You never really do.

CHAPTER 7

MARIA NUMBER ONE

Picture Jackie Brown.

Now imagine that she's white and that she's called Maria.

Got it?

Then add this: falling in love with the intensity of the blast of an atomic bomb.

That's how hard Dave was hit!

I wouldn't believe it myself; because we were talking about Dave here, it didn't make much sense! But love never needed sense to happen. We all know that.

After graduating college, Dave started to work as a trainee in a company near his hometown. Despite his reckless living, Dave did well in college and graduated without much trouble. He liked his new job and thrived at the prospect of learning and growing professionally, but he soon realized that he had a problem with taking orders or, generically, being bossed around. And that is never good.

Despite his inability to suck up, Dave soon became, as always, quite popular among his colleagues, though he refrained from engaging in close relationships with his fellow female colleagues. Regardless, the task proved to be quite difficult in some cases. There was some innocent flirting and a not-so-innocent encounter with one of the girls from the human resources department in the copy room. He admitted to me that he just couldn't pass up the opportunity of having his way at the copy machine. It was, after all, a classic. It happened only once, though, and sadly, it didn't live up to his expectations.

To my utter disappointment, Dave did not Xerox the girl's ass. He wasn't in college anymore, he told me sternly, trying to make a point out of it, I think. Honestly, I suspect that he beat himself up for not remembering to do it but was too stubborn to admit it.

The working experience seemed to add a degree of maturity to Dave's behavior, and although I wouldn't say that he had sealed a barrier on his past life, one thing seemed to be noticeable: he had changed.

Don't get me wrong. He continued to be his tortured romantic self, with the numb feelings and a need to live life to its fullest, for he was Dave. But now he seemed to have become aware of consequences. Maria was the one who brought that out in him. His actions always had consequences; he knew that. But so far, Dave hadn't cared about or anticipated them. He'd always endure them with more or less bravery, but he was not concerned with them. He didn't think ahead; that's how free he was.

Dave had sucked the marrow out of his college experience, as he had with all experiences that he'd come across in his life so far. I would always admire and envy him for that. Despite the recurrent numbness and the permanent dissatisfaction, in Dave's heart was a sense of fulfillment and the sheer satisfaction of having no doubts. Of knowing. He might not get what he wanted, and he might even end up regretting his actions, but he would live. He couldn't be any other way. By living to the fullest, he accomplished what most of us can't: he didn't miss out on life and he would always know, for good or for bad, what was out there to live for.

When he called me that afternoon after New Year's, saying that he needed to speak to me, I was far from guessing that he was about to pour his heart out and tell me all there was to know about Maria number one.

Our relationship was changing, and we were becoming friends. We'd accomplished that much.

He'd gone home to spend Christmas on the right side of the world—as I liked to call home—and he had seen her. It hurt like hell to see all her glorious indifference. That woman was proud; for that, she had my respect.

Dave was all jet-lagged. He'd arrived the night before and hadn't slept more than three or four hours. He looked like shit. After one look at him, I knew that he felt that way too.

"Hey, Izzy! Thanks for coming. How was Christmas around here?" Dave greeted while opening the door for me to enter his apartment.

"As bad as I expected it to be," I said, matter-of-factly, but I was smiling. I'd missed him; I realized it there and then. "And yours?"

"As good as I expected it to be," he said, closing the door behind me and crossing the room with wide strides toward the window. Then he propped himself up on the large windowsill and pulled a cigarette from the pack that lay there. While he lit up the smoke and gave it a puff, he motioned for me to sit down on the couch in front of him.

"Everything okay with your family and friends?" I asked, trying to bring him down to the moment, as he seemed lost in the clouds of smoke that he tried to blow out the open window.

"I saw her." Dave wasn't looking at me. "Maria," he offered after a while.

Dave and I had been a fixture in each other's lives since I had arrived at the other side of the world, which was how we insisted on referring to our current place of living, as a private joke to how we'd met. I'd been there for three months, so I had heard of Maria. I knew she had been Dave's girlfriend until he decided to move here and leave everything behind, including her. She was the woman who had had him on his knees. That much I'd known since Dave and I met, six months before. But that was about it. He'd mentioned her several times but just in passing. He didn't elaborate and just referred to her on occasion. I didn't push it; that was not how I worked.

That was why this time he offered me all there was to know.

He'd met Maria while he was working at the company where he first interned. She wasn't a colleague there. She was the manager of the bar where Dave and his colleagues hung out after work.

He'd been going there for a while when he saw her for the first time, crossing the bar with her confident walk, her killer smile, and that owner-of-the-world look in her eyes that only a self-assured woman can master. He felt his heart implode. It was that bad.

Maria didn't acknowledge Dave that day or any other day during the following month. That's how long it took him to work up the nerve to talk to her. It really was that bad.

"Did you speak to her this Christmas?" I asked him.

"I tried. She ignored me." He shrugged, eyes sad.

"What on earth did you do to that woman?" I asked in an even voice.

"I made her fall in love with me." Dave said this with a sad smile on his face.

He had. He'd turned her world upside down when he made her fall for him head over heels.

"How long did you date?"

"Around two years, give or take. We broke up when I told her that I wanted to live and work abroad . . . experience different things and meet new people."

"I see. So no chance of a long-distance relationship?" I asked tentatively.

"No. We don't work that way. We're both all or nothing."

"That's . . . radical." I was trying to figure out what I was missing there. Dave never offered details about Maria number one, and I always assumed that it still hurt him to talk about her. It did. Despite all the distance and the time that had gone by, it still hurt him to think of her.

"So you broke up still loving each other," I stated.

He nodded his head.

"There's something that I will always have trouble understanding," I said.

"What?" Dave looked confused.

"I'm not a romantic, you know that, but it always strikes me as sad when two people who love each other don't make it work." I realized the irony of my words as soon as they left my mouth. Who was I to speak? I had lived those words.

Dave lit a second cigarette, inhaling the smoke deeply and gingerly letting it out. "Some things just don't work. If they had to, they would."

"I wouldn't peg you for a fatalist," I sneered.

"I'm not," he said flatly.

He wasn't. He'd just realized that sometimes things just aren't meant to be, no matter what.

"Why do you think things between you and your Maria weren't meant to be?" I asked, ignoring his apparent reserve on the matter.

"We wanted different things for the same reason."

I studied my options cautiously. There was only one right question to ask, and guessing by Dave's posture, I had to get it right if I wanted to hear the end to that story. And I really did want to hear it.

"What was the reason?" I asked, taking my chance after briefly considering what I already knew about Dave. He was all about getting what he wanted, so if he mentioned reasons, that's where the problem lay.

"Age," he mumbled between a long inhale.

"Age?"

"Maria's forty-five now."

"Oh!" I said, trying my best to conceal my astonishment. I hadn't seen that one coming. Although I had suspected that she was older than he was, based on some of the few things he'd said about her, it had never, ever crossed my mind that she might be twenty years older than he was.

"It's okay. I know it's a bit strange for people in the beginning."

Strange was an understatement. It was freaking shocking, at minimum. And I am not one to be easily surprised.

As I processed the information, trying to make sense of what he'd just told me, Dave engaged in a monologue about his and Maria's story that was only interrupted by the lighting of cigarettes, one after another.

When Dave saw Maria for the first time, at the bar that she managed, he felt that a lightning bolt had struck him. The woman was pure sexuality on legs. She exuded confidence, charm, and sensuality. She had every man in the room drooling at her feet. As I said, picture a Caucasian Jackie Brown and you'll get a fair portrait of her looks. He had never seen a woman like her before, and he didn't have a clue about how to approach her. A month of severe drooling later, he summed up the nerve to talk to her and tried to charm her with his witty comments and bad boy tactics. Naturally, it didn't work. She was a woman, not a girl. And she was more than used to being hit on by all kinds of men. He'd seen her politely avoiding the flirting that some clients tried to engage her in, but it summed up to that. She seemed inaccessible and acted unattainable.

Dave's first attempt at talking to her had her eyeing him up and down and smirking at his boldness. Dave had never felt as stupid as he felt then, being dismissed with a mere look. He felt tiny and vulnerable. His heart had been shred into little pieces in just ten seconds, as only a real woman was capable of.

At this time, Dave was still rather smug about his easiness with the ladies and lacked the sense to understand when a woman was out of his league. Maria clearly was. She was stunning, with long straight hair and big brown eyes, with a body that would put most twenty-year-old girls to shame. She was smart, confident, and independent. I'm also certain that she was one of the most sensual women Dave dated.

She was also old enough to be his mother. Literally. Not that that was a problem to Dave. He was quite fond of older women. They were always more eager to give in to lust, and honestly, nothing beat the perks of their willingness to love.

However, Maria was unreachable, and that first encounter showed him that she was not the type of woman who would succumb to his normal antics. After that, she barely noticed him, and that made him feel worse than being ignored, for if she ignored him, he could have had the satisfaction of knowing that she at least acknowledged his existence. But she didn't. He knew that she didn't because when he had passed her on the street a few days later, she greeted him uncertainly, clearly not placing where she knew him from.

He felt demoralized, so he went to his uncle Casanova for help. Not that the man would understand his misery, but if anyone could find a way, it would be him. Dave told him all he knew about Maria and all he'd managed to find out about her too. In addition to her looks and attitude, he'd learned that she was single and that the few men that she'd been seen with didn't last long at her side and, apparently not by their choice.

"She seems quite a woman, Dave," his uncle said.

"She is. And I don't have a clue about what to do to even make her notice me, much less hunt her down."

"Ah, Dave, but you can't!" his uncle exclaimed, amused with his nephew's predicament.

"Can't what? Make her notice me?" Dave asked, confused.

"You're doing it all wrong, Dave! You can't hunt the hunter. You have to ambush him. Be the prey. Haven't I taught you anything?" His uncle chuckled.

Dave felt fourteen again. This was Clara all over again. He didn't have a clue what his uncle meant, but he prayed it didn't involve reading *The Art of War* all over again.

"Some women, Dave, are not for you to dazzle. They dazzle you, and they pick you; not the other way around."

"Okay, but how do I get her attention? Should I go up to her and tell her that she's old or that she has big ears?" Dave mocked. "It worked before . . ."

"Ah, Dave, Dave, Dave. You aren't paying attention! This is not a girl we are talking about. This is a woman who knows what she wants and how she wants it. From what you told me, she picks her men. She won't fall for those basic moves, especially from a twenty-three-year-old boy that still reeks of milk."

Uncle Casanova was, of course, right. Maria was the kind of woman that laid down the rules for men to follow. She didn't play games—at least not this kind.

Dave did the only thing, according to his uncle, that he could do in this situation and prayed for it to work. He approached her coyly and gradually imposed his presence on her. The daily greetings evolved into small talk, and when she seemed comfortable enough with that, Dave attempted to make her laugh, which he did quite successfully. Dave was hilarious. He had a wonderful sense of humor, and a woman loves nothing more than a man who can make her laugh. Moreover, he could take advantage of his young age and add a bit of goofiness to his jokes. Maria loved it, and Dave was thrilled when he realized that she came to expect her daily dose of laugh from him.

"You're so funny, Dave! I bet you don't have that much to complain about," Maria said with a wink, responding to Dave's silly joke about having no luck with the ladies.

If Maria were any other kind of woman, Dave would have hit her with a smart-ass comment and made a move on her, leaving her with no doubts about what he wanted. But she wasn't, so Dave kept his cool and hit her with the best coy lamb eyes he could master and a sad smile. This was it. Now that he'd gained her trust, he needed to let her know how he felt. However, with Maria a full frontal attack would only result in her dismissing him. Again. But a lovesick college kid with puppy eyes who made her laugh . . . Well, that was kind of cute. And cute and funny won't get you dismissed like an old dog.

Maria held his gaze, averting it only a few seconds later, leaving no doubt that she hadn't missed the meaning of his stare. She went around doing her business, and Dave left for the day, not knowing what to expect.

He kept throwing the puppy eyes at her subtly. He had to make it cute, not clingy. She liked it, whether it was the ego massage that she got from it or the possibility of her feeling something for him, the truth was that she liked it. This allowed him to gather up the nerve to take it a little further.

"Can I ask you something, Maria?"

"Sure, Dave."

"What would a guy need to do to take you out?" Dave started out, not masking the nerves that tangled in his stomach or feigning the trembling voice that came out of his mouth. If he'd attempted to pretend it, he would have never gotten it this good. "I mean, as a woman, what do you expect from a man? I mean, how do women like to be wooed?" Dave asked, expectantly looking into her eyes but quickly looking away once she stared back at him.

Maria smiled and studied him for a while before she answered him. "Well, Dave, every woman is different, so it really depends on what she likes." She was worrying her lower lip with her perfect white teeth to prevent the smug smile that threatened to escape her. She was playing him.

"Oh, of course," Dave mumbled, fidgeting with the cocktail napkin in front of him to avoid looking at her. Then he sighed in frustration.

"I, for instance, like a man that cooks for me," she added a moment later, her lips curled up in a smirk that caught only one side of her face.

"Cooks?" Dave asked.

"Yes, Dave. Cooks. As in, makes food for me." The half-smile never left her face. "I find it rather attractive." She turned away, heading to the restricted area of the bar, and he stood there staring at her sexy swing of hips, completely adrift.

*   *   *

"A cake?" Dave asked incredulously, looking at the phone in his hand.

"Yes, Dave. Bake her a cake and make sure you burn it," his uncle said patiently.

"I don't know how to bake a cake," Dave squeaked in desperation, regretting having called his uncle for advice. The man had lost it! He'd told him his conversation with Maria, and his uncle was telling him to bake her a cake.

"Even better, you won't have to make an effort to ruin it."

"But . . ."

"Dave." Uncle Casanova cut him off. "Trust me and bake her a cake."

"What flavor?" Dave asked, resigned.

"Women normally like chocolate," his uncle answered.

So that night, after three hours of intense wrestling with cake batter and a cookbook, Dave managed to produce a chocolate cake that resembled cow manure. Burned cow manure apparently.

Feeling ridiculous and clueless about what to expect, Dave left work a bit earlier the next day, to avoid the after-work flood of patrons, and went to the bar with the cake stored in a cake box that he tucked under his arm.

"You're early today!"

Dave turned on his heels toward Maria's voice.

"Yeah . . ." Dave started, embarrassed, running his free hand over his hair and down to the nape of his neck. "I got something for you . . . Well, not *got*. I kind of actually made it . . . so." Dave shoved the box in her hands while she smiled in a confused way at his rambling speech.

She looked at the small box in her hands, then set it down on the bar counter and opened it slowly, stifling a laugh once she set her eyes on the small turd that lay there.

Dave felt the humiliation taking over him but stood there stoically. "It's a chocolate cake," he explained.

She burst out laughing in his face. He would have blushed if he could, such was the mortification he felt.

"Did you bake this for me, Dave?" she asked, trying to compose herself and wiping the laughing tears from her eyes.

"Yes. You said you liked a man that cooked for you."

She looked him in the eyes, all traces of mockery gone from her face, and ran a hand over his cheek. "That is the sweetest thing a man has ever done for me, Dave," Maria whispered, and stepping closer to him, she gently pulled him by the nape of his neck toward her and kindly brushed her lips over his, giving him a sweet peck. "Now, let's taste this goody," she said, breaking the spell and moving to the other side of the bar, where she looked for a knife and two plates.

Dave exhaled deeply, realizing that he had been holding his breath. She had kissed him. A goofy smile crept up his face and refused to leave.

"You know I am old enough to be your mother, Dave, don't you?" Maria asked, not looking away from the cake that she tried ingloriously to cut. The turd was burned and hard as a rock. Eventually, she managed to slice it, and she handed one of the plates to Dave.

"So?" Dave asked, raising his brows.

"So this was sweet and romantic, but I am way too old for you, Dave."

"I don't have a problem with your age," Dave retorted.

"Well, I have one with yours," Maria stated sternly.

"Oh, I see. Now I'm too young for you! I didn't know you were so prejudiced," Dave said caustically, throwing the plate on the bar counter and storming out the door.

"Dave!" Maria shouted after him, but he didn't look back and she didn't move to follow him.

Once the sulkiness drained out of Dave's system, he realized how childish he had acted, proving Maria right in the worst way he could have. Not only was he young, but now he was also immature and spoiled.

There was only one thing to do. He called his uncle again.

"Hmm. Was it a chocolate cake?" the man asked.

"What? Yes, but . . ." Dave started.

Dave's uncle carried on as if nothing else deserved to be addressed. "And you burned it?"

"It looked like a turd! Do you want to know if it tasted as bad as it looked too?" Dave snapped, losing his patience.

"Dave, do you even know why I told you to bake her a cake?" his uncle asked calmly.

"Because she told me she liked men that cooked . . ."

Uncle Casanova cut him off. "Dave, Dave, Dave . . . You're smarter than that. If I wanted you to impress her with your cooking skills, which we both know are inexistent, I wouldn't have told you to bake her a burned cake."

"Well, why did you, then?"

"This is about the effort, Dave! She tells you that she likes men who cook for her and you bake her a burned cake. Another man would have cooked her a meal to get her to go to bed with him. She was dazzled by your effort and moved that you did it for her, not to get into her pants. It was a sweet gesture and was supposed to melt her, and it did. She kissed you."

"She kissed me out of pity!" Dave retorted.

"Trust me when I tell you that she didn't pity kiss you. You're a boy in her eyes, and she has feelings for you that she doesn't know how to handle; otherwise, she wouldn't have kissed you and then told you that she's too old for you and has a problem with your age."

"That doesn't make sense. If she likes me, why is age such a problem?"

"Because she's a woman!" his uncle said, exasperated.

"That's supposed to be an explanation?"

"Dave, accept this as the only fact you can be sure about women: you'll never understand them."

The tantrum Dave threw ended up not being that bad. After all, his biggest disadvantage was also his biggest ally. Being a boy worked both ways. Maria had a problem with his being so young, but that was also what she liked about him: his carefree youth. Therefore, once the initial display of wounded pride that Uncle Casanova encouraged Dave to pursue, to add credibility to his real feelings for Maria, was over, he had to get himself together and fight for what he wanted. Some days later, he showed up at the bar and told her he had something for her.

"Dave . . ."

"Don't worry, it's not another cake," Dave said sheepishly.

She smiled sweetly at his shy joke.

Dave handed her a piece of paper.

"What's this?"

"Well, you told me that you have a problem with my age, so I made you a list of the one hundred reasons why you should date me," Dave said with a smirk.

Maria couldn't help herself from laughing at this, and she unfolded the paper, which contained one hundred logical and illogical reasons that Maria should date Dave. From higher levels of testosterone to not being prone to a midlife crisis in the next twenty years, he made sure to list all absurdities that came to his mind. Because he could . . . After all, he was a boy.

"Dave . . ." she kept saying, a smile on her face as she read the one hundred reasons why she should date him.

"Come on, Maria. Give a guy a break. What do you have to lose? Come on a date with me!" He kept his pleading eyes glued on hers.

"Dave, I'm too old . . ."

"To have fun?" he interrupted. "Tell you what: I'll pick you up tomorrow after work and take you on a date. I promise you that if you don't have fun, I will never bother you again." Without waiting for her answer, Dave left her there with the cardboard in her hands and still smiling.

The next day, Dave took Maria to a carnival—yeah, clichés do work—and she had more fun than she'd had in a long time. At the end of the night, she took him to her bed and he had the time of his life. He was in love.

But she wasn't. Not yet anyway.

For a couple of months, their relationship was one-sided. In fact, only Dave was in a relationship. Maria made sure that their encounters, which involved a generous amount of steamy sex, were discreet and that there were no public displays of affection. In the beginning, Dave was fine with this arrangement, because he thought that time would break Maria's resolve and have her formalize their relationship.

It didn't. Whether it was her work or people's prejudice against their age difference, there was always some excuse to keep him hidden. All their time together consisted of torrid encounters and wild fun that were preceded by muffled moans and furtive looks and nods. He felt like her dirty little secret.

A few months had passed, and Dave found himself at a rock concert with his friends, looking from afar at Maria, who hung with her group of friends nearby and ignored him completely, as she usually did. But this time, standing there at the concert he'd invited her to and she declined because her friends were going, it felt worse.

He felt hurt and humiliated, and when she bothered to look back at him, she saw all that, plus his love for her. She saw his eyes pooling with unshed tears because of her. That's what broke her and made her lower all her defenses. She went up to him, grabbed his face with both hands, and pulled him into a kiss that had his friends hissing and howling around them. Her friends were dumbfounded, their mouths ajar.

They became a couple that night. Dave did everything in his power to win her love. And he did. She gave him her heart and her soul, and that's why she couldn't give him her forgiveness when he left her.

Dave and Maria's story lasted almost two years, which was how long Dave managed to keep his need for freedom tamed. His growing dissatisfaction with his job and the choking feeling of being in a relationship became his ever-present ghosts, and when he could no longer ignore them, he knew that his love for Maria had nothing left to give.

Soon the fire inside him was burning more than he could master, and he knew that he wanted what he did not have and that he needed to be where he was not at—their age difference finally becoming the burden that it always threatened to be.

"You still have feelings for her," I said, stating the obvious. "So why do you think you felt choked? Weren't you two happy?"

They were, but when Maria finally let herself love Dave, things became wont. He started feeling that tingling that told him he was missing out on life.

"It's hard to explain. She was like a bomb in my life. She literally rocked my world . . . I'd never felt that way for anyone."

"So what was the problem? Her age?"

"Our age difference became the problem. I wanted more out of life, and she wanted what she already had. Our choices were not compatible, so ending things was the only thing left to do."

I let his words sink in. His mood was lifting, and I could see a smile creeping on his lips. By then, I didn't know him well enough to see through him, but I knew him long enough to know the one thing that had made him leave a love that big.

"She wasn't the one," I mumbled, realizing that I'd said it loud enough for him to catch it.

"She wasn't," he said, eyeing me as the suspicion of how vulnerable and exposed he was to me flooded his mind. A flash of uncertainty crossed his face but was instantly gone. Then he smiled and shook his head, as if with that he dismissed the uncomfortable thoughts that haunted him.

"Honestly? I can't imagine what's like to be with the same woman for the rest of your life," he said.

He was baiting me. He wanted to be sure how much I had figured out so far. I could have just let it go, but I didn't.

"Sometimes I wished I didn't get you. You can't imagine yourself with one woman for the rest of your life, yet you keep searching for 'the one.'" There, I'd handed it to him.

"Yeah, well, you have to have a goal; otherwise, all the random sex and the meaningless women would have no purpose." He had his mischievous smile now fully pasted on his lips.

"And what would that purpose be, Dave?" I asked between laughs.

"To separate the wheat from the chaff!" he added.

"How biblical of you!" I said with sarcasm. "Since when do you have any hopes for women that you sleep with just for fun? Name one, just one, that started that way and become more than that."

"That is not the point, Izzy. You can only tell that a woman is different from the others if you know the others. There is no meaningful sex without meaningless sex, no good without evil, no love without hate . . ."

"You're so full of shit." I snorted. "Why don't you just admit that you can't keep your love stick in your pants?"

"Because I actually can. You, Izzy, of all people, should know that."

PART 2
KNOWING DAVE

CHAPTER 8

WHEN DAVE MET IZZY

A deck of tarot cards, a regular one at least, has seventy-eight cards. Twenty-two are called the Major Arcana. The remaining fifty-six are called the Minor Arcana. Arcana means secret. So when you hold a deck of tarot cards, you hold not the possibility of revealing seventy-eight secrets but the potential to unfold all the mysteries a soul can bear.

Reading cards comes as naturally to me as reading a book. Reading people through tarot cards, well, that just comes as natural as breathing. Regardless, I am a skeptical believer. I can neither bring myself to believe nor force myself not to. This being said, I can tell a person his past, present, and future if I have a deck of tarot cards in my hands. Or not. The tarot cards just make it easier to others. Truthfully, other than a keen ability to read people, I can't quite say that I have any mystic powers at all, despite others' faith in my capacities, Dave included, since that was how we met.

That happened in the beginning of a summer so long ago, at a friend of a friend's party, that I can neither place it nor time it, as with many other events between Dave and me. But I know that I had my cards with me. At that time, I always carried them in my bag. They were almost an extension of me. They were all I needed. It was all it took for us, and as I said, it was a long time ago. Despite my unawareness of the wheres and whens, I do remember that eventually during that night, one of my friends asked me to read the cards to her boyfriend. That's how it started, and although it was not the place, I agreed. I'd always been curious about him, and curiosity had always been my weakness, so I often indulged it. In addition, the guy was a skeptic; nothing has more appeal to me than a skeptic. Skeptics are so driven in not believing and finding holes in your predictions that they forget to mask their surprise when you pull a dirty truth about them from your divination hat.

My friend's boyfriend had many dirty truths to hide, and I didn't even need my cards to know it. But hell, the cards made it a lot funnier.

The guy was confused. He didn't love my friend, and I couldn't blame him. She was a needy person with low self-esteem and was constantly smothering him. He planned to leave her but still hadn't had the guts to do it, because despite all, nothing better had come along yet. Naturally, he also cheated on her, but I was expecting that, so there was a silent understanding between us that I would not address that issue directly, since it would cause problems that neither of us wanted to deal with. He knew that I knew, and we both acknowledged that neither of us wished to be the one who would let her know. I know I didn't.

Twenty-five minutes of fortune telling later, the guy was praising my supposedly mystic abilities and making sure that everything that I had told him would remain between us. To reassure him, I swore that I was bound by the equivalent of the attorney-client privilege of cartomancy. By then, I knew that what cards told me, they would also hold against me. So I abided by the common sense rules that dictated that what you don't know won't hurt you and that some things are just not yours to tell.

When I finished my consultation and we were both ready to return to the party, my friend knocked on the door and let herself in without waiting for my say-so.

"Umm, while you two were in here, I might have mentioned to one or two persons out there that you know how to read cards . . ." She started this with hesitation in her voice, clearly trying to access my reaction.

"Hmm. Did you?" I said, without giving away anything but mentally archiving the information about her boyfriend in a very remote area of my brain. I couldn't tell her anyway, but now I didn't even want to.

"Yeah. And there's kind of a queue of people outside asking if you could read the cards to them . . . please," she added.

"I see. They're asking if I can, and they are already organized in a queue. Of people." I purposely emphasized the last two words just to give her a piece of my mind without bothering to express it in words. She knew me well enough to know that I was silently cursing her. "How many are there?" I asked.

"I dunno . . . Around a dozen," she said evasively.

"A dozen? Are you kidding me?" I was trying but not succeeding at keeping my calm.

"Or thirty . . ." she muttered.

I froze, and it took me a minute of deep breathing to calm myself down and not break anything in her face.

"How stupid are you?" I breathed out in a low and menacing tone. "What am I? The fair fortune teller?"

"I don't know why you are being like this. It's not as if you don't like to do it. You carry that damn tarot deck around with you everywhere you go," she accused.

"Yes, I do. And I also happen to choose who I want to read cards to and when I want to do it," I snapped.

"Oh, come on. It will be fun. Don't be mad at me."

"I'm not mad. I'm furious. You know perfectly well that I don't like people to know I do this unless I want them to."

"Please?" she begged, looking at me with pleading eyes.

"At this point, I don't have much choice, do I? I'm either the witch or the bitch." I pointed this out in a now-controlled tone.

Therefore, I opted to be the witch. It suited me better, at least at that time.

One after another, people strutted through the room hesitantly and sat opposite to me, hoping to get answers that lasted them a lifetime.

The truth is that when people ask you to read them tarot cards, they are at least intrigued, and even if they are skeptical about it, they hold a speck of anticipation, or even dismay, that you might reveal something true about them. It's human nature. Moreover, it's not the future that disturbs people, because they aren't able to know if you got it right or not. At least not in that moment. It's their pasts. Once you read people's pasts, and assuming that you got it right, you will have their full attention and you'll have gained their trust—even when you don't deserve it. You see, vanity is the most common and shared flaw in humankind. All of us think of ourselves as unique, singular, special. And we are. In many things and in many ways, we are. But as humans, our passions, our flaws, our dreams, and our lives are bound to suffer from an enormous lack of originality. As such, our pasts are most likely burned by the same scars. Who hasn't had his or her heart broken? Who doesn't have someone important in his or her life? Who doesn't hold a secret? Who hasn't suffered?

When people are looking for answers and see themselves as completely original and unique, they tend to ask the right questions, and in their questions, you can sometimes see more of them than in anything else they will willingly give you. It's not what they tell you; it's what they want you to tell them that matter. So at some point, you've seen it before and you've heard it dozens of times before. And at that point, it all starts making sense and you don't need to guess anymore, for you simply know. As I knew with Dave.

Amid all the people who sat in front of me that night in search of revelations about their unique lives and fates was Dave.

He strolled through the room with a grin on his face, the same conceited grin that I would later identify as his charmer smile, and sat opposite to me, looking me straight in the eyes. *This is a first,* I thought. Most people so far had felt intimidated by me. After all, I was, to many of them, the keeper of the unknown. They thought I could crush their hopes with a word or imprint fears and suspicions in their minds, because people do tend to cling to the bad things you tell them and forget about the good things you hand them. It's the fault in our souls.

Dave, however, seemed oblivious to all that. His eyes missed the awe that most of the others before him had had, but they didn't hold the mockery of some as well. He was neither a believer nor a skeptic. I was, to say the least, intrigued by his attitude.

"I'm Dave," he said, stretching his hand toward me.

"I'm Isabella," I said, extending my hand for him to shake. He didn't. He captured it between his hands and kept his gaze on mine.

"Nice to meet you, Isabella."

"We'll see about that," I retorted with a grin, winking at him as I removed my hand from his grip. "So, Dave, is this your first time? With the tarot, I mean," I joked.

"With the tarot, yes. With you? Let's see what that card tell us," he joked back smugly.

Dave was not every girl's wet dream, I'll admit. He was an average-looking man, but he could make quite an impression on the ladies. I realized right there and then that what he lacked in looks, he pulled off in charm. As much of a cliché as he seemed, with his mix of typical bad boy looks with the tattoos, piercings, and sloppy clothes, when he opened his mouth, one just couldn't deny the allure. He seemed the kind of guy that could charm his way out of almost every uncomfortable situation that crossed his way or have the overconfidence to put himself purposefully in it.

I remained undaunted and serene in the face of his comment, letting the silence be my answer. He didn't flinch or seemed affected by it. It looked as if it was up to me to make the next move after all.

"I won't need my tarot to tell you that when it comes to me, you will only be having one first time tonight. Treasure it. Do you want me to explain the basics?"

"By all means, please do. I'm all in favor of the basics," he said with, I noted, a flirty tone in his voice. He had game; I had to give him that.

I took a deep breath and fired away.

"A deck of tarot cards has seventy-eight cards. You can divide them in two groups. The Major Arcana and the Minor Arcana. Arcana means secret. The tarot is a game of energies. It uses your energy and my energy to unveil the secrets of your past, your present, and your future. Any doubt so far?"

"Will you be able to tell me my entire life?"

"No. Why would you like to know something like that?" Without waiting for his answer, I continued. "The predictions normally don't seem to go beyond half a year. It's different with each person, but normally I wouldn't expect anything to happen after that period of time. But that is for the future. When it's the past that we're talking about, it will be entirely up to you."

"How come?"

"Well, your past can show events from last week or the last decade. It depends how those events have affected you."

The mocking flirty tone had abandoned our voices. He was becoming uncomfortable, which let me know that he had skeletons in his closet that he was afraid I would become aware of. Since he definitely wasn't gay or married, it was probably something about his family. Normally, it's about either the family or a lover.

"Okay, so how does this work? Should I ask you questions?"

"Let's start with a spread that gives us a general idea of your standing. We'll go on from there," I said, starting to shuffle the cards. "This one is called the big wheel, and it gives a general idea of all matters in your life."

When I finished shuffling the cards, I put them down in front of him and told him to cut them with his left hand.

"Why the left? Any particular reason?"

"It's closer to your heart." I started to lay the cards on the table. "Each group of two cards is placed in a house, and each house represents an aspect of your life." I looked at the cards and absorbed the information that I had in hands.

"So what's your verdict?" Dave asked, apprehensive.

"Guilty," I said matter-of-factly and without raising my eyes from the cards. I didn't need to. I knew by then that he was already fidgety.

"And here I was thinking I was innocent until proven guilty!" Dave mocked, attempting to lighten the mood.

"Well, Dave, I think we can both agree that there hasn't been anything innocent about you for a long time now." I didn't change my tone and kept my gaze on the cards. "First things first; I see here that there's a big change in your life coming up. Are you going on a long trip soon?"

"I'm leaving the country tomorrow to work abroad," he blurted out. And I had him. Two statements in and I had him.

"Hmm, nice. Where are you going?" I asked casually.

"To the other side of the world!" he said without a drop of hesitation in his voice. I guess that was all I needed to know.

"It won't be easy. Those things never are. But you will be fine. You will meet many people, but very few will make a difference. You seem to have a way with people, especially the ladies."

He tried to mask the conceited smile that was forming on his lips at my last sentence by thrusting his hands through his hair. He wasn't going to brag about it, but he liked the notoriety. My, my, isn't vanity a form of pride?

"You also seem to have a talent for teaching. Even if that's not your area, you would do well at it. You're a natural pedagogue."

You know what they say: "Those who can't, teach," I thought, but I refrained from adding those words. There was nothing to gain from teasing him at this point, and there was no chance that he would not interpret that as an insult.

"Your health is good, and there's really nothing relevant coming up in that department. But while your physique is well, your psychic seems constantly troubled. You think too much and tend to close yourself up in your thoughts. You also get a little moody, don't you?"

"I have my days. Who doesn't?" he said defensively.

"Fair enough," I stated before moving on. "There's a woman in your future."

"Just one?" Dave teased.

"Does that matter? Yeah, just one. Thank God that the others don't show up in here; otherwise, I suspect I would not have enough cards in my deck to go through all of them, would I?"

We both laughed at my tirade, and then I carried on.

"This woman seems to be a little different from what you're used to. She seems to be a mature woman . . ."

"Hey, I'm not picky. I do like older women. My mom's age is my limit, though."

I laughed at that, a true and genuine laugh. Hell, I think I even snorted.

"I can see that. If my cards are accurate, you just broke an older woman's heart," I said lightly, still caught in the playfulness of the moment. Once I saw the shift in his expression, I knew that I had hit a nerve. Hard.

He didn't let me pursue it, though.

"This other woman that you were talking about . . ." he urged me.

"Well, Dave, it's not that there won't be anything romantic about you and her, but that's actually not the point. She shows up in your cards as a wise woman who will guide you. She shows up in this house here." I pointed to the cards placed in house nine of the spread. "This house is the house of aspiration. It represents what you seek to gain your truth and what helps you to expand your conscience. Basically, it represents what gives meaning to your life."

"So this older woman will give meaning to my life, but our relationship won't be about love . . . She must be ugly as hell!" Dave deadpanned. I don't know if I should be intrigued or scared."

"Well, she is not old per se. In fact, she's probably not much older than you. But she is, well, kind of a seer, and she will sort of guide you and help you with your life, but it will be up to you to find the meaning in it. So it's not that your relationship with her won't be about romantic love; it's more than that. It's bigger than that or, rather, beyond that." I paused, bending my head slightly to the right. "Oh, but if it helps, I believe that she will be a brunette," I added.

"Aw, I knew it. That explains it. I have a thing for blondes!" he said, and I knew he was at ease again.

"Now, my favorite house of the spread," I said, pointing to a particular pair of cards. "Your fears and concerns." I raised my brows suggestively.

"I'm just gonna come clean on this one so that you don't humiliate me here." He paused for suspense and to straighten his face in an attempt at sounding serious. "I was afraid of the dark when I was little, and I really thought that eating carrots would make me shit orange," he joked.

"Was that before or after you started having problems with your father?" I asked, without a trace of teasing in my voice. "You two seem to have a tense relationship. And you seem to worry a lot about your mother."

I caught him by surprise there. His face dropped and became grave as his eyes lost all the spark they had held so far. So this was it to him; this was the fault in his soul.

"Yeah, my mom is great, one in a million. My father is not. Let's leave it at that, shall we?"

"Sure," I said, trying to focus my attention on another pair of cards as the realization of the oddness of the entire reading started to dawn on me. It wasn't being smooth and fluid. The information was coming out in chunks and didn't seem connected.

"What's the meaning of this card here?" Dave asked, trying to change the subject.

"That's the wheel of fortune." As I said it, it hit me. "Do you believe in fate, Dave?"

"I'm here, ain't I?"

"That's curiosity, Dave, not fate." Oh boy, had I ever been more wrong! "The wheel of fortune is the fate card. It means great force that is outside your control. No matter which way the wheel turns, it is impossible to change it, but if you accept that and live with what is handed to you, the ride will be easier."

"Ouch! So I have no choice?" Dave said, feigning an imaginary pain.

"You always have a choice, but there are things bigger than you, so sometimes, although you set your own path in life, you won't be able to deny feeling a sense of destiny. Some things are just meant to be. Like karma."

"Karma?"

"Yeah. What goes around comes around. Never heard of it?" I asked, smiling slightly.

"I was familiar with the word but not the meaning. Though I'd heard 'What goes around comes around' before. Does it work that way?"

"I hope so, in some cases."

"Just in some cases?"

"We can't always be good, whether we want to or choose to, Dave. And it's scary to think that every bad deed and every bad choice that we make will hunt us down. We should have some slack. Don't you think?"

"I don't know if I can see things that way. This world has too many bad people that never pay for their wrongs, and too many good people that only know misery, for me to believe that every crime has its punishment and every good deed has its reward."

"Well, you know what they say: only those who believe in witches can be bewitched," I voiced.

"So karma will only get me if I believe in it?" he asked.

"As I said, Dave, you set your own path in life. Your choices, your decisions, your wrongs and your rights are entirely up to you."

"Isn't that a bit contradictory with your tarot thing? I mean, you're telling me that I have free will, and here you are, reading me my future. So where do you stand, Isabella?"

"The tarot gives you directions, paths, and possibilities, but the choices are always up to you," I offered. "You can always alter them and redefine your paths. That's why I don't do long-term readings. They're pointless."

"So where does that wheel card enter?"

"You never had the feeling that no matter what you did, the outcome of a situation would always be the same?"

"Do you really believe in that shit, Isabella?" Dave asked, shaking his head depreciatively.

"This is not about what I believe in, Dave. But let me put it in a way you'll understand: how does it feel to live with the fact that no matter what you do, your father will never look at you differently?" I asked, wanting my words to feel like a sucker punch to him. As I'd said, we can't always be good.

Dave stared silently at me, letting the pain from my low blow fade away. I'd made my point. He now knew that I wasn't speaking out of my ass, and that this wasn't a two-way conversation. This wasn't about me, and earning someone's respect sometimes can't be done the nice way.

"Can I ask questions?" he asked, breaking the silence.

"Sure. Just ask what you want to know and I will lay out a spread."

Dave started to ask questions about his trip, his work, and even his love life. Things went smoother from that point on. Even the air seemed lighter, and we ended up laughing and cracking jokes about my predictions and Dave's fates. In the end, we said good-bye with the lightness of one-time encounters. I wished him Godspeed for his trip to the other side of the world.

I don't know how long we'd been in that room, but in my mind, it seemed that a long time had passed in no time at all. Maybe that was why Dave's reading kept haunting me for some time. Sometimes readings did; other times people did. In this case, I didn't know which. Or why.

Sometimes reading cards and reading people blurred in my mind. Most times they didn't and I knew exactly what I was looking into and what I was seeing. The deck of cards? Well, that just took away the awkwardness of people bluntly asking me how their lives would turn out to be and empowered me, in the eyes of others, with a tool that justified every statement I delivered about things most people would be able to see by themselves if they made the effort.

Why, then, couldn't I force myself not to believe?

Because I still haven't found a suitable explanation to foreseeing people's futures and them happening as I saw they would . . . whether I told them or not.

CHAPTER 9

THE WHEEL OF FORTUNE

Albert Einstein said, "Coincidence is God's way of remaining anonymous," and as I looked at the sea of clouds below me, I couldn't stop feeling the overwhelming sense of fate that chained me to those words. I was trapped in a plane, fifty thousand feet above the ground, and headed to the other side of the world; never before had I felt such an overpowering certainty that the paths that I was about to travel had been laid down for me long before. And I didn't mean it literally, though it was also true. I couldn't help myself from feeling that my life was unfolding right before my eyes and that my choices, my decisions, my will were all but mine. The wheel of fortune kept turning and had caught me in its spin.

I hadn't seen it coming.

When I met Dave three months before, I was far from guessing that the company that I worked for was about to offer me a position in their subsidiary in the other side of the world. The desire of working and living abroad was something that I'd been nurturing for a while, but I'd never considered going so far away from home. Strangely, or not, my first thought was of Dave, and my first certainty was that I had missed something in that cards reading three months ago. My only doubt was if it had been a what or a who.

As the time for my life to change approached, Dave became the inevitability that I had to face. My friends who were friends with Dave's friends undertook as their mission to spread the word that I was leaving to the other side of the world. The immensity of it dawned on me one night, a week before my departure, when I received a phone call from Dave's mother, introducing herself and asking me if I would be kind enough to take a package along with me to Dave. Apparently, the other side of the world lacked specific men's toiletries, and I noticed that my friends were very generous when it came time to give out my phone number. I, of course, expressed my availability for the task and agreed to meet her two days later. After all, I needed to know more about Dave, but in addition to that, I needed to prevent eventual damages to my reputation. I did not want to be known as the corporate fortune teller.

Meeting Dave's mother and his younger brother, with whom I fell in love instantly, was an experience, for lack of a better word. I can't honestly describe them in any other way than them being two fine ladies. Dave's brother was as gay as it gets, and our connection was instantaneous. Mind you, he was nowhere near the loud, feminine gay type, but the mannerisms were impossible to miss. And he was impeccably dressed, in case you were wondering. I would be.

During our rendezvous, time flew by without any of us noticing it. Dave's mother told me about the struggling times Dave was enduring on the other side of the world and, despite them, how enthusiastically he was facing the whole experience. He'd met a lot of people, as I'd told him he would, but no older woman yet. I couldn't help thinking that most certainly he already did, but only I was aware of that for now. Regardless, only time would prove me right. And the woman was not older, just wiser, I kept thinking to myself. After all, I was not even four years older than Dave was.

My encounter with Dave's mother and younger brother resulted in a quite interesting dynamic since I ended up reading their cards and being ensured that Dave would be told that those singular activities that I took upon were, well, on the private side of my life, and not to be shared with anyone else.

The day to leave finally came, and it was with joyful hope and a sense of power that I boarded the plane. During the long hours that filled the journey, I finally settled down from the turmoil of events that had been my last weeks and allowed myself to wander through my thoughts. The one thing I'd done to prevent the choking claws of destiny on me was resigning to it, because that's the only way you'll fight fate. After an entire day of traveling and feeling completely at loss with the jet lag, I arrived at the other side of the world no longer fueled with a sense of hope or power.

Just loneliness.

When you leave your country to live abroad, alone, no matter how well you prepare yourself or how mentally strong you are, nothing will appease the reality shock that will strike you the moment you realize that it's only you against a world that you'd never lived in. It's overwhelming.

So there I was, on the other side of the world, stuck in a hotel room with a list of phone numbers from a bunch of people that I'd heard of because they were friends of friends or friends of acquaintances, not people I knew. Except Dave. So I called him and prayed to God that he would invite me to dinner, for I was in desperate need of seeing someone familiar. He did. He took me to dinner and out for a drink.

After a dinner that Dave would later confess made him incredibly uncomfortable, we went to a Latin bar, where Dave tried to dazzle me with his dancing skills. At that point, I was still potential prey, not that he ever confessed that to me, and I couldn't blame the guy for trying, really. I'm no Miss Brazil, but I'm no ogre either. He invited me to dance with him, and our mutual uneasiness was immediate, as if our energies collided. We brushed it off jokingly by blaming my two left feet, but we both knew that that wasn't it. I normally had that effect on people, but in this case, it went both ways. We had that effect on each other.

That night, I met several of his friends and realized instantly when I was introduced to Dave's best friend and cousin, John, that he'd heard of me and of my singular activities. I never confronted Dave about it, though, not even when our friendship became so deep that I didn't need words to know his thoughts or filters to voice them out. I would gain nothing out of such confrontation, especially because, with life, I'd come to expect some things from people and learned not to blame them when they matched my expectations. Therefore, I'd expected Dave to have shared his cards experience not only with his family but also with his friends. In fact, I didn't expect anything else, which didn't mean that I would make it easier on him.

I didn't. Now that we shared the same part of the world, I needed him not to spread it around, and I needed him to make sure that his friends didn't do it either.

I made him assure me that he'd told no one about my cards, though it wasn't true, and I forced him to gain the courage to ask me to share this side of my life with his best friend, though John knew about it already. But that was not the point, was it? You see, as our friendship grew, so did Dave's sense of loyalty to me, which meant that he felt uncomfortable with keeping something that had such a direct impact on my life from me. Moreover, he feared that I would catch him doing it.

Dave's and my connection was not instantaneous or even natural. An invisible string kept us near at all times, but there was also an awkwardness that came along with it.

It took us awhile to adjust to each other. I guess that to Dave, it was a bit of an inner struggle adapting to me. After all, he never had the option of letting me in or not, for I'd been there all along. I knew his secrets before I knew him, and that wasn't something that he dealt with easily. I know I wouldn't, but I'm not an easy person, nor one that you would feel comfortable with right away. Apparently, I have a seriousness about me that intimidates people and keeps them at bay. So I've been told.

*   *   *

"So, Isabella, who would have guessed?" Dave said, sipping his coffee and voicing what we'd both silently dwelled on since I'd come to the other side of the world—how strangely life had brought us together.

"Well, Dave, I should have!" I said, and we both laughed because it was one of those rhetorical questions that, at least in our case, could actually be answered.

"You're funny!"

"You're right!" I said, winking at him.

"Do you think about it?" he asked, more serious.

"All the time, Dave," I said with a mischievous smile that let him know that my words had a double meaning. I was teasing him purposely.

Dave laughed uncomfortably. We were at a bar near my workplace. Dave had called and invited me to go for a drink after work. It was nice of him, especially because by now I was almost certain that he'd ruled me out as prey material.

"You know what I mean . . ."

"I do," I said, not offering further.

"You're not making this easy, Isabella."

"That's because I'm not easy, Dave," I said, still pushing him. I must confess that I was testing his levels of comfort with me. They weren't high at all, and that bothered me. I was used to having male friends who poured their souls out to me, guys that I could mercilessly tease to alleviate the heaviness of some of our talks. Dave, however, didn't seem able to handle that gray area.

Nevertheless, Dave accepted the inevitability of his relationship with me with the same resignation that people accept the wetness of water; as a fact. He showed me the way around things in a land that would be foreign to me until the very last day I stayed there. And he kept me company. So we quickly settled into what felt like an arranged friendship that strangely worked out for both of us.

I'll admit that that shook my beliefs, because I'm not a needy person or one that easily trusts or puts faith in others. I counted on nobody else but me. Until Dave. Because when you're so out of your element, as we were there, you tend to cling to some people. They become your sense of self, your everything. They become your family. Dave became more than that to me. Without me even noticing it, he became my person on the other side of the world. You know, the person you name when you fill out a form, the person to call if something bad happens to you. The person who will be there no matter what. Dave was my person. However, that didn't happen right away.

"So how was your weekend, Isabella?" Dave asked as he sat at the table where I had been waiting for him for the past five minutes.

"It was nice. Nothing special. How about yours?" I asked while I lazily drank my coffee. Dave and I would keep this throughout our lives whenever possible: Monday morning breakfast. This was where Dave and I would share our thoughts and our doings, doing our weekly balance.

"It was nice. John and I went to that bar that we went to last Thursday after you got off of work," he offered.

"The one where that Chinese waitress works? You know, the one that you were ogling?" I smiled broadly at him.

"Hmm, you got that? I thought I was being discreet," Dave said, a little embarrassed.

"Oh, you were, Dave. Only half the people there were on to you; the other half missed it."

He'd been discreet, but I wasn't going to let him know that. Telling him that I'd been on to him would be like those people that announce to the world that they are very sharp. Well, that's not very perspicacious of them, is it?

"I did not ogle her," Dave said, faking outrage.

"Okay, you didn't. You just drooled a little. But hey, I'm certain that she has her eye on you too."

"You think so?" Dave asked, trying not to smile.

"Yeah," I said, lingering on the word.

"That's great to know, especially because I already slept with her this weekend!" Dave said smugly.

"You're serious?" I almost barked.

"Guess!" Dave teased me. He liked to joke about my divinatory skills.

"You little devil! Well, tell me, then. You're not gonna spare me the details now, are you?"

"A gentleman never kisses and tells," he said, trying to maintain a straight face.

"Well, good thing we both know you're not a gentleman, Dave. Go ahead and spill the beans!" I goaded.

"Yes, I am," he insisted.

"Oh, come on. You just bragged about banging the girl. You might as well just go ahead and tell the whole story."

"Or we can talk about other things," Dave said, trying to evade the matter but still smirking.

"What are we going to talk about, then? My work is boring. Yours is not that interesting either. The weather is fine. I don't have a sex life, so we might as well talk about yours," I said matter-of-factly. "Assuming that you have one and are not just making it up!" I was baiting him.

"Nice try, Isabella. I'm not five, you know?"

"I know! You're not funny," I grumbled.

"Why do you want to know?"

"Why wouldn't I? Human nature is fascinating, and it's much more interesting to talk about that than to sit here trying to come up with matters to fill the inevitable silences that flood the conversations of two persons that don't know each other well. Don't you think?"

"Well, you're already ahead. You know a lot about me! I, on the other hand, know nothing about you," Dave countered.

"Well, there's actually not that much to tell."

"There's always something to tell," he said smugly.

"It's sad, Dave, but there really isn't." I shrugged.

"Oh, come on, Isabella! If you tell, I'll tell!" Dave's voice was full of amusement, and he winked an eye at me.

"Are you trying to bribe me, Dave?" I asked smugly.

"Everyone has their price, Isabella," he said, matching my attitude.

"True! But I'm not sure you reached mine. Yet," I said, adding the last word with deliberate slowness.

"Name your price," he challenged.

"You tell me the Chinese waitress story now," I said, and then I paused for suspense. "And whenever I ask you, no matter when, you will tell me what I ask you to tell me."

"What?" Dave asked, confused.

"Sometime in the future, I will ask you to tell me something about you, and you will have to tell me, no matter what."

"That's an odd request," Dave said, taken aback.

"It's as much as odd as yours. You're asking me to tell you anything about me now. I'm asking you to tell me something about you sometime. Same thing; different timing."

"I'll agree to that if you tell me something important about you now," Dave retorted.

"Okay, I'll tell you something about me that will make you own my soul. You will know how I think, what I believe in, and above all that, how I live my life," I said with my best straight face and an earnest voice. "Are you sure you're ready to hear this?" I added.

"Ready as I will ever be," Dave said, buying my faked seriousness.

"The only thing you need to know about me is that I live by a pair of truths: The first one, and I don't know who said it, is that assumption is the mother of all fuckups. Life hasn't proven me wrong on this yet. My father, however, taught me to always assume that the others are smarter than I. This way, I will always be at an advantage.

"I learned my second truth from Oscar Wilde, who said, 'Questions are never indiscreet. Answers sometimes are.' Experience, however, has shown me often that people tend to answer when you stop asking questions. Hence, I only ask when I cannot assume." I deliberately paused, exhaled, and added, "I also do like to think of my truths as complementary in the way that only contradictory things can be."

Dave looked at me with the utmost disbelieving look on his face, as I had expected him to, and shook his head. He didn't get me, but he wasn't supposed to anyway. Not if I could prevent it or at least delay it.

"Don't worry, Dave. This is not how this is supposed to work," I said, gesturing my hand back and forth between us. "Are you gonna eat that slice of cake?" I asked him, reaching for the uneaten cake that was in front of him. I don't know why, but to us cake always tasted better at breakfast.

"You told me nothing!" he accused, grabbing the plate before I had the chance to steal it from him.

"On the contrary, Dave. I told you everything."

"It doesn't even make sense. First you say assumption is bad. Then you say you assume when you can't ask. That's clearly a contradiction. Where do you stand after all?"

"Where nobody can reach me, of course!" I laughed.

"That's rubbish. I still don't know a thing about you." He was clearly a bit annoyed with my little stunt.

"Dave, if you think about it, you'll see that you actually know plenty, and I just told you the most important thing there is to know about me. You're a smart guy. Figure it out. What were you expecting, that I tell you my favorite color? Or about the men in my life? The names of my pets, perhaps?" I joked.

"That probably would have been more revealing."

I chose my words carefully. "No, that would have been easier. I told you before that I'm not an easy person."

A mischievous smile crawled upon Dave's lips, and he stared at me defiantly. "You know, Isabella, you keep saying that, but I'm afraid I'll keep forgetting it. I have this problem with remembering things, so I might just start calling you Izzy. You know, as a short name for Isabella." Dave was teasing me, content with his smart-ass pun.

I arched a brow and stared right back at him with what was, I hoped, a fierce enough expression to discourage him from his intents. But believe it or not, at that precise moment, "Easy," from Faith No More, started playing on the radio. We both laughed at the coincidence—it was impossible not to—and Dave made an act of saying it was a sign. And whether he believed it or not to be a sign, the truth is that Dave never stopped calling me Izzy ever since. After all, we didn't want to mess with the beyond, did we?

It grew on me. The nickname, I mean. And though other people started to use it as well, it was something that held a special meaning between Dave and me only.

*　　*　　*

"Don't think that I forgot," I said.

"About what, Izzy?"

"The Chinese waitress," I clarified.

"Yes, Izzy?"

"You were supposed to tell me your story with her last Monday, but you never did," I accused.

"If I remember correctly, you were supposed to tell me something about you, Izzy, and you never did," Dave countered.

"Yes, I did. I'm not to blame if you can't keep up with me, Dave. And stop with the Izzy thing. It's starting to get annoying." However, I was smiling even as I said that.

"Okay, Izzy," Dave snorted.

"Funny! What happened with the waitress?"

"Why, Izzy!" Dave said with an affected voice. "I thought you only asked when you couldn't assume. And this story with the waitress is quite obvious, don't you think?"

"My, my, Dave," I retorted in the same scornful tone. "You were listening! Well, what can I say? I'm a woman. So I'm just gonna go ahead and exercise my God-given right to be illogical."

"That's a good one!" he noted, appreciating my joke.

"The Chinese waitress, Dave. I'm waiting here," I scolded.

"Why are you so obsessed with the Chinese waitress, Izzy?"

"Honestly, Dave? I don't know, but something tells me that there's more to that story, and I just want to know if I'm right.

"Is it your sixth sense?" Dave asked, half-amused.

"Perhaps," I said with a wink.

"Well, okay, then." He shrugged, resigned. "John and I went up to the bar, and after a while, I started talking to her. We got along. She told me what time her shift ended. I waited for her. We went to her house and had sex. End of story."

"That much I could have guessed, Dave!" I shrieked.

"Well, that much is all there is to tell," Dave said. "She was kind of easy, you know?" He laughed his ass off. The bastard.

"Why her, then?" I asked as soon as he stopped laughing. It took him awhile.

"What do you mean?" he asked.

"What was it about her that made you pick her out?"

"You know, the usual: nice boobs, great ass . . . God, why are we having this conversation?" He was visibly uncomfortable.

"She didn't have boobs. She was as flat as an ironing board. And I don't think that that thing at the bottom of her back classified as an ass. So cut the crap."

"You checked her out, Izzy?" Dave smirked.

"Of course I did, Dave. I'm a woman! That's what we do. We check each other out!"

"So . . . what did you think?" he asked, wiggling his brows.

"Honestly? I think you picked her up for some weird reason. She wasn't all that hot, and you could have done way better than her. And I'm just curious about that reason."

"That's it? You're curious to know why I picked up some random girl in a bar?"

"That's it! Now, Dave, pray tell," I urged.

Dave eyed me with an amused look on his face, but he was still hesitant as to whether he should share his reason with me. I took my chances.

"You picked her up because there was something about her that you just had to see, didn't you? Some detail that made you feel drawn to her, ain't I right?" I asked, looking at him sideways. "You're about the details, not the whole."

"It was the way she swung her hips," he whispered. "It had a flow about it that I found beautiful . . . and provocative."

"Was it worth it?"

"Yeah, it was," Dave said absently, apparently lost in the memories of his night with the Chinese waitress. "She did things to my . . ." For

106

no other reason than an inexplicable attack of shyness (yeah, go figure, right?), he stopped.

"To your . . . ?" I urged him.

"You know . . ." he said, still bashful and raising his eyebrows and rolling his eyeballs in the universal gesture for "duh."

"I don't, Dave! Are you talking about your arm? A hand, maybe?" I joked, making an act of feigning ignorance.

"Very funny, Izzy."

"Come on, Dave. Say it. Say it," I pushed with a defiant smile plastered on my face.

"My love stick!" he finally barked.

"God, you did not say that!" I cried, covering my mouth with my hands in fake disbelief.

"What? What's the problem with saying love stick? Do you want me to just be plain out rude, is that it?" he snapped, embarrassed.

"You know, Dave, there are adult words you can use to refer to your genitalia. Like penis. Come on, repeat after me, pe . . ." I couldn't finish and burst out laughing instead. "I swear to God, I had not pegged you for a prude!" I snorted.

"Izzy, if there's one thing I'm not, it's a prude!" Dave said, his smug smile showing up.

"I have no doubts about it. In fact, I'd even bet your love stick that you aren't,"

"It's not yours to bet," he retorted childishly.

"That's exactly why. I don't care what happens to it." This earned a laugh from Dave. "But I think it's safe to say that most women would prefer to care for a man with a penis instead of a love stick, you know?"

"Never underestimate the power of the love stick, Izzy."

"Dave?"

"Hmm?"

"Do yourself a favor and never, ever, refer to your penis as the love stick in front of a woman again."

"Well, when you put it like that . . ."

"Dave, independently of how I put your love stick, if you keep advertising it like that, it will always come out short. Pun intended!" I snorted aloud. I had tears rolling down my face at this point.

"You're not gonna let it go, are you?"

"As long as I am Izzy, I will never let your love stick go!" I mumbled between two laughs. "Did that sound as bad as I think it did?" I asked, still laughing. I couldn't even breathe properly, and it took me awhile to.

"How did you know?" he asked after I calmed down from my fit of laughter.

"About what?"

"About the details," he said, summarizing his attraction to random women into all that it was: picking out the element of beauty that mattered the most.

"It takes one to know one." I said, winking at him and changing the subject without giving him the chance to ask me any more questions.

One thing we learned right away once the initial awkwardness between us started to fade away: we felt drawn to each other because, despite all our differences, in the things where we didn't collide, we weren't alike; we were the same.

CHAPTER 10

FRIENDS WITH BENEFITS

I was never one to notice the moment when I fell in love or the moment when I knew I had become friends with a person. Nor was I one to believe that those moments could be isolated from the stream of complex feelings that both love and friendship inspire. Until I met Dave. I remember the precise moment that we became friends, real friends. That's when Dave became my person.

"Why didn't you come, Izzy?"

"I wasn't in the mood!" I said sheepishly.

"How would you be in the mood? You don't let yourself go. You don't relax. That's why you didn't come."

"Jeez, Dave, I'm sorry, you don't need to act like this is a big deal. I didn't even think you would notice my not coming. You had fun, didn't you?"

"I did, but it would have been better if you had come! You're not an easy person, you know?" Dave mocked, but there was a sweetness in his voice that I had never heard before.

"Thanks for reminding me . . . I just wasn't in the mood, okay?" I said, taking mental notice that our brief exchange, from an outside perspective, might not be interpreted as a conversation about missing a party. I snorted while trying to contain a laugh, but I didn't say a word about it. Dave would feel awkward about it. He still did. He said I had a dirty mind. I knew I just had a quicker mind. He thought the same things; I just said them first. Or plainly said them.

"What's wrong with you, Izzy?" he asked, concerned.

"A lot of things, as you might have noticed by now." I attempted to joke, but I lacked my usual poignancy. "But today I think I'm just a little blue. Girl stuff, you know?" I said, trying to play it down.

"Are you dressed?" Dave asked. We were talking on the phone.

"No, Dave. I'm hanging around the house naked. It's a little habit of mine," I teased. What can I say? When I see a will, I find a way. Even when I'm sad.

"You just can't help yourself, can you?"

"You make me sound like a pervert, Dave," I said, grimacing despite the fact that we were on the phone.

"Just have that ass of yours ready in five minutes, because I'm picking you up and we're going for a walk."

"Hmm, I don't know . . ."

"Izzy?"

"Yes?"

"Did you hear that?" Dave asked.

"Hear what?"

"Me hanging up the phone and leaving the house. Move!" Dave shouted in my ear. Then he hung up on me. I didn't hear him leaving the house, though.

Dave did these things. If you were feeling blue, he would spend the day cracking jokes and making you laugh. If you were moody and had cramps, he would show up at your door with a bucket of ice cream. He would eat most of it, but still, it was the thought that counted. Though I must confess that he did a great job at swearing that he felt sympathy cramps and that he was bloated and ready to spawn like a salmon. He was sweet, and he would simply try to sweep you off your feet without your even noticing. He couldn't help himself.

I understood quite well the allure surrounding Dave. There was a pull to the easiness with which he met new people and made friends. He really was a great guy, and he was witty, smart, and funny, despite his occasional foul moods. He wasn't hard on the eyes either, but that was something that grew on you. I told you before that he wasn't every woman's wet dream; in fact, Dave wasn't the type of man that women found terribly handsome at first sight. Because he wasn't. He was six feet tall with a wide frame. With his broken nose and the disheveled brown hair, Dave was what most women would call an interesting man. And there was something appealing about him that had you guessing. He had me confused, though.

Once Dave showed up at my house, we went for a walk and ended up at a shopping place doing stupid things like trying on sunglasses and funny hats. I suggest you picture this in movie mode—you know, with cheerful music playing in the background, people laughing, happy dogs, sunny day, a lot of green and a fountain, and Dave and I having fun and messing with each other. You know, the whole shebang. Oh, add a little slow motion if you intend to visualize us running and jumping. I always do that; it feels right and looks better. Don't you think?

Well, in truth, the shopping area was a crowded street filled with gray stores with flashy signs that tried to make you aware of their daily promotions or, simply, of their existence. You pictured a park and golden retrievers, didn't you?

We walked around for a while, cracking jokes and sharing the latest events of our lives. We did enter an accessories store, hence the sunglasses and the hats, but that was it. We did not run around chasing each other, or move from store to store trying multiple out-of-style accessories or clothes; nor did we share ice cream. And the only background sounds that we had were car horns and the mash of incomprehensible voices of people that all looked the same speaking out loud. But we did have fun, though, and after a long walk we ended up at a coffee shop that sold lousy coffee and nice cakes.

"Feeling better?"

"Yeah, thanks!" I said, nodding my head as I sat in the chair opposite Dave's. We were in a secluded corner of the shop. We always chose those places; they suited us.

"No need to thank me. That's what being awesome is all about," Dave mocked, winking an eye at me.

"True. But you do know that more than your awesomeness, what I truly admire is your modesty. Now there's a virtue!"

"I know! It's so hard to be this modest when I'm so amazing, and intelligent, and funny . . ."

"Yeah, I don't know how you manage all that!" I mocked.

"With great effort and prideful humbleness."

"God, cut the crap, Dave!" I snorted, laughing.

"You wanna hear something funny? It took me ages to understand the meaning of the expression!"

"Cut the crap?"

"Yeah! When I was little, it didn't make sense to me. I thought of it in a literal way. Someone cutting crap with a knife! Sometimes I still imagine that when I hear it, you know?"

"You don't cease to amaze me, Dave! Now I'm certain that Einstein must live in that head of yours!"

"Are we being sarcastic, Izzy?"

"No, we are being ironic, Dave! There's a difference, you know. Hey, I have to get you a nickname or something. You keep calling me Izzy."

"Get me something instead."

"Pardon?"

"Get me something. You know, when people offer something as an alternative to stuff—like, 'Can I get you a coffee or something?' 'Wanna grab a beer or something?'—I always think of saying this. And I finally had a chance! Thank you, Izzy, from the bottom of my heart, for making it possible."

"I would say you're very welcome, but I honestly think that that kind of gratefulness is not deep enough. Why aren't you grateful from a deeper part of your body? I just made a wish of yours come true."

"I can be thankful from the bottom of my scrotum if that's your will, Izzy!"

"See? That has an added depth. Now I feel rewarded."

"I love this meaningful talk! It's so hard nowadays to find someone with whom to share all these profound thoughts!" Dave said, attempting for an intellectual pose.

"It's refreshing, isn't it?" I concurred. "Got it! I can call you Duh; it's a nice short name for Dave! Don't you think, Duh?"

"Hmm, I don't think it would be very practical. It would be confusing, and it would seem that you have a speaking disability." Dave started to mimic me. "Duh, come here! Duh, do this! See? It's confusing. I won't be able to tell what I'm supposed to do, and it will seem that you are drunk all the time. Not very ladylike of you, Izzy."

I was laughing so hard by this time that I didn't even try to speak, so Dave continued with his rambling.

"Tell you what. You can call me Steve!"

"Steve?" I managed between two gasps and wiping the tears from my eyes in an attempt to compose myself.

"Yeah. My great-aunt Carol says I look like a Steve. She never gets my name right, and she even says that it's not her fault that my parents named me wrong. She says I couldn't be more of a Steve if I tried, whatever that means."

"I so want to meet your whole family," I managed. "You don't have a second name? You're just Dave Poe?"

"Ah, Isabella Maria, not all of us are blessed with graceful name combinations as yourself!" Dave retorted with his best fake Italian accent.

"I swear to God, Dave, I'm not telling you anything else about me again. Ever!" I said with amusement.

Dave continued with his scoff but with a British accent now. He was unstoppable. "You ungrateful child! Thou shall not renounce your Christian name."

"I should have known better than to tell you my name. I just handed out ammunition for you to mock me to death!" I said with exaggerated drama.

"Well, Izzy it is, then!"

"You never gave me much choice, did you?"

"Come on. Just admit that you like it when I call you Izzy. It's cute!"

"Yeah, it matches me. I'm all about cute!" I said sarcastically.

"You are more than cute," Dave said without a trace of mockery in his eyes, pinning me with his stare. We weren't laughing anymore.

"Hi, guys!"

I turned my head toward the sound, letting out the air that I'd been unwittingly holding escape my lungs in a long but silent exhale . . . and allowing my heart to calm itself down from the blow.

"Hi!" I greeted with fake enthusiasm, still a bit dazed with the intensity of the brief moment that Dave and I had just shared.

In front of us stood a colleague of mine from work.

"I hope I'm not interrupting, but I saw you guys in here, and I was dying to have a coffee. And I don't like to sit by myself in these places. Mind if I join you?" she asked.

"Not at all," I said. "Just grab a seat."

"You must be Dave," she said, reaching out her hand to greet him. "Isabella talks about you all the time!"

"Does she?" Dave asked with a smile and a raised brow, as if assessing the possible meanings behind her words.

My colleague was a nice and kind girl who didn't swear and was always polite. She lived her life with controlled joy and, enviably, had no greater expectations than to get married and have babies, for she was one of those persons who was blessed with the possibility of living a normal life. To add up to her normalcy, she was beautiful, yet she lacked the sparkle that made women like her light up a room just by smiling. She was truly unaware of her looks, and she had a shyness and an innocence about her that made men like Dave crave to unravel such purity. She was a good girl, you see. And there is no greater allure than to corrupt that kind of woman. To any kind of men.

As she sat at our table, I noticed the shift in Dave's demeanor immediately. I'd seen him eyeing girls before, but this was the first time I saw him release what I would thereafter call the Charm Beast on one. Of all Dave's prowess, this would become one of my personal favorites. But not at that time, though.

I sat there silently, seeing the events unfold in front of me as if I were watching a play. I saw their exchange subtly evolving. Dave was leading her on with his sweet talk and his charming manners, and she was being hopelessly seduced. She didn't stand a chance.

I noticed that his posture was different, carefully studied to look totally relaxed and at ease. His voice had an added roughness about it that did things to your insides, or maybe that was just from all the coffee I had drunk. His gaze held a disturbing confidence that pinned you down and made you feel exposed. And he topped it all with a careless attitude and that smug smirk of his in such a way that few women would honestly stand a chance against his charm. Well, not that few, but it sounds better if I say it like that.

But the point here is that my colleague wasn't one of those few women. So I saw her react to his every assault with genuine emotion and complete ignorance about the fact that she was being played right into his trap. She thought he was funny and friendly, and she clearly loved the attention. I said it before, and I'll say it again: he had game!

After a while, Dave was openly flirting with her. There was no need for subtlety there, just patience.

At some point, she went to the bathroom and we were left by ourselves. When Dave stopped staring at her ass, which only took place after she sashayed her way through the coffee shop and disappeared toward the ladies' room, his gaze fell on mine. I'm certain that what he saw in my eyes left him with no doubts about the meaning of the words I told him next, just as I had no doubts about the reach and implications of his words right after that.

"Not her, Dave!"

"Okay."

It might seem trivial, but that's when I knew we were truly friends, when he looked into my eyes at that moment and I saw that honesty and loyalty—and that me and us were more important than anything else was. Dave had become my person, you know, the one that will be there for you. No matter what.

When my colleague returned to the table, Dave's attitude was entirely different. He was still attentive and friendly in his polite way, but his posture was no longer the one of a hunter.

Things had changed.

After this event, our days were filled with stories, ridiculous rambling, nonsense talking, mocking, and everything else that allows two people to really know each other. Dave and I didn't become inseparable; we became indispensable to each other, though in different ways.

I became Dave's confidant, support, and counselor. He would trust me with his secrets, his concerns, his conquests, and his doubts; and he would seek my opinion, my advice, and my words concerning almost every event of his life. I became the woman in his cards, and without either of us even noticing it, I became the woman in his life as well.

Dave wasn't that to me. Sure, I shared my problems and concerns with him and sought his opinion in many situations, but I didn't do it out of need. I did it out of trust, because Dave had become my possibility. I told you already that I'm one of those persons. I try my best not to depend upon anyone, because I know that the only person I can rely on is myself. Now I knew I had Dave as well, because if I wanted or needed there was that possibility. He was that possibility.

*   *   *

"Hey, Midget!" John greeted me, mocking my almost five feet tall stature, as he always did, as he and Dave stepped into my house. I sound taller, don't I?

"Hey there, Little John!" I retorted, as I always did, stepping aside to let them in. "Dave," I acknowledged as he walked past me and nodded his head at me.

John was Dave's cousin, housemate, and best friend, and he was also the reason that Dave had come to the other side of the world. Dave hadn't come for him, rather because of him. John had been living and working there for almost two years then, and he was living the life. He had a nice job, plenty of spending money, and a different girl in his bed every week. That had been enough to spike Dave's curiosity and will to come see it himself. It had been enough to make him leave Maria.

John was a fine young-looking guy. He was six feet four, hence the Little John joke, and he had a pretty face and a toothpaste commercial smile. He was one of those men that women either fall in love with or nurture. He was carefree, fun, and practical. He had a keen inability to brood over problems or situations, letting himself be consumed by guilt or remorse for the things he did. He couldn't be more different from Dave if he tried, and that's why they got along so well. It was really one of those cases that fit the adage that opposites attract. They complemented each other very well. If they were gay, they would have been the perfect couple. I couldn't tell them that, naturally.

"So, Midget, how's work?" John asked me, slumping down on my couch.

"There's not much to tell. Same old thing," I said, smiling and shrugging my shoulders.

"Hey, how come he calls you Midget and you're all smiles and dimples, but I call you Izzy and you're always nagging me about it?" Dave asked with an almost outraged tone in his voice.

"I'm cuter than you, you clown," John answered, goading Dave purposefully.

I laughed. Dave was always pointing out the niceties that I did or had toward John. He was kidding, of course, but he was right. John fostered my maternal instincts. To me, he was like a big kid that I felt compelled to take care of. At some point, I used to say that if he were smaller, I would even carry him around. Thank God he wasn't, because I honestly think I would. Carry him around, I mean.

As with Dave, I lost count of the women John bedded, though my relationship with him was very different from the one I had with Dave. In fact, John only searched for my shoulder in extreme cases, which was either when he'd met a special girl or when he wanted to dump her. Yup, that's how special they got. And he didn't exactly search me to look for my advice or my opinion, but rather to voice his conflicted feelings. Contrary to Dave, he didn't dwell on those feelings for long or heavily. In fact, I was always under the impression that once they had left his mouth, they no longer haunted his thoughts. He was that carefree.

"How are things with that jackass of a colleague you talked about last time? Need us to go break his teeth or something?" John asked, all macho.

"You can go break his something instead," I said, and Dave and I laughed. "You're right! This is fun!" I stated, looking at Dave, who was still laughing at our private joke.

John pouted. "I'm feeling left out."

"Grow a pair, will you?" Dave mocked.

"The guy is still a jackass; no change there," I informed them. "And now he stares shamelessly at my boobs!"

"Doesn't he have anything better to do?" John asked.

"Are you saying that my boobs aren't nice to stare at, Little John?" I asked, trying to maintain a straight face.

"I wasn't saying that, Isabella," John stammered, suddenly flustered. "Hmm, I was just . . ."

"Oh God, relax! I'm just messing with you!" I said, smirking while Dave laughed at John's abashment.

"You treacherous Midget!" John mocked pointing a finger at me.

"Man, you should have seen your face!" Dave said, slapping John on the back and still grinning.

I picked up my purse and looked in the mirror to see if any final touches were necessary. Nope. I was all set to go.

"Hey, I'm ready! Shall we go? Do I look okay?" I asked all at once, looking down at myself.

"Yup!" the boys said in unison, raising themselves up from the couch and heading for the door. They seemed eager to go, so I assumed that I looked okay.

We went to a party at a club downtown. When we arrived, the place was already packed. I never felt comfortable in places like that, so the only thing to do was drink my ass off. That always worked.

John and I engaged in a series of tequila shots while Dave remained faithful to his beers and two or three whiskeys. It didn't take me much to get wasted. And when I did, I was dancing all over the place. So was Little John. And we rocked at dancing together. At least that was my perception. In my head, we looked like Fred Astaire and Ginger Rogers, though eventually, I do remember seeing Dave laughing like a maniac while he watched us. What can I say? Alcohol does that to a person.

I was actually having fun. But I sobered up a little when a colleague of mine from work (there's always one around, usually when you're not on your best behavior) came to ask me to dance with him. I wasn't able to refuse him. Sometimes people in some situations need to be handled with care. That was one of those.

He was a nice man, always kind and attentive, with nice manners. But unfortunately, it was a slow dance, and he was fat and pink as a pig, and he was drenched in sweat. I couldn't push from my mind the idea that the poor guy looked like a nerdy pervert, especially when he pasted himself to me and I felt all those soft and moist meats bobbing around my small frame. I was grossed out, but mostly I was truly scared about the physical possibility of being sucked into his body or choked in his lard. My eyes searched for Dave or John in hopes that one of them would free me from that meat loaf embrace, and I found them laughing their asses off at the bizarre scene. Neither of them came to my aid, and I thought I would be stuck there, literally, until the end of the music. I can only thank God that mobile phones with cameras weren't popular yet; otherwise, they would have captured the moment for posterity.

Fortunately, one of Little John's friends came to my rescue and disentangled me from the tentacular wet lard of my colleague. John's friend was a funny guy who rambled endlessly. He seemed nice. I liked him. However, when I shared my opinion of the guy with Dave, he seemed to thenceforth find countless flaws as to the guy's character. He didn't do it overtly, but I noticed that after a while, I had developed the idea that the guy was a man whore that slept with everything that moved. And bragged about it. To everyone. And might have had, or might have, sexually transmitted diseases. Lovely, wasn't it?

After a few moments of my being in the guy's arms and dancing with him, Dave showed up and grabbed me by an elbow, pulling me away and staring down at the guy in a blatant display of protectiveness. Or was it possessiveness? The guy backed away, raising his hands defensively and shaking his head, leaving us by ourselves on the dance floor. When I was about to open my mouth to protest, Dave raised a brow at me, clearly annoyed, and yanked me through the crowd. I didn't say a word and followed him obediently.

I was a little flustered after that, so I settled in by Dave and John while they talked to some girls. Little John sometimes told the girls I was his sister, oblivious to the pain and memories that those words evoked in me. When the girls showed their surprise at our complete absence of resemblance, and they were not referring only to our height, John normally offered very inventive reasons for the fact. From us being fathered by different men, mine being a midget, to genetic problems that allegedly made our entire family suffer from an incapacity of resemblance disorder, or my being adopted from a village in Papua New Guinea where people didn't grow more than five feet, John always had a plausible justification to give away. I played along because I didn't want anyone to pry in my well-kept life. Dave played along too, protecting my privacy. But if someone asked if the two of us were siblings, our denial would be so vehement that people wouldn't dare ask anything else. But if they only questioned our relation, Dave would simply say that we were just friends.

It always bothered me when people said that. It seemed they were playing down friendship, as if everything else were more important, when normally it wasn't. But it bothered me even more that Dave said it. We weren't just friends. We were real friends, with all the good and bad that came along, with all the difficulties and concessions inherent to such fraternity, though we said it wasn't one. For when it comes to real friendship, you don't hold back, you don't hesitate, and you don't offer or take from your true friends less than all. That's where the real benefit of friendship lies.

CHAPTER 11

THE ELEPHANT IN THE ROOM

Here's the thing: why can't a man and a woman simply be friends? Not "just" friends. Friends! Simply.

Human nature, I know, yet frustrating nonetheless.

It's a common assumption that a man and woman who are seen together have or will have something going on between them. Some people even say that a true, honest, and disinterested friendship cannot subsist among members of opposite sexes. Others exclude the possibility of such a friendship entirely. In fact, to those who defend such a limitative point of view, the only friends a man can have are called other men.

I don't agree.

And I'm not talking about those friendships where you go out for coffee and share bits and thoughts about life and the world. I'm not even talking about those friendships where you hold each other's hair in turn when you puke because you just had too much to drink. Or those where you complete each other's sentences because you spend so much time together that you can guess what the other person is going to say.

I'm not talking about those.

I'm talking about the friendships where you know each other so well that you sense what the other person is thinking because sometimes you cannot even part your own thoughts from theirs. They become the same. I'm talking about the friendships where you don't just share your deepest and dirtiest secret; you share your soul. I'm talking about the ones that when a person calls you in the middle of the night saying that he needs you, you just say you're coming, and it doesn't matter where that person is.

I'm talking about Dave and me.

It wasn't always like that, though, and I'm not going to lie. It wasn't easy either, because when you strip bare your soul like that, you'll get hurt at some point. It's almost inevitable, yet it's necessary.

When Dave and I became friends, we became almost an item. Looking back, it was fair and expectable that people assumed that we were lovers of some kind. We knew so much about each other that at some point, even to us, the lines sometimes got blurry. This was because our friendship, with all its coincidences, had been abnormally fast and much too intense.

We didn't have the time to let things flow and mature naturally. We weren't given that chance. So in a matter of a very few months, we had a bond so strong that I accepted without struggle the fact that Dave had already become more important to me than many of my family members or oldest friends.

How did they blur? The lines, I mean.

Human nature, you'd say.

Lack of it, I'll tell you.

*   *   *

"So, Izzy, you and Dave, huh?"

"Dave and I what?" I asked, pretending that I had missed the innuendo. I was having lunch with my nice colleague, the one from the coffee shop that I forbade Dave to hit on. Yes, forbade. In case you missed it at the time, I wasn't asking him, though it was the first time I ever purposely interfered with Dave's life. The second, and last, happened many years later and almost broke us apart. Almost.

"You know. Don't play dumb with me!"

"No, I don't know. Why don't you enlighten me?"

"Aren't you guys dating?" she asked, all smiley.

"No," I denied sternly.

"Oh, I see. It's one of those friendships with benefits kind of thing," she said, as if reaching a brilliant conclusion.

"You might say so, but if you're trying to insinuate that the benefit is us having sex, then I'm sorry to disappoint you. The real perk of our friendship is that we can count on each other."

"So you're just friends? There's nothing more going on?" she asked, visibly surprised by my revelation.

"No, we're really friends," I almost barked. There it was again, the annoying insinuation that friendship wasn't enough. Apparently, though, if you added sex to it, it would become something worthy and you could drop the "just." Hell, you could even add some air quotes to it and top it with an annoying wiggling of brows while you voiced the word "friends."

"Okay, okay. There's no need for you to get mad," she said, looking uncomfortable.

"I'm not mad. I'm just tired of everyone assuming that." I sighed forcefully.

"Don't get me wrong, Isabella, but it's kind of natural that people assume that. I mean, you're always together and you seem so close."

"We are close, but not that kind of close. And I get it that people think that, but that doesn't mean that it doesn't wear me out. It's been awhile now, so it's kind of obvious that nothing is going on between us, don't you think?"

"Yeah, but didn't it ever cross your mind? You and Dave . . ." she suggested hopefully.

"No," I lied.

"I don't get it! You guys look good together. Why don't you date?" she asked, and I could tell she truly wanted to know.

"Because it's not like that. Some men you date, and some men you don't."

"What does that even mean?" she asked, a bit exasperated.

"You don't have many male friends, do you?" I asked with a simper.

"I have friends, but apparently my notion of friendship is a bit different from yours," she retorted defensively.

"Oh, I have no doubt that it is," I whispered. "I just think that not every man is for you," I followed in a more audible tone.

"Honestly, I just really don't get you guys. You're both single, you obviously get along more than most couples, and I'll say it again: you look good together."

"Not every relationship between a man and a woman is about romantic love. Just because you're close to a man, it doesn't mean that you will work as a couple or that you have to jump each other's bones! Didn't it ever cross your mind that maybe we got along so well because we're not having sex?"

"Why do you think sex would complicate things?"

"Because we're not those kinds of people."

"What kinds of people? The ones that have sex?" she teased, seeming immediately uneasy and guilty with her mischief, which was quite endearing. She was such a nice girl.

"No. The ones that fall in love," I explained.

"You have never been in love, Isabella?" she asked, looking almost horrified at the prospect.

"The point is not if I have ever been in love but rather if I can fall in love." *Again*, I thought. "And no, before you ask, I don't think I could fall in love with Dave."

"Why not?"

"Because we are too much alike, especially as far as the bad parts."

"But wouldn't that be a good thing? You could help each other, understand each other . . ."

"No, we wouldn't, and that's the whole point. We would never trust each other!" I said, cutting her off in the sweetest tone I could manage. She didn't get it.

"How come? Honestly, I think you're both just scared of the feelings you have for each other," she said.

She would never get it. I realized that there and then. I also realized that, like her, many other people wouldn't either. It simply wasn't worth the trouble. You can't make people understand what they don't want to believe in. It's like trying to explain the joys of parenting to a person who never wanted kids. But that doesn't mean that you cannot have fun trying.

"He farts around me," I said, doing my best to conceal the grin that was threatening to betray my faked seriousness.

"What?" she asked, shock blatantly starting to dawn on her.

"Dave farts around me. You know, big, loud, and smelly farts."

"Oh!" she said, realization seeming to finally hit her. "Oh, gross!" she added right after, as if she were truly nauseated.

Apparently, farts, like the truth, can also set you free. Pun intended.

Whether I grew tired of people's surmises or not, the reality was that I was well aware of the meaning of my colleague's words. I knew that people looked at us and assumed that we were a couple or that we were simply screwing around. Honestly, it didn't bother me. As I said, it was expectable, and at some point in your life, you just learn to accept that. Dave, however, didn't handle it so well, and his uneasiness toward the subject not only became obvious to me, but it also started to get me fidgety.

Dave did his best to ignore the issue, and his stiff posture prevented me from doing what I always did in these situations, which was lighten them up with humor. Dave didn't allow any room or ease to do that. Any joke or innuendo about the matter was met with discomfort at the very least. It was strange. We had become so close and intimate in so many levels of our lives, yet we couldn't address something that was silently smothering us.

It was worse for me, though. Dave had his women, his conquests, his easily made friends, and everything else that allowed him to vent. I only had him. It wasn't fair.

Time didn't make it easier for either of us. Even Little John started to eye us with suspicion. He wasn't flagrant, but I noticed that there was something there, mainly some quizzical looks now and then when our interactions looked like the ones of an old couple. I knew he didn't get it either. He didn't understand how we could spend so much time alone just talking, with nothing else going on. But foremost, he couldn't comprehend why not.

At some point, with all the outside pressure, doubtful looks, and all my loneliness, I started to question it myself. Dave wasn't the only person I knew there, but he was the only one I had allowed myself to be known by on the other side of the world.

Therefore, I wasn't that surprised when the myriad of conflicting thoughts and feelings started to take over my rationality. I realized that

Dave was becoming attractive to me, that I was seeing more than I should in our small exchanges, and that I was missing out what I shouldn't see in the whole picture. So inevitably, I lost my touch, my keen ability to read and see Dave's intentions and feelings just by watching him. He became an enigma. Not in the whole but in the parts that concerned me and us . . . I simply didn't know anymore.

It frustrated me. But above all, the lack of control over the situation infuriated me, though I managed to keep the building tension that I felt between us well tamed.

But there were moments, though.

Moments where our gazes would lock and we would immediately avert them, because neither of us could bear whatever was passing there. Moments where I would become uncomfortable seeing Dave pick up a girl. Moments where Dave would shift moods while I talked about a guy that I found interesting.

Sometimes they were worse. Sometimes we would go out with Little John and one of his girlfriends, and out of nowhere, Dave would suddenly coil up in himself and give everyone the cold shoulder. That confused me, because I just knew he was stupidly brooding over the fact that he had looked at us and seen what everybody else saw: a couple.

Those were the hardest times, for they were filled with mixed-up signals and unspoken accusations that we didn't know what to do with or how to address. Moreover, the growing pressure did nothing but worsen things, though Dave kept ignoring the elephant in the room with the same lightness that he'd managed to deal with the matter so far. After all, he had the means to unwind it. But not me. So I just dwelled on it relentlessly.

Until I could not do it anymore.

This wasn't our human nature calling upon us; this was the world telling us that we were lacking in that department. There was nothing primal or instinctive in our attraction, if there was ever one, or if we could sum up our feelings toward each other to that. We were that tangled.

There are only two ways to solve this kind of affliction when a friendship is at stake; either you get it out of your mind or you get it out of your system.

Guess what we did?

*   *   *

The music was blasting through the columns, and we were barely able to listen to our own thoughts, much less any kind of conversation.

Little John had his flavor of the night (yes, it was one of those periods where they didn't even last a week) drooling all over him, and it wouldn't take him long to become intimately acquainted with her, though he seemed a little conflicted over something. He was dragging the final blow unnecessarily. The girl didn't need any more convincing, but maybe he did.

"You should be careful there, Little John," I teased, motioning my head discreetly toward Friday (trust me, after a while you just don't have any more imagination left to name them, so why not just stick to the obvious?).

"What?" he asked me, confused.

"You can drown in all that drool that girl has pooling in the corner of her mouth."

"Yeah, you think?" He smirked.

"What are you guys conspiring over there?" Dave asked, joining our conversation as Friday eyed me with a menacing glower from a distance. We had already moved to a much more soundly bearable place by then.

"Friday is giving me the look!" I blurted. "I swear to you guys, one of these days I'm going to take a beating because of you. I'm small, and I'm not a brave person. I can't stand physical pain."

"Who's Friday?" Dave asked.

"Isabella's amusing nickname for my lovely friend for this evening," Little John explained, his voice drenched with sarcasm.

"She's losing her touch, don't you think?" Dave teased, speaking to Little John as if I weren't there. "She used to have these witty nicknames. That was some funny stuff, good material. Now it's all gone. We're stuck with clichés and unimaginative monikers. I tell you, half the fun of picking up girls is gone now."

"Now that you mention it, I realize that long gone are the times of Under Woman, Sleeping Booty, Darth Vart—"

"Blonde Girl or Meats Loaf," Dave interrupted. "And before either of you two dare to say it, I still think that the woman was not fat; she was voluptuous! And, last but not least, Little John . . ."

"Hey, I'm not on that list! My nickname is a term of endearment," Little John whined. "Isn't it, Midget?" He faced me.

"Of course it is, sweetie!" I said with fake outrage. "But then again, they all are." I snorted.

"Why haven't you ever called me Robin Hood?" Dave asked.

"Why would I?" I asked back.

"Come on, Izzy! Little John? Robin Hood?" Dave asked, brow raised as if trying to make a point.

"Hmm, too obvious. But I confess that I considered going for Robin Wood, given how you name your little fellow downstairs—God forbid that we say the word penis!—but then I thought that there was nothing heroic about the way you stick your love around. You're not actually stealing from the rich to give it to the poor in any way. You're just keeping it all to yourself. I could have gone with Sheriff of No Toughing Ham, though."

"That's not fair," Dave retorted.

"Wait a minute there! What did he name his penis?" Little John asked me eagerly.

"Don't you dare, Izzy," Dave threatened, sticking a finger right in my face.

"You're such a girl, Dave," I mocked, knowing that it would annoy him that I said that. He hated when I said it. But it was true! He was such a girl sometimes, but he never understood what I meant by that, and he always took it as an insult. It wasn't. Dave felt and reacted in many situations as a woman: emotively, fully, and sensitively. And that was all but a flaw, for that was where most of his humanity lay. "I'll take it to my grave, I swear!" I said, diverting the subject and holding up my hand before Dave had time to throw me one of his deadly glares.

"I'll pay you, Isabella," Little John said, grabbing his wallet to make the offer more believable. He remained unaware of Dave's and my brief exchange of looks.

"I can't, Little John! He'll hit me; I'm sure of it."

"He won't hit you! You're a girl. And moreover, a midget girl. Tell me. Go ahead," he urged me.

"I'm a boy to him. He will have no mercy! I bet he'll even try to hit me in my proverbial balls," I teased, and when my gaze fell upon Dave's, I froze because he was deadly serious staring at me.

Little John did not miss this exchange. He turned on his heels and went over to where Friday stood to deliver the final blow, I assumed, since he was nowhere to be seen right after that.

As for Dave, he was pissed. He ordered vodka and didn't say a word for a while. I ordered a pink drink. The times for Dave and I to get shitloaded drunk with whiskey were still to come. So pink drink it was. Because pink is pretty and cheerful, pink drinks always make me happy, especially when they come with those little umbrellas. And cherries.

Five pink drinks and three whiskeys later, I decided that the elephant that was standing between us could also be pink. Mind you, elephants only come in neutral tones, but I can't honestly blame alcohol for my poor decision making. I can only blame it for my color blindness.

"You do see me as a boy, don't you, Dave?" I asked tentatively.

"Izzy," Dave said in a warning tone.

"Come on, Dave. We have to talk about this."

"About what?"

"Stop being evasive," I snarled.

"I'm not," he said sharply.

"We have to talk about us. This," I said, gesturing a hand between us.

"There's nothing to talk about," he insisted. Dave wouldn't pass on a fight or any kind of direct confrontation. Yet when an uncomfortable situation or a real problem posed as a threat to his manicured reality, he would avoid it like a plague. I was the opposite.

"Do you find me that unattractive?" I mocked.

"You know you're not unattractive. You're far from that," Dave said, not looking at me.

"Yet you see me as a boy," I joked.

"It's not like that, Izzy," he countered. "And it's you that sees me like a girl, not the other way around."

"Oh, come on, Dave! You know that that's not what I mean when I tell you you're such a girl," I said, almost incredulous.

"What do you mean, then?"

"That you feel things like a girl would. But I'm not saying it in a bad way."

"Well, I don't like it. It makes me sound weak."

"You're all but weak, Dave."

Despite the seriousness of our conversation, the booze was now striking me hard. I was having trouble focusing, and suddenly I felt compelled to laugh. So I did. I laughed like a maniac. Dave looked severely pissed at me then.

"You're drunk!" he stated.

"I am not!" I said in mocked shock at the accusation.

"Come on—let's go home," he said, reaching for my elbow.

"I don't want to go home! I want to stay here and finish our conversation," I said, stomping my foot.

"What do you want to say?" he asked, seeming slightly amused with the childish tantrum I was throwing.

"I want to talk about this thing going on between us. This thing that is blurring our friendship," I said defiantly.

"And what would that be?" Dave said, stepping closer to me, his hand still on my elbow.

"Well, I think you're a great guy. And we spend all this time together and we talk . . . a lot and about everything."

"That's what friends do, Izzy." He was clearly uncomfortable, but he didn't flinch or retreat from where he was standing, which was too close.

"Yeah . . . I know. But . . . the thing is . . . I mean . . ." I was rambling, disturbed by the proximity.

"Just say it, Izzy!" Dave said hoarsely.

"I feel attracted to you!" I blurted, holding his gaze.

"Izzy . . ." Dave groaned.

Everything happened quickly then. But to me, it was all in slow motion. It still is, because there are some moments in our lives that stay engraved as the memories we created of them in our minds, and not as the instant we actually lived.

That's why I clearly recall Dave letting go of my elbow and raising both hands to rub his face with them, in a gesture that was meant to prevent me from seeing the smug smile that he was trying to conceal from me.

"I'm not saying that I'm infatuated with you, Dave," I said, all drunkenness gone from my system.

"I know, Izzy. We're friends, and I don't want to mess that up." Dave was fighting the corner of his mouth that was forcing its way up conceitedly.

"I don't want to do that either! But I needed to tell you because this was bothering me, and if we're friends, we need to be able to talk things through. No matter what."

"I get that!" He sighed.

"I don't think you do. I'm telling you that I'm attracted to you, but nothing else. I don't want to date you. I don't want a relationship with you. I'm not talking about that . . ."

He cut me off. "Izzy, it's not smart to mix things. I don't want to ruin what we have."

"Me neither! I don't want to go to bed with you, Dave. You can't handle a friendship like that. I can, but you can't. So don't worry, because that's not what I'm suggesting." I was almost amused.

"I think it's better if we just go home. We've talked, we've cleared things up, and this won't change anything between us."

"I hope not," I said, trying to conceal the growing anger that I felt building up inside me. Between the alcohol and the roller coaster of emotions that ranged from anger to amusement, I was already a mess when I followed Dave through the mass of people still hanging at the bar.

When we finally exited the bar, we stood outside facing each other; the only thing between us was silence—thick, heavy, choking silence.

"I'll see you tomorrow," Dave finally said, looking me straight in the eyes. I averted his gaze, but I was still able to see the smug smile crawling up his lips as he turned on his heels to leave.

"Bye," I said curtly, turning as well, and walking in the opposite direction toward my building door, which was literally the next door. But I stopped and turned on my heels just when I was about to reach it. I just had to hear him say it. "Dave!" I shouted, though there was no need for that. Dave was just a few feet away.

"Yeah?" he said, turning in my direction but not coming forward to where I stood. That's when I noticed he was still in the same place where I'd left him.

"Remember when we met? The deal we made?" I asked.

"Deal?"

"Yeah, that sometime in the future, whenever I wanted, I would ask you something about you, and you would have to tell me, no matter what?"

"Yeah," he acquiesced.

"Well, Dave, this is the time," I said, sighing deeply and biting my lower lip.

"What do you want to know, Izzy?" Dave asked, swallowing hard.

"What do you feel about me? For real!" I asked, staring right into his eyes, despite the distance that stood between us and that each of us was keenly aware of maintaining.

"You don't need me to tell you that, Izzy, because you already know!" Dave said, staring right back at me.

I remember breaking the stare and walking away toward my house. The turmoil of emotions had taken over, and I felt relieved that all that weight was now off my chest. But I also felt my pride wounded so much. I had lowered all my defenses, and that bothered me. I had trusted too much in our friendship and told Dave how I felt. He had told me nothing in return, and he had left me there hanging and exposed.

However, the worst part had been realizing that he just couldn't help himself. Once I voiced that I felt attracted to him, his ego rocketed. I couldn't help but feel hurt by his cocky attitude. I was furious too. It was burning me up inside that Dave, despite not wanting to ruin our friendship, couldn't suppress the urge of gloating at the fact that I too had succumbed to his charms.

I hadn't, but most of all I didn't want to. And he didn't get that, as he didn't get what I had told him. He didn't get that I needed to get this out of my mind so that nothing would pose as a hindrance to our friendship. He didn't get that, contrary to him, I needed that matter dealt with and well resolved in order to proceed. And I needed him to shove that elephant wherever he wanted to, because it was not going to stay in my room.

As expected, the next day was terrible. So were the following weeks. Things had changed, and awkward was the only word to describe how we felt around each other. We didn't know what to say or how to behave. No conversation was relaxed, and everything felt uncomfortable. We didn't laugh as we used to, and we didn't joke with the same easiness. We had broken an important boundary in our friendship, but one thing we both acknowledged: neither of us was willing to lose the other, so we endured all those awkward moments and forced our presence on each other.

We went out, and we pretended to have fun. We went to Monday morning breakfast, and we forced conversation on each other. Dave made sure to tell me about every detail of his every conquest, and he even added stories about his past. It was at one of those breakfasts that he told me about his first disastrous threesome. Dave desperately needed things to go back to normal; he didn't realize that we could only go forward or nowhere at all.

We went forward. I guess that nowhere wasn't an option for either of us.

One awkward day, similar to all the others that had preceded that one, Little John invited us for coffee. I never knew if he was aware of Dave's and my uncomfortable times, but if he was, I must say that he fooled me well. He was not the type of person to try to solve other people's problems. He lacked the tact and the will to do so.

The three of us met at our usual coffee shop, and from the moment Little John started to tell us his latest tales, the air felt lighter, the moods switched, and all awkwardness between Dave and me was gone. It was something that I couldn't explain, but Little John had that effect on me; whenever I felt bad, sad, or mad, Little John's presence made it all go away. I never knew why he affected me so much, and I never told him; it would freak him out. Dave knew, though, and he would take me to Little John whenever he thought I needed him.

Our friendship became stronger after this shake-up, despite all the doubts and uncertainties that were still hanging in our minds. We both knew that from the moment Dave turned his back on me on the street outside that bar, he was convinced that I was in love with him. I never bothered to enlighten him otherwise. I honestly didn't care to, and I didn't think it would matter. Dave's ego was bigger than my need to set things straight, especially when by addressing them, I would only make them worse.

He would get there by himself. Eventually.

So I left it to God.

CHAPTER 12

MORE THAN WORDS

Attraction was no longer an issue. I had cleared it out of my mind, and we had moved it out of our way.

Our friendship continued to grow, and we even added some conquests to our weird dynamic. Touching was one of them. Dave and I never touched each other purposefully. So the first time we did, it was something that we would both remember. We hugged. The first time I went home on vacation after a year of living abroad, Dave asked me to hug him. I did. It might seem ordinary to most people, but to us it was extraordinary. From then on, we would always hug when we were apart for long. Sometimes Dave would just hug me because he felt like it or threaten me that he would because he knew that I typically hated being hugged. I was never a fan of public displays of affection, but truthfully, I didn't hate Dave's hugs. In fact, I came to cherish them.

Dave's dissatisfaction toward his job also grew. He complained more and more about the uneventful routine that filled his days and the underlying, smoldering conflict between his boss and him.

"You have to keep your cool, Dave."

"I know, Izzy, but I'm dying here. Boring is an exciting word to describe my work. I'm tired of doing the same thing over and over again. And that guy is a prick. One of these days, I'm going to lose it and give him a piece of my mind. Or something."

"You're smarter than that, Dave. Don't buy a war that you cannot win," I warned him.

"I'm not buying a war, Izzy. But it should be illegal for someone who's supervising the work of other people to be so mentally challenged."

"A lot of people would be in jail by now if stupidity were illegal."

"Speaking of illegal, I met someone," Dave said.

"I like the sound of that! I say illegal and you tell me that you met someone. Is she's an illegal worker?" I joked.

"No, she's a—"

I cut him off. "A drug dealer?"

"No, she's a—"

"An illegal circus dwarf that swallows swords by night and traffics weapons by day?" I continued.

"Just shut up, will you?" Dave barked.

"Oh, come on. I still had a few more," I complained.

"You want me to tell you about her or not?"

"Just spill the beans, will you?" I said, resigned.

"She's a lawyer."

"Fancy! You're finally going after the smart ones!" I said, winking an eye at him.

"You're such a snob, Izzy. Just because she's a lawyer doesn't mean she's smart—or that the girls I normally date aren't."

"I can hope, can't I? For crying out loud, Dave, I'm getting tired of your dull dates. There's no thrill there. Everything is as expected. No effort is needed. I know that you're not after their brains, but a little excitement wouldn't harm you. Don't you get bored?" I asked.

"Hmm. A bit, yes. I miss being in love, you know?"

"Ah, Dave, always the romantic! It must be hard to search for love in the arms of a different woman every week!" I mocked.

"You're such a . . . witch!" he said, as he used to so many times.

"Are you ever going to call me a bitch? I'm just wondering, you know."

"As much as I might want to, I'd rather keep the suspense. It bothers you more."

"Spoiler!" I said, grimacing.

"You had me fooled now; I thought that you were going to call me party pooper!" Dave knew that I always laughed at the sound of poop. Pun intended.

"I've grown! I've overcome my poop phase, and I'm on my shit phase now. Now, give me the small print on the lawyer."

"Oh Lord! You're just going to make lousy lawyer jokes the whole time, aren't you?" Dave complained.

"I object! Where did you get that idea?"

"Give a guy a break, will you?"

"I'm late. I have to go to work. But I will want to know about that lawyer. You'll need my verdict, after all," I said, gathering my things to leave and tossing some money on the table to pay for my coffee. "You're still up for lunch at the end of the week?"

"Sure."

We had lunch on Friday (I'm a woman; I know it was Friday because I remember that I was wearing casual clothes. In case you were wondering). Two of my colleagues joined us, and Dave behaved. He was well tamed by then. And it would have been an uneventful lunch if it weren't for the mark it represented on our friendship.

During our meal, a woman walked through the restaurant. She was tall and blonde and she looked around my age. She wasn't particularly pretty, but she was attractive and had presence. She was one of those women who do not go unnoticed. She strolled around the place, clearly looking for someone, and when she passed our table, she accidentally bumped into me. It was just a brush, actually. But it was enough to make Dave look at her. They exchanged a brief greeting—one of those head nods that you give to people you're not very familiar with and never know if it will be reciprocated, so you opt to make it discreet in case it's only you making the greeting.

Once she passed, Dave's gaze met mine for a brief moment, but it was enough for him to know that I knew. Subtle smiles ghosted our lips in sign of acknowledgment, and we both returned to the conversation that my colleagues were having without our silent exchange being noticed.

When we were exiting the restaurant a while later, I turned to Dave, making sure that my colleagues, who were walking in front of us, weren't in ear range, and opened my mouth to ask what I already knew. Dave cut me off before I had a chance.

"Yes, Izzy, that was the lawyer I told you about the other day. Do you have any more questions?" All we could do was laugh.

We had reached that place in our friendship where words had become unnecessary because it was more than words; it was simply beyond them. The few safety barriers that stubbornly remained had fallen, and we both silently acknowledged it. From here on, we could only free-fall into each other's soul. If there was any other path, neither of us cared or bothered to look for it.

After that, we could have entire conversations with just a dozen words. Now that I think of it, those were always odd conversations to whoever watched them. They seemed a lot like those mobile phone calls without a strong network signal, where you only hear disconnected words. We were like that sometimes. Other times we didn't even need words at all, because just by looking at Dave's face, I would know what was going on in his head.

That's how I knew that the woman in the restaurant was the lawyer Dave had mentioned earlier that week.

Dave had met her during a work meeting at his company. As far as a woman went, she filled most of Dave's requirements—at least the physical ones. Adding to the tall and blonde that I already mentioned, she also had a nice rack to sum to the whole assemble. In my defense, I must clarify that those were Dave's words, not mine, though in this case, I could attest the veracity of his statement. She did have a nice rack.

She and Dave hit it off right away, though at the time the conversation was strictly professional. Nevertheless, as you can imagine, Dave managed to unleash the Charm Beast on her. Apparently, she wasn't that impressed, which gave me hope that maybe Dave had finally found a match.

*   *   *

"What are we going to do about this lawyer? Any strategies?"
"We, Izzy?"
"Yeah, we're a team!" I said, smirking.

138

"Izzy, you have to get a life, you know?"

I gave him a quizzical look and shrugged my shoulders. If he only knew.

"Yours is enough for both of us! Besides you're gonna need my help to get the lawyer. If she's smart as I think she is, this is going to give us some trouble."

"Don't you have faith in my skills?"

"I do, but I have bigger hopes for her brains."

"What? You're rooting for her? What a great friend you are!"

"I'm not rooting for anyone; I'm just wishing for some entertainment!" I deadpanned.

"You know that I always have your best interests at heart. I'll try my best to entertain you," Dave said, sarcastically.

One thing was for sure: the hunting season was officially open!

Dave had managed to get her office number and called under the pretext of having a doubt about something that had been discussed on the meeting where they had met. She wasn't available at the time. Her secretary took the message and said she would call him back as soon as possible.

She didn't.

I was thrilled.

Finally a breath of fresh air! A woman who wouldn't simply succumb to Dave's charms! Of course, many didn't, since we already established that Dave was no Adonis, though he was an interesting man. But it adds to the drama if I put things like that. We've been through this before, remember?

She called after three days, which teaches us that we can never be thrilled for too long. Or can we?

"Am I speaking to Dave?"

"Yes."

"This is . . ."

"I know who you are. I wouldn't forget that voice. And that's not the only thing I haven't forgotten about you." Dave would always shoot to kill, as you can see.

She snorted but didn't flinch for a second. "I got your message. So you had a doubt?"

"Yes, I didn't know if you preferred Japanese or Italian," Dave said. He wasn't even bothering to aim. This was Rambo style.

"Come again?"

She walked right into that one, and I must say it was such a waste not to use it, but that was neither the time nor the woman.

"I was wondering if you preferred Japanese or Italian, but we can go somewhere else for dinner, if you prefer," he continued, sure of himself.

I must say that at this point, the only thing that occurred to me was that he must have thought that hand grenades were good to hunt, because that was such a blast!

"I see," she said. "So it was that kind of doubt."

"It was. Care to enlighten me?" Dave asked, all smug and cocky.

"Well . . . 'The only limit to our realizations of tomorrow will be our doubts of today,' which I believe is kind of self-explanatory, don't you think?" she said. "I trust that was all, but please feel free to contact me if you need any more . . . enlightenments." She then hung up on him.

Dave stood there dumbfounded, with the phone in his hand and his mouth ajar. He had suffered blows to his macho ego before, but I must say that this one was very classy.

"I still can't believe that she quoted Roosevelt to you!" I managed to say as soon as I stopped laughing.

"What?" Dave asked, facing me and stopping to pace my living room back and forth. Eventually, he just let himself drop onto the couch.

"You know, that thing about the limit to our realizations being our doubts, that's a quote from Franklin Roosevelt, I think."

"Who knows that stuff?" Dave shrugged, indignant.

"Smart people, Dave!" I smirked.

"Says the woman who likes to watch *Pretty Woman*! Izzy Her Majesty, the queen of romantic comedies!" Dave mocked.

"What's wrong with sappy movies? They're funny, entertaining, and have happy endings. I don't see a movie to get depressed; I have my life to do that for me."

"We're not going there again. Watch all the crap you want; I'm never gonna understand that brain of yours."

"You're not supposed to." I winked at him.

"Well, just show me some compassion here," he grumbled.

"What? Your ego is hurting? Is it very painful?" I teased.

"The only pain I feel is in my ass, and it has your name on it. And maybe some lawyer's also. You're gonna help me out or what?"

"Now that you've put it so nicely, I feel inclined to do just that," I continued in my ironic tone. "You're lucky that I like this lawyer woman, and that I'm already having too much fun to let you ruin this for me."

"We wouldn't want that," Dave mumbled.

"If my memory doesn't fail me, there's a part missing in that quote from Roosevelt. That quote is about faith, not about blowing people's hopes. It's something about moving forward with faith and strength. I think," I added pensively.

"So she was telling me to pursue her?"

"Nah. She was blowing you off. What were you hoping to accomplish with those cheesy lines and that cocky attitude? Didn't your uncle teach you anything?"

"We hit it off when we met, and then there was that exchange in the restaurant the other day . . . I thought she was interested," Dave explained.

"She might have been then, but now, with that smooth move of yours, I'm not sure . . . Hey, you might as well have showed up naked at her office and told her to just get it over with because you were in a hurry."

"I'm no ogre," Dave said, acting dumb and . . . Ogre-like.

Women, whether they're smart or not, don't fall for the cheesy lines; they fall for the guy that tells them. It's mainly the attitude that counts. Most women like self-confident men, men who know what they want and are not afraid to say it. But above all, most women like to be pursued. Nothing is better to a woman's ego than to have a man at her feet. Mind you, always at but never beneath them.

However, when aiming for a smart woman, the compliment has to be about her brains, because that's the asset that she values the most.

"So what do you suggest I do now, Izzy?"

"Pursue, Dave. Pursue!"

And he did. He called her office the next day, and she answered the call immediately. I must confess that I was a little disappointed.

"Dave, to what do I owe the honor? Are you in need of further enlightenment?" she asked with sarcasm, naturally.

"I am," Dave replied smugly.

"And what would that be? I was under the impression that we had clarified all there was to clarify yesterday," she said, her tone showing her amusement.

"It's not exactly a doubt, in case you were thinking of quoting Roosevelt again. It's more of a predicament, actually."

"A predicament? I'm not sure if I'm more impressed with your use of big words or with the fact that you did your homework and went in search of whom I quoted."

"If I'd known you'd be so easy to impress, I would have suggested a Big Mac."

"Excuse me?" she said, perplexed, I'm certain.

"I'm kidding! We're going to Italian," Dave said matter-of-factly.

"I don't recall accepting your invitation to have dinner with you."

"I don't recall you not accepting it either. In fact, judging by your words, I assumed you were giving me hope. Wasn't that what Roosevelt was aiming for?"

"You have a strong case there, but I'll have to pass."

"Why?"

"I don't mix business with pleasure."

"Me neither. And since we don't have any pending business, I don't see how we would possibly be mixing what we don't have anymore with what we could be having . . . plenty of," Dave added with a throaty voice.

"You're a bit full of yourself, aren't you?"

"I would expect an intelligent woman as yourself to be able to distinguish confidence from conceit."

"I, however, didn't expect a conceited man such as yourself to be able to take no for an answer . . ."

"You have so little faith in me!" Dave said, cutting her off. "Just so you know, I would take no for an answer if I believed that was what you wanted, but I don't think it is."

"Is that so? Conceited and presumptuous! Don't your virtues have an end, Dave?"

"Why don't you find out for yourself?"

"Give me a good reason to," she teased.

"I don't need to anymore," Dave said.

"And why is that, Dave?"

"Because you're already having too much fun!"

"Dave?"

"Yes?"

"My answer is still no."

"I'd be disappointed if it weren't," Dave said, hanging up after they said their good-byes.

Dave didn't call her again during that week. According to him, she needed to feel the loss. Meanwhile, he had something to entertain him. Apparently, there are some things a man is not supposed to deny himself during his existence, namely a contortionist, unless he has stronger or nobler motives for depriving himself of such a fantasy, of course. And so far he hadn't.

After a week, he resumed his cat and mouse game and kept it up for two weeks, until she finally caved. He took her to an Italian restaurant, but the date was far from satisfactory. She didn't let her guard down, and at some point, the conversation became an exhausting mental ping-pong.

"I don't know, Izzy. I think I'm losing interest."

"Of course you are! If you lose interest, then you don't get to be dismissed," I joked. "Nice strategy. I like it."

"It's not that. She's not all that interesting after all."

"Quitter!" I mouthed.

"You're just enjoying this too much, aren't you?"

"Ah, Dave, you know me so well!" I exclaimed. "Why don't you invite her to have dinner at your house?"

"She's not ready for that yet. I have to break her defenses first. You know that when they step inside the cave (yup, Dave and Little John were that corny and named their apartment the cave! Actually, that was the short name for The Love Cave), they only get out to see the light of day." He wiggled a brow at me while pairing it with a devilish smile.

"Ah, there's nothing that I admire more than a man who can give a literal meaning to the adage that there ain't no such thing as a free lunch! In this case, dinner," I added.

"Do you have any suggestions on how to break the lawyer, miss smart-ass?" Dave asked.

"She is, I hope, a smart woman. You just have to outsmart her, beat her at her own game, but never let her know that you did it."

"You sound like my uncle! Care to be more specific? I think I can only deal with one cryptic person in my life."

"Don't worry, I'm not gonna tell you to bake her cake. I think you should bake her a pie!" I said with a serious face.

"What the . . . ?"

"Just kidding!" I said, laughing in his face. "Now, seriously, just keep up your game. Women like persistence, unless you're a creep, which I'm certain is something she doesn't suspect yet."

"That's it? Keep on pursuing her?"

"Well, you can up the game a bit and tease her a little more. You know, invite her for coffee and throw some sexual innuendos at her; see how she reacts. And pretend that you're spellbound."

"What?"

"You know, let her catch you inadvertently gawking at her, avert your eyes when she looks at her . . . You know."

"She'll fall for that?" he asked skeptically.

"She's smart. She's playing hard to get. She'll look for the details and will listen to what you say. If you do it right, she'll be thinking that she has tamed the bad boy. And that's why she'll fall."

"You're telling me to pretend that I'm infatuated with her?" Dave asked, looking at me with a mix of awe and admiration. "You know, Izzy, if you wanted, you could be a really bad person!" He looked uncertain as to whether he had just insulted or complimented me.

"I know. I chose not to be one a long time ago, though," I said matter-of-factly. "But, Dave?"

"Yeah?"

"Mind that when smart women fall, usually they fall hard." I looked Dave in the eyes and sighed. He gave me a comforting smile and squeezed my hand.

It didn't take Dave a week to have the lawyer having dinner at his house. Just for fun, I baked him a pie for dessert. Things went smoothly, and after they had their meal, Dave pulled his most idiotic trick from the hat and invited her to dance. How or why that always seemed to work, I will never understand. I used to tell him that women were just eager for that awkward moment to pass, and to avoid any more shameful memories, they just jumped right into the sex part.

Apparently, some didn't.

The lawyer danced with Dave, and when he finally gathered up his courage to kiss her, she wasn't shy about it. They fell on the couch, entwined around each other with such a fury that you would think that they would combust. Suddenly, when Dave was about to cop a feel under her blouse, she stopped him, stood up, and said that she had to leave. And she left! Just like that.

"She was panting, Izzy! That was so damn exciting!" Dave said, all elated and running a hand through his air.

I burst out laughing.

"What are you laughing about?"

"I can't believe that you fell for that!" I snorted.

"Fell for what?"

"She's playing you! I liked her already, but now I think I'm in love with her," I joked.

"She's not," Dave said, annoyed. "I was there! She was all flustered and panting. She wanted me. Bad!"

"Oh, Dave, you're so hot. Oh, I can't resist you! I have to go before I lose my mind! Oh, Dave!" I mimicked, going all *When Harry Met Sally* on him.

"No way!" he barked, but I could see that uncertainty was already flooding his convictions.

"Way, Dave!"

So what does a man with a wounded ego do? He restores his honor. What else?

He invited her for dinner again. This time, there was no dessert and no dancing. They both knew why she was there. She was only under the illusion that she was in charge. Dave seduced her mercilessly and had her in his bed spread wide as an eagle in no time.

"It was lousy."

"Hmm, that bad?"

"Izzy, she didn't even touch my love stick!"

"What? You're kidding me! Not even a brush just to give it a feel? Wait! Is it that small that she couldn't even find it, Dave?" I raised my hands to prevent the incoming pillow from hitting me in the face.

"Very funny!"

"What? It is funny, Dave!"

"Seriously, it was such a lousy lay. What a disappointment!"

"I'm disappointed too. Hey, maybe she was just nervous or having a bad day. Or you suck in bed."

"Shut up, Izzy! It was boring missionary sex. She was moaning all the time, and she looked like a corpse just lying there. You know what she asked me in the end?"

"What?"

"She was all flustered, with watery eyes and shit, and she asked if I had felt it too!"

"Felt what?"

"Apparently, *it*."

"Oh God! She didn't!"

"She did! Like if there was something special going on between us. I was so bored with her that I just turned around and went to sleep while she lay there sobbing. Can you believe that? She was all emotional and crying! Finally, I heard her leaving in the middle of the night. Thank God she didn't stick around for breakfast."

"I was having so much fun! I would have bet one of my lungs that she was going to be hard to get . . . What a disappointment!"

"You're telling me that? I was the one who had to sleep with her!"

"Oh, come on! It couldn't have been all that bad."

"At least I got to empty my balls!"

"See? Every cloud has its silver lining," I said, giving him a reassuring smile. We went on talking about the latest movie Dave had seen.

The lawyer called Dave a few times afterward, but eventually she left him alone without too much drama. Dave moved on to the next girl, who was, if I'm not mistaken, Brazilian. And in case you're still wondering about the contortionist I mentioned back there, I'll shorten it up for you and share the visual that was stuck in my head from Dave's descriptions: banging a pretzel. And that's about it.

CHAPTER 13

DAVE'S SECOND MARIA

I had heard of Dave being in love, and I had a fair image of him out of love, but so far I had never truly seen him fall under a woman's spell—until Maria number two came along.

She showed up in his life as all women that apparently mattered seemed to make their entrance in Dave's heart; she burst in unexpectedly and with no sense at all. As I would refer to the occurrence later on, she popped. The women who made a difference always showed up out of nowhere, as if they materialized out of thin air to become the object of Dave's full attention. Hence, they popped.

He saw her walking down the street during some pagan festivities in one of those ethnic neighborhoods that abound all over the place. She walked with a smile on her lips and eyes adrift. And that's what drew him: her detachment. In that instant, the word ceased to exist, everything else blurred and she was the only thing tangible out there and in Dave's mind. *Pop!*

It took him a month to see her again, though. And only then, when she stood there in front of us, enveloped by the crowd yet so free of it, did he gather the courage to tell me about her. He rambled incoherent sentences about having seen her before but not telling me anything, saying how beautiful she was and how he needed to find out her name.

"You like her," I said, my mouth ajar, not hiding my astonishment. "You really like her!" I added, a smirk already forming in the corner of my mouth.

"I don't even know her," he countered.

"But you like her. She's different!" I stressed.

"I just told you I saw her once. How can you tell she's different? You're just fishing around, aren't you?" Dave questioned hesitantly.

"Nope!" I smirked fully while rocking back and forward on the balls of my feet, trying to cloak the smugness that was crawling up my face. Dave raised his brow at me questioningly.

"What?" I shrugged.

"Tell me!" he demanded.

"You wish, lover boy!" I mocked, but I acquiesced once I took a full look at his pleading eyes. "I know she is important because you want to know her name. Whenever you or Little John say their names or want to know them, I know they're important."

"That's it?"

"That's it," I said. "Otherwise, you just refer to them by their professions, their nationalities, funny nicknames . . . You know, nonpersonal stuff."

"I had never thought of it that way."

"No shit, Sherlock," I mouthed, turning around to where Mystery Woman (hey, at this time, we didn't know her name, so no harm done) stood with her friends, dancing. "What are you waiting for? Go talk to her!" I urged Dave, attempting to shove him to the dance floor.

He didn't even flinch. He just looked at me with sheep eyes.

"Are you kidding me?" I asked, amused with his sudden lack of confidence. "Just get your ass out there and go ask her name." I finally managed to push him to the dance floor and settled on one of the bar stools to get a first-row view of the spectacle that I was undoubtedly about to witness.

It's amazing what attraction can do to a person. It can make you a fool or a king, it can make you desperate or hopeful, or it can burn you or save you. But that was unimportant; what really matters is what a person can make out of it. You can own it, tame it, succumb to it, or simply run from it, but never, ever mistake it for love. That's the biggest risk and the most common mistake we're bound to make.

Dave was no different; not only was that kind of misperception an inherent trait of his character, but circumstances were also compelled to contribute to the equation. Being alone can be a tricky thing.

Sitting at the bar, I took advantage of my privileged position to examine the, so far, Mystery Woman. She was tall and elegant, and her long hair had a coppery tone. Dyed, no doubt about it. She was pretty, but there was something off about her. I looked further to see if I was able to put my finger on it just by watching her, but apart from deciding that I really didn't like her boots, I got nothing else.

"Why, for God's sake, is Dave doing an impersonation of Michael Jackson on the dance floor?" Little John, who had arrived without my noticing him, asked with undeniable amusement plastered on his face while he watched Dave.

"Is that what he's trying to achieve?" I asked, tilting my head to the right and frowning.

"That was a moonwalk right there," Little John said, motioning his chin in Dave's direction. "He's trying to score a girl, isn't he?"

"Yup. But he's not succeeding."

"You think so?" Little John asked sarcastically.

"She doesn't seem impressed. Hell, she doesn't even seem to have noticed him so far."

"Who's the girl?" Little John asked, trying to see over the cluster of people.

"It's that one with the fluttering gown and the green boots. And coppery hair," I offered, doing my best not to point at her.

"The one that looks like a hippie?" he asked scornfully.

"Hmm. She doesn't look like a hippie. She looks more like a . . ." I hesitated, not quite finding the right word.

"A fairy?" he said tentatively, cutting me off.

"That's it! That's exactly it!" I squeaked, adjusting in my stool.

Dave joined us a while later, drenched in sweat and looking uncomfortable, as if he had something big up his ass.

"So? What's her name?" I urged.

"Maria, but she prefers Mary."

"Well, that's convenient! You won't be in trouble if you call her by your ex's name," I pointed out.

"Are you already assuming that she is going to be my girlfriend?" Dave asked, surprised.

"Mary the Fairy!" joked Little John, who was listening to our talk.

"Don't start!" I admonished him, trying to keep a straight face. "What else did you two talk about?"

"That was it. I asked her for a cigarette and asked her name."

"Why didn't you talk to her?"

He didn't answer me. He just gave me one of his sheepish stares and looked back to where Mary the Fairy (that was kind of funny!) stood. Yup, it was that bad.

During the next week, we engaged in true and shameless detective work to find out who exactly Mary the Fairy was. It turned out that I knew a girl who knew a girl who knew Mary. Unfortunately, she wasn't willing to share Mary's phone number with me. Allegedly, she found me unpleasant. Go figure! Fortunately, she had a strong appreciation for Little John's looks and was pleased to make his acquaintance. So after some seductive persuasion and a series of unfulfilled promises later, Little John managed to get Mary's number. In exchange, Dave did the dishes for a whole month.

When he called Mary out of the blue, she didn't remember him but accepted his invitation to have dinner nevertheless.

As expected, dinner was a failure.

Dave showed up at my house after dropping her home without a good-bye kiss or even a hint of hope.

"She's different." That's all he said when I opened the door.

"Don't take this the wrong way, but I've seen you looking more . . . attractive," I said, eyeing him up and down as he stormed through my apartment. He was wearing some faded jeans, All Stars, and a fitted dress shirt. And he was sporting a mustache with a goatee. Not his best look, I must tell you.

"She must like me for who I am . . ."

I just raised a brow at him while putting my arms akimbo to emphasize my unspoken thoughts. There was no need to waste words with his bullshit. This was me he was talking to.

"So . . . cards?" I asked, searching for my tarot deck without waiting for his answer, which was frankly quite irrelevant since I had already decided that I wanted to see what my cards had to tell about Mary the Fairy.

Spread after spread, we were able to draw a pretty close portrait of Mary. If you believe such things are possible, of course.

Mary was, or seemed to be, a detached person. She didn't think or act like normal women. She didn't follow the same rules or obey the same order. She had the speck of attention of a goldfish and the keen ability to erase from her mind everything that didn't somehow please her. That simple. And that's why when Dave called her again to invite her to a picnic, she had a hard time remembering him. He was devastated, but he didn't lose hope. We had decided that Mary the Fairy needed a persistent approach. Dave had to pursue her until he found out something that she liked and go for it.

Luckily, she liked picnics—a lot. And that was it. They started dating. There was no anguish, no long chase, or even a glint of suspense in their relationship in the beginning. They went to the picnic, ate, and at some point kissed and made love in the outdoors. It was so boring that the only memorable thing about it was a bee sting in Dave's butt, due to its exposure to the elements and wildlife, if bees can qualify as such. I must admit that it did make me wonder if Dave's butt resembled a flower or smelled like one. Dave was thrilled nevertheless—not with the bee sting, of course. And I had never seen him like that. He was shitting puppies and butterflies out his ass, which sported a swollen buttock for some days, and I swear to the smaller deities, his pupils started shaping like hearts . . . or deformed balls. He was disgustingly in love, yet it was fun to watch and even more to mock.

Mary was the first girl that Dave introduced to me as his girlfriend, and I must confess that it was awkward as hell, even with Mary being such a scatterbrain. A veil of uneasiness shaded our interaction, and it remained there for a long time. In fact, it stayed there until almost the end, which was when we started to get along. I guess it made sense that way.

Things with Mary were fast but lasted long. Dave's priority, once they started dating, was to make the woman fall in love with him. This was Dave's obsession. It wasn't a need to be loved or to tame women' hearts; he just had to reach that point where they fell for him head over heels, as if that were his life mission or something upon which his happiness depended. Then he'd lose interest and move on. There was some drama in between, of course, but he would move on. He always did.

"You think she's the one?" I asked Dave.

"No. She's not the one."

"It's been what? Five weeks?" I stated more than asked.

"More or less."

"And you already know she's not the one? That was fast!" I stressed, my eyes wide open as if in wonderment, though I wasn't surprised at all.

"Yeah. That's something you just know."

"Just like that?"

"Yeah, just like that. It's something you feel in your gut."

"I have to confess that that's something I've heard from several of my male friends over the years and I still have trouble understanding."

"What's the difficulty?" Dave asked, surprised.

"I just find it strange that it's something that you just know. I'm not the sensitive type here—as we both know—but I find that rather disturbing. I don't have one single girlfriend who, after five weeks of dating a guy and being in love with him, has told me that she knows in her gut that he is not the one."

"That's because women believe until the end! Men don't. We're practical. Things either click or they don't."

"And they didn't with Mary," I stated.

"They don't," Dave said.

"So now what?"

"Now we're gonna move in together!"

I believe that in that moment and as an effect of my utter bewilderment at Dave's words, my eyes must have turned scarily huge. In fact, Dave seemed to be genuinely afraid that they would jump out of their sockets, because he made a reflexive move as if to catch them in midair. I didn't say a word. I didn't need to.

"It's the right thing to do. It's time I leave John's house. Mary and I get along just fine, and I spend all my free time at her house anyway," Dave explained.

"Now that you got yourself all convinced and believing in those plausible arguments, do you want to hear my opinion?" I asked, trying my best to maintain an impartial expression.

"Spare me the lecture, Izzy. I know that you think I'm rushing things—that I will soon get tired of Mary and will be dying to break things up with her but will not know how to because I will be living with her. I know you think I'm making a mistake . . ."

"I don't! I think it's not a bad idea," I said, cutting his rambling short.

He stood looking at me, his mouth ajar and suspicion all over his face. He was having trouble believing my words, yet he knew I wasn't joking or lying.

"You know, Dave, for someone who is so certain of his own wills, you seem to feel strongly about the thoughts you assumed I would have on the matter . . . and I just heard of it!" I didn't bother masking the sarcasm that was dripping from my voice. "I think that's what psychologists call projective identification. You know, when you attribute to other people your own thoughts and feelings . . . or something like that," I added.

"Don't talk to me like that!" he snapped in a husky voice, looking deadly serious.

"I'm sorry," I said after a brief pause, meaning my words. If there was one thing that Dave and I had learned in our friendship, and being the kind of people we were, it was that in order to move forward, we had to sort out our divergences and apologize. Always. So it could take us seconds or it could take us months, but we would speak things through, say what there was to say, and forgive what there was to forgive. Forgetfulness might come or not.

"I want to do this, Izzy! I'm in love with her."

"I know, Dave," I acquiesced with a muffled laugh, noticing that the tension that had marked our words so far was already lifting.

"I know you understand me, Izzy." He sighed.

"I do. I know you're in love with her, but you don't love her and never will. I know you won't rest until she loves you. And I know that you're desperate for a change in your life and this is the closest you can get to that now." I grabbed his forearm gently to reassure him that I knew what powered his decision and that I would be there, no matter what.

"Sometimes I think you know me better than I know myself," Dave said, almost whispering.

"Sometimes I think that too," I whispered back.

We didn't discuss the matter further. Dave moved in with Mary two weeks later, and things didn't change. Dave seemed determined to leave the main aspects of his life untouched. We kept diligently fulfilling our Monday morning breakfast ritual. We saw and talked to each other almost every day. Dave shared his problems and his worries with me, and he continued to ask for my advice and my opinions in almost every aspect of his life. We talked about everything, and our roles in each other's lives remained pristine, as always. But he lived with Mary, though she was never a presence outside their cocooned living. He kept that part all to himself, as an appendix of his life, because at some given point, it would simply be removed or, if necessary, extracted. It was that far-fetched that sometimes I would even doubt Mary's existence if it weren't for the few times we were together at some dinner parties or casual encounters where our coexistence was, naturally, marked by awkwardness.

Mary was uncomfortable around me, and I did not discourage it or make a great effort to counter that trend. Neither did Dave. As with many other women before and after her, Mary was bound to suffer from the insecurities inherent to having a boyfriend who already had a girlfriend, although platonic, with whom he shared almost everything. And since I was no troll and had a complicity with Dave that most women knew from the start that they would never achieve in their relationship with him, they, as with Mary, chose to see me as an inconvenience—to put it kindly.

However, in Mary's case, I must admit that things were slightly different. At that time, I suspect that Dave still held the belief that I was or had been infatuated with him, and due to his overinflated ego, he just couldn't convincingly deny any frontal accusation on the matter. It also didn't help that on one or two occasions, we had our tantrums in front of Mary, and if that weren't enough, Dave bitched about it to her for two or three days. No woman wants to spend that much time hearing about the fight her boyfriend had with his friend, who happens to be a girl and whose shoulder he searches for whenever he needs one. Mind you, I'm just playing the devil's advocate here. This is not my vision of things.

Actually, this was a subject Dave and I never had a word about. He never told me or insinuated what Mary thought about me. Though I knew it right away after we had cleared things up and made our amends in the aftermath of one of our lovely quarrels to which Mary had her first front-row view. It was not what he said about Mary being disturbed by our scuffle, that much I had already assumed, but rather the way he stirred uncomfortably in his seat, avoiding my gaze. That's when it hit me, and I just knew that she thought I was in love with him. She'd probably even given him shit about it, and he hadn't been able to denied it, because he thought the same thing as well. But I let it go . . . again. Why? Because we were bigger than that, and I kind of thought it was entertaining seeing him all fussy and convinced about it. His discomfort was far worse for him to handle than the truth, so why not let him suffer a little with the inflations of his own ego? Besides, there would be more Maries and more fights, so there really was no point wasting it all right there and then.

However, so that we're clear on one thing here, you'll have to know that when Dave and I fought, we were either feast or famine. We had no middle terms. We either went all cold war on each other and didn't utter a word, discussing the matter later, or we made a festival out of it, with some restrained violence associated to it, if necessary. And then we would also discuss the matter later. Now that I recall it, we always discussed the matter later, and we would do it politely, for both of us were somewhat susceptible when it came to those kinds of sorrows. Funny, huh?

Apart from these incidents, and as I already stressed, Mary's presence in my life was quite faded, though I often discussed their relationship with Dave. Mind you, there was no surprise or unexpected developments there. Things went down exactly as they normally did. In the beginning, Dave did everything in his power to make Mary fall for him. Eventually she did. Hard. He romanced her, dazzled her, and swept her off her feet. I have to be truthful here, though; he had no merit in her fall. Mary fell in love with Dave because she wanted to or had decided she would.

You see, Mary was a singular creature who inhabited her own little world and followed her own logic and rules, if there were ever any. She might seem lost or detached, but with time I realized that in her own different way, she kept afloat and didn't drift all that much. She just seemed to. She was always kind to everyone, despite her constant lack of recollection of people and situations. To put it simply, she was plainly spaced-out, but there wasn't a hint of stupidity or dumbness about her— quite the contrary. Despite all her alienation, she was smart and had one of the strongest intuitions I've ever came across. I saw it as a defense mechanism. Amid all that apparent absentmindedness, Mary was alert and in tune with the universe. She would sense and feel when something was wrong and react to it by closing herself off to whomever or whatever triggered her suspicion. That's what she did with Dave, though he acted as boyfriend of the year around her. In case you were wondering, that's not what she did with me, because when she let her intuition work on me, that's when we started to get along. For as much as you tried, you just didn't connect with Mary. She connected with you.

"She's closed down on me again, and what's worse, I don't even care!" Dave said.

"You think she knows that you're not in love with her anymore?"

"I think she suspects," Dave mumbled. "Shit! I really can't have that kind of drama right now."

"Why don't you just end things and save yourself all that unnecessary drama?" I asked.

"It's not the best time! You know I have a lot going on in my work and my life. I just can't do it . . ."

"You just won't do it . . . but I get you," I said reassuringly.

"This is all so exhausting. I'm losing my strength. It seems that wherever I turn, there's a plot to bring me further down. Nothing comes out well. We both have our own agendas. It's so damn frustrating."

"Dave, people and things have the importance that we give to them," I said softly. "Just calm down. Take it one day at a time and things will get better."

"You promise?" he asked me, his eyes pooling hope as if I held any power in the outcome of his future.

"I swear!" I replied, not managing more than a rueful smile.

Dave didn't end things with Mary. He let their relationship drag on through pits of silence and muffled frustrations. It wasn't all bad, though. Apparently, the sex was great. When they didn't connect or find any link that would justify the persistence of their relationship, they would replace it with sex. Therefore, they essentially humped like rabbits—all the time and everywhere. Not even the fact that they were caught in some public places once or twice made them stop their sexual escapades. Their sexual life was so intense that after a particular strenuous weekend, Dave had to hobble to our Monday morning breakfast.

"What happened to you? You look like you ran a marathon. What's wrong with your knees?"

"I skinned them."

"Do I want to ask how?" I questioned, hesitation in my voice.

He smirked conceitedly at me and shrugged.

"What did you get yourselves into this time?" I asked, already smiling in anticipation.

"You know, the usual. But we stayed at home this time. Mary is still a bit embarrassed about being caught on the elevator of that store near the market."

"That was not your brightest idea, but it was funny." I grinned.

"I think so too, now that I look back. But at the time, being surprised by those ten or fifteen people in the store when the elevator doors opened and I was with my pants down and grabbing my girlfriend's boobs wasn't all that amusing."

"I can just imagine your face!" I smirked.

"Yeah . . . Note to self: never trust the stop buttons on elevators again!"

"I would add, on department stores or any kind of places prone to have security around that would immediately jump to action to free allegedly trapped persons."

"Yeah, I might take your suggestion on that. Those guys were fast!"

"I don't know why people complain about security!" I concurred. "But hey, that's old news. I'm curious about your knees. What happened?" I asked, dropping my eyes to the said body part as if I were able to see through his pants.

"I literally spent the weekend on my knees! Too much friction, if you know what I mean," he said smugly.

"Good God! Why don't you guys just talk or see a movie? Do the dishes. Clean the house, for God's sake. One of these days, you're going to break your love stick, Dave. I mean it! You should . . ." I stopped my rant min sentence, my mouth agape as an ashamed Dave focused his eyes on the floor and refused to meet my gaze. "Oh. My. God!" I punctuated, realization dawning on me. "You broke your love stick!" I exclaimed loudly.

"Izzy!" he admonished me, shushing me with his bulging eyes.

I burst out laughing, and that's all I did for a while. I laughed and laughed and laughed.

Then I laughed some more.

It took me some time, but eventually I managed to compose myself and force the facts out of Dave, who was quite pissed at me by then.

"You do know that it didn't actually break, don't you, Izzy? It isn't exactly a bone . . ." Dave was attempting to gain the upper hand, but I just flashed my scornful smirk at him and winked my eye, urging him to continue his tale.

"I don't know exactly what happened. But in short, we were at it, you know, and I started to feel that there was too much . . . moist. You know. Wet is one thing, but that was a river down there. So I looked down and saw blood everywhere . . ."

"Bloody hell!" I squeaked.

"Yeah . . . and it was Sunday!"

"Dave, we're not gonna go there!" I admonished him before he had the chance to start humming U2's "Sunday Bloody Sunday."

"What did you do?" I asked, stirring in my chair nervously and propping myself forward on the table.

"We stopped, of course! We didn't know where all that blood was coming from. I mean, whom it was coming from."

"Oh my God!" I exclaimed.

"At first, we both thought it was Mary's. We thought that she had some kind of cut."

"And then?" I urged nervously.

"And then she fainted. Well, almost fainted."

"What?" I grunted.

"Yeah, she's very sensitive with that. She can't see blood."

"But was it hers?"

"The blood?"

"Of course the blood!" I cried, exasperated.

"No, it was mine! Once I managed to clean us up a bit, I saw that I had a cut—well, actually, it was more like a blown blister—on the head of my love stick, and it kept gushing blood."

"Yuck! And Mary?"

"Mary lay on the floor with her legs tossed up and white as a ghost."

"God! Did it hurt?" I asked, grimacing to suppress the cackling that I felt building inside me again while my mind was picturing the situation.

"No, it just kind of pumped. You know, like when you have an open wound and it seems that your heart is beating there. It felt like that. But there was so much blood!"

"How did you stop it?"

"Well, I thought of trains and other things that don't make me hard."

"Hmm?" I asked, raising a questioning brow.

"Trains, excessively hairy women, bugs . . ."

"For crying out loud, Dave, that's not what I was asking you. I was referring to why you had to shrink it." I practically yelled this as I cut him off.

"Well, that's obvious," he said, rolling his eyes at me. "Izzy, if I had any doubt about it, now it's gone! Now I know that all my blood literally goes down there. It's impressive! I only managed to stop the bleeding once my love stick shrank."

"Really?" I voiced, astonished.

"Really!" He said, nodding his head concurrently for emphasis.

"Have you noticed that these things only happen to you, Dave?" I asked, almost without changing my tone, although we had been silent for almost a minute then.

"You think?" Dave inquired thoughtfully.

"I have never heard of any guy skinning, blistering, or generically injuring his dick from excessive friction before. Not even horny adolescents that wank their puberty away!" I stressed.

Dave looked at me flatly, and then a smug smile slowly crawled up one of the sides of his mouth and stayed there.

"Go ahead! You can say it; I am the most interesting person that you know, ain't I?"

I just smiled back. Fully.

Dave and Mary lasted more than a year. Apart from the mad sex, their relationship boiled down to a long list of inexistent conversations, unheard claims, and a forced connection that neither of them was brave enough to break. Mary didn't do it; she opted to recoil to that little place of hers and shut down the outside world. Dave didn't do it either, for he didn't have the heart. Mary was just a small fragment of the wrongs that were filling his life back then, so at some point, he had no heart; he didn't leave her for the single reason of it being practical to him. That's why he stayed when every ounce of him screamed to go. He dwelled on it relentlessly. He might not have had a heart at the time, but he had a conscience.

Yet no conscience can prevent life from happening when we fail to assist our fates, as Mary and Dave did. One day Mary got a job offer back home, and she had no reason to decline it when Dave found no will to ask her to stay. You just don't turn down a better world and a better life for a man who doesn't love you back. And I have to admire Mary for that because even more than Dave, she loved herself.

CHAPTER 14

IF YOU DON'T GO, YOU NEVER GONNA KNOW

"Hmm. Hello?"

"It's me!"

"What the . . ."

"I need you, Izzy."

"I'm coming!" I said, my eyes shooting open as a rush of adrenaline yanked me from my sleep at the sound of Dave's torn voice.

"I'm at home."

"I'll be there in twenty," I muttered, hanging up the phone.

I pushed myself up on the bed until I reached a seated position and rubbed my face with my hands to force the remains of my sleepiness away. My heavy eyes searched for the alarm clock on the bedside table. It was five thirty in the morning. I had been asleep for less than two hours.

I sighed deeply and turned my head toward the warm naked body that lay beside me in my bed, whose name I wasn't quite sure of anymore, and nudged him slightly.

"Hey, wake up! You have to leave . . . now!" I said, sharply. I stood up and tossed a shirt over my head to cover my nakedness and then proceeded to pick up his disheveled clothes from the floor, throwing them at him. God, I hated it when they ended up staying the night!

As soon as he was gone, I took a quick shower, and I must have flown to Dave's house, because the next thing I remember is knocking on his door.

He was a mess.

He had dark circles under his eyes, not that I needed to see them to know that he hadn't had any sleep yet, and he looked devastated.

"Do you want any coffee?" he asked hoarsely as I walked past him and entered the kitchen.

"Please!" I muttered, trying to assess quickly what I had to deal with.

"I talked to her. There's someone else!" he offered.

I nodded my head to let him know that I was following the meaning of his words.

He had called Mary, so I will need to ask you first if you know how hurricanes happen. In case you don't, all you need to know is that for a hurricane to form, at least three things are needed. You will need heat; that's your fuel. You will need heat to combine with atmospheric moisture; that's your propeller. And you will need wind; that's your propellant. And of course you will need a preexistent weather disturbance; that's your trigger.

Dave had them all, which meant that there was no way to prevent the major storm that was coming.

It might sound odd to have Mary as a trigger at this point, since when she left, Dave's first feeling was one of relief. A weight had been lifted from his shoulders, and I hoped the resulting lightness would at least help him stay afloat.

It didn't.

Dave's life at the time was turmoil. He hated his job and his boss, and his revulsion toward both was at a boiling point so high that each day that passed uneventfully made me fear the next one even more.

He wanted out. Back home, on the other side of the world, his family seemed to be crumbling like a sand castle at high tide due to the constant conflicts over Dave's grandfather's inheritance. Being so far away, Dave hadn't been able to attend the funeral, which enhanced his inability of coping with his grandfather's death. To add to all this, his father was going to have a child with his new wife, and that had sent his mother into a depressive spiral since the woman knew no middle terms; she was either high or down.

Then there was Mary—or rather the hole she had left and that I had neglected to register. Mary's absence from Dave's life was something that I had not given a second thought about. Seeing Dave breathe again had made me forget how near the edge he always balanced. Moreover, he had made a fast comeback to his previous ways and had already christened his and Mary's bed with the moans of other women. Within a month, I counted at least three new conquests. All uneventful and passersby, but nonetheless he had taken some time to pursue them. Well, in truth, he only pursued one of them—and not for long—but nonetheless, he took the trouble. The other two were just more motivated to jump his bones . . . at the same time (and yes, this time things went down better, or at least longer).

Mind you, in no way was I convinced that he had forgotten Mary already, though I knew he had never loved her. Admittedly, I just thought he missed her and was still hanging on to the illusion of their last days, when everything was how it never had been between them.

I knew that he maintained contact with Mary. They had parted on good terms, and I knew Dave just couldn't help himself from feeding the tiny flame that still burned underneath the mess that had been their relationship, because only once their love had gained an expiration date did everything between them become more intense, more vivid, and less real. Yet better. When Mary left, she left crying not for the love that she was leaving but for the one that she had never truly had with Dave.

Again, they didn't exactly break things off either. That was something that neither of them seemed able to do. They just couldn't utter the final words, even when they had no reason to hang on to them. But now that I look back, I can see that Dave had nothing else to hang on to, so he hung on to what could have been.

"What did Mary tell you?"

"She told me that she had met someone." Dave said this with so much angst in his voice that I felt my heart shrink at the sight of him so vulnerable. It pained me.

"Okay, but is she seeing the guy or has she just met him?" I asked with exaggerated sweetness in my voice, as some people do when they talk to small children.

"Izzy . . . it's a girl! She met a girl."

"Oh!" I gasped. Not many things can actually shock me, but that one almost made me pee my pants. "Oh," I gasped again. Nothing else would come out.

"I'm shitting you, Izzy! Hey, I still have a sense of humor." He managed to let out a muffled laugh, but the smile didn't reach his eyes.

"For Christ's sake, Dave!" I cried, but I smiled nevertheless, pretending that I was going to punch him.

"She met some guy at her new job, and she's interested in him." He offered this with the same suffering tone that he had used the first time he had said it.

"You know that was bound to happen, don't you?"

He sighed deeply and ran his hands through his hair, as he always did whenever he tried to mask any deep emotion that threatened to come out unattended. His eyes were full of loss and fear, and he looked defeated.

"Yeah, but I always thought that it was going to be me first or that I wouldn't care," he confessed.

"Do you really care, Dave? Because if this is only a whim, you have to let her go," I said, holding his gaze.

"I do. Honestly, Izzy. I do! This is not a whim. I don't know what to do. I just want her back." Despair was dripping from his voice. I had never seen him like that. He seemed that he was about to either jump or to fall. Again, it pained me.

"Okay, let's just think things through," I said, trying to calm him down. "She left about four months ago? You didn't exactly stop living your life. Why do you think you want her back now?"

"Because I love her. I really do!" Dave ranted. "I've been missing her like crazy. I've been telling you that. And no, I'm not saying this because I think I'll lose her."

"Okay, okay. Calm down. I know you've been saying that you miss her and all, but I never thought that you felt so strongly about it." I was trying to find a way to reason with him.

"I do, Izzy! I know that I've been screwing around and all, but you know that that doesn't mean a thing. It's just sex."

"I know. You don't need to explain that to me."

Dave paced the room a few times before he sat in front of me with his head hanging down and framed by his hands. He looked so powerless and fragile that I had trouble finding the man whose soul I almost couldn't tell apart from my own. For the first time ever, I didn't know how to comfort him, so I let his pain sink in, for no amount of words would make things better. Not with Dave.

"I don't know what to do here. I've never been in this situation before," he said eventually. "But I know one thing: when a woman gets interested in another man, you're gone. She doesn't change her mind." He raised his head and looked at me.

"That's true," I concurred matter-of-factly, which made Dave flinch in his seat. "Mary is different, though. You never know what to expect from her." I added, trying to alleviate his pain.

"You think?"

"Yeah, I do. If she were any other woman, I would tell you that she was a goner, but as this is Mary that we're talking about, I think that anything can happen." I was stating this truthfully.

Mary was indeed one of a kind, and I had never seen her follow anyone, let alone feel like anyone, so there really was a possibility there.

"That's my hope too."

"Has she had any kind of involvement with the guy yet?"

"At first, she told me that she didn't. But I kept insisting until she told me they had kissed." His voice was laced with pain, his face a mask of disgust.

"Okay. That's not good." I regretted my words as soon as they left my mouth, and Dave winced as if I had stabbed him. This was one of those moments where people just can't handle the truth and, as a friend, you have to be gentle. So you either lie or omit, whichever comforts the most. "I mean, it might even be good. It's a way of getting it out of her system."

"You think?"

"It's possible," I said, trying to sound convincing. "But what do you plan to do? You're here and she's there, across the world."

"I'm going to her," Dave said hesitantly, which should have raised my suspicions right there.

"Okay, but do you have any holyday left? When are you planning to leave and for how long?"

There was a pause. Dave inhaled deeply and looked me in the eyes; I knew what he was going to say before he voiced it.

"I don't intend to come back, Izzy."

"What?" I muttered, shock dawning on me as I felt the sound of his words hitting me and freezing my heart.

"I'm not coming back," Dave said defensively. "We've talked about this before. You know that I'm not happy here. I've not been happy here for a long time. And now with this going on with Mary and all the fuss with my family back home, I just can't stand to be here anymore!"

"Dave, just think things through. I know that we've talked about leaving. You know that this is a phase. We all go through that from time to time. It's normal. But it will go away," I reasoned.

"It won't, Izzy. We both know that it won't. And I want to go. I need to go. I want to press the eject button and leave this place."

"And go after Mary?" I asked, defeated.

"Yes, and go after Mary. Because if I don't go, I never gonna know!" He all but shouted these words.

I knew what he meant, but I failed to understand it. Dave and I couldn't be more different in that aspect; he put himself out there and would take whatever life had to give him. I, on the other hand, was yet to see the day when I would leave everything and everyone behind to go after what I wanted. Or whom I wanted.

We let the silence fill the space between us, and we sat there sipping our already cold coffees. Dave's coffee was really bad. I snorted a little at the thought of that while feeling the dreadful goo slide through my throat. How could anyone ruin something so simple?

"What?" he asked, raising a questioning brow at me.

"I'll miss your shitty coffee!" I mocked, letting him know that everything was okay between us.

"I bet you will." He winked at me.

I would. I would miss him terribly because he was already a part of me. The idea of being there on the other side of the world without him frightened me like hell. He had been there from the beginning, and he was about to leave. Me. I was about to lose my person, my possibility. Yet I knew that he had to go and that I couldn't and wouldn't try to dissuade him. This was something that he needed to do, and no amount of reasoning would change his mind. I just didn't want him to do it for the wrong reasons, but that was something that he had to realize by himself.

"Hey, how was last night?" Dave asked.

I was drinking my coffee when the question caught me off guard, causing me to choke. I almost coughed up a lung.

"Wrong pipe," I offered, still trying to compose myself. "Nothing special." I was trying to dismiss the subject.

"But you went on a girls night out last night with that colleague of yours, the one with the nice boobs, didn't you?"

"Yeah. We ended up just having dinner," I answered, trying to sound relaxed.

"You didn't go to that new bar, the one you were talking about the other day? You said you wanted to try it."

"We just passed by. I didn't even get to see the place properly. She had things to do early today. And apparently so did I!" I used a scornful tone on the last part to divert Dave's attention.

"I'm sorry, Izzy."

"Shut it, Dave. Don't even dare apologizing!" I admonished him in a playful tone. "Hey, you wanna go for a walk and drink some real coffee instead of this shit?" I asked, smirking.

"Sure, let's go. I don't know how you even managed to drink half a cup of that," he said in a playful tone, looking at my mug with fake disgust.

We exited his building and inhaled the morning air. Life as we knew it was about to change.

Dave had made his decision and soon started to act on it, so if I had ever had a hope that he didn't follow through with it, it faded away in thin air.

The first thing Dave did was hand in his resignation letter and quit his job. And since he had nothing to lose, he did it in style. Well, he did it in Dave's style. He stormed into his boss's office, shoved the resignation letter in his face, and spoke his mind. It might not seem like much, but it turned out that almost three years of pent-up frustration and no sense of accomplishment can really make you say nasty things. The man was caught off guard, so he was rendered speechless and just stood there, mouth ajar, taking all the shit Dave had to give him. Apparently, it was quite a lot of shit. If that alone didn't do the trick, in the end, Dave turned on his heels, ready to leave his personal hell behind, walked three steps toward the door, and stopped mid-stride. He bent slightly and let out an excruciatingly long and loud fart. It was the ultimate release. Then he resumed his step and slouched out the door without looking back. Classy, huh?

The second thing Dave did before leaving was sleep with almost every girl who was on his wish list. There weren't that many, since he hadn't been shy before Mary showed up, and yes, he did have a wish list. It wasn't an official written down and numbered list, but both he and Little John had their fair share of women they'd called dibs on.

I don't know how many women he crossed off that mental list of his at the time, but I remember one in particular, not only because she was one of my company's secretaries but mostly because I have soft spot for Dave's stupid sex stories.

Dave and the secretary had exchanged some flirty looks on occasion, so it didn't take much for Dave to seduce her and have his way with her. Nothing remarkable there, right? Well, the thing is, the secretary had a huge amount of pubic hair, like seventies-style Afro wig pubic hair, according to Dave, who admittedly had issues with body hair.

I must confess that I always pictured him bent over the girl, his hands on her hips and about to pull down her underwear. When he does it, he's assaulted by a bulky Afro wig that jumps from her underwear and stands about three inches from her body. Funny, right? Oh, but there's more! Dave was so perturbed by the pubic hair that he turned on the autopilot and jumped the girl as quickly as he could. If he had had to, he would have managed to fake his orgasm as well. She was kind of pretty, so it mustn't have been all that hard, even with the hair and all. I think.

As soon as it was over, which was rather fast, Dave made sure she covered her modesty—all three hairy inches of it. She didn't quite understand at first that there was not going to be any more action there. She tried to fondle him and to snuggle for a bit, but Dave just turned his back on her and pretended to sleep, hoping that she would get the clue and leave. She didn't. And the worst part was that she woke him up after a while to help her remove her tampon, which she had forgotten about and that was now, with all the pushing from Dave's love stick, lost inside of her.

He didn't help her.

Quite memorable, right?

I must confess that it took me awhile to pass by the girl unaffectedly, since I kept picturing her Afro wig . . . and the lost tampon. Priceless!

You might be asking yourself by now where Mary stood in all this. Wasn't Dave about to go back to the right side of the world in pursuit of her? Well, yes, but Mary had never told him that she would be waiting for him. Moreover, as Dave had put it so bluntly, love and sex are two very different things. Yet the real reason behind it all was simply that Dave had never loved Mary, nor had he ever had a wounded ego before.

Notwithstanding, in less than a month, Dave packed up his life and his belongings and was ready to leave. It all happened fast. Too fast. As the day approached, I felt my world getting smaller and I couldn't stop the dread from filling me. I feared for Dave. I feared for what he was about to endure. I feared for myself.

When the day came for Dave to leave for the right side of the world, he, Little John, and I had lunch together. Dave told the secretary story, and we all laughed as we hadn't in a long while. We laughed as we did in the old times. He looked carefree, and I had no doubt that he felt that way too. He was happy.

Then came the good-bye.

We were all fidgety. Little John lightened the mood by cracking a joke about finally getting rid of Dave and having the girls all to himself. He did this while patting him violently on the back.

I stood on the sidewalk waiting my turn, and when it came, Dave and I hugged as if it were for the last time, despite that we knew we were permanent fixture in each other's lives and that this wasn't forever.

"I don't how I'll make it without you!" Dave whispered desperately in my ear before he put me back down on the sidewalk.

I locked my gaze with his and gave him a knowing nod because all my words were trapped in my throat. He nodded back with a fake smirk on his lips, sighed deeply, and walked toward his fate. It ripped my soul apart to see him disappear down the street, taking a piece of me with him.

"Godspeed, Dave!" I gasped finally.

PART 3
BEING DAVE

CHAPTER 15

BETWEEN HERE AND NOW

"If I had to tell your story, I would make it about your wanton life."

"Am I that shallow?" Dave asked.

"Not at all! You're that deep," I said flatly.

The memory of that conversation and of Dave frowning at the sound of my words then, as if digesting them, flooded my mind as I reread the message that I had received from him that day. It simply said, "I miss you so, so much now, Izzy."

I replied, saying the only thing that could comfort both of us in the face of his despair: "I am here; I am always here."

Dave had been gone for almost four months now. I missed him terribly.

We e-mailed back and forth and talked over the phone occasionally.

He was still a mess, and I was still at a loss.

Things with Mary had gone exactly as everyone expected them to go: poorly. As soon as he met with her, he realized he didn't stand a chance, but he begged for it anyway. Mary was adamant, though. She killed all his hopes with a single stab; she was in love with a better man, and whatever they might have had was now long gone.

It was a tough blow, and after all he'd been through lately, it was the last straw for Dave's fall—the last push to throw him over the abysm that attracted him so much and which he fought so fiercely against. But not this time, though. This time he was weak and was suffering. So he fell. Hard. The wound in his chest was open and bleeding too much, but mind you, the cut was not in his heart; it was in his ego.

You see, when someone breaks your heart, the pain is almost unbearable. Something in you changes; it's almost impossible not to. Almost. But when your ego suffers the blow, it's not the pain that is intolerable or the change that comes with it that marks you; it's the burn from the wound in your pride, the very core of your self-reliance. And that's a stain that no other love will wash out if you're proud.

And was Dave proud!

Dave had never been left before. He had never endured the excruciating pain of being rejected and replaced. And he had never begged. His ego was immaculate when it came to those kinds of scars. Until then. He didn't know how to process it.

Because he didn't know what else to do, he chased Mary for a while, all but pleading for her to take him back, despite her constant rejections.

"Izzy, it's me," Dave said as soon as I picked up the phone.

I jumped as soon as I heard his voice. "Dave!"

"I fucked up!" he blurted, his voice dripping pain.

"What happened?"

"I went to see Mary yesterday . . ."

"Again, Dave?" I growled.

"I know, Izzy! But I just don't get it . . . How can she be like that? How can she simply not love me anymore?" His voice was full of grief and spite.

"You have to let it go. Let her go," I reasoned.

"I can't! Every time I meet someone new and I think I'm over her, I realize I'm not. I'm stuck here, and I can't let her go. It's her, Izzy. She's it for me." Dave was arguing with the most haggard voice I recalled hearing from him.

"She's not, Dave. She never was!" I pleaded with him.

"I'm miserable," he muttered.

"Oh, what am I going to do with you?" I asked with a sigh. "I know it hurts, but it will go away. It always does."

"I just don't know what to do. I miss you so much . . ."

"I miss you too, stupid! Why did you have to go away to where I can't take care of you?" I mocked, attempting a playful tone that ended up only sounding resentful.

Dave just sighed.

"You can't keep doing that to yourself, Dave. You have to move on."

"But I love her."

I exhaled deeply and ran my fingers through my hair with my free hand as I slid my back down the wall until I was sitting on the floor with my knees bent. This was going to take me some time.

"Dave, I know you think you do, but you don't. You never did. It's not your heart that is broken; it's your ego. You're always the one who leaves and ends things. You're used to having the final word. This is just new for you." I paused to allow my words to sink in.

"I know you. If you keep doing this, if you keep begging Mary to take you back, you will regret it so much later on. You're too proud to be doing this, and you will feel bad about yourself when you look back and see that this was nothing but a whim."

"It's not a whim," he mumbled.

"It is, Dave! And you know it! What were you going to do if she took you back? Do you really think you could handle the idea of her having fallen for another man? Do you really think that it would last? Do you even want it to last?" Even though we both knew that there were no doubts in my questions, I asked them anyway.

"You just want to get back with her to prove yourself that you're in charge, that you can make her love you again," I continued. "Don't do that. Don't go that way, Dave. You're better than that. You're such a great guy. You're funny, you're smart, and you're interesting. It's her loss, not yours. You know that I don't give away compliments . . ." He knew it was true. When I complimented, which was rare, I truly meant it.

"You know me so well, Izzy . . . I need you so much," Dave whispered. "I would give my left pinkie just to hug you right now."

"You would miss it later," I whispered back.

Eventually, the idea of having been dismissed by Mary started to fade from Dave's mind as he tried to heal his wounded ego in the way he knew best: women and drugs.

As things got heavier to handle, he just retrieved to his dark place and cut all ties to this world. I stopped receiving news from him—no e-mails, no phone calls, nothing.

I was worried. I had never seen him like that, and worse, I was not around to control the damage. I kept writing him, if for nothing else, at least to reassure him that I was always there and that I knew what was going on. But at some point, I had to stop and respect his distance. Sort of, at least. In the absence of Dave's news, I ended up talking to his mother, who was worried sick about him. So was I, which made me take my annual leave earlier and go back home, to the other side of the world, to find a broken Dave. He was a shadow of the man I used to know, but he still refused to accept that his coping mechanism wasn't the best.

As far as I was able to tell, and to put it bluntly, he was fucking his pain around and mixing every drug and drop of alcohol he got his hands on. I was terrified that he'd lost control, but I kept faith that he hadn't. I scolded him gently about it, even though I knew that that would only keep him further away. Fortunately, it didn't take him long to realize that he couldn't keep up with that kind of life. The women, however, were another story.

"I want you to meet someone, Izzy, just to see what you think of her," Dave said as we walked down his street after having had lunch at his house.

"Hmm?" I mumbled, raising an inquisitive brow at him.

"She's a friend. We've known each other since we were kids. She used to live next door to me until we were fourteen, then her parents moved, but we kept in touch all these years . . . more or less. And now she's back!"

"That's a nice story," I said, amused. "So did you cop a feel or just exchange saliva with her during puberty?" I asked, trying to keep a straight face.

"You're so gross sometimes, Izzy . . ." Dave tried to snarl at me but failed miserably because his last words were already filled with laughter.

"I love it when you try to pull the prude card on me!" I teased. "It doesn't suit you, you know?"

"It's not like that, Izzy. She was special, you know? She was my platonic love, the girl that I never touched."

"But whose bones you want to jump right now! How platonic of you."

"You're ruining it for me!" Dave accused.

"No, I'm not," I snorted, amused. "You already knew that I was going to tell you this. You want me to talk you out of it! You're afraid you're going to ruin things beyond repair if you sleep with her."

Dave looked at me askance and shrugged, resigned with the fact that I could read his mind so well.

"You want to hear something funny?" he asked, breaking the silence that had followed my sharp exposure of his misgivings.

"Do I?" I asked skeptically.

"Her name is Maria!"

"You are shitting me!" I all but barked.

"I am not." He raised his hands in a conciliatory gesture.

"For crying out loud, Dave, no more Marias! I mean it! What is it with you and the Marias? Some kind of *West Side Story* obsession or something? Enough with the Marias!" I demanded, joking of course but not sparing him the drama.

"Hey, you are Maria as well . . . Isabella Maria!" Dave said with a bit of guile in his voice and winking his eye at me.

"I might be Maria, but I'm not that kind of Maria. I'm the exception!" I stated, deadly serious and frowning for emphasis.

Dave looked me in the eyes and opened his mouth to say something that never left his thoughts because his phone rang at that precise moment; it was the New Mary.

We met her for coffee downtown.

New Mary was unlike anyone I've met before, yet there was something familiar about her. Really. She was nothing like Dave's regular women, but then again, what woman was? Sure, she was pretty and seemed nice and intelligent, but she was also driven, committed, and a free spirit. I liked her. Moreover, I got why Dave had never touched her; she simply wasn't that kind of girl. She was not immune to Dave's charm, but there was something about her that made Dave respect her in a way that I had never seen him respect a woman before; they had history.

New Mary and Dave had known each other since forever. Most of their childhood memories were either linked or tangled, and their relationship was tainted by sweet innocence. They had never even so much as kissed. Yet it was obvious that they both held dearly to the idea of having something unique between them. That was why Dave was so conflicted in the face of the possibility of having New Mary in a way that, so far, he had just dared to dream of.

The stakes were too high, and Dave couldn't bring himself to fairly appraise whether the bliss of having New Mary would overcome the risk of losing her forever.

My holidays were over before any developments of New Mary's story became known, and though our time together had been limited, we found our way back to each other. We always did, as time ended up proving to us repeatedly. It didn't matter when it happened or where we were; we always managed to meet each other.

By then, however, Dave was so lost that he thought he had no other remedy than to find himself first. So he packed his backpack and decided to travel the world on a personal quest. He had no job and no one to go back to, so it made sense.

During his time abroad, he had saved some money with no defined purpose. Now he had found one.

He traveled for about a year. In some places, he stayed only a few days, and in others, he thought he would spend the rest of his life. He had no plan and no other goal than to wander the world until his life started making sense or something else provided that revealing epiphany that he searched for. He knew that eventually he would find whatever he was looking for.

He traveled across at least three continents, and he walked across dozens of countries. He found misery, poverty, luxury, and injustice in some of those countries, but he found beauty in all of them. Dave had that knack. He was about the details rather than the whole, remember? Therefore, he was prone to find whatever grace he could in even the most hideous of places. He was, after all, a romantic.

Dave met tons of people during his travels, yet most of the time, he felt truly alone. He liked it, though. He even started to crave the loneliness at some point.

I kept track of him, or at least I tried to, through the postcards that he sent me from time to time. They showed beautiful landscapes and exotic places and said more or less the same thing: "I still haven't found what I'm looking for!" He would always start with a brief reference to what he'd been up to, and it would bear similarities to U2's music—for example, "I have climbed a big mountain." The he would follow it with the dreaded words. This could have become one of our private jokes, but we both knew that it wasn't as funny as Dave tried to make it.

Dave also phoned, but that was even rarer and always rushed. We had so much to tell each other that we always ended up saying nothing at all. It was frustrating.

When Dave strayed near the other side of the world, we decided to meet halfway for a couple of days.

I almost didn't recognize him. He was so thin. His face was hidden behind a thick layer of beard, but his hair was practically shaved.

After we managed to untangle ourselves from the fierce embrace that held all our unspoken words, I eyed him up and down.

"You're so skinny! And what's with the hair? Shaved head and long beard?" I asked, confused.

"Lice. Don't ask!" Dave added before I had time to interrogate him about how he'd managed to catch lice. I rendered myself silent on that one, though I was itching to know. Pun intended.

We spent our time together strolling through the unfamiliar streets and talking each other's ears off. We had so much to say that we both had the feeling that even a lifetime wouldn't be enough for us.

"Hey, tell me about New Mary! What happened with her? Did you sleep together?" I asked, after hearing Dave talk about rivers and churches and people who got lost in both.

"Well, New Mary became Almost Mary. Nothing happened. I guess we both got cold feet when the time came."

"Hmm. Really?" I asked, hearing the pinch of disbelief in my voice.

"Yeah. We had a moment, though."

"A moment? I love moments!" I said excitedly. "It's something you always remember, don't you think? You can forget everything else, but you never forget those times when the world seems to freeze and it's only you and the other person. Those seconds are precious! They tell you more than words."

"If I didn't know you better, I would peg you for a romantic, Izzy," Dave sneered.

"I'm not a romantic, Dave. That's your department! But I am a poet," I retorted, smirking.

Dave slowed down a bit and tilted his head slightly to the side, throwing me an inquisitive look.

"Not all poets are romantics, Dave! Some of us find poetry outside the heart," I clarified, raising my voice since I had not slowed my pace to match Dave's. He was now behind. "Tell me about the moment," I said.

Dave smiled and picked up his pace so that he could catch me.

"It was a moment fit for a movie!" he started, knowing exactly that he was about to make me despair to hear the end of the story. "We went together to Little John's parents' hometown. I had promised them that I would visit, and she had things to take care of there. So we decided to go by train together. Our car was a bit crowded, so we just wandered around the train and ended up in a car that was practically empty. At some point, she was walking in front of me and turned to say something. In that moment, the train curved abruptly and she lost her balance. As she fell backward, I grabbed her. It was instinctive. When realization dawned on me, I had her lying in my arms and I was bent over her. Once our gazes locked, all we could do was stare into each other's eyes. Then, a second later, she bit her lip and I felt her breathing getting heavier, her chest rising up and down . . ."

"Did you kiss her?" I interrupted, not managing to endure the suspense that Dave was so obviously torturing me with.

"No." He sighed. "When I was about to, some assholes started fleering and howling; it ruined the moment. Stupid teenagers."

"Aww," I let out, not hiding my disappointment. "That would have been such a great kiss, Dave!"

"It would, wouldn't it?" Dave asked, resigned.

"Too bad. Maybe next time." I shrugged.

"Hmm. I don't know. Maybe. I kind of like it that nothing ever happens between Mary and me, you know? It's frustrating yet thrilling at the same time. She's kind of my perfect love—the one that was never ruined or tainted but without the burden of being the one that got away."

"I get that. She's different. There's something about her."

"You said that about Mary, too! The Fairy," he added, answering my questioning raised brow.

"Yeah, but I was referring to her personality. New Mary is different because you seem to be different around her." I couldn't quite put my finger on it.

"We all want we can't have, Izzy." Dave dismissed it, shrugging.

"Someday, Dave, you will join the rest of us in this world, and then maybe, just maybe, you will be able to see what's been in front of you . . . all this time." I stopped mid-stride to look at him while I spoke.

"What's that supposed to mean?" Dave asked, scowling at me.

"Exactly what it meant. That you idealize too much. You fantasize about love, and most of the time, you fail to actually live it because you're too lost in your ideals to see what's right there in front of you."

"You're one to talk," Dave snapped.

"Let's not go there, okay? I'm sorry. I didn't mean to criticize you. Let's just drop the subject." I conceded because I didn't want to start a fight that would lead us nowhere. After all, you cannot force open the eyes of those who do not want to see.

Our time together seemed to be over almost as soon as it started. We spent those few days sightseeing and talking about everything and nothing in particular. That was what was so great about our friendship; we always talked as if we'd never been apart. So when we said good-bye once again, it was with heavy hearts but also with the certainty that we would meet again between here and now.

Dave continued his soul-searching journey for a few more months, and though there wasn't really a moment that he could later define as being the turning point for him, I always attributed that feat to Aisha.

Well, not so much to Aisha as to the fervor with which she lived her life. That singularity about her marked Dave deeply. Years later, Dave would call upon his memories of his time with her to help him cope with one of the most difficult moments of his life.

Aisha crossed Dave's path around his eighth month of traveling, and she was the epitome of freedom. She was a thirty-five-year-old Brazilian belly dancer who had left her husband and her boring life as a Realtor to travel the world, earning her living as a dancer. She was happy and carefree. She lived in the moment and nurtured no worries or regrets. She lived fully.

Dave saw her dancing one night at a world dance festival in an European capital and couldn't take his eyes off her. She saw him too. When she was finished dancing, she strolled to where he sat and introduced herself.

"I'm Aisha. I like you, but you already know that," she offered bluntly, without a trace of shyness in her voice.

"Yes, I do," Dave retorted smugly.

"Are you going to tell me your name or will I have to force it out of you?" she asked, resting her arms akimbo.

"That will depend on how you plan to do that," Dave said, dragging out his words and his eyes across her body while moistening his lips with his tongue in a clearly provocative gesture.

She looked him in the eyes, the corner of her mouth twitching slightly in what resembled half a smile, and then she bent over him, resting one hand on his shoulder for support and putting her mouth near his ear. Slowly.

"In a way that will take you a lifetime to forget." She sashayed her way back through the crowd.

Dave followed her without a second thought.

Dave and Aisha shared a week of intense passion and total surrender to each other. I wouldn't be far from the truth if I said that in those few days, Dave gave himself to Aisha in a way that he had yet given himself to any woman, or would there from give himself, to almost every other woman in his life. Almost.

Their affair was raw and primitive submission to desire and lust. But strangely, it was also love . . . of a sort.

They told each other their stories, about their lives and everything in between. No fear was left behind, and no moment was spared.

Sure, their love, as with others that Dave had experienced before, had the stain of an affair with a scheduled end, and that naturally made things easier. But that wasn't it, or at least that wasn't all. There was also Aisha, and she was unforgettable, to say the least.

She was a life lesson to Dave, one of those persons who marks your life and carves a place in your soul.

Dave didn't fell in love with her, mind you; he fell in love with the way she lived her life, with the way she completely surrendered to any challenge and the intensity she put in everything she did. She sucked the marrow out of live fully. It was breathtaking and enviable to see someone live so freely. To see someone live so passionately . . . so much.

Those few days they shared were lived with ripping passion and no thoughts about the aftermath, for it simply didn't matter. So when they parted ways, they did it with the same simplicity and straightforwardness that they came together. They said good-bye and wished each other the best of lives and happiness, and then they went their separate routes, knowing that that would be it. They would never see each other again.

After Aisha, Dave continued his journey, but he already had a destination in mind: home. It took him around four more months to get him there, though. I would have liked to tell you that he used that time to sightsee or contemplate things, but that wouldn't have been truthful or fun, would it?

Dave used that time to make his own version of *Around the World in Eighty Days*, the classic by Jules Verne. However, as you might have guessed by now, it wasn't exactly around the world that the remainder of his journey took him, nor was eighty, even to Dave, a plausible or accurate number to wager on.

I'm not talking about days, in case you were wondering. And they mattered; they all did. That was something that I learned right from the start with Dave: all women that he slept with mattered. Whether they were there for a moment of passion, as an anonymous body in a strange bed, or women he fell in love with, they all counted because they all ended up making Dave who he was. And he knew it.

His would never be a story solely about love, though he chased it mercilessly. Or about the paths he had taken. Or the choices he made in his life. None of that would have a meaning per se; nor could it be untangled from all the women that he had and would bed and the crudeness with which he lived his life.

That's how deeply rooted they all were, and that's why, if I had to tell Dave's story, I would make it about his wanton life.

CHAPTER 16

FOR WHOM THE BELLS TOLL

As the bells tolled, I sighed deeply, trying to dismiss the thought that harassed my mind: how I utterly disliked every little thing about weddings. They just weren't my thing.

Yet there I was, in Dave's arm, standing pretty in a gown and high heels and crossing the church threshold with a fake smile plastered on my face. The roar of congratulations and cheering was almost deafening. I couldn't blame people. When everyone had stopped hoping, the unexpected had happened.

Even Dave and I had been caught off guard, and I guess we were still a little flabbergasted with the whole thing. But I guess that it's always like that, isn't it? When you least expect it, life throws you a sucker punch. I smiled at the thought, letting a shred of my amusement cross my lips as I looked up and met Dave's gaze. He smiled back, and I tightened my grip on his arm as my other hand held firmly the rice grains that I was supposed to throw at the newlyweds as a symbolic gesture of my wishes of prosperity to them. Little John was now a married man!

Who would have guessed?

Little John, of all men!

It happened stealthily. So stealthily that even Little John was caught off guard, and he realized that he was completely and hopelessly in love.

Little John was not one to befriend women on an uninterested basis. Sure, he had friendships with women, but not the deep kind. Even his female friends in whom he had no romantic interest, such as myself, struggled to get a semblance of closeness when it came to him.

That's why Cathy was such a surprise.

Cathy had known Little John from the very first day he had set his foot on the other side of the world. She'd been there for a year then. They shared an office at their company, and with time they ended up sharing much more than that. Cathy was funny, witty, smart, and soon became skilled at interpreting and knowing Little John's moods, thoughts, and needs. She became a constant in his daily life and someone he unconsciously asked for advice, comfort, and uncomplicated fun. Being around her was easy and effortless; being around her allowed him to be himself. Of course, the fact that Cathy weighed 220 pounds also helped Little John's easiness around her. The thought that she was a woman never crossed his mind. After all, she was simply . . . Cathy!

Well, as it happened, the other way around wasn't all that straightforward. Cathy was in love with Little John long before he even started noticing that she was not just Cathy. She hid it well, but not enough. The constant whirlwind of women, though meaningless women, in Little John's life started to pain her beyond reason and up to the point that she knew she had to do something to change that. And she did. She stopped feeding her unrequited love for him, and she reinvented herself.

She lost almost one hundred pounds in a year, and she started liking herself first and foremost, before anyone else. Little John included.

At first, Little John was Cathy's greatest supporter, encouraging her to go to the gym and to wear tighter clothes to show off her figure. But then, when he stopped being the center of her world and she started dating, a pang of jealousy descended upon Little John, though he masked it as a friend's spite for her sudden lack of time and availability toward him.

At the time, after spending an entire lunchtime listening to Little John bitch about Cathy's selfishness and self-centeredness now that she was all thin and pretty, I mocked him. I told him that if I didn't know him any better, I would think that they were just sour grapes. Turns out that I didn't know him any better.

After some torturing months of tasting his own medicine, which basically resumed to enduring Cathy's parade of dates, Little John started considering that maybe, just maybe, the thing with Cathy wasn't just friendship. It was pure, raw attraction now that she was all hot and pretty, his brilliant mind—yes, I am being sarcastic about it—decided. So he needed to put an end to it and get back to his easy and uncomplicated life. After all, he was no Dave.

But it wasn't that simple. Cathy was a smart girl—God bless her— and she knew Little John well enough to know that he was trying to get her out of his system. She decided there and then that if she was going to have her heart broken, at least she was going to have it broken on her terms.

Funny thing about making men wait: they don't stand it very well, and they tend to fall. Little John fell hard. When he finally was trying to get Cathy out of his system, he realized that that would simply imply taking his system down—shutting it off. He was in love with her.

Mind you, this was the soft romantic comedy version I'm giving you here. Reality wasn't so kind on Cathy and Little John. Before they rested their hearts and decided that they belonged together, they managed to do a lot of damage to each other. Love is a hard thing to admit to when there's too much resentment in between. So I've heard.

They managed it, though. And now there they stood, getting married and vowing eternal love and fidelity in front of their families and closest friends.

God, I hated weddings!

"And you are?"

I turned toward the voice coming at me and was faced with a skinny gray-haired lady.

"Oh dear, I thought you were a boy! You girls nowadays with those boy haircuts. It's impossible to tell you apart." The woman was smiling at me without a hint of scorn.

I was currently sporting a short haircut, and though I was petite, I had curves and did not look like a boy, I can assure you, especially because I was wearing a dress! So I reacted to those words in the only possible way: I smiled back.

"I don't think I've seen you before, darling," she carried on.

"I'm here with Dave . . . Dave Poe," I offered, eyeing the crowd in search of Dave, curious to see where this conversation was headed.

"Dave? Who's Dave?" she asked, apparently confused. "Oh dear! Don't you mean Steve?"

"Steve?" Then it dawned on me. I was in the presence of dear old Great-Aunt Carol! "Oh, you must be Dave's and Little John's Aunt Carol! Am I right?"

"I am, my dear. And you must be Steve's girlfriend!" she shrieked.

"No, I'm not Steve's . . . Dave's . . . I'm not his girlfriend! I'm Izzy," I mumbled, taken aback by the question.

"Oh dear, never say that!" she chided, cutting me off. "No wonder you're not his girlfriend. You're selling yourself short, going around saying that you're easy. No man respects an easy girl."

"What I meant is that my name is Izzy, a short name for Isabella. I'm friends with Dave, and he nicknamed me Izzy. We met when we were both living abroad," I explained quickly, trying to gain some control over what seemed a madman's conversation.

"You had me fooled for a while! So you're friends with my nephew Steve! You're not married, my dear, are you?"

I was about to open my mouth to retort, but dear old Great-Aunt Carol didn't seem very interested in a two-way conversation, and I must confess that I was a bit too awestruck with the whole thing to have the necessary wit to catch up with the woman.

"I didn't think you were, you poor thing! Don't worry, there are plenty of men out there who like older women." As she carried on, she eyed me up and down as if assessing my age. "Nowadays lots of women marry after they're thirty. You're not forty yet, are you darling? You don't look like forty."

At this point, I have to tell you that there wasn't a pinch of sarcasm or venom in the woman's voice. She was not, contrary to the way it might sound, being mean. She was an eccentric woman with no kind of filter whatsoever. Either you could be offended by her diarrheic comments or just play along. She was pretty hilarious and, what the hell, I had to see where that was headed.

"Unless you play for the other team!" she squeaked. "Oh darling, no babies for you, then. No matter what they say, that's just not natural. The kids get confused. Imagine them in school saying that their mother is called Mary and their father is called Patricia. It just won't do!"

"I don't play for the other team," I clarified, as soon as I managed to cut through her mad rambling. There was no way I would ever be able to catch up with her. She jumped from one subject to the other without any kind of logic or warning.

"Good for you, sweetheart!" she said with clear relief in her voice. "What do you think of my nephew Steve?" she asked, changing the subject. Or not. Who knew?

"We've been good friends for a while now, so I pretty much think Dave is a gem. Precious, no doubt about it!" I managed to elaborate.

"Oh dear, not you too?" she asked, disbelief tinting.

"Come again?" I asked, confused.

"Why do you people insist on calling him Dave? He's clearly a Steve, don't you think?" she asked with a pinch of outrage in her voice.

The absurdity of the whole talk flashed through my mind in the few seconds that it took me to decide just to play along. Why the heck not?

"Now that you mention it, I can see that there's something Stevie about him. I wonder what," I retorted, rejoicing with my witty pun as I stressed the words Stevie and wonder.

She eyed me quizzically as if truly seeing me for the first time and tilted her head slightly, winking at me. Had she caught my joke?

"Izzy! I see you've met Great-Aunt Carol," Dave said, approaching us with a big smile plastered on his face and interrupting our moment. "Aunt Carol, this is my friend Izzy."

"Why, Steve, I already knew that! We've been talking for the last fifteen minutes!" Great-Aunt Carol said dismissively. "You know, she's not married! Why don't you date her?" she asked bluntly.

Although we should have seen that one coming, given Great-Aunt Carol's proven straightforwardness, I must confess that we were both caught off guard. I'm sure our widened eyes held a hint of panic, and for a moment, neither of us was able to answer her.

"Because we're friends, Aunt Carol," Dave finally said, rolling his eyes while I tried to control my imminent fit of laughter.

"One more reason! You don't want to marry a woman you're not friends with," she lectured.

"Too bad I'm already taken," I said quickly, winking my eye at Dave, who mouthed a silent thank-you to me behind his aunt's back.

"Oh, good for you, darling! And where is the lucky—"

"John is calling us, Aunt Carol!" Dave interrupted, dragging me out of there before I had to elaborate further on my half-truth.

"Your aunt is something else, Dave," I said as soon as we were out of her ear's reach.

"She's getting crazier as she ages, but she is quite funny—if you don't take it personally, of course."

I agreed with a nod of my head as Dave led me away from the sea of people that crowded the wedding reception area. When we were finally alone, in the gardens, he just smiled at me. I had arrived from the other side of the world the previous day, and I was tired and jet-lagged. We hadn't seen each other for almost one year, and we still hadn't had the chance to be alone and catch up. The last time we'd been together had been those few days when Dave was making his soul-searching trip across the world. So much had happened meanwhile.

Dave was back home, and he had founded his own company, with a little help and encouragement from his relatives. Though he was just starting up, things were going quite smoothly. He obviously was tailored to be his own boss. He was happy and confident, and the wound in his ego had healed. The scar was there, though.

"God, I have so much to tell you," Dave said, running his hands through his hair. "I like your new haircut. It suits you! You look like a sixteen-year-old horny teenager." He tousled my hair affectionately. "Or a pixie! Yeah, you look like a pixie . . . You're just missing the pointy ears," he added, one arm grabbing me firmly in place around my waist while his free hand ruffled my hair fondly.

"Hey, stop it, you moron!" I shrieked, trying to evade his clumsy round of tenderness and nudging him in the ribs playfully. "You're messing up my hair!" I pouted.

We stared at each other with stupid grins on our faces, just letting everything sink in.

"You first," I urged. "Tell me all the details of your trip and what you've been up to!"

"You already know that."

"Those e-mails don't count. I want the juicy details, not your rushed mentions of this and that," I scolded, making myself comfortable on a garden bench and patting the place by my side so that he would sit next to me and talk away.

Dave told me about Aisha, how she simply had opened his eyes and given him a different perspective of life. She had a joie de vivre that was contagious and made you want to live in the moment, leaving every worry behind. Although quite tempting, that was also very dangerous, especially in Dave's case. We didn't dwell on that, though.

He also entertained me with the stories of his last months of traveling. He had endured so much and discovered so many things. One thing was for sure; he had significantly increased the number of stupid sex stories in his portfolio, to put it lightly. He almost, and I emphasize *almost*, took part in an orgy. When I asked him what made him change his mind about it, he just said that some things were not meant to be. I told him that I would bet my left pinkie that most of the participants in the "event" were men and that that was what made him back out. He smiled and dismissed the subject. Some things never changed.

He, however, had changed. I could tell. He was calmer. But he was still my Dave.

"What do you think about this?" I asked, referring to Little John's wedding.

"I think it's great!"

"Really?" I asked, surprised.

"Yeah. I think they look great together and that he really got it right this time. She's the one for him."

"Don't get me wrong, because I also think that they look great together, but I just thought that you would have doubts about it," I offered, not hiding my surprise. "You know, this is Little John we're talking about."

"People change, Izzy, especially when you find the right person for you," Dave said, matter-of-factly. "And I do think Little John found his soul mate in Cathy."

I eyed him skeptically.

"What?" Dave asked, raising a defiant brow at me.

"Nothing! I just never thought you would accept all this questionless. You know, being away and not having had a front-row view of the whole drama . . ."

"There are some things in life that you just don't question. You accept them because you know . . . No, you *feel* they're true. This is one of them. Simple." Dave shrugged.

You know those times when you feel in your gut that something just doesn't add up and you choose to ignore the feeling and later on you wish you hadn't? This was one of those times for me.

"What about you?" I asked, focusing on him instead.

"What about me?" Dave asked, looking a little startled.

"How have you been in the ladies department? Your last e-mails didn't say much," I said, fishing around.

"You know . . ." he said, stretching out his words and then smiling shyly at me.

"Are you trying to play coy with me, Dave?" I mocked.

"I wouldn't even dare, Izzy," Dave said earnestly, raising his hands in surrender.

I grinned fully at him, and he smiled back at me while we held each other's gaze. We were plainly happy to be together again.

"Dance with me, Izzy!" he said, reaching out and grabbing my hand.

"No way! We dance terribly together, Dave," I said, trying to withdraw my hand from his grasp.

"Come on, you wimp! We're gonna make history today," he joked.

"Yeah, and I'm not even drunk enough to forget about it," I grumbled as Dave dragged me back to the wedding reception area.

The band was playing a slow song, and Dave reached out for my waist and pulled me to him while I rested my hands on his chest. Eventually, and as expected, I stomped on his feet, but he didn't complain. We swayed to the rhythm of the music while Dave made me laugh with all the silly comments he made about everything within his line of sight. We were actually pulling it off! We were dancing together!

We were so excited with our achievement that we decided to dance until we dropped. So when a song ended, we just stood there on the dance floor happily teasing each other as we waited for the next song to start. Until the band decided to play Rod Stewart's "Baby Jane." As the first chords hit me, the world just froze, crystallizing me along.

"Don't, Izzy!" Dave said, pulling me toward one of the ends of the dance floor and trying to snap me back to the present. "Don't let that guy ruin this day for you! He's a moron, you hear me?" He said this sweetly, and brushing the backs of his fingers over my cheek while he stared into my eyes, searching for me.

I blinked, oozing out of my stupor and realizing that Dave was holding my head between his hands and was now stroking my cheeks with his thumbs, his face full of concern. He wasn't used to my moments of weakness. They were rare, but when they hit, they normally knocked everything out at their passage.

I sighed deeply, letting out the air I hadn't realized I was holding, and moved away from Dave's grip and stare.

"I'm at a wedding, ain't I? My day is already ruined!" I mocked, forcing a smile on my lips that I was sure never reached my eyes.

Dave grabbed my arm and spun me toward him, so that I was facing him. "I know you're tough as nails, Izzy, but you still let that guy get under your skin. You already know what I think about it, so I'm not gonna lecture you on that again."

"Good! Because I really don't want to talk about it right now . . . Who on earth sings this song at a wedding, for crying out loud? Don't they pay attention to the lyrics?" I tried to regain some composure.

"Okay, I'll tell you what: you and I are going to dance to this song together and are going to have a blast doing it. It's going to be so epic that whenever you hear it again, the only thing you'll remember is the two of us here and now!" Dave pulled me toward him in a dramatic dance gesture, which I had no way to escape from.

Dave twirled me, twisted me, rolled me, and waltzed me in every possible way around that dance floor until I was laughing aloud. I was so dizzy that even if I tried, I don't think I would be capable of reliving all that that song meant to me. It held some of my best memories, but those lyrics had painfully turned into poetic justice for me. Ain't life a bitch?

We danced through a couple of songs more and then decided that we needed a break. I followed Dave off the dance floor and through the maze of tables before we headed to the gardens again. Once we reached our secluded bench, he eyed me mischievously as he patted his trousers pockets, searching for something.

"I've got just what you need right here," he said.

"Oh, I like it when you talk dirty to me!" I scoffed, winking an eye at him.

"You . . . witch!" Dave retorted, and opened his hand to show me what he was so happily referring to: a joint.

"Are you serious? We cannot get high at Little John's wedding!" I scolded him, trying my best to sound convincing.

"Of course we can! And this is light stuff anyway. You're not gonna turn your usual stoned self."

I stared at him, still undecided but very enticed. We hadn't done this in such a long time, and I missed our goofiness.

Dave lit the joint and took a drag, letting the smoke out through his nostrils. Then he passed it to me so that I would have a hit at it. I'd never been a skilled smoker, so I had to take it slow and step by step. I passed it back to Dave, and we were at it when we heard footsteps approaching us. We were already a bit stoned, so we didn't have it in us to cloak our doings. Well, truth be said, I didn't have it in me since the rush of being caught made me have a fit of laughter.

"You're so busted!"

"It's not what it seems," I snorted between two laughs.

"You devious Midget!" Little John joked, pointing his finger at me and resting it on the tip of my nose. "And you, my best friend and cousin, blood of my blood, hiding to get high at my wedding party . . . without me! I'm wounded!" Little John sneered, not sparing on the drama. He took the joint from Dave's hand and had a puff.

"You can't get high at your own wedding," I reasoned, because somehow I thought that it was something I should say. Wise advice from a stoned friend.

"Why not?" Little John asked.

"Huh . . . I really can't think why not, but I thought I should say it. You know, like something your mother would tell you . . . Don't drug yourself when you get married . . ." I laughed. I was as a high as a kite. Light stuff, yeah, right.

"Nope. Still not convinced . . . Man, this shit is good. Where did you get it?" Little John asked Dave, handing him the joint.

"The usual place . . ."

"Yeah, in the supermarket! In the pot . . . tery isle," I sneered. And yes, still laughing.

"I guess this is the highest the Midget can get!" Little John joked, and the three of us laughed our asses off.

"Cathy will be mad at you if she sees you stoned," I finally managed.

"You're right! She's gonna be so pissed at me that I didn't go get her to smoke with us," Little John pondered. "I'll tell her that you were about to kill it when I arrived."

"See?" Dave said, facing me. "That's true love. I told you."

"You should know it, lover boy. You're next!" Little John teased, patting Dave on the arm. "Shit, I have to head back. My wife is waiting for me," he added, all solemn and serious.

Dave and I laughed at Little John's display and watched him head toward the reception area. We were there for a while just enjoying the blaze, the floaty feeling of dreaming with eyes wide open. Well, not that wide considering the circumstances.

As we drifted back to reality, I scooted closer to Dave and nudged his shoulder with mine. "So?" I said.

"So what?" He crooked his head back, looking up to face the sky, which was now dark.

"So when are you planning to tell me about this Helen woman?"

"Who told you about Helen?" he asked with a clear pitch of annoyance in his voice, changing his position on the bench in order to face me.

"Well . . . everyone but you!" I snarled, holding his gaze.

"What did they tell you?" Dave asked, a bit too startled.

"That's not important. What's important is that you're not telling me something. I want to know what and why, Dave," I said, sure that by the tone of my voice, he knew I was serious.

Dave sighed sharply and ran his hands through his hair before he faced me. When he did, his eyes were uncharacteristically devoid of doubts, yet he was nervous.

"I'm getting married in three months, Izzy."

CHAPTER 17

TOTAL ECLIPSE OF THE HEART

Many women passed through Dave's life, and I heard about a great number of them, saw very few, met less than a dozen, and became friends with none. Most of them felt uncomfortable around me. Some of them sought my approval. Others were jealous of me, and I am certain that not a single one understood the nature and depth of our friendship. "You are one of my pillars," Dave told me once. And he meant it.

Helen, however, had an entirely new vision on Dave's and my relationship; she saw right through us.

Helen had been Dave's first client once he'd set up his company back home after his year around the world. The minute he saw her bursting through his office, something in him broke. The way he described it to me, it was as if the walls around his heart had been shattered as he stood in front of her feeling utterly vulnerable and exposed. It was terrifying, yet the most intense feeling that he had ever experienced. It was beyond lust, passion, or love itself. It was a total eclipse of the heart.

She felt it too, though she was not that kind of woman. You know, the kind that falls in love at first sight.

Dave's women had the peculiarity of not fitting stereotypes. Sure, he had a thing for busty blondes, but what man doesn't? The only thing that Dave's women had in common, now that I think of it, was that they had nothing in common. Whatever detail drew Dave to them was most likely exceptional and most certainly unique.

Helen, however, was someone entirely different. When looking at her, it was impossible not to recognize one thing: she had class. She was not a beauty, but no one seemed to notice it because she also had what very few women managed to pull off: charm. Helen had class and charm. It was a hazardous and overpowering combination, to say the least.

She was about the same age as Dave. She wore her hair in a classy blonde bob and was the spitting image of elegance and grace. Yet there was something real and attainable about her that made her not look perfect. Whether it was the way she would snort loudly and throw her perfectly coiffed head back when she really laughed or the way she would bite her manicured nails when she was nervous, it made her human. It made her irresistible as well.

It seems hard to pair Dave with such a woman, given his lifestyle and personality. However, once you saw them together, it seemed almost inevitable. Almost.

They had met under professional circumstances, and though Dave knew better than to blow his company's first job and mess it up with romantic gibberish, he couldn't care less. Helen overshadowed everything in between Dave's heart and his reason. He never stood a chance—but neither did she.

Dave's first response to Helen was to avoid her. The extreme reaction he had felt when he'd met her frightened him beyond measure, so he refrained from meeting with her in person and tried to communicate with her strictly, and whenever possible, through e-mail. In between, he sought to hold on to the shred of common sense that still hadn't abandoned him when his heart had been irrevocably and totally eclipsed.

That didn't work, though—not with him and certainly not with Helen.

You see, under her charming and classy appearance, Helen was assertive and feisty, which also captivated Dave. She was way far from being a damsel in distress or a fragile and frightened kitten. In fact, lioness would be more appropriate to describe her. She knew what she wanted and had no problem fighting for it, as I came to realize. And she wanted Dave from the moment she met him. She wanted Dave as she had wanted no man before him: desperately, totally, and madly. Therefore, after exchanging several e-mails with him requesting a meeting that seemed impossible to schedule, she just showed up in his office and invited him to have coffee, using that imperfect charming way of hers.

Dave didn't have it in him to refuse the invitation, and for the first time ever, he truly became the prey. He knew it right away. He felt nervous and insecure, not knowing how to act around her. Not even his uncle Casanova's advice had any impact on his behavior. And since he'd left me out on this one, I too was unable to provide him any kind of solace. When I learned about the situation, Dave was already engaged to be married in three months.

Sure, Little John and Dave's mother had told me about a Helen and that Dave was head over heels about her. But none of them had spilled their guts about the hasty engagement. Later on, Dave enlightened me to the fact that I had been the second person that he'd told about it. Little John had been the first, and he knew better than to break that piece of news to me.

Dave was so sure about it. I had never seen him like that, and I was impressed. Whoever this Helen was, she had him by the balls.

In the beginning, Helen took the lead. She was the one offering the invitations and pursuing Dave, but always in her endearing charming way. To Dave, the only good thing from that was that Helen didn't know him well enough to see that he was simply rendered to her. She just thought he was not that interested, which turned out to work for him instead of against him; Helen doubled her efforts. Dave had a great poker face, though, I'll admit. If you didn't know his telling, you would find it very hard to read him, and Helen, well, she would always be a little dyslexic in what concerned Dave, to put it kindly.

*   *   *

"Tell me how you met. How was your first kiss?" I asked eagerly.

"Izzy . . . that's lame," Dave grumbled, a bit coy.

"No, it's not! You know I like to hear that stuff. Just indulge me, will you?" I pleaded.

"What do you want to know?" he asked, still a bit hesitant.

"Every dirty detail!" I said, hearing the mischief in my voice.

When Helen took Dave out to have coffee on that first day when she just showed up at his office, he was sure of one thing and one thing only: he had never met a woman like her. And he had met his share of women in his thirty-year-old life.

Helen was confident and self-assured, and she made everything sound interesting with the unpretentious way she talked and gave her view of things. It was a gift, as I came to realize.

"I don't know how to explain this any other way, Izzy, but it's like she could make butterfly hunting interesting. I'm always interested in every little thing she says. It's . . ."

"Magic?" I interrupted.

"Yeah, that's it!" Dave said, eyeing me appreciatively.

"The Police have been there and said that already," I said.

"What?" he questioned, not catching my joke.

"Every little thing she does is magic. Everything she do just turns me on," I sang, bobbing my head from one side to the other to the rhythm of the song.

Dave opened his mouth, a little flabbergasted, and then closed it without saying a word. Then he just laughed aloud.

"God, Izzy, I missed your wit! That's exactly it . . . I hadn't thought of it, but I guess that that song basically sums it up."

"Well, at least you gathered up the courage to ask her if she'd marry you in some old fashioned way," I teased him.

Dave was taken since their first encounter. He'd been mesmerized from the first time they'd met, but he'd been completely at a loss, taken, from the moment he sat across from Helen at the coffee shop she took him to.

Since that day, he had wanted nothing more than to know Helen and everything about her. He'd dated other women and fallen for them, and he'd owned their hearts, which had been enough. However, that wasn't enough with Helen, because he realized that with her he needed more. He needed to own her soul. That's why he had no doubts that she was the one for him. Right from the start.

They left that coffee shop with a dinner date scheduled for the next day. Helen's initiative, naturally. Dave just muttered two-syllable words, tops, during their time together at the coffee shop. At the time, sentences were out of the question. Fortunately for him, that only aided in making him pull off the mysterious man type.

When he drove her home after their dinner date the next day, he decided that he would not rush things. He opened her door for her, helped her out of his car, and escorted her to her building entrance. When she didn't glance at him nervously or wait for him to try to kiss her before wishing him good night and entering the lobby, he was at a loss. Wasn't she interested in him after all? Had dinner gone that bad?

It hadn't, because she called him the next day, and later on, she would confess to Dave that she'd been afraid that if he kissed her, she wouldn't be able to stop herself. She wanted to know him better before she slept with him.

"Hi, it's Helen!" she said as soon as Dave picked up the phone, preventing him from even saying hello.

"I know," Dave offered smugly.

"Oh." She sighed. "I really enjoyed our dinner last night, and I've got tickets to this indie band festival that is going on downtown, and I was wondering if you would like to go with me . . ."

"Sure."

"I can pick you up. I have tickets for next Saturday."

"Okay."

"Okay, I'll see you Saturday," Helen said enthusiastically, pausing briefly afterward, as if waiting for Dave to say something. Which he didn't. "Bye, then," she uttered, not seeming to know what else to say.

"Bye."

See? What did I tell you? Two syllables words, tops!

"God, Dave! Was that all you said when you were around her?" I asked, astonished.

"In the beginning? Yeah . . . that was pretty much it," he admitted.

"She must be a tenacious woman to manage all that eloquence," I jeered.

"You have no idea!" he said with a dreamy look on his face; I'd never seen that expression on him before. He didn't have it bad; he had it worse.

Their next dates were a repetition of their first on the non-kissing part but with an increasing pent-up sexual tension that they visibly tried to ignore.

"I can't even describe it to you, Izzy. It seemed that I was back to puberty all over again! The simple fact that she accidentally brushed me or touched me made me get a hard on!"

"You're joking, right?" I asked, incredulous.

"I'm not. It's that sad," he said sheepishly.

"That is so . . . not you!" I stated.

"You have no idea, Izzy! Helen is mind-blowing. I never felt this way before. It's overwhelming . . . It's almost as if I need her to breathe."

"Wow!" I managed, not knowing what to say to that display of surrender from Dave.

"It scares me to death. I don't know what I would do if she left me," he admitted.

"Is that why you asked her to marry you after you'd been dating her for only two months? You were trying to secure her?"

"Well, I guess that counted too," he admitted shamelessly. "But mostly, I knew she was the one, so it made no sense wasting time when I finally had all I wanted right in front of me."

"Wow . . . again," I muttered with an inch of skepticism in my voice that did not go unnoticed by Dave.

"I hate it when you're like that, Izzy!" Dave snarled.

"Like what?" I asked, startled.

"Cynical," he said bluntly.

"I'm not cynical. I'm just . . . impressed!" I countered.

"Don't give me that shit. This is exactly why I didn't tell you about Helen in the first place! I knew you were just going to undermine and diminish my feelings for her."

"And how, pray tell, did I manage to accomplish that if I didn't utter a word about it, Dave? Where is this coming from? Why do you always assume the worst from me?" I asked, wounded.

"You have only yourself to thank for that. After all, you kept telling me to always assume the worst from people. That way I would never be disappointed, only surprised. Remember?" Dave said sarcastically.

"Why are you trying to pick a fight with me, Dave? What have I said?" I asked in a low and icy tone, looking him in the eyes.

"It's your attitude. You don't need to say anything . . . It's just that condescending look you have."

"Condescending? Try astonished, perhaps! What do you expect from me? You tell me that you're getting married in three months, to a woman that you've known for four, and whom I only heard about now, and I can't even be surprised? Wow, that's plain stupid, to say the least!" I threw at him. "Want me to jump on the cheerleading squad and say I'm happy for you just because you want to hear it from me? I'm sorry, Dave, but I'm more the type of friend that tells you the fucking truth!" I picked up my things and bolted out of the restaurant where we were having lunch, not looking back. A bit dramatic, I know, but sometimes, to make a point, you have to either go big or go home. So I did both! Pun intended.

It took Dave two days to call me. I wasn't mad at him anymore, but I was still sulky.

"What's the truth?" he asked me as soon as I picked up the phone. Unbelievable! Only Dave would brood over the last thing I said to him for two days and then call me to ask what I meant by that.

"God, you're such a prick!" I snapped, but I knew that he could tell from my tone that I had a smile on my lips.

"It takes one to know one . . . Come on, Izzy, let's make friends," he joked.

"I'll think about it," I said, trying to sound distant.

"Are you playing hard to get?"

"Oh, just go eat a dog, will you, Dave?" I snapped, amused, though.

"What on earth is that? Who says that? 'Eat a dog,' Izzy?"

"Just shut up!" I barked.

"Listen, I'm sorry I said those things to you . . . but you know I value your opinion, and I really want you to like Helen."

"Dave, I get that. I really do. But you have to understand that I will only be able to have an opinion about her once I get to know her. Until then and until I understand this total eclipse of the heart of yours, I can't and I won't honestly tell you that I'm happy for you."

"Total eclipse of the heart? You're inspired today! What's next? All's . . ."

I cut him off. "I mean it, Dave!"

"I know, Izzy, and I wouldn't expect anything else from you," Dave said, all mockery gone from his voice now. "That's why I want you to have dinner with Helen and me tonight at my place."

"I already have something scheduled tonight," I explained. "Can we make it tomorrow? You know my time here is a bit tight . . . There are actually other people in my life besides you!"

"Sure, no problem," he agreed. "But, Izzy?"

"Yes?"

"I'm the most important, ain't I?" Dave joked.

"You wish!" I said, hanging up the phone.

The next night, I met them at Dave's house. Helen was doing the cooking. I was a bit anxious, I'll admit.

Dave opened the door and gave me a quick hug. I followed him to the kitchen and saw Helen, in all her splendor, for the first time ever. It was a sight. Really. I couldn't help feeling a bit awed.

"Hi Izzy. I'm sorry—Isabella! I know that's Dave's nickname for you, and I heard so much about you that I feel like I already know you!" She babbled, a sincere smile on her face.

"Hi Helen. You can call me Izzy. I hope he only told you the good things!" I smiled back, taking the hand she had stretched toward me.

"That wouldn't leave me much to talk about, would it?" Dave mocked.

"Dave!" Helen scolded him, smacking him playfully on the arm.

Dinner was delicious, but for the first time since I could remember, I had a taste of my own venom. Helen, in her classy and charming way, observed Dave's and my interactions attentively throughout the whole meal. That in itself was not a first, but the comprehension that flashed through her sharp eyes made me feel naked; she was assessing me, and she seemed to be getting it almost right. Almost.

"So, Izzy, Dave tells me you're going back in a few days."

"Unfortunately, all good things come to an end, so . . . here I go again," I said, shrugging.

"You like it there? Do you ever plan on getting back home?"

"I don't love it there, but it's not that bad. It gets better if you think of it as temporary because—to answer your question—I plan on coming back in a couple of years."

"Why hadn't I heard about it before?" Dave asked me in a serious tone, raising an expectant brow at me.

"We've talked about this before. I don't have a date . . . I don't even have a year defined. I'm just saying that I intend to come back in two or three years, but that's it. Nothing more."

"Move your ass back here as soon as possible, you . . . witch! It would be great having you here," Dave jeered sweetly.

"And have to suffer you on a daily basis again? No, thank you! I'm paying Helen here good money to put up with you. You didn't think it was love, did you?" I scoffed, winking my eye at Helen.

She smiled politely back at me, and Dave threw me a piece of bread and proceeded to stick his fingers through my face holes. It was something Dave just did. Luckily, he still wasn't completely at ease around Helen; otherwise, he would've stuck his fingers in my food and in my drink, as he also usually did.

"You're so gross! Stop it!" I scolded him, laughing.

Helen seemed amused with our interaction, but I couldn't help wondering how she felt about it. After all, this was the polished version of us, and something told me that she'd have plenty of time to see the cruder versions of us as well. That, I was certain, she wouldn't like.

"So do you think you'll be able to come to our wedding?" Dave asked me, making Helen turn her full attention to me, which freaked me out a bit.

"We both know how much I'd love to, Dave," I said, and we exchanged silent glances full of irony and did our best not to laugh. "But I most likely won't be able to come. If I'd known about it sooner, I might have been able to work out something, but with such short notice, I don't think it will be possible. Sorry!"

"I understand. It's too far away . . . and this was a bit last minute." Dave was pouting.

"Are you planning to have a big party?" I asked, turning to Helen and ignoring Dave's childish attempts to make me feel bad over not attending his wedding.

"No, we want to do something simple. We don't want a big celebration. Just the closest friends and family, of course," Helen explained.

"That sounds nice. But you don't have much time to plan things. Do you think three months will be enough?"

"I don't think it will be a problem, Izzy. I know exactly what I want, which is something very simple that won't involve much planning. And we're not having a religious wedding, so we just have to handle the legal formalities, which is rather quick."

"Nice! Dave, you'll be a man, soon," I mocked, faking a grave and solemn air that made Helen laugh.

Dinner went on uneventfully. We talked about everything in general and nothing in particular. Helen grilled me about our times together on the other side of the world, and my cautious answers did not go unnoticed by her. She was, naturally, very gracious about it and did not show any kind of resentment in face of my reservations.

Dave was happy to see that Helen and I seemed to be getting along. I'll admit that it didn't take me long to understand Helen's allure. She was everything Dave had mentioned and more. I genuinely liked her, and I wasn't surprised when I realized that they did look good together.

"Oh my God, look at the time!" I cried. "I have to get going. I hadn't realized it was so late." I stood up and looked around in search of my purse. "We're still on for breakfast tomorrow, right?" I asked Dave as my eyes met his and a ghost of a smile ran across his lips. I knew exactly what he was thinking . . . because I was thinking the same. So I nodded almost imperceptibly in agreement, but apparently not enough that Helen would miss it. And there, right there, that nod, that was my unforgivable mistake with Helen. I knew it right away.

"I'll walk you, Izzy," Dave said, standing as well and fetching the keys, which were lying on the kitchen counter. "It's a bit late for her to go alone," he offered in the face of Helen's questioning look.

I opted to remain silent, hoping naively that it would remedy Dave's and mine, apparently and in Helen's eyes, blunt admission of twisted complicity. It didn't, though. I knew it because when I said my good-byes to Helen and tried to give her one of those awkward hugs that you give to people that you don't actually know but who are close to people you know very well—you know, those hugs where you grab the person's upper arms to prevent him or her from coming any closer and lean forward so that you only touch each other with your shoulders—she just grabbed one of my hands between hers, squeezed it slightly, and said with a plastic smile, "It was so nice to meet you, Isabella."

She never called me Izzy again.

Dave was as oblivious to this exchange as I expected him to be. He was in love with Helen, and he had unknowingly given the woman her first shred of doubt about the lengths of his love for her; Dave had just shown Helen that to him it was far more important to know what I thought of her than to hear her opinion about me. It was so important that he couldn't wait to meet me the next day for breakfast and learn it then, and so important that it wouldn't even place as a choice to Dave.

Mind you, though, Helen was perfectly aware that it was not me but rather my opinion that came first instead of hers. And that's exactly why she never forgave me. Helen, as many other women before her, made that same mistake; she blamed me for Dave's inability to open up and share his life with her. Because I existed in Dave's world, he would never let her in completely. I was the space thief, the mind reader, and the ultimate hijacker of souls. I was the barrier that prevented her from owning Dave completely.

So no, she never forgave me for that, but she never hated me for it either. You see, Helen was a good woman, and because she saw right through Dave and me, she knew that she could never hate me while she loved Dave; we were part of each other.

"So?"

"Hmm . . ."

"Don't be difficult, Izzy. Just tell me what you thought of Helen!" Dave demanded as soon as we stepped outside his house and were alone. "You know I'm dying to know."

"It's such a nice evening. Don't you just love the way the stars shine so bright here?" I asked, purposefully stalling just to make him beg.

"I'm gonna kick your ass, Izzy," Dave threatened.

"No, you won't," I teased.

"Yes, I will," Dave said, taking hold of my head and messing up my hair while I shrieked and tried to escape his vicious grip.

"Stop it, Dave!" I laughed. "Okay, okay, I'll talk," I conceded, lifting my hands in mock surrender.

"Spill," he urged as we started to walk, walking past my car and going for a stroll while we talked.

"Yes . . . lover boy," I jeered, but then I got straight to the point. "I like her."

"I could've guessed that on my own. You always like them," he sneered.

"I can't blame you for having good taste. You do! Flawless taste, actually. Your women, with rare exceptions, are always . . . fine," I said, uncertain of my choice of word.

"Fine? That's what you think? Helen is *fine*?" he asked with disbelief.

"You don't need me to tell you that you've got yourself a lady there, Dave!" I said, pulling off my best accent and placing a hand on my hip for emphasis.

"No, but I need you to tell me that I'm doing the right thing here." He hesitated, putting into words what we were both dreading; I, that he made me tell him the truth; him, that I did exactly that.

"Tell me your story, Dave," I said.

"Helen's and mine? I told you already."

"No. You started to, but you never finished it," I corrected him.

"What do you want to know?"

"Everything that's important to you!" I deadpanned.

Dave kissed Helen for the first time on their seventh date. He took her home and escorted her to her building door, as he always did, with absolutely no illusions that it would be any different from the other times where he had done exactly the same. Helen would walk right into the building without hesitation, and she wouldn't even flinch. This time, though, when she seemed about to do just so, she turned to him, looked him straight in the eyes, and asked him, "When are you going to kiss me, Dave?"

Dave didn't fly to her; he materialized on her lips. And he never let her go from then on.

Once they kissed, she just grabbed his hand and took him upstairs, to her home and to her bed. They'd slept together almost every night since then, and Dave couldn't get enough of Helen.

It was such a consuming feeling that he sometimes felt that he needed her simply to breathe, as he told me countless times. From here to marriage was a small and inevitable step that neither of them even questioned. Dave woke up one morning and looked at Helen's face as she slept peacefully beside him, and he simply knew that he wanted to wake up to that for the rest of his life. He didn't even wait for her to wake up. He shook her until she started grumbling, and as soon as she managed to open one eyelid, he told her that he wanted to marry her. He never asked her, and I guess she never felt she needed to be asked. It felt like the natural thing to do.

"It scares me," Dave confessed. "I never felt this way for a woman before. This is different."

"Different how?" I asked.

"Well, for starters, sex with Helen is just mind-blowing!"

"She's that good? And here I was thinking she might be a prude," I teased.

"Not even a bit," Dave retorted, winking at me. "But her being good in bed it's not what is enticing at all . . . Well, maybe a bit. I do like that under her polished and classy appearance, she is a little volcano."

"Don't!" I cut him off, smiling. "Do not put images in my head. You know better than that. You're handing me ammunition to scoff you."

"Don't even dare!" he grumbled. "Where were we?"

"You were telling me about how steamy it got between sheets with Vesuvius Girl!" I joked, succeeding in getting a rise out of Dave, who just silently scolded me with a raised brow and an almost menacing look in his face. "Okay, okay, I'll shut up," I conceded.

"Things are different with Helen. She just makes sense in my life. She makes it better . . . What, Izzy?" Dave barked as soon as he realized that I was about to explode into a fit of laughter. Which I did.

"I'm sorry . . . but all I can think of is Helen telling you how much she lava you!" I shrieked, erupting in a fit of laughter again.

"Are you done?" Dave asked after a while. He was clearly not amused, which made me realize that I was seriously crossing the line.

"I'm done! Sorry! Please continue," I said, dropping my head and gluing my eyes to the ground in hopes that the bogus guilt move would placate Dave's ire.

"Jeez, Izzy. Sometimes you infuriate me!" he vented, letting out a prolonged sigh.

"I'm sorry, really. Come on. You were telling me why you found Helen so appealing."

Dave eyed me, still a bit annoyed, but he eventually conceded.

"She's just everything I ever dreamed, Izzy!" Dave stated bluntly, leaving me speechless.

We continued our walk in silence for a few minutes. I guess we were both letting Dave's words sink in.

"So this is you grabbing hold of your dream and living it?" I asked finally.

"Yeah, I guess so."

"Doesn't the whole marriage thing scare you?"

"You know what, Izzy? It doesn't! In fact I'm kind of looking forward it to it."

"I'm sorry I won't be able to come . . ."

"I know you are. Even knowing that you hate weddings, I know that you'd like to attend mine. And I'll miss you there. You're one of those persons that I really wanted there."

"Don't make me feel worse about it, you racketeer!" I joked. "So who else are you inviting?" I was attempting to lighten our moods.

"Just family and close friends, as Helen mentioned. We don't want anything big."

"Well, given the size of your family, that won't be an easy task. Hey, are you going to invite Almost Mary?" I asked out of nowhere.

"Almost Mary?" Dave voiced, as if trying to place my words. "Huh . . . I don't know. I really haven't thought about it. Do you think I should?"

"You're asking me? She's your friend, well, your platonic love . . ."

"Hmm. Too inappropriate, perhaps? I don't see her that much nowadays . . ."

"You don't? That's a pity."

"How so?"

"It's a shame if you lose that special connection you have. That's all I'm saying," I said, coming to a halt and boring my eyes into Dave's. "Don't let it happen, Dave. Don't let petty things get between you two."

"Are we still talking about Almost Mary and me?" Dave asked, a bit baffled by my words.

"Who else?" I smirked, winking at him and resuming my march.

We walked back to my car, engrossed in meaningless talk about everything that came to our minds and teased each other, as we normally did.

"So, Izzy, don't think you're off the hook," Dave said as we reached my car. "You still haven't told me what you think . . ." His voice trailed off, and he stuck his hands in the pocket of his trousers.

I sighed deeply and raised my head to face him. "A couple of weeks after you started dating Mary the Fairy, you told me that you knew that she was not the one. That it was something you just felt in your gut. Remember?"

"Yeah," Dave answered hesitantly.

"Do you feel in your gut that Helen is the one?" I asked.

"I do!" Dave retorted without a trace of doubt in his voice while his trademark smug smile crawled up his lips.

"There's your answer!" I announced as I opened the car door and prepared to hop inside.

"Thanks, Izzy. I'll see you tomorrow morning!" Dave was clearly relieved, and he turned and jogged toward his house.

I sat behind the wheel and turned the key in the ignition, starting the car, and eased out into the street. As Dave's house was left behind, I let the pang of guilt that was building in my conscience consume me as I pondered whether I should have given Dave my honest opinion. As I dwelled on the matter, which occurred often over the years, I always came down to the same conclusion: it wouldn't have mattered, and I would have only succeeded in making him sad.

That's why I didn't tell Dave that I felt in my gut that Helen was not the one; she was so much more than that. She was one of those few remarkable women who would be the one to a thousand men. She just wasn't the one for him. Helen, as with all eclipses, was doomed to be a passing phenomenon.

CHAPTER 18

ALL THE PROMISES WE MADE FROM THE CRADLE TO THE GRAVE

Somewhere along the lines of time, someone said that there are moments in life that define us. Somewhere along the lines of Dave's existence, he chose to see most of those moments as clichés, because our lives are necessarily bound to suffer from an inescapable lack of originality. So birth, death, marriage, divorce, falling in love, heartbreaks, sickness, and healing came to him as the inevitable promises that we make and break from the cradle to the grave.

Dave married Helen, as he knew he would. And he promised her that he would love her and respect her, in sickness and in health, in good times and in bad times, for all the days of his life, until death did them part. He meant all those promises at the time.

More than meaning his vows, Dave felt genuinely happy about them. I could even see it in the wedding pictures he sent me, and that made me feel better about the whole thing. It's hard to explain, but though I didn't think Dave was making a mistake, I also thought that this wasn't the right thing for him. Regardless, I felt that that was something for him to find out, not for me to tell him. And that's what bothered me, for we normally didn't keep those kinds of thoughts from each other.

Now, since Helen, I did. I wondered if Dave did too.

I guess that, as I was to her, she also became a shadow in Dave's and my relationship. That's why when he called or wrote, we rarely spoke about Helen. Although she was constantly hovering over us, we managed to keep Helen distant enough from our closed reality at the time—so distant that I'll admit that I often forgot she even existed. And deep down, I would be lying if I didn't admit that I liked to believe that she went to more trouble than I did to achieve that degree of convenient amnesia.

"Izzy!" Dave shouted as soon as I answered the phone.

"Dave!" I shrieked excitedly. "I tried to call you last week. How are things?"

"Are you sitting down?" he asked flatly, not giving away if what he was about to tell me was good news or bad news.

"I am now. Fire away!" I urged, sitting down on the nearest chair . . . just in case.

"I'm going to be a father," Dave said in the same flat tone he had used so far.

I gasped, and there was a small silence between us.

"Are you still there, Izzy?" Dave asked, breaking the silence.

"Are you happy about it?" I asked hesitantly.

"I'm thrilled!" he finally said, with so much happiness that it almost infected me as well. Almost.

"Then congratulations!" I exclaimed, trying to sound excited.

"If I'd told you that I wasn't happy, what were you going to tell me? That you were sorry?"

"Probably," I answered honestly.

"You're the only person I know who can get away with saying such crudities, Izzy," Dave noted with amusement.

"I don't actually get away with it; I just don't have that many friends I can say these kinds of things to. In fact, that's probably why I don't have that many friends," I joked.

"I'm happy, Izzy! I'm really happy! I feel like I'm gonna burst!" He said it in such a way that I could sense all his enthusiasm from thousands of miles away.

"Doesn't it scare you? A baby is something big!" I told him, not bothering to mask my concern.

"It's not that big . . . They're quite small when they're born. Besides, Helen is the one who's going to have to shit the watermelon, so I'm not that concerned," Dave joked.

"Shit the watermelon?"

"Well, that's what my mother said when I was born, that giving birth to me was worse than shitting a watermelon. Hadn't I told you that already?"

"I knew that you were no angel to see, according to your grandmother, but I didn't know the watermelon part. Pity. That might have been handy back when we met."

"Were you going to be lame to the point of nicknaming me watermelon?" Dave goaded.

"No, I was going to be awesome to the point of nicknaming you shit!" I countered, laughing.

"You . . . witch!" Dave blustered.

"Hey, do you already know what you're having?"

"A baby! We're having a baby, Izzy!" he cried out condescendingly.

"Funny! What is it? Boy, girl, cat, dog, parakeet?"

"It's a panda bear!"

"Pray that it's not a female panda bear; otherwise, you'll spend a fortune on hair removal."

"Let's just stop here. This conversation is getting completely nonsensical, even for us, and it's not cheap to call you there," Dave said, laughing.

"Hey, you'll be a wonderful father. You know that, don't you?"

"You think so?"

"Yeah, I really do," I said sweetly. "Hell, even I would like to be your daughter!" I added jokingly to dismiss the sentimental tone that the conversation was starting to have. Dave played along.

"Just admit that you just want me to ask you who's your daddy!"

"Dave, I'm sure that that sounded as bad in your head as it did when you actually said it . . ."

"Oh, just shut it!" he huffed playfully.

"You still haven't told me if it's a boy or a girl."

"We still don't know. Helen is just seven weeks pregnant. It's still too early to tell. Hey, don't mention it to anyone. We're not telling people," he confided.

"Hey, what am I, then?" I asked with false resentment, secretly fishing around for Dave's sweet words, which followed right after.

"You're my Izzy! I just had to tell you first."

"Ohhh!" I groaned, all mushy-like.

"You're getting soft, Izzy. What's going on?" Dave asked, a bit concerned. "You're not one to fall for this bullshit."

"That's because you're not giving me bullshit. I'm your Izzy, and we know it."

Helen had gotten pregnant right after they married. I didn't understand this urgency in their relationship. They seemed to be on a restless race against the clock. They met, married, and got pregnant in less than ten months. Why the rush? Why pursue the sense of fatality that their relationship kept piling up?

I didn't get it, not even when I asked Dave about it. At the time, he just eyed me, seeming confused by my question, and said that all of it made sense to them. I didn't ask again for a long time, but when I did, Dave told me the truth.

You know when you see someone adding layer after layer of crap on himself and being ecstatic about it because he just doesn't have a clue or simply doesn't care that he's doing it? Good! Because that's not what I thought Dave was doing. When I looked at Dave's life, I got the feeling that he was fast-forwarding a chapter in it, and I just couldn't understand why. At some point, I had to conclude that he didn't know it either; he was simply living with all he had . . . because it apparently all made sense to them.

Dave and Helen's marriage seemed like something out of a magazine. Even with all the distance that stood between us, I got that idea. They were social and active, even with Helen being pregnant and their being newlyweds. They were always attending dinners and going to parties, and Helen blended right in, becoming a part of Dave's life and closest circles. At some point, she was even a Poe.

Then their lives changed when the baby was born.

The baby was a girl. They named her Tess, though when she was born, autumn had already stripped the trees of their leaves, leaving them bare. Tess means late summer, in case you were wondering. Helen liked the earthly and simple allure of the name. Dave liked that she had Helen's blonde hair and his brown eyes, and that that combination reminded him of chilly nights and early sunsets.

Once Dave told me why they were going to name the baby Tess, I couldn't help thinking that Helen, rather than shitting a watermelon, had shit a poem. They had waited for the baby to be born to choose her name. They had picked some that they liked already, but they were waiting to see her face first to feel what she looked like. Yes, *feel*. I had told Dave that she would look like a knee. All newborns look like a knee to me. Dave didn't think it was funny. I didn't tell him that I wasn't joking.

When I first met Tess, she was about to celebrate her first birthday. I'd seen Helen pregnant when I had gone home for my annual leave the year before. She was more of a charmer than ever. She truly gave meaning to the aphorism that pregnant women glowed. She kept her elegant and lean figure and held only a tiny bump at seven months of pregnancy. And she glowed—so much that they probably didn't have to pay any electricity bills during the nine months she hatched the baby inside her.

"Here, Izzy, hold her," Dave said, handing me Tess, who started crying once I held her. "She'll shut up—don't worry. She's just shy because she doesn't know you yet." He seemed amused by my uneasiness. "Right, Tess? Don't scare Aunt Izzy away!" Dave said sweetly to Tess, grimacing to make her laugh, which she eventually did. But she kept stirring on my lap, visibly restless to be held by Dave, stretching her little arms toward him.

"Just take her back. She doesn't stay still," I complained, handing her back, to her relief as well as my own.

"It's just a baby, Izzy! She won't bite you . . . yet," Dave mocked. "Here, baby, come to Daddy." He grabbed hold of Tess and kissing her sweetly on the cheeks.

We'd been strolling around at one of the city parks and had decided to rest on one of the few empty benches that were sheltered by the trees. It was a nice place, but at that time of day, it was a bit crowded. People liked to go for runs and walk their dogs at dusk. It was still summer, but you could already tell that the days were getting shorter. Dave had picked me up at my place, and then we had gone to his mother's to bring Tess along with us for a walk. She didn't walk yet, so we just pushed her stroller. Between Tess's mood swings and tantrums, we were trying to drink our coffees and have a conversation. Once we sat down on the bench, Dave took Tess out of the stroller and kept pushing her toward me. I kept handing her back to him. She seemed to enjoy our silly game.

"I never thought I'd live to see this day, Dave!" I said, shaking my head to cloak the smile that was starting to curl up on my lips.

"What?" he asked, intrigued.

"Nothing, really. It's just that I never thought I would see you so completely and utterly subdued to a woman," I stated, winking my eye at him and motioning my chin toward Tess.

"What can I say? It was love at first sight!" Dave joked, fondling Tess's head. "But seriously, Izzy, this is just something that you can't explain. You'll only understand it when you have children of your own," he added, eyeing me steadily.

"You're not giving me the baby talk, Dave!" I scolded him.

"I'm just saying that this is something you have to go through to know about. It changes your perspective of life. And I think you should have kids. You'd be a great mother!"

"I already have kids; I have you! And I don't even need to potty train you anymore," I teased him.

"I'm not joking, Izzy. I really think you would be a great mother."

"Yeah, I'd be like the Virgin Mary, except for the virgin part . . . I wonder if I would be able to pull off an immaculate conception, though? You know, since the man I'd like to be the father of my children is already taken, I guess I would only settle for the Holy Spirit now. Or I could go for a sperm donor. What do you think?"

"You're too proud, Izzy! Too proud!" Dave snarled.

"Proud? You, of all people, saying that, Dave!" I almost shouted.

"Don't play dumb with me. You know what I'm talking about. This isn't about having babies," Dave riposted. Then, after a brief pause: "Have you seen him since you've been back?"

"No!" I snapped, annoyed by his question.

"Good!" he spit back sharply.

We sat on the park bench for a while, just playing with Tess. Neither of us was in the mood to dig further or have an argument about the past, though the subject kept brooding in our minds. Eventually, we let it go and resumed our walk as if nothing had been said.

I'd lived on the other side of the world for seven years, three of which were shared with Dave, who, in the remaining four, had managed to travel the world, find his soul, get married, and become a father. And settle.

Dave seemed to have settled. He was living a life that even in my wildest dreams, I had never pictured him in. He was a husband and a father, and he worked diligently in his solely owned company, which was growing slowly but steadily. If I didn't know him any better, I would say that he was tamed and that he had succumbed to the inevitable routines of life so that he could keep his promises.

But I did know him better than that. Much better. I knew him well enough to know that if there was any constant in Dave's life, the one thing that one could rely on when it came to Dave was that he didn't settle. He lacked that appetence.

But now he had Tess and Helen, and I was back home for good. My time abroad had ceased, and I had a life to pick up from where I'd left it. Most of it at least. But that's another story.

Dave and I fell easily into our dynamic once I moved back from the other side of the world. Having him in my life again on a daily basis gave me a sense of belonging that I hadn't felt for a while.

Dave also felt more grounded once I was back in his life. And Helen felt the full blast of my—I assume—inconvenient presence coming into her organized life. Until then, I'd been a shadowy presence that only really haunted her once a year when I came home on the holidays. Sure, she was aware of our calls and e-mails, but I was so far away that she could easily dismiss the weight that she felt our friendship had over her relationship with Dave.

Now she couldn't ignore me anymore. Now I was a full-time ghost, and I liked it; I felt that it suited me.

Mind you, Helen's and my relationship, or lack of it, to put it properly, was in no way tainted by any kind of animosity. Helen was always polite and nice to me, as she was to everyone. But that was it. There was no evolution in the way we interacted. Every time we were together, it felt like the first, and we both dealt well with that. So did Dave. In fact, he wouldn't even address the matter or go as far as to simply notice it. I guess that he felt that things worked out fine like that to all of us.

Dave's apparently settled life went on uneventful for some time. For some time, Tess seemed to appease his urgency of living on the edge and cloud the detachment that he progressively felt toward Helen.

"You're late," Dave grumbled.

"Sorry. I couldn't find a place to park," I said, slumping on the nearer chair while I placed my bag on the unoccupied one right beside it. "Great, you ordered for me already!" I saw my toast and latte in front of me.

"I didn't. Once I entered, the guy just nodded his head and mumbled, 'The usual?' He didn't even wait for my answer," Dave explained, a bit annoyed.

"So? We're regulars. We have been coming here almost every Monday for the past . . . what? Three years now, right? Of course they know our order! We always order the same thing!" I pointed out. "Did you not want a bagel today? Are you feeling brave enough that you'll ask for a croissant?"

My teasing was met with Dave's silence and gloomy mood.

"What's bugging you? Problems in paradise?" I asked.

"No. Things are fine with Helen . . . It's just . . . this," Dave said exasperatedly, motioning his hands toward our food on the table.

"What's this, Dave?" I asked, mimicking his gesture.

"Predictability, I guess."

"Hmm. We're not becoming predictable. We simply settled into having small habits," I said, choosing my words with caution.

"No, we've become predictable, foreseeable, expected. Dull. We're dull, Izzy. I bet you can guess the entire day I have ahead of me in less than a minute because, sadly, you won't need more than that to describe the day that I'm about to have. I wouldn't even be surprised if you guessed what I'm having for lunch."

"Dave, I know what you're thinking about just by the way you move, but that's because I know you too well, not because you're predictable. So do you want to talk about what's really bothering you?"

"This is bothering me. It seems that I'm living on the clock, that I'm fulfilling a schedule, that everything is programmed. Fuck! I make love to Helen on Sunday mornings after my mother comes by our house to pick up Tess to play at her house." He sighed, infuriated.

"You know that I have to ask . . ."

"At eleven, Izzy! Every Sunday around eleven, I bang Helen!" he growled, cutting me off and answering the question he hadn't let me finish. "Because my mother always comes around ten thirty and takes about twenty minutes to pick up Tess's things and get her out of the house. Then we go to our room, take our clothes off, and have lousy, boring, and unexciting sex. Then we take a shower and go to my mother's for lunch. Every Sunday, Izzy. Every fucking Sunday!"

"I see . . . Routine is killing you, isn't it?" I asked, but I wasn't really asking.

"It's not that I don't love Helen anymore; it's just that everything is so dull. I feel numb. If it weren't for Tess, I . . ." Dave lifted his gaze to meet mine so that he wouldn't have to say the rest of the sentence aloud.

"Why did you rush into marriage with Helen? What was it that made sense to you at the time?" I asked.

Dave sighed deeply before he faced me again and started to talk. "Remember that friend of mine who went to visit me when I was abroad?"

"The journalist guy?" I offered.

"Yeah, that one. Well, he dated this girl for ten years, and they looked so good together. They were an item. Whenever I thought of what a relationship should be about, I thought of them. Then, after ten years, they decided to get married. They got married, and after three months—three lousy months, Izzy—they filed for divorce. They don't even speak to each other anymore nowadays."

"Why did they divorce?"

"They just realized that they couldn't live together . . . something like that. How can you date a person for ten years and not know that you can't live with her?"

"And after four months of knowing Helen, you knew you could live with her?" I ventured.

"No. But I figured that I wasn't going to waste my life like that. So I did what felt right to me at the time. And Helen felt so right. More than right. She felt perfect. So I knew that if I was gonna do it, I just had to go big. I couldn't hold back!"

"So you just plunged in headfirst?"

"Is there any other way to live, Izzy?" Dave smirked.

"So this is what's troubling you? That you're . . ."

Dave cut me off, completing my sentence. "Not living, Izzy."

"Ah!" I sighed, the full blast of realization dawning on me.

Dave was not living. He was a passerby in his dull life, and his restlessness had started to get the best of him. In the beginning, it was just the small things; he would spend more time at work or lose himself in longer runs. But then he started to linger around here and there, losing track of time, until he finally gathered up the strength to go home. Sometimes he went to my house just to be there by himself. He would come by when he knew that I would be busy, and even if I wasn't, I would just let him be. When he simply wanted company, I sat beside him reading a book or making small talk, and when he wanted to talk, we would turn his blooming silences into all-night conversations. Helen didn't like it, but she opted to overlook Dave's alienation; she knew to pick her battles, and this one was one she had known from the start she would never win.

Things got better. Dave had these moments, but then he would snap out of them and Helen would have her husband back.

As I watched Dave's ups and downs, I kept asking him the one thing that was left for him to answer: "How much longer?" He always answered me with a shrug.

Eventually, the moments of detachment from his life became less and less soothing, and the so far silent abysm, whose edge he had threaded for so long, called for him. And Dave whispered back.

The call came in the form of women. Don't get me wrong. Dave, of all men, hadn't turned blind once he had met Helen. Women were a constant temptation to Dave, but Helen had brought along with her a numbness to that part of him. No pun intended. Of course he looked at other women and occasionally even flirted a bit. But it was all innocent. He never let things go too far, and he never allowed temptation to catch him off guard.

Unfortunately, women reminded Dave of a carefree existence that belonged in a past that he now craved more than anything.

*   *   *

"Come on, Izzy! What's the big deal? It will be fun. I'm the one who should be worried about it, not you."

"This is stupid, Dave. I'm not going to lay down a spread to see which trainee you should hire!"

"Why not, Izzy? It's as good as any other criteria that I might use. They're trainees. They don't have any experience. The cards are perfect to know which is the most adequate for me to hire."

"I don't need my cards to tell you which one you should hire," I countered.

"That's not an informed opinion!" Dave barked.

"On the contrary! It's quite informed if we considered all the knowledge I have on your life," I barked back.

"That is low," Dave grumbled. "Why don't you just indulge me? Come on Izzy! Please?" he begged, flashing his charmer smile at me.

"Really, Dave?" I scolded. "You're throwing that smile at me?" I tsked him, shaking my head in disapproval.

"What? Can't blame a guy for trying!" he mocked, a bit constrained.

I looked him in the eyes and raised a scolding brow at him while I rested my arms akimbo for emphasis. He almost cringed, as if I had hit him, and even amid his goofiness, I couldn't help noticing how interesting a man he had become. Don't get me wrong; I had always found him interesting, even him not being every woman's wet dream. And yes, I do like to emphasize that. But at thirty-six, Dave's charm was blooming. He had a few gray hairs that gave him character, and he had a stillness about his facial traits that to the unknowing eye made him appear mysterious. The fact that he took good care of his body didn't hurt either. His shoulders were wide, and he had the kind of arms that when they enveloped you, you felt you could live there forever because there was no better place in the world.

"Dave, do everyone a favor and just hire the girl you feel less attracted to," I said, dismissively.

Dave didn't listen to my advice, but he didn't want to cheat on Helen either. So he suffered a painful and blue-balled existence every other day at work, especially when the trainee sported cleavage. She was a double D.

"I've seen it before and said it before, but I just have to say it again: God was very generous with that girl!" I mocked, plopping myself onto the couch in Dave's office and resting my feet on the coffee table in front of me. Not very ladylike of me, but I did it just to annoy Dave, who was anal about it.

"Make yourself at home, Izzy," he said sarcastically.

I just smiled teasingly at him.

He finally caved in, raising his eyes from the computer monitor in front of him and piercing me with a reproving look. "Get your feet off my table."

"So, Dave, feeling a bit . . . blue?" I joked, looking at the trainee in the adjacent room. "So that's how cleavage is supposed to look, huh?" I sneered, taking my feet off the table.

Dave rubbed his face with the palms of his hands before he rested his gaze on me. He looked tired.

"How much more shit about it are you going to give me, Izzy?" Dave asked, sighing.

"I don't know Dave, but after all these months, I must confess that I still find it funny." I shrugged. "That's just too much boobs for only one woman!" I concluded, eyeing the trainee again.

"There's no such thing as too much boobs for one woman," Dave remarked. "Forget about the trainee! I've got a new client that's messing with my head. She invited me to have coffee at her house . . ." He sighed.

"God! What is it with women nowadays? And what is it with you? Are you wearing a new perfume . . . or shamelessly producing outrageous amounts of pheromones? Every week you tell me about a new woman!"

"I don't know what's going on, but I swear that I'm not looking for it! It just happens," he justified.

"You might not be looking for it, but you're sure open to it, Dave."

"You think so?" Dave asked honestly.

I nodded my head affirmatively, giving him a sympathetic smile. How much longer would he hold up? Temptation around him kept increasing and though Dave was no angel, he was no cheater either.

Mind you, Dave had cheated before, but he never did it lightly or searched for it. Dave, in all his restlessness, was never one of those men who viewed women simply as another notch on their bedposts. Not that it made him feel any better about it, but Dave had never cheated because he couldn't say no; he cheated because he had no reason left that prevented him from saying why not.

A couple of months later, Dave, Little John—who was finally back for good from the other side of the world with his Cathy and a Little John of their own—and I went out for a nostalgic get-together to celebrate my big forties.

"And here's to the cutest forty-year-old Midget we know!" Little John mocked, raising his glass at me and wiggling his brows.

"You wicked men! In about three years, when you two turn forty, I'll be the one laughing!" I threatened.

"Why do I always get scolded because of the things Little John says?" Dave asked with an incredulous tone, rolling his eyes at me.

"Old habits die hard!" I smirked. "And don't raise your voice at the elderly," I playfully snarled at him, hitting him in the arm. He flinched, as he always did, pretending that I had hurt him.

"I missed this!" Little John said, grinning at us.

We stood at the bar counter, our gazes locked as we mirrored the nostalgic smiles we saw on each other's faces and I just knew that we all felt the lumps in our throats getting bigger. No one seemed to find the words to fill the silence between us.

"I'll drink to that! And to being forty and hot as hell!" I said, rising my shot glass and my eyebrow, defying them to contradict me. The hangover was going to be a bitch, but you only turn forty once in a lifetime. Or you simply never do.

"You sure are! One hot Midget coming up!" Little John said, clinking our glasses together. Dave followed right after, and before we dropped our heads and our drinks back, the three of us exchanged a conspiratorial smile.

"I think I'm drunk!" I announced several shots later.

"Already, Izzy?" Dave said. "You're getting old! You used to put up a little more fight."

"Bite me!" I barked.

"Ah, now we have feisty Midget coming up! I like it!" Little John mocked. "Hey, Izzy, now that you're forty, are you going to deviate and seduce inexperienced young men?"

"Pfff! Been there, done that!" I said, winking at him. Or at least I think I did. Maybe I just closed both my eyes at the same time.

"Is she serious?" I heard Little John ask Dave, who just shrugged and laughed at him.

"Hey, speaking of deviating young people . . . Little John, have you met Dave's trainee?" I asked mischievously.

"I've seen her boobs."

"You've seen her boobs?" I asked, surprised.

"Well, I saw her, which is basically the same as seeing her boobs . . . You just can't get past that."

"And?" I urged.

"And that's it! I saw her, hence I saw her boobs, and hence I couldn't see anything else," Little John explained. "How do you manage to get any work done?" he asked, turning to Dave.

"Once you get past the boobs, you notice the legs," Dave offered absentmindedly.

"She has great legs!" I agreed.

"So it's boobs and legs?" Little John asked.

"No," I said. "She's boobs on legs!"

"Nice!" Little John whistled. "Hey, I'm having an epiphany! I'm picturing myself entering Dave's office one of these days and finding a disheveled trainee smoking a cigar by the window." He paused and then winked at me. "Stationery all over the floor and Dave's desk cleaned off . . . You know, like someone just knocked everything off it hastily." He donned a faraway look and stretched out his arm to give it a little drama.

"That's so good! Can we share that fantasy?" I asked Little John. "Will you call me if that happens?"

"I'll call you on the dot! And you do the same thing if you come across that scenario."

"That's not going to happen!" Dave said, laughing. "I'm a married man!"

I snorted. Loudly.

"Am I missing something here?" Little John asked, visibly confused.

"Tell me something, Little John," I urged. "Are you and Cathy happy? Do you miss your life before Cathy? You know, all those women, exciting sex . . . the game?" I asked.

"I am happy with Cathy, but I'm not gonna lie. Sometimes when I meet someone, it's tempting. The thought crosses my mind, but that's it. It never stays there longer than a moment, because Cathy just flashes over it and I can't picture my life without her." Little John said this matter-of-factly.

Dumbstruck, Dave and I looked at him.

"Wow!" I managed to say. Dave just mouthed it.

We drank all night. It was a monumental binge for old times' sake. We talked about our lives, we shared old stories, and we promised to do it again regularly. When we left the bar, it was late, and we sat outside talking and waiting for the booze to wear off before we finally hailed ourselves cabs to drive us home.

The last coherent action that I remember was sinking down on my bed still dressed. Then I blacked out.

I don't know how much time passed before I started to hear the buzzing sound of a phone ringing. And we all know that a phone ringing in the middle of the night rarely carries good news. I looked at the screen of my cell phone and saw Dave's name on it, feeling a pang of adrenaline that made my heart race before I pressed the answering button.

"Dave," I acknowledged.

I was met with that exhaled silence that seems to last a lifetime and that normally precedes the worst news you can ever receive.

"Little John died in a car accident, Izzy," Dave blurted, just before his sobs engulfed the blow that my heart had just suffered and swallowed all the air that was left to breathe in the world.

CHAPTER 19

LIVE AND LET DIE

Little John died a good death. One without suffering. One without noticing it.

On his way home, in the middle of the night, Little John was killed by a drunk driver who rammed into the cab we'd seen him hop into while waving good-bye to us, all of us oblivious to the fact that it was his last.

They said he died instantly.

They said he felt no pain.

They said it wasn't our fault.

And Dave and I told each other the same things over and over again as we coped with Little John's death in our singular way, because our minds, although not that great, didn't just think alike; they thought the same.

So to let Little John die, we decided to live as much as we could and as best we could, because we now knew for sure that life simply wouldn't wait for us. So live and let die was all that crossed our minds. Live and let die.

Have no illusions, though; our best was very close to our worst. We cared for no wounded, for no consequences, for anyone but ourselves. We had Little John's death as a catalyst, and we had it as an excuse as well. After all, all's fair in love and war, right?

"Remember Aisha?" Dave asked me at one of our many breakfasts a couple of months after Little John's death.

"Aisha?" I asked, rummaging through my memories.

"The belly dancer I met when I made my yearlong trip . . . when I came back from the other side of the world . . ." he offered tentatively.

"Ah, yes!" I exclaimed. "The woman who lived every day as if it were her last."

"Exactly."

"What about her?" I asked, since Dave was offering nothing else.

"I've been thinking about her . . . about the way she lived her life."

"Because you suddenly found out that you want to belly dance your way around the world?" I joked.

"Izzy!" Dave scolded. "I'm serious! Why do you always have to joke about everything?" He seemed exasperated.

"Because I have a great sense of humor," I said flatly, gesturing him to carry on.

"I envy her. Her courage, her freedom, her passion," he said after a while.

"I envy her too. But I can't help thinking if her courage isn't but cowardice, her freedom but a prison, and her passion just indifference? Damn, that sounded really poetic!" I said as soon as the meaning of my own words dawned on me.

"Quick, write it down before you start springing butterflies out of your ass as well!" Dave joked, bursting into laughter.

"Asshole!" I mouthed, throwing him a bread crust that lay on my plate. "And I'm the one that jokes about everything?"

"As if you had that much to complain about," Dave accused. "I'm the one who's always been the victim at yours and Little John's hands!" The smile fell from his face as he mentioned Little John.

I smiled weakly back at him. We rarely mentioned Little John. Both of us acknowledged him silently, but we almost never spoke of him, both of us carrying his death on our consciences and mourning him wordlessly. But it was worse for Dave. Far worse.

Little John had shared Dave's life and blood from the beginning. He was his cousin, his best friend, and a part of him. And though I knew exactly what Dave felt because I too had lost a part of me before—the best part of me—I had already learned to survive without it. Dave hadn't.

"Don't you ever think we're missing out on life?" he asked after the heavy silence that had fallen upon us lifted a bit.

"All the time!" I answered, quickly and without hesitation.

"Why don't we do something about it, then?" he asked, looking me in the eyes and fidgeting.

"Who says we hav . . ." I started, stopping as soon as the meaning in his words reached me. "What are we really talking about here, Dave?" I asked in a whisper, studying his embarrassed face and almost forgetting to breathe. Almost.

Dave had been invited to teach a class at our town university, something related to art and management. It was a prestigious post, the acknowledgment of his work as a businessman in his field. I was proud of him, but I didn't tell him that. I didn't have to; he knew it. So I just nudged him in the ribs and told him not to sleep with the students.

The invitation had come right after Little John's death. At the time, Dave was too numb to see the impact that something like that could have on his growing company. He didn't care either. But I put my foot down on that one and even joined forces with Helen to convince him to grab the opportunity.

Eventually, he came around and accepted the invitation, and once he started his lectures, he was thankful that we had taken the trouble of pestering him into doing it. He felt truly accomplished, as he had never felt before. I told him that maybe that was his true calling, recalling the time when we'd met and the spread of tarot cards I had laid down for him then.

He loved the impact that his words and his teachings had in the young minds before him. However, more than that, he loved the feedback he got from his students because it made him feel young and carefree again.

"Something happened, Izzy," Dave finally said, averting my gaze.

"You're sleeping with someone, aren't you?" I asked, astonished, mostly at myself for having missed it.

He didn't answer me for a while, so we just sat at our usual table wordlessly.

"Are you going to give me shit about it?" Dave finally asked, breaking the silence.

I sighed and shrugged. "What would be the point in that? You don't need me to preach about it for you to feel bad about yourself for doing it. You already do an awesome job at it by yourself, and honestly? The only thing that I really want to know is if it was worth it!" I smirked.

Dave smirked back at me.

"So pray tell, lover boy, who's the lady?" I asked.

"Well . . . this is kind of different."

"Isn't it always?" I asked smugly. "Hey, it's not a guy, is it?"

"Please, Izzy!" Dave barked.

"What? I'm just asking . . . Plus, it wouldn't be your first," I said, raising my hands defensively as soon as I saw Dave's frown.

"It's not a guy," he assured me. "But I can guarantee you that even to my standards, this story is . . . weird, to say the least. And you of all people know how weird I've gotten before."

"Stop teasing me and just tell me who you are doing! Are you sleeping with one of your students?" I questioned, a bit dazed.

"Well, not quite!" he said. Mysteriously, I should add.

Dave had been teaching for three months, and he had already become one of the students' favorite teachers. No surprise there. After all, Dave had his charms, and he was young in spirit and in age.

Unsurprisingly as well, he was often invited by his students to go for a coffee or to a dinner party around the campus. And that's when it started, in the aftermath of one of those dinner parties.

His whole class had decided to make a class dinner. All the teachers were invited, but many didn't show up. Dave did, and he even went to the bar with his students when the dinner was over.

The music was loud, and the bar was crowded with undergraduates. Dave blended right in, and even though he was older than most of the patrons, he didn't clash. His acquired charm gave him a cool and casual look. According to the female student body, Mr. Poe was hot.

"Mr. Poe, are you married?" a girl with long white-blonde hair that he hadn't seen approaching him asked in a provocative tone.

Dave was alone by the bar, facing the dance floor and drinking his whiskey.

"Excuse me?" Dave asked, not sure if he had heard her right.

"She asked if you were married." A second girl, with short black hair, seemed to have materialized out of thin air, and she stood next to them, holding the blonde girl's hand.

"I am," Dave answered, a bit dumbfounded.

"But are you happily married?" the brunette asked, making a show of moistening her lips with her tongue while the blonde bit her bottom lip.

"Come again?" was all Dave managed to voice.

"Oh, we intend to . . . Mr. Poe." The brunette said, turning her back on Dave and dragging her friend with her.

Dave stood perplexed for a while, trying to process what the hell had just happened. He remembered the girls from his class. They sat together in the front, but he had never paid them much attention.

"Are you serious, Dave?" I said, incredulous. "You're kidding me, right? That did not happen."

"I'm not shitting you, Izzy. It happened just like that."

"Are you telling me that they just approached you out of nowhere, struck up that porn movie conversation with you, and then left you hanging there looking at their asses while they sashayed their way through the crowd?"

"Well, they went out on the dance floor and danced together. They put on quite a show." Dave sighed, clearly disturbed by the memory.

"Really? And what then? What did Chip and Dale do next?" I asked, stressing my lip.

"Chip and Dale?"

"Who cares? Do you honestly think I give a shit about their names? Just tell the rest of the story!" I urged him.

Chip and Dale dazzled the entire male student body . . . Well, all the male bodies at the bar, to be precise. There wasn't a single straight man who remained unaffected by their performance, and even the gay men stared at them, if not out of envy at least out of curiosity.

Once their little show was over, they hung around the bar for a while, evading all male attempts to strike up conversation or simply offer them a drink. When the interest seemed to have vanished, they passed by Dave, winked at him, and walked out the door.

Dave saw them in class the next day. When he finished his lecture and the students were leaving the classroom, dropping their papers on development of arts careers on his desk, Chip and Dale let themselves fall behind, and when they dropped theirs, the brunette said, "Mr. Poe, if I were you, I would read our paper first."

"And why is that?" Dave asked flatly.

"You'll find it quite . . . inviting," she said in a tantalizing tone. She then left, shadowed by the blonde-haired girl.

The first thing Dave did once he was alone was go through their paper. It was a perfectly normal paper, but at the end, they'd put an address, the following day's date, and a time. It was an invitation to show up at their house, and it didn't take a genius to know that it wasn't to have tea.

Dave dwelled on the matter the entire day and the entire night. He didn't close his eyes for a second that night, hearing Helen's soft snoring and looking at her sleeping peaceful face. He struggled, he debated, and he argued with himself until he finally accepted that he had no reason left to prevent him to go and know. To go and live again.

Yes, one could say that he was just being weak. He had Tess, and he had the obligation to respect Helen; he had promised her that much. But those were not reasons. Those were hopes, vows, obstacles, or even consequences, but they were not reasons. There would only be one reason, one single motive, that would prevent Dave from cheating on Helen: love, true love for her. He had none.

So the next day, ten minutes after the scheduled time in the paper, Dave was at the given address, knocking on the door. A few seconds later, but enough for Dave's heart to skip several beat, two smug faces were smiling at him after the door opened.

"Why didn't you tell me anything? How long have you been keeping this from me?" I demanded.

"Seriously, Izzy? That's what bugs you?" Dave asked astonished.

"It bugs me that you didn't trust me," I said sulkily after a small silence.

"Come on, Izzy. You know perfectly well that I trust you with my life!" he reasoned.

"So what, then? You couldn't possibly think that I was going to give you shit and try to persuade you not to do it," I retorted.

"That's exactly why I didn't tell you. I knew you wouldn't. I knew that only you would understand my distorted lack of reasons and that you would stand by me, without judging me, independently of my decision. So the least I could do was to respect you, man up, and not drag you with me on this one." Dave had averted my gaze, and there was a bit of pain in his voice.

"You idiot! Where's the fun in that? And anyway, who would ever believe that I didn't know?"

"I would know!" he said weakly.

"You still haven't told me how long has this been going on. Oh, and where's the weirdness about the whole thing? A threesome with two of your students? That wouldn't be a first for you. The threesome part, I mean."

"Ah, that's not the weird part . . . The weird part is that it isn't a threesome!" He laughed.

Apparently, the thing had not been going on for long, just two weeks, but it was intense, to put it lightly. And since Dave had obviously been busy, we hadn't had the chance to get together lately, so this was basically the first time we had met since the whole thing happened, apart from our conversations over the phone.

"What do you mean it's not a threesome? What do you do then? Just bang one of them?" I joked.

"Yeah!" He shrugged, nodding his head. "I bang one at the time . . . while the other one watches."

"No!"

"Yes!" Dave laughed, amused with my incredulity.

"No!" I said again, too dumbfounded to say anything else. "What do you mean by watches?" I finally managed.

"Sits nearby and observes attentively!" he mocked.

"What . . . How . . . Huh?" I grunted.

"It's the weirdest thing. They don't touch each other, and they don't touch me at the same time. So while I'm with one of them, the other one is sitting nearby and watching us."

"That's a bit creepy. So she just sits and watches you?" I asked, amazed. Dave nodded his head. "And then what?"

"Then when I'm finished with one, we wait for a bit—you know, to regrow my love stick—and then I do the other one. And the other watches."

"That's it?" I asked, incredulous.

"That's it. Every time! And they never let me alone with just one of them. And they told me to never try to contact just one of them. Oh, and they always call me Mr. Poe!"

"Now that's weird! Are they a couple . . . Mr. Poe?" I snorted.

"I don't know! I've never seen them together. The closest to that that I've seen them was at that bar, when they danced. But even then, they just teased. There wasn't anything explicit going on. I've never even seen them kiss."

"Sick," I mouthed. "So you've been with them . . . what? Four, five times?"

"Five!" Dave said, after thinking about it for a bit.

"Isn't it strange to have someone watching and waiting for her turn?" I questioned, my curiosity getting the best of me.

"In the beginning, yes, but then it kind of aroused me seeing the other one watching."

"Mr. Poe is kinky! Hey, are they pretty?"

"They're twenty years old, Izzy! Nothing bounces off of them."

"Nice, Dave. Thank you for just making me feel old! I asked if they were pretty, not how generously gravity handles their boobs and asses."

"The blonde one is cute. The brunette not so much, but she has this kick-ass attitude about her that is so alluring," Dave said, daydreaming.

"Hey, are you being careful? If they catch you, you're gonna get in trouble, right? You're not supposed to sleep with your students . . . Mr. Poe."

"Who said we get any sleep?" Dave joked. "But yeah, you're right. This is completely against the rules, and it won't look good if I get caught . . ."

"No shit, Sherlock!" I mocked.

"I think I prefer Mr. Poe."

Dave's weird sex triangle ended not long after he told me about it. He and the girls agreed that it would be wiser to end things before anyone found out.

The girls' performance in the bedroom did not affect their grades in the class. What? Dave was an impartial man, even given the circumstances!

This was the first time Dave cheated on Helen. He felt bad about it, as he knew he would. But the thrill that came along, the sense of freedom that filled him at the time, made it worth it. Or at least it eased the burden he felt on his conscience and gave some rest to his grieving soul.

There were others, of course—not many, but enough to feed Helen's suspicion slowly. He never touched the busty trainee. My guess was that it made no sense to live Little John's fantasy without him. I covered for Dave, and now I was aware of his indiscretions right from the start. After all, what would be the point in that?

After Chip and Dale, all the women who crossed Dave's path gave him hope and made him think that his life was about to change. Each time, each new woman, made him decide to leave Helen and fight for his own happiness. But then he wouldn't. At the last minute, he would pull back and return to Tess and Helen. Every time.

Dave was thirty-eight, turning thirty-nine, and age was being very kind to him. At the beginning of the new school year, he had met a colleague at the university, where he still gave his lectures as a guest teacher.

She was vibrant, full of life, and younger than he was. Not by much, though. They got along very well, and at first it was an honest and disinterested friendship. Until it became more. Then he met her younger sister, and things got complicated.

"I need your help with something, Izzy," Dave said.

"What?" I asked flatly. "Not my house again . . . You've already been there two times this week!"

"You're counting?" Dave asked, almost indignant.

"I'm not keeping track! But it's kind of hard not to notice it when I have to stall to go home because you're using my spare bedroom to bang your colleague."

"Thanks, Izzy, for putting it so nicely!" Dave said sarcastically.

"Spare me the aggrieved look, Dave! What do you need?" I asked sharply.

Dave sulked for a bit before he spoke again. "I need you to come with me to a dinner party."

"Helen's not available?" I questioned.

"Helen's not invited!"

"Ah, that kind of party! Who's going?"

"My colleague and her sister and some of their friends."

"And you need me because . . . ?" I asked, dragging out the words.

"Because I need a buffer," Dave explained.

"Care to elucidate me on this one?"

"As you know, the sister doesn't know that I'm involved with her sister, my colleague, and my colleague doesn't even dream that I've became very fond of her sister . . . and I need to keep it that way if I want a chance with the sister. And I do want a chance with the sister, Izzy!" he added.

"This is way too confusing, even for you Dave! Let me see if I've got this. You need me to go with you to this dinner as your date—what are we going to be this time . . . cousins?—so that none of the girls feels comfortable enough to get too cozy around you and expose you."

"Exactly!"

"But hadn't you already managed to convince them not to talk about you with each other?" I asked.

"I did, but this is the first time since I met the sister that I'm going to be with both of them again at the same time . . . so I'm not sure how they will react. And I don't know how well they know each other . . . so I don't want to risk it. Will you come?" Dave pleaded, giving me his best begging face.

"Dave, this is getting too messed up! Why don't you break up with your colleague?" I suggested. "In fact, why don't you stay away from both sisters?"

"I still haven't had the chance to talk with my colleague. This was all very sudden," Dave explained. "The sister thing . . . But you have to meet her, the sister, not my colleague. You'll get it when you meet her. Please, Izzy?"

"The things I do for you!" I cried out, feigning exasperation.

The thing was, Dave was having an affair with his colleague. And of course he had thought her to be the keeper of his happiness and that he was going to leave Helen this time. However, while he was going through his usual inner debate about leaving Helen, he met her sister and was rendered speechless, to put it bluntly.

He described her to me as an angel, not only in beauty but mainly in character.

Dave managed to sweet talk the sister and keep her from speaking with her sister, Dave's colleague and lover, about him. And because Dave's colleague was also in a relationship, she wasn't exactly in the position to be talkative about her affair with a married man.

Convenient, don't you think?

I, on the other hand, must admit that I was very intrigued; I had never met an angel before!

Have you ever had one of those moments in life that challenge you? Where things are put in perspective and you are compelled to act, knowing that your action, your decision, will interfere with other people's lives and change them inevitably or even drastically? Who hasn't, right? I always thought of my life as one made of those moments, especially when I met the sister that became the angel. Or was it the other way around?

Dave and I went to the dinner party, and I finally met the sisters, though one of them was already quite familiar with my spare bedroom. Dave's colleague was one of those persons who had a compelling personality. Everyone seemed drawn to her. Her sister, though, was a completely different case.

She exuded calmness and kindness, but you wouldn't feel as drawn to her as you would to her sister. Her sister was about fun; she was about something else. Goodness, I guess.

Dave sat beside me, but soon he was engaged in a conversation with the person sitting in front of him. I sat back and observed, not feeling in the mood to engage in meaningless conversations with strangers.

As if sensing my apathy, the sister came and sat by me; we started to talk. I could tell she did it for me, not to please Dave and not to make a good impression on me. It was just one of those things you sensed. So though I was not particularly in the mood, I talked to her about everything and nothing in particular. It was one of those uneventful conversations that you are unable to reproduce after it's over, because it held no pungent significance, so you just forget about it almost instantly. Nevertheless, there was one thing: throughout the entire time we talked, I couldn't manage to erase from my thoughts, though I kept trying, how heartfelt and kind she was.

But she wasn't just a good girl—one of those that are so compelling to corrupt—she was also a good person. One of those genuinely good persons that you don't come across often in life. And she was falling for Dave, if not fallen already. And from what he had told me and what I then saw in her, I could tell that it tore at her. She was at war with herself; her heart and her conscience were in a restless battle about surrender. Which one was going to come down first? Which one was about to lose?

I was lost in these thoughts when I caught her stealthily glimpsing at Dave with guilty eyes, and I knew then that my decision was made.

For the second and last time, I was about to purposefully interfere with Dave's life. So I leaned forward, and touching her lightly on the forearm for comfort and looking her straight in the eyes, I whispered, "He's been sleeping with your sister, and he's never going to leave his wife."

CHAPTER 20

IT'S FUNNY HOW FALLING FEELS LIKE FLYING, FOR A LITTLE WHILE

Here's the thing with freedom: it's overrated. We all crave it, we all long for it, but when we finally attain it, most of us just don't know what to do with it. Come to think of it, freedom sums up to a heavy burden, an illusion, because when we finally catch a glimpse of it, our first feeling is fear and our first impulse is to hold on to anything that will give us our customary sense of belonging.

When I left that dinner party with Dave, after crushing the sister's heart and hopes and, with any luck, setting her free, I was perfectly aware of the possible consequences of my actions. I just wasn't ready to face them. So I said nothing about it to Dave.

When Dave tried to contact them, he was faced with silence and rage. The sister didn't want to speak to him again, and the colleague broke it off with him. Neither of them gave him any reason or alluded to knowing about his antics with both of them, though it was implicit. I sighed in relief and waved away the nagging fear of Dave finding out that I was to blame for all that.

Therefore, throughout his confusion, angst, and lack of understanding about the sister's sudden withdrawal, I remained mute. Throughout his astonishment, hurt, and disbelief about his colleague's inexplicable contempt, I did not utter a word.

And throughout all that, my guilt or my fear—which one was it, anyway?—grew bigger and bigger, and when I thought I had no space left in me to house it, I would find one more free inch to accommodate it. And then one more. And then another.

"Hey! I wasn't expecting you!" I said as I opened the door.

Dave stormed into my house abruptly, not giving me time to react. Then I saw the rage on his face, and I felt all my blood draining from me. He had found out.

"Do you know who I just ran into, Izzy?" he asked, his voice as sharp as knives.

I said nothing. I just stood in front of him, trying to gather up the courage to speak.

"By the look on your face, I can see you already guessed!" he continued. "That's right! My colleague's sister . . . you know, the one you told that I was having an affair with her sister and that I was never leaving Helen."

I still said nothing.

"In fact, that's why they never spoke to me again. Makes sense now, doesn't it? And here I was brooding over this, trying to understand what had happened, when I could have just asked you!" Dave said sarcastically.

"It's not what you think. I can explain," I managed, realizing immediately how pathetic I sounded.

"What?" he mouthed, disbelief still vivid in his eyes. He was still hoping that it wasn't true, that there was another explanation.

"It's true," I started.

"Why, Izzy? Why the fuck did you do that?" Dave shouted, cutting me off.

That was quick! I remember thinking. Dave went from disbelief to astonishment and from there to rage, in less than ten seconds. Not bad.

"Don't shout at me!" I cried back.

"All this time and you just let me brood over this without saying a word?" he shouted. "What the fuck, Izzy? Why did you say that to her? But mostly, why did you do this to me? Why?"

"I'm sorry, but I had to!" I said, starting to feel the trembling in my voice.

"You had to?" Dave snapped. "You had to, Izzy?"

"She was a good girl, Dave . . ." I started.

He cut me off. "I know! That's why I liked her!"

"No, Dave, that's why you wanted her!" I said firmly.

"Same thing!" he snarled. "And what's with the I'm never leaving Helen comment?" He snarled again, pacing my living room and running his hands through his hair.

"It's not the same thing, Dave! You were just going to fuck her and dump her like you do every time! And she deserves better than that . . ."

"Are you judging me, Izzy? Who the fuck are you to judge me?" Dave shouted, out of his mind.

"I'm not judging you! I'm just saying things as they are!" I shouted back, not managing to keep calm.

"Are you? Who died and made you the owner of the truth? Why don't you turn all that clairvoyance at yourself before you point your finger at me?"

"This is not about me, Dave," I tried to reason.

"Isn't it? Why did you tell her that I was sleeping with her sister? That I was never leaving Helen?"

"Because she deserves better than to fall for you and be left hanging . . . You were just going to break her heart."

"Now you're Madre Teresa?" he asked with acridity.

"For fuck's sake, Dave!" I cried out, exasperated. "Just get your head out of your ass and join the rest of us down here in the world." I sighed loudly. "Stop fucking with people's lives and man up! You can't keep cheating on Helen, breaking all these women's hearts, and telling yourself that it's all right!"

"You're such a hypocrite, Izzy! Since when do you care about Helen? You never even liked her. You helped me cheat on her!"

"You're right. I don't give a shit about Helen! I never did. and I never will. And I did help you cheat on her, and I did cover for you, and I did all that willingly! But none of that makes it right!"

"Now you're worried about making it right? Now?" Dave shook his head in disbelief.

"I'm not trying to make anything right, but there's a limit! And to me, the limit was that girl. If I even hoped you might fall for her, I would not have said a thing. But you weren't going to, Dave, and we both know it . . ."

"No, Izzy, you don't know. You thought, as you always do, that you knew! Because you think you're always right and full of shit, but you're not! You're just bitter and can't see beyond it."

"Is that so?" I snarled. "Tell me something, then: Were you in love with that girl? Were you going to leave Helen to be with her? What was different this time? What did she have that was going to make you finally take that step?"

"You didn't let me find out, did you?"

"For the love of God, Dave, grow up!" I snapped. "Stop sabotaging your marriage, grow a pair, and ask Helen for a divorce!"

"You're such a . . . bitch!" Dave bellowed, and we both fell silent for a second as his words dawned on us, making us both gasp. But he continued nevertheless. "At least I'm ruining my own marriage, not other people's marriages! You're not so fond of doing the right thing when it comes to you, are you? It must be great to be able to live with double standards!"

"Fuck you, Dave! Just fuck you!" I shouted.

"Yeah, I thought so! It's not that great to hear the truth about yourself, is it? At least I'm trying with Helen. I might fuck it up, but I'm still there when she needs me!"

"This isn't about me. This is about you and your fucked up way of messing up people's lives!" I said, all the bitterness in the world dripping from my words. "And don't even pretend that you give a shit about Helen, because you don't! If you did, you would have already divorced her. You would have broken things off with her before you broke her. But no, you keep doing the same shit over and over again because you enjoy feeling sorry for yourself! Why don't you feel sorry for your daughter instead? She has you for a father! A man whore!"

"You leave Tess out of this!" Dave said, slowly and with so much hate in his voice that I flinched when he stepped up to me. We were only a foot apart. "I am not to blame for your messed-up life and all the shit that you cling to in order to justify your bitterness! Don't you ever fuck with my life again!"

"Get the fuck out of my house!" I cried, stepping back.

Dave locked his gaze on mine and shook his head. We both had unshed tears prickling our eyes. He turned his back on me and left my house, slamming the door on his way out. The last thing he said: "Goodbye, Isabella."

I sank to the ground and swallowed every single tear that threatened to fall from my eyes, my heart, and my soul. I feared that if I let even one of them fall, I would never be able to stop them again. I felt so trapped. Wasn't the truth supposed to set you free? Clearly, freedom is overrated.

Dave didn't call or show up. And neither did I. Not that week, or the following, or the one after that. That's when I stopped counting the weeks and started counting the months.

One.

Two.

Three months.

Dave still didn't call. I didn't either.

One Monday morning, after the fourth month had passed, I drove by our coffee shop to see if he would be there, at our usual table. He wasn't.

My birthday passed, the third one after Little John's death, and Dave said nothing at all.

A few days later, I ran into Helen at the supermarket.

"Hey, Helen!" I greeted uncomfortably.

"Isabella!" She said, not masking her surprise.

"Everything okay?" I asked politely, looking around.

"He's not here," she said. "I'm fine." She sighed after my "Oh!" when I acknowledged Dave's absence. "And you?" Helen asked.

"I'm fine," I answered, and we fell silent. "Tess?" I asked.

"Tess is great! You know, all grown up and opinionated," she offered, clearly glad to be able to voice a sentence with more than three words.

I smiled politely back at her and nodded my head, signaling that I knew what she was talking about. "Well, I have to get going. It was nice to see you," I said, walking past her.

"He's sad," Helen said as I walked away from her, making me slow my pace. I nodded my head almost imperceptibly and resumed my walking. I was sad too.

For days, I entertained the thought that Dave would call once Helen told him that she had run into me at the supermarket. Had she told him? I decided she had. Helen's biggest flaw was her love for Dave. Despite the shadow that I cast over their relationship, Helen knew that Dave was miserable without me, as I was without him. And it pained her more to see him like that than to endure our complicity, our friendship, our dependency on one another, and her exclusion from all that.

Dave didn't call, though. Neither did I.

One more month came and went.

Then one weekend, in the very early hours of the morning, I woke up to the sound of my phone ringing. It was Helen.

I felt the familiar pang of adrenaline rush through my system and the air around me getting thicker. I grabbed the phone and was about to press the answer button when instinct prevented me from doing it.

Helen had never called me before, not a single time in the nine years we'd known each other. And I had never called her. Not once. Not ever.

I breathed deeply and exhaled slowly, trying to calm myself down, trying to think through all that. Why was Helen calling me when she had never called? Especially now.

Had something happened?

Something must have happened.

And then it occurred to me that something had indeed happened but Helen didn't know what. That was why she was calling me. She wanted to know if I knew anything about Dave, if I knew where he was. And she must have been desperate if she was calling me. If there was one thing that I knew, it was that Helen, with all her kindness and class, would never call me if something had really happened to Dave. She would tell me that he was sad, and she might even tell him that she had run into me at the store and that I was sad too, but she didn't have it in her to call me and tell me that he needed me . . . more than she thought that he needed her.

I understood. It was simply too much.

I exhaled deeply again. The wheels in my head were starting to turn, and things were getting clearer. If she called me, I thought, she'd called everyone else already, and that must include the hospitals and police stations . . . What if he had been in an accident in the middle of nowhere and still hadn't been found? *Why would he be in the middle of nowhere?* I thought. How would I know? We hadn't spoken to each other in six months. I sighed. There was only one way to find out. I picked up my phone and dialed Dave. He answered when I was about to hang up.

"Izzy," he said with a hoarse voice.

"Helen is looking for you . . . She called me," I said hesitantly.

"Oh! I fell asleep and lost track of time. I was just looking at her missed calls and trying to come up with something to tell her. What did you say to her?"

"I didn't talk to her. I figured that if she was calling me, she had already called everyone else and she didn't know if anything had happened to you," I explained. "That's why I'm calling you . . . What do you need me to tell her?"

Dave sighed, and I could sense the uneasiness in his voice when he requested a favor. "You don't mind?" he then asked.

"I never did, Dave," I muttered.

"Thanks," he said, and he hung up the phone after lingering for a moment in the silence that stood between us.

I went to the kitchen and made myself a cup of coffee. Then I called Helen and told her that Dave was sleeping in my spare bedroom. I told her that he had showed up at my house last night and we had gotten drunk and made our truce. In our stupor, neither of us had remembered to call her or text her, letting her know of Dave's whereabouts.

She thanked me and asked me to tell her husband to call her when he woke up. I told her that I would deliver the message to Dave as soon as he woke up. And then I hung up, noticing that not a shred of guilt pinched at my conscience for having lied to Helen.

I went back to my room and dressed quickly, anxiety flooding my body. I couldn't stay there, so I went outside, sat on the doorsteps, and waited, immersed in my thoughts and unable to focus on anything other than the thumping of my heart. When I saw Dave's car approaching, my heart raced faster, if that was even possible.

He had already seen me.

Dave stepped out of his car and stood rigidly staring at me. I stared back at him and stood up, my arms crossed in a strange self-embrace. He began to walk the small path between us with slow and unsure steps first, and then, when he saw me walking toward him, he just let go of all doubts and ran to me. And I ran back to him, throwing myself in his arms.

I don't know how long we stayed there, entangled and soothing each other. My eyes were prickling with the same unshed tears that had outlived our fight.

"I'm sorry. I'm so sorry, Dave!" I muttered into his chest, almost unable to breathe, such was the force he was holding on to me.

"I'm sorry too." He hushed me, running his fingers through my hair and kissing the top of my head. "You stubborn, stubborn, Izzy!" He sighed.

"Look who's talking," I joked lightly. "Let's go inside." I grabbed hold of his hand and pulled him along with me.

Once we were inside, he ruffled my hair and bumped his shoulder goofily against mine, never letting go of my hand.

"Pest!" I cried out.

"Witch!" he cried back.

And with that, we fell right back into what we were, as if nothing had happened, as if nothing had been said. But it had, and though none of us wanted to talk about it, we knew we had to eventually.

"You're a jerk!"

"I missed you too, Izzy!" Dave grinned.

"How was life without me?"

"Great! Couldn't be better. All that peace and quiet, you know, from not having you constantly nagging me . . ."

"That bad, hmm?" I winked at him.

"Yeah, that bad . . . Yours?" He laughed.

"Same thing, though I did hear that you were kind of sad," I probed.

"I heard that you looked kind of sad," he countered.

"I see that we had the same informer," I said, and Dave nodded his head. We exchanged an ashamed smile, acknowledging Helen's kindness.

"Hey, I talked to my father!" Dave said, changing the subject.

"What? When? Why?" I stammered, surprised by his news.

"Well, I had been thinking about it for some time—we discussed this, remember?—and I decided that I had to at least try to make my peace with it. So I went to talk to him, met my teenage brother, and spoke my mind." Dave shrugged.

"And?" I urged.

"And that was it. He didn't say much back. Just stood there shaking his head with a patronizing smile on his face . . . and I realized you were right. I can't expect him to change, because he never will. I just have to accept that and learn to live with it."

"And have you?" I asked.

"I'm working on it." He smirked, locking his gaze with mine.

We stared at each other for a moment, acknowledging that the time for us to make amends had arrived. We had to talk about what had happened.

"I'm sorry about the things I said to you . . . I didn't mean . . ." I faltered.

"You meant every word you said to me, Izzy," Dave said flatly. "If there's one thing I know about you, it's that you always mean the things you say."

"Oh!" I gasped. "I did mean them," I admitted. "But I didn't mean to be so harsh. I did want to hurt you, though."

"You did hurt me. We can't say you went easy on the words . . . or rather, you kind of did go *Izzy* on them!" he joked, but the smile never reached his eyes.

"I'm sorry . . . for hurting you," I stammered.

"I know. And I'm sorry for hurting you too."

"So . . . am I forgiven?" I asked sheepishly.

"You have been for a while now." Dave grinned, averting his eyes from mine coyly.

"What? Why haven't you called me, then?"

"For the same reason you didn't call me!"

"You thought that I still hadn't forgiven you?" I asked, perplexed. It hadn't occurred to me.

"Well, you didn't call. I thought you were still mad at me . . . You're kind of scary when you're mad. And when you're not as well," he joked.

We laughed and grimaced at each other, falling silent for a bit. We wanted to savor the moment.

"You know what the hardest part was for me?" Dave asked, not waiting for my answer. "The betrayal. Knowing that if you wanted to, you could deceive me without it even crossing my mind."

"I didn't betray you, Dave. I omitted . . ." I said, weakly.

"It sure felt like it, Izzy. And I'm not referring to your telling that girl that I was banging her sister and all. I'm referring to afterward. Why didn't you come clean? You had plenty of opportunities to do it. Fuck! I was bitching about it to you every day."

"I know, and I'm sorry about it, but as time went by, it just made less and less sense to tell you. It wouldn't change anything, and eventually you would forget about it."

"I know, but it was a low blow, Izzy."

I acquiesced. "Are you hungry? I can make us some eggs," I offered after a small silence.

"Yeah, I'm starving. It's been a long night, and I need my stamina back," he noted smugly.

"You are just dying to tell me about your new conquest, aren't you?" I mocked. "You're getting careless, though. What possessed you to fall asleep at her house?"

He grinned and mischievously winked an eye at me. I threw an oven mitt at his face in response.

She was a twenty-something flight attendant who just wanted to have fun and had no wish to be the owner of Dave's heart. Smart girl, right? Dave, on the other hand, had no wish whatsoever to give her his heart or hold hers in return. And that, that carefree and no-strings-attached exchange between them, made Dave realize that he couldn't carry on like that. Helen deserved better, much better, and he had to let her go.

"It's strange, but I feel like I hit the bottom in my marriage . . . but without all the angst and degradation that normally comes with it. It's more like a sense of freedom," he said. "Do you remember that music from that film about a decadent country singer . . . You kept singing it over and over again."

"Funny how fallin' feels like flyin', for a little while," I sang, tapping my feet.

"Yeah, that's the one! It keeps coming to my mind. I know I'm falling, but it feels like flying. Does it make any sense to you?"

"Dave, that music could be the soundtrack of your life right now!" I sneered.

"Yeah . . . but I also keep thinking about that last part, the one that says that it's only for a little while."

"Don't you ever think what Helen would do if she found out?" I asked. "Do you think she knows?"

"I used to think about it, but I don't anymore. I think that sometimes she suspects . . . but then her suspicions just seem to fade. I think that she has too much faith in me."

"What do you plan to do now that you've finally realized that you can't keep going on like this?" I asked.

"I'm going to find the best way to work things out with Helen, without unnecessary drama . . ."

I cut him off. "Dave, there is no best way to resolve that marriage of yours, and if you keep stalling, the shit will most likely hit the fan."

"Not if I can prevent it."

Turns out, he couldn't.

When Dave went home that Sunday morning, Helen was waiting for him. She was devastated.

When I called her to tell her that Dave was sleeping at my house, Helen, in a boost of rage after we hung up, decided to come there to wake up Dave herself. When she arrived there, she had a front-row view of Dave's and my reconciliation and, of course, the meanings behind it.

Neither of us had even noticed her.

Neither of us ever did.

CHAPTER 21

DAVE'S LAST MARIA

"Helen called you a bitch."

"Ouch! Do you think she meant it?" I asked out of curiosity.

"Nahhh." Dave dragged out the word. "I think she just wanted me to tell you that she had. She knew I would, and I guess we owe her that much."

"I guess we do," I agreed, shrugging. "Hey, are you off to bed already?" I asked when Dave got up from the couch.

"Yeah. You're not coming?"

"Not yet, pumpkin. I have to finish this first," I said, motioning my chin to the laptop that rested on my legs.

"I swear to God, Izzy, you call me pumpkin one more time and I'm going to do nasty things to you!" he grumbled, but he was smiling.

"You promise?" I asked, raising my brows suggestively while Dave rolled his eyes at me. "What? We're living together! I'm entitled to have a term of endearment to call you. And I'm not calling you something as cheesy as *love!*" I shouted as he left the living room and headed to the bedroom, still grumbling. "You know I like my vegetables!" I added, shouting, knowing that he still could hear me. I heard the door slamming, and I couldn't help from grinning; Dave loved to be theatrical.

The next day, I woke up to the smell of coffee. Dave still made awful coffee and, against all common sense, persisted at the task.

"Good morning, sunshine!" he said as I walked into the kitchen.

"I'm not drinking that shit, pumpkin," I said, passing him by without grabbing hold of the mug he was trying to hand me.

"Ah! Such a lady! Such manners!" Dave said, apparently unaffected by my rudeness.

"Not all of us can be Helens, you know?"

"I'll be in the living room ignoring you, okay?" Dave said, disregarding my tantrum and turning his back on me. That simply.

Dave and I had been living together for almost two months, so by then he was more than used to my bittersweet attitude upon wakening. He wouldn't even be bothered to be mad or offended by my occasional crude retorts. After all, that was how we were with each other. And that was how I wanted to remember us.

Even now, after three years have passed over this memory of us living together, this is how I want to remember us: teasing each other. So I smile slightly while I keep my head dropped almost to my knees and nested between my hands. And I breathe. I breathe all the air that I can, as if it is about to end anytime before my next breath. Why are these places always so impersonal? Why do we have to hold our hearts and our souls in cold places like this? Why is this waiting so agonizing? What can we do but hope?

Right now, all I want is not to be here, holding my soul, waiting, and relying only on hope. I want to hold on to that time when we were living together and it seemed things were finally going to be okay.

Even we were okay. Throughout the adversities, the changes, the happenings, the setbacks, and the mishaps, we remained immutable, we found each other, and we remained okay.

But right now, we're not okay, and I don't know how I will find Dave between here and now, or if I will find him there again.

And all I can do is wait and hope.

But all I can think is *what if*?

What if things had been different? What if this was how it was supposed to happen? What if this was how it was meant to be?

What if?

Those words haunt me now, but back then—on the day Dave asked me, "What if, Izzy?"—I had no doubts.

Dave had been struggling to keep those thoughts at bay for so many years that at some point, he thought that they had been gone for good. So at first, when it was only the glimpses and the occasional absentmindedness, he didn't pay attention to them. They were just inconsequent flashes that popped in his head and went away faster than they had appeared.

But then they became more. They became an itch, an urge, and an affliction.

That's when I started to notice them, but I didn't ask. I saw them too, but I wanted him to know, to be sure. I didn't want to plant ideas in his head. Therefore, I did nothing. I waited instead.

As time inevitably passed, I saw the conflict grow inside him . . . What if?

He dwelt on it. He let himself be consumed by angst, by doubt, by uncertainty, and by fear before he came back to the same question, repeatedly: *What if?*

Unlike all the other situations in his life where he had plunged headfirst because he simply needed to know, Dave didn't let the unknown lead him this time. He feared the consequences of knowing more than the blessings of ignorance, for this was all or nothing and there was no coming back, no possible remedy. That's what he thought, because this was Dave. Therefore, necessarily, there had to be some drama, some flare. Otherwise, it wouldn't be worth it; otherwise, this wouldn't be the one story of all Dave's stories that Dave always told better than I did.

He always started it by saying that it was August and it rained.

Then he would say that the smell of earth filled the air as he lounged lazily on the couch. He was thinking about her. Lately it was all that he thought about. At first, it was only the small things: how she couldn't stop laughing at one of his stupid jokes, how she bit her lip when she was thinking, what she had said about a song.

But then he couldn't stop noticing the big things as well: the way she laughed when she really laughed, how her hair always came loose on the right side first, the way she talked about things.

Then he just couldn't simply stop noticing. All this time and suddenly he couldn't stop noticing. Sure, he had noticed before, he had always noticed; she was a woman, he was a man. He noticed! But not like that. They were friends. Sure, there was the ever-present underlying attraction. But there was also a limit, and he had never crossed that limit. He had been close, but he had never crossed it, because from there on, there was no coming back and too much was at stake.

What if she didn't feel the same? What if their time had passed? What if it didn't work? What if he was wrong?

But what if he wasn't?

Time wasn't doing anything to appease his torment. Each day that passed, the doubt weighted more, his feelings burned more, and he grew more desperate.

To think that she had always been there, within his reach, and he had missed it. Or maybe he just didn't want to see it before and now she was all he saw.

Dave exhaled deeply and ran his hands through his hair. He couldn't continue like this. As much as he feared it, he had to do something. He eyed his mobile phone resting beside him on the couch and picked it up, sighing deeply one more time. He searched for the number he knew by heart and pressed call.

"We need to talk," Dave said as soon as I picked up the phone.

"Okay."

"Are you at home?"

"Yes."

"I'll be there in twenty," he said, hanging up the phone.

Twenty minutes later, he was knocking at my door, not giving me much time to dwell on the matter.

He walked in with an unsteady pace and avoided my gaze.

"So?" I urged as Dave stood mutely in my living room for more time than I found reasonable as a prelude to any kind of conversation.

"Have you ever thought *what if*, Izzy?" he blurted out, in a way that made me think he was feeling actual physical pain.

"So many times that I lost count, Dave!" I answered honestly.

"Did you reach any conclusion?" he asked, fidgety.

"Well, I concluded that the answer to that question normally depends on the conclusion you're after," I said, half-serious.

"Don't go cryptic on me, Izzy. Don't do that to me, not now . . . please," he begged, all flustered.

"Ah, I see! We are having one of those conversations!" I said, realization dawning on me. "For real!" I added.

"I guess we finally are," he said, sitting down on the couch at last and patting the place next to him, indicating that he wanted me to sit there. I didn't. I sat on the other end of the couch, and that wasn't lost on him.

"So . . ." I said, my lips curling slightly despite all my attempts not to smile.

Dave smiled coyly at me and sighed deeply. "God, this is difficult!" he said, exasperated.

"It's only me, Dave. Go ahead . . . Say what you came here to say!" I encouraged.

"Will you tell me what I want to hear then?" he asked hopefully, attempting a charming smile.

I laughed and shook my head no. "I'll say what I have to say if there's anything to say," I offered, winking my eye at him.

"That seems fair!" He nodded. "I'm kind of nervous, which is stupid, but I am." He sighed again. "Well, for a while now, I've been noticing . . . I've been feeling different about . . . God, I sound like a girl!" He grumbled to himself.

"I'd noticed," I said, trying to ease up things for him.

"How long have you known?" he asked, startled by my easiness.

"Known what?" I asked, pretending to be dumbfounded.

"Come on! You already know what I came here to tell you, don't you? You're not gonna make me say it, are you?" he pleaded.

"Every single word of it, Dave! And you're very lucky that I'm not making you kneel in front of me and spell it out. Go on . . . I'm waiting here!" I urged as he looked at me, thwarted but perfectly aware that I was not making a request.

He inhaled deeply before he started to speak.

"I am a fucking cliché! It took me years to realize that the woman of my dreams had always been in front of me and I was too blind to see her . . . Satisfied?" he asked, resigned.

"Very much!" I smirked mischievously.

"You are a wicked woman!"

"I would say that's why you love me, but given the circumstances, I guess that's something I shouldn't be saying right now."

"You know . . . all the fun is gone now. Here I was, thinking I was going to surprise you! I can't keep any sort of secret from you!" Dave threw a pillow at me. "Why didn't you say anything to me?" he asked, a bit wounded. "Why did you let me go through all this alone?"

"Because you had to figure it out by yourself! I didn't want to put any ideas in that stubborn head of yours . . . and I wasn't sure myself. I suspected it, but that was all—a suspicion, a possibility."

"You weren't sure? But you are now, aren't you?" he asked, apprehensive.

I gave him a reassuring smile and said nothing.

"This is very confusing to me! I never fell in love like this. Hell, I don't even know if I fell in love or if I've simply been in love all this time. It's completely different . . . It's calm and warm but consuming at the same time. It's not like those other times, when I felt as if I had been run over by a train and everything was intense and passionate, and then one day just wasn't anymore. Now I just know. Really know," he said, standing up.

"Are you sure?" I asked, smiling.

"It's strange, but even with all these questions, I know that I have never been surer of anything in my life!" he said, locking his gaze with mine. "And now what? What am I supposed to do now?" Dave asked, moving slowly toward my end of the couch.

"Now you get your lady!" I joked.

"Come here, my little witch!" Dave said, grabbing hold of my hands and pulling me toward him in a swift movement that had me landing in his arms.

I hugged him fiercely before I loosened our embrace so I could crook my head back and look him in the eyes. He smiled sweetly at me. Raising myself on my tiptoes, I stretched out my hand toward his face and tapped his nose lightly with the tip of my forefinger. "Behave," I whispered. "And now go turn that Almost Mary of yours into a Definitively Mary!"

"She's out of town. She'll be back over the weekend, though!" he offered, letting go of me.

"Ah! So you'll have to wait a couple of days to declare all that love . . . Do you think you'll manage and not combust?" I teased him.

"I've managed this far, but I'm scared to shit of it . . . Do you think she feels the same?" he asked fearfully.

"Hmm . . . I think you might have a chance!" I winked and smiled broadly at him. He sighed in relief.

"You'd better be right; otherwise, you're gonna hear from me," he threatened playfully, his eyes resting on the television remote. "Hey, let's watch a movie!" Dave plopped himself down on the couch again.

"Only if I can pick it!" I said, grabbing hold of the remote before he had time to do it. "I made pudding. Do you want some?" I asked, while I surfed the channels in search of the ones that had movies.

"You made pudding? Nobody makes pudding! People bake cakes," he said, his eyes glued on the television screen.

"Lots of people make pudding!" I countered.

"Is it one of those box puddings?" he asked.

"No! I made it from scratch," I said proudly.

"Hmm. How bad is it?" he asked, still looking at the screen, but I could see the smirk on his face.

"It's not that bad, actually. But it looks shitty." I shrugged.

"Don't you want to grab some for me?" he asked, and I just looked at him and raised my brow. "Pretty please?" he tried. I raised my brow even higher. "Fine, I'll do it myself! But I don't know where things are!" He groaned and stood up, heading to the kitchen.

"Atta boy!" I mocked, swatting him on the backside when he walked past me. "And you know exactly where everything is. You lived here for two months last year, so don't give me crap, pumpkin!" I scolded playfully.

I heard the commotion in the kitchen as Dave went through the cabinets and drawers in search of what he needed.

"Izzy?" he shouted.

"What?" I shouted back.

"What do you think is best? A plate or a bowl?"

"It's pudding, Dave. You use a bowl, for Christ's sake!"

Dave always liked the pudding part of the story best. He said it gave the most faithful portrait of us. Though I agreed with him, I always liked the other part more because it was an open window to Dave's soul. At forty-one, still nothing scared him more than having to deal with his feelings and saying them aloud. After all he'd been through, he still didn't trust himself to be sure that what he felt was finally for real. And the irony of it wasn't amiss either. For someone who had spent most of his life trying to feel, Dave was scared to death when he finally did.

Dave's last Maria, who'd gone from New Mary to Almost Mary to Definitively Mary, was scared too. She shared Dave's fears. If things didn't work, they wouldn't be able to simply go back to what they were, because that would be hopelessly gone by then.

They'd known each other since they could remember. She was the girl next door, the platonic love upheld in the glass dome, the girl that had been there all along and the one that had never left that special place in Dave's heart, where only she had been allowed to enter at a time when they were still innocent enough.

None of it could be more cliché even if Dave had tried.

So when Maria said all that to Dave, she finished with the one question she needed Dave to answer: "What if things don't work out, Dave?"

Dave gave her all the answers she needed when he responded, "What if they do, Maria?"

She launched herself into his arms, and that's where she's been ever since.

Dave had finally found his heart, and this time it was for good. After all the women, all the heartbreaks, all the illusions and eclipses, he had finally found the person he had never been looking for, who had always been there and didn't need to be found.

After they'd been together for almost a year, I recall asking Dave if he still looked at other women. He told me yes, of course. If he was at the supermarket and a hot girl crossed his path, he inevitably would notice her and think she had a nice ass or nice rack, but then his mind would immediately go back to wondering where the hell the dish detergent was.

That made me laugh. Things had changed, but he was still Dave, after all.

To think that that day over three years ago, when Dave left my house after we made our peace, he still thought that he could prevent life from happening. But that day he went home to a devastated yet dignified Helen, who asked him for a divorce. She didn't demand any explanations from him, and she didn't even ask him why. But she asked how many and if I'd known all along. That's the thing about Helen; she had never been able to read Dave, but she had always been able to see through us and through our friendship. She had never feared me as a woman, but she had always been terrified of me as a part of Dave's soul.

Dave told her everything, mostly to appease his own conscience and lighten the burden of having to carry in his heart the burn that Helen's pained eyes left there when she looked at him with utter disgust.

At first, I couldn't understand her masochism, and I even scolded Dave for telling her that much. What good would it serve her? What was the point of hurting her beyond the inevitable? Then I realized that she needed something to grab on to so that she could hate him. She didn't need anything to despise me, though.

Dave left their home the next day, after a night on the couch, and moved into my spare bedroom for two months, until he straightened out his life. Tess, who was almost nine at the time, had no alternative but to watch her mother's pain up close and personal and grow her own, making hers and Dave's relationship a very hard one. She stopped talking to me at some point.

Though not that dramatically, even Dave's family nurtured Helen's pains. She was, after all, a Poe. Dave and I got sideway looks from Dave's cousins and uncles and an epic reprimand from his mother. Yes, I was reprimanded too. Somehow, after Little John's death and in Dave's family's eyes, Dave and I had become sort of an entity. Sometimes I even suspected that some of them thought of us as just one person, though lodged in two different bodies. Ultimately, I even found myself waiting for the day that Great-Aunt Carol would call me Steve. Yet I was not a Poe . . . I was just part of one. And I don't know exactly why or how, but apparently judgment and morals sort of belonged in my part and hence were my responsibility. So I got scolded as well when Dave's extramarital activities reached his mother's ears. The only good thing about it was that we felt like we were fifteen again.

*   *   *

I can't help but snort when the memory of Dave's mother's furious face comes to my mind. Now it's somewhat funny, but then it had been scary as hell. I sigh. Those were strange times, and this is definitely a strange place to be remembering all this, though right now all I have are memories.

"I'm going to grab some coffee. Do you want me to bring you some?" someone asks me.

"Sure. Thanks," I say, raising my head.

I look across the impersonal room and see Maria curled up alone in one of the corners. Had she been there all along? I didn't see her when I came in. I stand up and make my way up there.

"Thanks for calling me," I say.

She looks up, apparently confused by my words.

"Helen wouldn't have . . ." I offer.

"Oh!" she says, understanding finally.

I sit beside her, and we remain silent. Dave and Maria have been together for more than a year now. It's been a little over three years since Dave's marriage ended, and up to today, nothing much has changed. We still have our Monday morning breakfasts, though we go to a different place every week because we don't want to conform. When you reach forty, you'll get it. Maria and I are not friends, but she respects Dave's and my friendship.

The only actual change is that Dave's heart stopped a few hours ago and he is having emergency surgery right now, while we, his family and friends, wait in the hospital waiting room. I look around and can't help thinking that we look like the shrapnel of a bombshell. We're all scattered around the room, bearing the pain on our own and dealing with the nagging fear all by ourselves.

We've been told that the odds aren't good.

But in these times, there's always God, so we pray, hope, and wait.

"He'll be fine!" I say, trying to reassure both of us. "Besides, neither God nor the devil would know what to do with him, anyway," I joke, and Maria gives a little chuckle.

"God, Izzy, I'm so frightened! What if . . ."

"He'll be fine. Nothing is going to happen!" I'd cut her off midsentence, and then we were both out of words.

We stay like that for what feels like an eternity. Meanwhile, I sip at the coffee that someone brought me, and Maria sits there unmoving. She's terrified. I am too, but I know he'll make it—because I can't bear it any other way.

"You want to hear something funny?" I ask, breaking the silence. I'm not looking at Maria, but I know she is listening, so I just keep on going without waiting for her answer. "When Dave and I lived abroad, there was this guy there that Dave and Little John were sort of friends with. He was a total player, always chasing girls . . . You know, the whole notch in the bedpost kind of guy. But he had this thing about him. When he took girls to his house, he always asked them to strip from the waist down first. If they were hairy down there, he would ask them to shave themselves with a shaver that he had bought just for that. Otherwise, he wouldn't touch them. And they did! They always shaved!" I say, letting a snort escape.

Maria looks at me, dumbfounded. "Is there a point to that story, Izzy?" she asks, a bit wary.

"None whatsoever!" I say, and she chuckles. "But it's a stupid story that always makes me laugh when I picture the girls' faces when the guy is handing them the shaver . . . and we could use a laugh right now." I shrug, and she starts laughing.

"It *is* a stupid story!" she says, still smirking. "Why didn't they refuse?"

"For the same reason they obliged!" I tell her.

"Because they desperately want to get laid?" Maria whispers tentatively, looking around to see if anyone can hear us.

"Because they think that if they do it, he will care more about them," I say, while nodding my head no to her question.

Maria smiles shyly at my answer.

"You know, Izzy, Dave told me once that you had a way of seeing things that made them seem clearer. Now I see what he meant by that."

I give her a faint smile, acknowledging the compliment.

"When I met you the first time, I had this feeling about you. It was like something told me that you were different from any other girl that Dave had spoken about."

"How come?" she asks, looking at me, her curiosity spiked.

"He respected you; that was obvious. But what got my attention was that he moved differently around you. I can't explain it better. But at the time, I recall that even then, the thought of you being the one—as Dave likes to put it—crossed my mind."

She smiles a bit. "You know, Izzy, I thought the same about you . . ."

"I would be surprised if you hadn't!" I deadpan, not missing that she tries to mask the jolt that my unexpected words cause her. "Maria, I still haven't met a woman that is perfectly comfortable with Dave's and my friendship. And I get it. I do." "No, that's not what I meant. I do get your friendship. It's just that when I met you back then, I thought that there was something between you two. I just didn't get why you didn't date. You seemed to get along so well. You know, with all your private jokes and your nodding and stares that speak volumes without you two uttering a word. Sometimes it seems that there's a talk going on between you guys and nobody else can hear it. It's . . . unnerving."

I smile at her rambling. "Have you figured it out?"

"Have I figured what out?" Maria asks, confused.

"Why we never dated . . ." I offer.

"Yeah, you're just friends!" she says, unconvinced.

I correct her. "No. We're friends."

"Why do you always say that? I've heard you say that before."

"Well, because that's what we are. The 'just' sort of devalues how we see each other." I sigh. "Does our friendship bother you, Maria?" I ask finally.

"Honestly, Izzy?" she replies, not looking at me, and I know I'm not supposed to answer her. "I would be lying if I didn't tell you that sometimes it does." She exhales. "I get it that you two have come a long way and that you have this weird connection . . . but sometimes I can't keep from questioning why am I not enough? Why does he need you so much?" "Would you be more comfortable if I were like Dave's surrogate sister or something?" I venture.

"That's another thing!" she exclaims. "If anyone asks you if you're brother and sister you both just say *no* with so much drama that nobody dares to continue on the subject." She sighs, fidgeting. "What if Dave got it wrong, Izzy? Doesn't it ever cross your mind? What if you're the one? What if you're the one that who has been there all along and he just doesn't see it?" She finally asks.

I exhale deeply, letting out the air that I hadn't realized that I was holding. I turn to her, locking our gazes and making sure that she will listen to what I'm about to say.

"Maria, you're asking the wrong questions," I tell her. "Dave and I are friends because that was what was left for us to be. We are not siblings because, though we feel like that about each other most of the time, Dave is too loyal and respectful of my memories to dare claim that place in my soul. You see, Maria, my only brother died when I was seventeen. He was my whole world, the best part of me and my soul. There's no replacement for that. That's why Dave and I never refer to ourselves as surrogate siblings or talk of our friendship as a fraternity."

"I'm sorry, Izzy. I didn't know . . ." she mutters uncomfortably.

"And we were never lovers either," I continue, ignoring her sympathies. "Because we both gave our hearts to other people at a very young age without even realizing it. He gave his to you and I gave mine to a man who I'm still not sure deserves it. And you can't give anyone else what doesn't belong to you anymore." I shrug. "So we're friends. The best we can and know how to be, and a bit messed up sometimes. That's why time and space never made a difference to us. It never mattered if we were near or far, if we didn't speak for six months, or if we were together just once a year. We always overcame that and managed to find each other in between."

Maria looks at me almost reverently, and I see that she is at a loss for words.

"And that's where the difference lies," I continue. "Because Dave and I meet in that place between here and now, and that's how we find each other. But you, Maria, you have been there all along. You simply never abandoned that place. So don't doubt if you're enough or if you're the one, because you're that and much more." I tell her, omitting the part that she just isn't *all* there is to be in Dave's life.

"Thanks, Izzy," Maria says.

We stay silent for a while after that, considering my words and all their meaning.

"We were making love," Maria says, almost a whisper.

"What?" I ask, unsure if I heard her correctly.

"Dave and I were making love when he had the heart attack," she repeats, mortified.

"You're serious?" I ask, the oddity of it making me start to laugh—until I realize that she is serious.

She nods her head and starts laughing too.

Dave's mother gives us a reproachful look that only spikes our fit of laughter, so it takes us awhile to steady ourselves throughout the uncontrollable muffled laughs that assault us before we can utter a word again.

"Dave never disappoints! He gives wantonness an all-new meaning!" I joke, and Maria just nods again, the smile leaving her lips, though.

"So it's that simple? You never had feelings for each other?" Maria asks suddenly, letting me know that after all I had just shared with her, uncertainty is still burning her up.

I stare at her, taken aback by her unexpected query and the myriad of possibilities that it holds and that I do not wish to address, though she's still asking the wrong question. My mind races back to that night on the street, many years ago, when I asked Dave what he felt about me, for real, and he told me that he didn't need to tell me what he felt, because I already knew. He was right. I knew. All this time I had known.

While I ponder what to say to Maria, a young doctor looms at the waiting room entrance. His hands are in his robe pockets and his eyes are searching the room, not knowing whom to turn to. He's nervous, but he is not avoiding our pleading eyes, so I have all my answers.

My eyes drift back to Maria, and I manage to force a ghost of a smile to pass my lips, hoping that it alone will be enough to comfort both of us before I answer her question, glad that she didn't ask the right one.

"Not a single day in our lives!" I lie.

THE END

ACKNOWLEDGMENTS

If my words were meant to be read just by you, you would have made them worthwhile already, my dear friends.

Moreover, because sometimes thank you is just not enough, these words are meant solely for every one of you.

So my honest thank you:

To my Little Swallow, for pushing me to follow my dream. If there was ever an impulse, it came from you.

To dear Great-Aunt Carol, for the great brainstorming and tireless enthusiasm. But above all, for asking me for rain and making me realize that I could make it fall. If there was ever support, it came from you.

To my Favorite Minion, for letting me watch you read my manuscript and making me believe that it was that good. If there was ever assurance, it came from you.

To De Pruis, for letting me keep you company on your boat rides and for being a romantic. If there was ever hope, it came from you.

To Miss Battle, for helping me keep track of time and for loving the balcony scene as much as I do.

To BG, for playing the drums.

To my brother, for believing. If I have faith, it's because of you.

To my True Poet, for your infinite patience, crazy ideas, and constant support. Without you, this book would never exist. So if there was ever a reason, the reason was you.

And to Nino Funfa, for helping me make the queen proud. If there was ever a Dave, I owe it to you.